Patient: Crew

HANNAH KAPLAN

ISBN-10: 069240886X
ISBN-13: 9780692408865
Available on Kindle and other Devices

Kapcom Publishing
2015

DEDICATION

For the voices in my head:
David, Clif, Christine, Jennifer, Jacob & Farrest.
You are my heart, my love, my life.

Table of Contents

1.

Momma died when I was three months old, leaving me to be raised by my grandparents. I was always told Momma and me could have been twins. Albee said we had the same wispy blonde hair and sad eyes. Pop would say we were both as skinny as rails. I was an unwanted addition to the people of Sunny, Texas, and this caused a sick feeling of rejection that has rooted itself in my memories. *If God were kind to evil she would have died with her Momma*, was the consensus of the women in town. *She's nothing more than an evil talisman sent to keep us in line*, was the men's. The children were warned to stay away, and never look me in the eyes. I was evil spawn and could curse them with a mere glance. Even the schoolteachers avoided me.

Sunny was the city to a hundred farms covering thousands of acres. It was a small community of hard working, God fearing people. Pop was the Mayor and the largest landowner in the county. The people of Sunny loved him despite his wanton daughter and her evil child. Blame for the rotten offspring was laid upon Pop's first wife—Momma's mother, she took her own life before Momma was a year old. Albee was Pop's second wife. She was pleasant enough, but it always felt as though I was in the way. There was never a moment of bonding or small talk. She made sure my clothes were clean, tummy was full, and homework finished. I questioned Albee about Momma on one occasion when she seemed a bit more approachable.

"Why go about digging up rotted bones? Best to let sleeping dogs lie. What that child did to her father, your grandfather, is unspeakable," she snarled. "The way she acted towards men was shameful."

"Is she the reason kids don't play with me? Why nobody likes me?"

"It don't help matters none that's for sure," she said. "Your problem is that you're too damn quiet. People don't trust other people who don't know how to communicate proper like. You need to learn how to talk to people."

I couldn't think of anything I hated more than talking to the other kids in school. The girls only wanted to talk about clothes or boys, neither of which interested me in the least. I considered both a waste of time. I didn't care what I wore as long as it was comfortable and capable of keeping up with me. The boys were far worse. All they wanted to talk about—in-between the spitting and scratching—was cars. I liked reading fiction. I checked out every new book from the library, and lived the adventurous life of a different person every month. I had many friends, but none were real. The one time I questioned Pop about Momma, he clammed up and looked as if he were fixing to cry. Needless to say, I never asked again.

I spent my free time with Pop. Like most farmers we lived in town. Monday thru Saturday we were up at dawn filling our bellies before heading out to the farm. During the school year, Pop would pick me up at the end of the day, and I'd do my homework in the truck bed on our way back to the farm. On Sundays, we slept until seven, which was half the day according to Pop. Albee would make pancakes and poached eggs for breakfast. By eight-thirty we were dressed in our Sunday best and on our way to The Church of Christ, along with half of Sunny. The other half was Baptist. Pop leaned more to the Baptist belief, but Albee was born in the church and never intended to leave it. They spoon fed religion and faith to me from the beginning. I don't have any thoughts on the subject.

I enjoyed the days spent with Pop. He taught me how to plow, and run the combine during harvest. When the sun went down we headed home to shower and present ourselves proper at the supper table. Albee was a good cook and there was always plenty to eat. All in all it was a good life. I behaved at school, made good grades, did my chores and did not argue with authority. I was content to follow a structured schedule until my eighth birthday, when I met Jim.

"My name is James Robert Long," he said, and shook my hand. If I were skinny as a rail he was downright scrawny. Jim and his family were new in town and were living with his Aunts in the Parker house. Jim's mother Pilly, and his Aunts Polly, and Picky were triplets. "Dad lost his job. We had to move back so him and me can farm the land, and put food on the table again. Momma says its family land, always has been always will be. I turned eight two months ago. That makes me older than you. I'm an only child because momma and daddy's blood don't mix."

Albee pushed her finger into my back in an attempt to make me speak. The problem was that I couldn't get a word in edgewise.

"Aunt Polly says your Momma put a curse on Uncle Peter with her wanton ways, and it killed him dead making her a widow fer life. She said they took your Momma and burnt "

Albee grabbed his arm. Jim's mother cupped her hand around his mouth as Jim struggled to complete the sentence. "Hush your mouth this second young man," she admonished. "We will not talk about such things on Shanna's birthday." She took him by the hand and led him away.

"What's he talking about?" I asked. Albee gave me a look of pity. I was too young to understand what he was saying and why it was a secret.

It was the best birthday ever. Jim and I talked and played while the grownups reminisced about the good old days. Albee and the sisters were best of friends and for that reason he was allowed to play with me, and look in my eyes. He had the most beautiful blue eyes. Pilly and Picky were there that day, but Polly had stayed home. "She's not the forgiving type," Jim would explain.

We became an inseparable duo. We shared everything. He told me secrets about the sisters that would force all three to confess during the invitation song six Sunday's in a row. I told him about Albee's chewing tobacco habit, and even went so far as to show him her spittoon. With Pop being the Mayor, and an elder in the church, I possessed an endless stream of gossip about the town folk. My days were no longer structured, and I no longer had time for Pop or the land. My world revolved around Jim.

We kissed for the first time on my tenth birthday, and when I turned eleven he told me the truth as he knew it. He said it had all started with my grandmother Zeffie. She was one of the hill people. We all knew people lived in the hills although most of us had never seen one. They lived well beyond the farmlands and deep in the brush inside dugouts created by digging into the hills. They stayed to themselves. You'd hardly ever see one of them except on the rare occasion, and only out of desperate need. I remembered seeing two of them at our front door when I was very young. It was a man carrying a woman. The man tipped his hat despite his full arms and asked for Pop to help the sick woman. Pop kissed Albee then told her to lock the door behind him. It's funny how little moments of time will stick in your mind as if they have a purpose. What I remember most about seeing those people was how the woman stared at me. She must have known my grandmother was one of her people.

"Zeffie and your Pop met in town," Jim said. "After they were married she got pregnant with your Momma. She was seventeen years old, and a few months away from giving birth when she started talking to the air. Aunt Polly said she talked to evil spirits that no one else could hear or see, and that's why she shot herself. It was that the evil told her to, is what Aunt Polly says." He looked at me with concern. "Stay tough."

"I'm tough. Tell me what happened to Momma," I said, but I wasn't tough. I was sweating with fear, wanting to know everything, and simultaneously wishing there was nothing to know.

"Aunt Polly said your Momma started acting the same way Zeffie did when she turned seventeen. She would wander around town talking to imaginary friends. They said she'd dance barefoot in the middle of the street without any music. Polly said it was the dance of Jezebel. Mom doesn't talk about it much, and Aunt Picky don't give a flip, but your Momma's about all Aunt Polly can talk about most days."

"Do you think it'll happen to me?" I asked.

"What?"

"Nothing," I said, not really wanting to know. "How'd Momma die?"

"Your Pop built her a house behind the farm, and it got burned down," he said.

"They burned her?" I started to shiver though it was a hundred and six in the shade that day. I couldn't believe what I was hearing.

"They didn't burn her, they burned the house, and she died from the smoke," he said.

"She didn't die. She was murdered," I said. "Why? What did she do that was so bad?"

"I don't know," Jim said.

He was lying—I pushed, "I want to know what she did!"

10

"It had something to do with her giving sex favors to men, and Uncle Peter's heart attack," he said.

"She gave him a heart attack?" I asked "Is that how he died?"

"He was coming home from her house, and made it as far as the Parker house front porch before his heart stopped. He was sprawled out, face up on the concrete and his pants were unzipped," Jim said. "The sisters won't talk about it around me, not even Aunt Polly'll talk about such things. The three of them give each other looks. Freaks me out when they talk without words."

"Have they ever talked about my father or who he was?" I asked.

"No," he said, "they never say anything about him. I think that's the part that scares them the most." Jim was never comfortable with the subject of my family and he avoided it from that day forward. If I went near the subject, he'd stop talking all together.

Time went on, and memories faded. Jim matured into the town's "Golden Boy", and I was seen less as the evil spawn and more as Shanna—Jim's girlfriend, and the granddaughter of Farrest and Albee Green. Aunt Polly adopted a four-year-old boy named Jason, after his mother died of cancer. Jason's father had died in a farming accident before his birth. Aunt Picky, the only nurse in town, suggested the adoption, and the sisters agreed Polly would be his mother. Jason softened Polly's heart. The sisters loved that boy like blood, and he soon became Jim's Shadow. Wherever Jim was, Jason was.

We met Vicky at Jason's winter school concert. He sang in the choir with her little sister Maria. Jim and I were a grade above Vicky in school, but in a small town age doesn't matter as much as attitude. Vicky had attitude to the moon and back. She was a troublemaker. She would sneak into the nearest store during a school trip, buy a pack of cigarettes, and then we'd skip out on the trip, smoke, cuss out loud and dream about a future we had no control over. We became our own little clique.

Jim and I celebrated our sixteenth birthdays with Vicky and her boyfriend. Jason and Maria tagged along as usual. Aunt Picky let Jim borrow her car to drive us all to Sweetwater for burgers and a movie. We couldn't get the little kids into an R rated feature so we settled for some Disney flick. We made the kids sit down front while us adults hung out on the back row. It wasn't long after the movie that Jim had dropped off the others, and we were alone and naked. That night would be the first time for both of us. Six weeks later, Vicky and I were in the girl's bathroom at school shocked by my positive pregnancy test. It felt as though my life was over before it had a chance to begin. We had committed the sin of fornication, and all too soon the proof would be in the swollen belly.

Jim bought rings and drove us to the courthouse in Abilene. To get married in Texas both parties must be over the age of 18, neither one of us could muster enough courage to tell anyone so we brought documents of consent, on which we had forged the names of our legal guardians. Both of us would rather go to jail than face any of them. We sat on the steps outside the courthouse contemplating the criminal act we were about to commit.

"What's the worst thing that can happen?" I asked.

"Jail," Jim said.

"Pop finding out is worse than death row."

"The sisters are worse than that. There are three of them."

Jim and I walked into the courthouse and down the long hallway to the Justice of the Peace. He went to the reception desk. I went to the restroom. Five minutes later I was sitting on a toilet full of blood—fully relieved. We left the courthouse without a marriage or license. Neither was necessary. That night we cuddled on a hay bed in Jim's barn.

"We should've gone ahead and done it," Jim said. "I want to go back to the courthouse get married and get out of this place. I don't want to live here. We're going to do nothing but rot and die, right here."

"We'll get out of here," I said. "Someday."

"When?" he asked.

"When the time is right."

"Promise?"

"I Promise," I said, as he pulled me close to his chest.

"Stay tough," he said.

"I'm tough."

Thirty days after my seventeenth birthday I left Sunny alone. Albee and Pop were at the breakfast table as I sped passed them and out the door. I revved the engine of my '72 VW Bug and blasted the car radio but nothing would help me that morning. I could not let this happen to Pop—not again. The pain he'd felt was palpable when the good folks in town brought up Momma and what she had done. It would be better for them to think of me as dead and go forward with their lives, than to endure the chaos that was living inside me. I didn't know where I'd go or what I'd do when I got there, but I did know that I had to leave. I've often wondered what Albee must have thought when I didn't come home that night. How upset was Pop when he realized I was gone? What did she say to calm him down? The voices increased in volume as I drove east on I-20, and soon after that I began to understand them. Two weeks prior they had sounded like a fuzzy A.M. radio broadcast. That's the point at which I blacked out. I didn't know how I'd lost my car or how the truck driver found me.

2.

*B*eing ambidextrous enabled me to pitch, write, eat, bowl, and golf using either hand. This little fact never sat well with my school teachers; it only served to increase their fear. They (at times not tactfully) would let me know that I should only use my right hand because the left side was evil. In my eyes, it was no big deal and simply something I could do. When it came to being a scribe for the voices that made a home inside my head; it was this little oddity that changed my life. I could write what two voices were saying simultaneously—one voice with each hand—on two separate pieces of paper and finish a session in record time. It was Marla's idea. Doctor Marla Todd was the director and a part owner of a private, Dallas drug clinic. She said a truck driver saw me walking down the highway in a daze, put me in his truck and brought me to the clinic. She gave me a bed and never left my side.

For the first few days, she held me as the voices echoed through my head. I begged her for hours on end to do something that would make them stop. On the third day the voices calmed becoming a background mumble in my head. I woke up and Marla was still asleep in the chair next to my bed. When I touched her hand, she jolted up out of the chair.

"I'm sorry," I said. "I think they're quiet now."

"What does it sound like in your head?" Marla asked. "How many voices are there because I believe there are four?" She steadied herself upright and grabbed her notes and pen. She wasn't sure how much lucid time to expect. "When did it begin?"

"It started before my seventeenth birthday. Can you make them go away?"

"From what I can make out you are hearing four idiosyncratic voices. I would lay odds that not even one of these voices belongs to you." She must have seen the utter confusion in my eyes because she stopped and took a deliberate deep breath. "I'm Marla Todd," she extended her hand.

"Shanna Green, pleasure to meet you. I'm sorry for the last few days."

"Don't apologize for something you can't control," she said. "Promise me you'll never do that again." I nodded. "It's me who should apologize," Marla continued. "I should have taken you to a hospital instead of this den of drug addicts. I have been studying schizophrenia for the better part of my life. Most Psychiatrists, using the DSM, would diagnose you as schizophrenic. Hell most of them would think you were faking because of the way you can come in and out of it so smoothly."

"What are you talking about?" I asked.

"Be that as it may, I kept you because I can help you," she said indifferent to my question. "Not necessarily as a diagnostician, diagnosis is by definition a categorization of symptoms and we all know that no two therapists could or would agree, but more as a behaviorist." She reached into her bag, took out a couple of books and laid them out for me to see. "Here is a case study of a woman hearing voices. She is otherwise, healthy, mentally and physically, displays no paranoia, and has no desire to hurt herself, or others. She simply hears voices, and these voices do not in any way manipulate her." She pointed to a book written by Betsy Holder. "This poor woman had seen multiple doctors before seeing Doctor Holder—who I might add is an extraordinary doctor, not to mention my college roommate. Every Doctor put her on medication; none of the medications stopped the voices, but Betsy did. I'm getting ahead of myself let me explain."

Over the next few hours, Marla gave me a crash course in psychiatric diagnosis. She agreed there were certain people who heard voices that were properly diagnosed as schizophrenic. She also explained that there were many other patients who heard voices and are not mentally ill. She was convinced that I fit into the latter category and saw me as a link between her theory, and fact. I felt that I was no different from Zeffie and Momma—bat shit crazy. Marla considered the voices real, and believed they served a purpose. I would not attempt to explain the sum of Marla's medical hypothesis and conclusions. My mental health is not meant to be the subject of this story. I will tell you, that I have never been formally diagnosed, and that I have no doubt (in theory) that I am mentally ill. A diagnosis is a label. Labeling is limited, inconsistent and at best, an unnecessary evil.

"These voices brought us together. It's our job to figure out what the purpose is," she said. "Will you agree to be my test subject?"

"Test subject? Like a lab rat? Are you going to drug me, stick needles and stuff in me?" I was standing and ready to run.

"No, no, no," she laughed, "just the opposite actually. I'll set you up in a room at my house so that I'm not forced by any laws to give you medication. I practice behavior modification. I live with my husband Tim. He's a great person…works for the government. I've treated other patients in my home. I'll admit it's a little unorthodox, but it's better than being committed. If I take you to a hospital, you will be committed."

"Government?" I put my shoes on. "You want me for a government experiment?"

She laughed again, so hard that I could hardly understand her words. "Oh heaven's no—this is not—you will not be a government experiment. Tim works for the CIA, in foreign affairs. He has nothing to do with my

"Three hours," she said. "But that number will be raised. Not only that, but I think—no—I know it's the solution to lessening their activity."

From that moment on, when the voices began to speak I sat on the floor with a pad of paper propped up on each leg. With a pencil in each hand I transcribed what they said, simultaneously, two at a time. After writing what they say, they go to the back of my head and hum, allowing me the freedom to go on with the rest of my day.

Time went by at a steady pace as the voices in my head grew to seven. I spent my days always prepared for dictation. I was able to get my G.E.D. through Internet courses, and Marla (as my physician) monitored the test. I studied Marla's library of books and learned as much as anyone would want or need to know about how the mentally ill brain works. When I became bored with those books, I would read Tim's on the criminal brain. I learned nothing about the normal brain. The voices continued their daily chatter, paying no attention to my needs. They talked when they wanted to talk; I had no control. Each session was a different phrase, song, lecture and so on. Some sessions lasted hours some minutes. I no longer tried to be attentive to what they said. It bored me. When they talked, I went to an empty space deep within my mind. While the rest of my senses were tending to the voices and their needs, I was in a place of my own making, my solitude. I began to venture outside the house and it's grounds after five years. The panic I felt agitated me. I imagined every eye on me watching my every move waiting for me to show the crazy.

"Everything you're feeling is normal," Marla said. "This is your first public encounter since hearing the voices. Firsts are scary for everyone."

"What happens if they want to talk, and we're out?" I asked.

"Never go out unprepared. We put notepads and pencils in your bag," she said.

"So let's say we're picking up some groceries and in the middle of the dairy isle one of them starts talking, then another chimes in. Am I supposed to sit down right there next to the milk and start writing?" I chuckled. "Do you think that would draw attention?"

Marla burst out laughing, "I can see the crowd gathering now. Oh, God help us." She wiped away the tears her laughter had caused. "We need a signal."

"Like what?" I didn't find as much humor in the probable scenario as Marla.

"I don't know," she said. "What if you whisper something to me like it's getting loud in here; that'll only work if you're close by. If we are separated, but can still see each other, put your fingers in your ears and I'll know what's happening. Find a bathroom or go to the car and wait for me, whichever is faster. If you're alone do the same just be sure to lock the doors."

When we went out Marla made sure I had a car key, and I made a habit of scoping out the nearest bathroom. Unfortunately, the voices did come forward about forty percent of the time. Nevertheless, we went out together at least once a week. I learned my surroundings, acquired a driver's license and Tim bought me a car. I never went far from the house when I was alone. On those days, I would drive to a nearby park and sit on the swings dreaming of what life might have been like with Jim. *We would have a house on the land. Vicky would be our closest neighbor. Jim would wake up with the roosters and give me a kiss before pulling up his boots. I would make a breakfast of fresh eggs, and home baked bread. We would have had a future and planned for a family.* Our life together was grand in my dreams, but I had no illusions of that dream ever coming true.

Marla began to show a greater interest in reading the sessions and putting them in a certain order. She never suggested I should read them, nor was that something I wanted to do. I had no interest in the voices.

"You need to name them," she said after an extremely long session.

"What?"

"I said," she spoke louder. "You need to name them."

"I heard what you said. I just don't understand why you would say it." I stretched my legs, fingers, and aching back.

"My point is that, well, um," Marla hedged.

"Go ahead and say what you're thinking, you're going to anyway so let's just cut to the chase. I'm starving and I'd like to catch some TV before it gets too late." I stood in my arms crossed leg out defiant pose daring her to speak the wrong words.

"I've been reading your transcripts a bit more seriously over the past month. I believe they—your voices—have something important to say, and I need to know who is saying what in order to put their phrases together. I hear rhyming, but I believe it's from two different sources," she scratched her head and fumbled through the notebooks. "There are statements and poems and demands and then just lists of numbers. Wouldn't it be easier to understand what they were saying? We could give each of them a name to reflect their own unique personalities?"

I turned away from her, stomped into the kitchen, and made a snack. I walked by Marla and her pile of notebooks on my way back to the bedroom, and noticed she had typed the sessions, and written commentary beside them. "You're writing a book about me?" I asked. "Is that why you want me to name them? For your book?"

"What did you expect?" she said. "I never lied to you. I told you that you were a test subject. I've never lied to you"

"You never said you were going to write a book about me!" I yelled.

"It's not about you," she said. "It's about Patient: Crew. Don't you think that's better than Patient: Shanna Green? No one will ever know it's you. You have to trust me on this. I'm protected by the law."

"Trust isn't given it's earned!"

"Surely I've earned it by now," she remained calm. Her tone was steady, flat, and devoid of emotion. I was her patient, she the Doctor.

"Maybe it's time I left. I should leave now so your book won't have an ending. Who in the hell wants to read about a crazy bitch who hears voices anyway?"

"Do you have any idea how many people you could help?" Marla asked. "What if other people who hear voices can write it down, the same as you do, and have the freedoms you've acquired because of it? Don't you want to help others that are like you?"

"What in the hell is going on in here?" Tim asked as he walked in on our argument. "You're going to wake the dead for Christ sake."

"I'm done with this," I said and left while Marla attempted to explain the situation to Tim. After slamming the bedroom door behind me, I sat on the bed eating my snack and accepting what was being asked of me. She wanted me to make it personal. I had been successful at distancing myself from the voices for the better part of seven years, and now she was asking me to name them like pets. If I named them I would have to know them, and I did not want to know them. I wanted them to go away. I wanted to hate them as much as they'd caused me to hate myself.

I was able to finish my snack before the voices came forward again. As my hands began to write I closed my eyes and left realty. I let myself see the relationship with Marla. She'd nurtured me and allowed me to exist in a semi normal state of being. I was not a prisoner; still she controlled my every move. Free to leave, but unprepared for life without her. The session filled forty-four pages and lasted two hours. I put the notebooks down and thought about where I would be without her. Without her, I would have been sent to an asylum or worse, if there were anything worse. Would I have known to write what they say?

"Shanna," Marla knocked on the door. "Can I come in?"

"It's your house, do what you want." She came in and sat at the foot of the bed. "I shouldn't have yelled at you," I said.

"I should have discussed the book with you. We're even Steven."

"Are you still going to write it?" I asked.

"Yes," she said. "We would have never come so far with your case if not for the books Doctors have written. You need to understand and trust that I would never put you in any sort of danger. No one will ever know the book is about you unless you want them to know."

"Never."

"Then, they won't. I promise."

I began to explain each voice. She listened and took notes while I named them. "The Poet always rhymes, everything he says is poetry. Then there's The Singer, he sings everything, and some of it rhymes. Sometimes he makes up music, and sometimes he uses music anyone would know, but with different lyrics. The Professor is the technical one he talks like a teacher. The one that says cool, and groovy man sounds like an old strung-out hippy. When I started writing Joseph started speaking. I think he's their leader. The last one preaches so he'll be The Preacher." There was an uncomfortable pause when I'd finished.

"Is that it?" she asked. "Is that all of them? Six?"

"There's another. We can call her Mother because she's the only woman."

"We need a vacation." Marla stood up, gathered her notes and headed out of the room.

Tim wanted to go to Hawaii. Marla wanted Galveston. They forced me to be the tiebreaker. Since I had never been out of Texas or on a plane, I chose Galveston by car. Tim accused the women of having an alliance. We left on a Friday morning and by six that evening we were on the beach. The sun was setting as we finished our picnic dinner, and Marla topped off her glass of wine.

"Whoa. Whoa," Tim said.

"What's wrong?" Marla asked.

"That's your third glass."

"So?" Marla quizzed.

"So maybe we should take it easy. I'm a federal agent," he shrugged his shoulders. "I'm just saying."

"You're always just saying," Marla laughed as she got the last word. "You and your badge are on vacation."

That is what I loved about Tim and Marla. They argued but never fought; they bickered at each other without raised voices and angry tones. Marla told me they had met in college. Tim said it was love at first sight. Marla claims to have stalked him for two years before he got up enough nerve to ask her out. Tim joined the Army Special Forces, and Marla continued her medical education and became a Psychiatrist. Tim served his time in the army, retired and became a C.I.A. agent.

After my second glass of wine, the crew came forward with a vengeance demanding immediate attention. Marla saw it. Tim was confused. I was searching for my writing tools. When the session ended the setting sun had been replace by a rising moon. Marla was still next to me on the blanket. Tim was gone.

"How long?" I asked.

"Two hours."

"Where's Tim?"

"He went back to the room."

"Spooked?" I asked, knowing Tim had never witnessed a session in progress.

She nodded. "He knows what you do. He wasn't shocked, but there's a difference between knowing and seeing."

Tim and I were far from what one would call close. We had a pleasant, cordial relationship. We joked with each other, and both liked to watch the Cowboys play football. He was fun to be around when he was around. He traveled at least once a month and spent several weeks at a time overseas. I never asked him about his job, or the C.I.A. He never asked me about the voices. We were comfortable with each other, and the last thing I wanted to do was screw it up.

"Nothing ever stays the same," I said.

"What do you mean?" Marla asked. "Nothing has changed. Tim is, and will be no different with you than he was before." When Marla and I returned to our suite Tim was there to greet us.

"Are you ok?" he asked.

"Yes," I said. "You?"

"I'm good." Nothing else was said. Tim remained the same.

3.

Marla's first book was published without fanfare in our eighth year. She signed her share of books at the local bookstores, and her sales were fair on Amazon. Tim and I were proud of her, and her first commercial publication. She bought a new car and took us all on a shopping spree with the first royalty check. Ten months later her editor called to say the publisher wanted another book. He said the first book was in its second printing, and it was time to plan the next because of its growing popularity. The editor also insisted on her including at least one hundred pages of the patient sessions.

"Why do they want more of the sessions?" I asked.

"I'm not sure," Marla said. "Tim's on the internet trying to pinpoint a reason. My editor said they wanted more of the sessions that's all I know."

"Who exactly are they?" I asked. "And why the sessions? Did they say sessions, or did they say writings?"

"Hold the phone Agent Green," Marla laughed. "Tim, or should I say your partner, has already grilled me. Jeez you two are cut from the same cloth."

"Good job," Tim said to me as he came into the room. "Always get more information than you give."

"Did you find out anything?" Marla asked.

"It seems you have a small cultic following," Tim said. "You, and your patient. It isn't unusual for this to happen with these sorts of books. There's a few blogs discussing it, nothing radical. I can't see how it would hurt to write another. Try to keep it technical."

"People are blogging about the book?" Marla asked. "What kind of things are they saying?"

"They speculate about the real patient and who it might be. Is it he or she? Stuff like that," Tim said. "There are only a couple of blogs with a few followers. It's not a mob of people, just a few. Nothing to worry about." He looked worried to me. Then again Tim always looked worried.

"I guess I shouldn't be unhappy that people like the book. They are discussing it. That is a good thing, right?" Marla asked, seeking our approval.

"Right," Tim said. "You get that second book finished. Damn the torpedoes baby."

"What about you, Shanna? I won't do this without your blessing."

"God knows we have to do something with all those notebooks piling up in my room," I said. "Go ahead and write it just make sure no one knows I'm the patient."

It took three months for Marla to finish the second book; six months after being published—Ceely Masters, an ex-lawyer turned pop-culture courtroom sideshow host, called. The show's producer explained that Marla would be their psychiatric expert. Marla was schmoozed to the point of no return, and by the time she was off the phone they had booked her for the live show via satellite link with a local Dallas-Fort Worth TV station.

Marla spent six days straight in her office researching the defendant du jour and his crime. Tim and I took up the slack on cooking and cleaning. When the crew started talking I locked myself in the bedroom, Tim never questioned me. On the seventh day Marla emerged from her office.

"I don't believe my brain can handle another moment of Wayne Perkins." She propped herself up against the kitchen wall. "What's cooking? It smells fabulous."

"It's called Shanna and Tim's fabulous chicken," Tim said and kissed Marla. "Tell me good Doctor, have you developed a theory?"

"I believe I have," Marla said. They hugged and kissed while I kept my attention on the pan of chicken and mushroom sauce.

"Would you like to share your theory with us?" Tim asked.

"No," she said with a wink. "You'll have to wait with the rest of the world"

"Oh come on," I argued. "Not even a hint?"

"No," she said. "How can it be a newsflash friend if the friends already know?"

We had a good laugh. It was the last meal we three would share. The next evening a limo and driver were waiting at seven. Marla was driven to the studio where makeup and wardrobe was anxiously awaiting her arrival. The Ceely Masters Show spared no expense.

"We've both watched this Ceely woman's show," I said. Tim and I were pacing the floor and chewing our nails. "She's ruthless. What if she disagrees with Marla's diagnosis?"

"Her theory," Tim corrected. "Marla doesn't diagnose. She saves that for Doctors of the body. Marla treats the mind."

"Theory," I said. "Whatever. What if that she-devil disagrees with her? She'll gut her alive via satellite link."

"Marla's a smart woman. She can hold her own," Tim said. "But just in case it's a boxing match we should make popcorn."

"It's going to be a bloodbath," I said.

Fifteen minutes before the show was set to air we nuked a bag of popcorn. I was nervous and could see that Tim shared my fear. We both wanted the best for Marla. Her book could and would see bigger sales by virtue of her

"The twelfth of December to be exact," Ceely said. "The first one was published on December eleventh of two thousand and nine."

"That sounds right," Marla said.

"It is right," Ceely said with arrogance. "I have both books in front of me."

"Get to the point," Tim said to the TV screen.

"Shush," I demanded.

"All I'm saying is what the hell does it matter?" Tim argued.

"You are familiar with the State of Texas vs. Perkins murder trial in the courts today, am I correct?" Ceely asked.

"I am familiar through internet research," Marla said, careful to cover her ass. "I have not followed the trial daily."

"I see," Ceely said. "Your book is based on a patient that hears voices."

"Yes," Marla said. "The book is a guide for other Doctors and Therapists to use in their own clinical studies."

"You mean to use on their own patients," Ceely corrected.

"No, I mean as a guide."

"Is Patient Crew schizophrenic?" Ceely demanded.

"My patient has not been diagnosed as schizophrenic," Marla answered gracefully.

"It's a simple question," Ceely laughed. "You claim to be a specialist in schizophrenia yet you don't know if the subject of the book is schizophrenic?"

"By definition, my patient shows symptoms of schizophrenia, but we control the voices. I don't know of any schizophrenic patient that has achieved this level of control without medication."

"Well Doctor, that sounds like double speak to me. Tell me Doctor Todd was Patient Crew in your care on the night of June first, two-thousand and ten?"

"Yes," Marla said.

"I'm going to read a paragraph from the first book of Patient: Crew," Ceely said. "With your permission."

Marla was not seen but I could hear her muddled tone of agreement as Ceely continued. "Let me remind you friends that this book, the first book of Patient: Crew," she held up the book. "This book was published on the eleventh of December, two-thousand and nine. The voice known as The Poet speaks: *Give me peace. Let me be. Leave now Lisa or you will see devastation caused by the real me.*" Ceely looked at the camera, "On the same page the voice known as The Singer says: *Once there was a little girl who married whom she loved. Six and eight of forty-four North of thirty-two twenty-six with a point ninety-one six seventy-eight. She turned and found the one she loved was filled with nothing but hate. West of ninety-nine, and forty-three with a point ninety-eight and six eighty-four.*

I don't know how this gibberish could be called a song but no matter, the words and numbers greatly concern us." Ceely closed the book and looked through the camera lens at her television friends. "The video you will see is the first interview with Wayne Perkins. It was recorded on the second of June, two thousand and ten—the very night that he murdered and dismembered his young, beautiful wife Lisa."

The video began. Marla could be seen looking down at a monitor off camera. Ceely began to quote The Poet. "*Give me peace. Let me be.*"

A detective interviewing Wayne Perkins was listening to his prisoner "I just wanted some peace and quite you know. I just wanted her to let me be, so I could get some sleep," Wayne said while crying pitiful, selfish tears.

Marla remained stoic as Ceely continued. "*Leave now Lisa or you will see devastation caused by the real me.*"

"I warned her," Wayne said. "How did you warn her?" the detective asked. "I told her if she kept on me she might push me too far, and I knew her life would be devastated if she saw the real me," Wayne said. The video stopped.

"Do you have a comment, Doctor Todd?" Ceely asked.

"No," Marla said. "I'm curious what the point you're obviously trying to make, is."

"You are correct," Ceely smirked. "Very observant of you, but I guess that's why they call you Doctor." Ceely twisted in the chair for her close-up. "The song that we read, of the voice called The Singer, included a series of numbers. Producer Ann studied those numbers, and has discovered they are the GPS coordinates for the very house Wayne Perkins shared with Lisa. The same house where he murdered Lisa, and blamed the voices. We'll be back friends.

"Tim got up slowly, and looked straight through me. "Be back in a second. Don't let it start without me." He returned carrying his laptop.

"What's wrong?" I asked. "What does Wayne Perkins have to do with me, or the crew?"

"Not sure," Tim said while keeping one eye on the TV, and one on the laptop.

The show returned. "Welcome back friends, and welcome back Doctor Todd," Ceely said with a smirk that morphed into her usual sanctimonious smile. "Is Wayne Perkins Patient Crew? Did he tell you a year in advance of his plans to murder his wife?"

"No!" Marla said. "I don't understand what you are implying."

"I am not implying. I am inferring. I am stating a fact. Your book, Patient: Crew, either foretold or told of Wayne Perkins entire murderous plan even down to the GPS coordinates for the house in which the murder would take place." Ceely looked at her TV friends. "Side note: Wayne and Lisa Perkins didn't move into this house until

February of two-thousand and ten. That is two months after the first book of, Patient: Crew, was published. Doctor Todd will you tell us how you came about this information? Who is Patient Crew?"

"You are trying to fit a square peg into a round hole," Marla said, her voice becoming weak.

"Again Doctor Todd," Ceely glared at her. "Are Wayne Perkins and Patient Crew one and the same?"

The music from the commercial break started and Tim called Marla from his cell—it went straight to voicemail. He held the phone close to his face, typing on the screen with his thumbs and sent a text.

"What did you say?" I asked.

"Leave," Tim answered.

"You think it's true, what she said?"

"You need to pack light and fast."

"Why?"

Tim moved the laptop enabling me to see its screen, and the Internet homepage of the Ceely Masters show. In the center of the page was an ongoing discussion about that night's show.

Tim's phone rang. "It's Marla," he said, and went into the kitchen. I continued to read the discussion. One person's comment said the voices had predicted the winning lottery numbers for every drawing held in the United States on March thirteenth, two thousand eleven. Another comment stated that The Professor foretold a massive earthquake in India a year before it happened. My heart was pounding. My breathing became shallow and cold.

Tim came back in a panic. "Pack now!" he said.

It took me ten minutes to pack a small suitcase. We left through the kitchen door that led to the garage. There were no windows, yet Tim cautiously unscrewed the light before leading me (wrapped in a blanket) to the backseat of his car.

you'll have enough money to sustain, and you have the deed to your grandparent's farm."

"You're sending me back?" I asked.

"You're going home," he said.

"This is my home. You and Marla are my home. I'm not ready for this to end, not yet."

"Shanna—move forward."

"I don't want to," I said. "Why don't I have a choice or at least a say in all this? It's my life, and I should have a choice."

"You need to suck it up girl," he demanded.

"Because I'm going back to Sunny the same way I left, with no other choice," I retorted.

"You need allies, and sometimes it's easier with a head start. These people know you. The only time you'll have to account for is the last ten years. Keep it simple, and close enough to the truth to sound true."

"You don't know those people, they dig deep, wear you down. They'd sooner see me dead than coming back."

"Get more information than you give," he said. "People love to talk about themselves. Manipulate the conversation and lie without guilt because those lies will protect everyone. Keep going forward, don't look back."

"What if something bad happens to Marla?"

"Be ready to cut and run without baggage. Do you understand what I'm saying?" Tim asked.

"I get it."

"If, and when, the shit hits the fan you'll wait for word from me before making any moves. I will find you, trust it."

"Ok."

"Keep your mouth shut and the fortune telling to yourself."

"I can't tell the future! I only write what they say, and I don't control them they control me."

"Since you are the only one who hears them you're the prophet. You, those voices, are a commodity. There are people who'd pay a lot of money to own you. There's not a person or government in the world who wouldn't want to see three steps ahead of the rest of us. You might want to start being more attentive to what they say."

"When do I leave?" I felt my body empty itself of the fear and dependence it had relied upon for the past ten years. Sending me back to face the destruction of my own creation was cruel. I was being forced to stare into the faces of judgment alone.

"After breakfast," he said. "I have eyes and ears everywhere, don't worry. You'll be safe, and soon enough you'll come to terms with it." Tim lit the stove's flame and started frying eggs. My hearing faded as the crew took over. I looked around the room and realized there was no hiding place. Tim saw my frustration, and stopped cooking long enough to help me find the notebooks and pens. I sat at the small kitchen table watching Tim cook as the crew took control of my hands.

My mind wandered. I began to imagine a homecoming parade as the prodigal daughter returned home to a welcoming town. I was led down Main Street on a float. The people held signs that read, **Welcome Home Shanna**! Jim, Vicky, Jason, and Maria were running beside the float. Pop and Albee were standing in the crowd of people watching as I passed by. None of them had changed; it was as if time were frozen while I was away learning to exist among them. I waved and blew kisses; they smiled, waved and began to chant, "We love you Shanna. We love you Shanna." The float turned. The town disappeared and we were on Pop's land. The people who had been on the street were now standing around me. The trees surrounding what was left of a burned down house lifted me out of the float with their branches, and put me down in the middle of a huge pile of hay. Pop and

Albee were the first to light the hay on fire. Jim, Vicky, Jason and Maria held hands as they lit a fire together. The crowd cheered. The flames jumped around me.

I woke up screaming. Tim was standing above me holding my hands down and trying to bring me out of a state of terror. "It's ok Shanna," he said, his face an inch away from mine. "You're safe."

"I'm not safe," I said still shaking. I wiped away tears I didn't know I had cried. "I can't go home. I don't have a home."

"I never said it would be easy," he said and went back to his cooking. "Don't get dramatic, you'll find allies. Life has gone on without you, but you can gain another spot for yourself. You'd be surprised how short a person's memory is."

"What should I do with the sessions?" I asked. "What if someone finds them?"

"Burn them, eliminate the risk."

"I've put us all at risk."

"Remember what I told you about disconnecting? Take out all the personal and address the person," Tim continued to coach. I had disconnected from my past when I left ten years earlier. I never called home not even to hear their voices before hanging up. I'd not written a single letter and had not expected to return. Now that I was, I had no desire to reconnect.

The transportation was an eighteen-wheeler with an enclosed trailer. The driver was a middle-aged, balding man who said nothing outside a soft you're welcome after I'd thanked him for helping with my bag. Neither Tim, nor I showed emotion during our brief goodbye. Thirty miles west of Dallas we stopped, and ate without conversation. I got the impression that he'd been instructed (by Tim) to leave me alone.

"My name is Shanna," I said as he finished his coffee. "Could we stop at the cemetery on our way into town?"

"Do you know how to get to the cemetery?" he asked without offering a name.

"I can show you." That was the extent of our one and only conversation. A few hours later, we'd exited the highway and headed down the cemetery road that separates the farms from the town. The big truck slowed to a stop, and I got out for a look around. Since the dead had always outweighed the living two to one in Sunny I had to walk up and down the rows a couple of times before finding the graves. When I saw the white picket fence, I knew Pop had the last laugh. Surrounding the graves of Albee, Pop, Momma, and Albee's only son, who'd died in the war, was the snow-white picket fence that Pop had built around Momma's house. Other than myself, it was the only thing that survived the fire. It was freshly painted and cemented into the ground, no gate, no entrance, or exit, and a thick layer of concrete covered the plot. Above the names on the stone it read; *tarry not, for even the dead won't linger here.* This was my family, and I was the only one left.

"It looks fine Pop. I mean the fence and all. I'm not sure about that big ass slab of concrete covering everything. I guess you probably figured I was already dead and buried but still, flowers would have been nicer. I guess you're mad at me. There isn't much I can do about it now. I know that I should have written you, and I'm sorry for that—I didn't know what to say, I did the best I could. You should have told me about Momma, and maybe then I would have been better prepared for what happened to me. Still, you were good to me, and for that I thank you."

The setting sun cast an orange glow over the concrete covered graves giving them a golden shimmer that made the fence look like white bleached cotton. I felt my blood warming, home sweet home. In the distance, I heard the truck's diesel engine roar. I started down the hill and was halfway when I saw the truck at the end of the dirt road turning onto the highway. At the entrance to the cemetery sat a silver hybrid car that looked more like a kid's toy. The title was in the passenger seat, and the keys in the ignition.

"Yes," I laughed. "This'll fit right in."

4.

*I*t took two hours to unpack, and settle myself inside Miss Black's little house. Two weeks later it still smelled of decayed flesh. I had been told that she was dead for at least forty-eight hours before they found her rotting corpse in the bathtub. True to his word, Tim had arranged delivery of all my belongings, some used furniture, hygiene essentials, and enough food to keep a family of six fed for a year. He'd also arranged for a lawyer from Abilene to settle my grandparent's estate, and as promised I'd received the deed to the land along with the little money they had saved. Albee had sold the house in town after Pop died, but the land was mine. My plans were to live in the rent house and farm, if all went well I would consider buying my own place. I continued the daily sessions for the crew. My mantra had become write what they say and they'll go away. I wouldn't call it a blessing, but it did help pass the time.

The south winds blow the orange sands of Lubbock through the plains every spring, and the dust storm of two thousand twelve was a doozy, making it impossible to leave the house. The local news reported it to be the worst sandstorm Sunny had seen in forty-five years. Then one day I woke up, and the winds had changed direction. They had blown in a rainstorm, some fresh air, and a visitor.

"Well now, aren't you a sight for sore eyes." Mrs. Charlene Davidson was one of Albee's best friends. She looked the same as she had ten years earlier with the exception of a cane that helped her balance. "Jesus have mercy on my soul, I never in my wildest imagination thought I'd see you again, and there you are standing right in front of me. Did you visit your Pop? Bless his heart.

He would love nothing more than to trade places with me right this second. I don't know whether he'd slap or kiss you, both I recon." She pushed past me into the living room. "Did you go visit your Pop? Did I already ask that? I'm losing my mind. I swunny not a single hair on your head has changed, not one iota. Spitting image of Anna Ruth." She was breathing deep and hard as she examined the little house. The floors creaked, and the cane made a thunk sound that was followed by her feet shuffling from room to room. She picked up the knickknacks for a look see here and there, giving a little "hmm" as she made her assessment of the decorations. This was to be my first impression. Half the town would hear about it by Sunday morning. I took my time, chose my words carefully and tried to behave in a manner Albee would have seen fitting.

"It's so good to see you Mrs. Davidson, and yes I've been to the cemetery. I wouldn't come into town before paying my respects. The graves look lovely don't you think?"

"It could do without that fence, but all is forgiven in the end."

But not forgotten, I thought.

"My, but you have fixed the place up. You painted and cleaned out those windows so good it made me want to cry when the dust rolled in." She sniffed the air like a cat on the prowl. "I see you took care of that putrid smell too." She sat on the sofa, rolling her thumbs and smiling at me. "Truth be told we've all been lurking around here while those Mexicans were unloading the moving truck a couple weeks back," she whispered the word Mexican.

"Oh my goodness. I'm so sorry they disturbed you. It's my fault they didn't talk. I told them not to. I didn't want them to raise a ruckus, and I don't think they understand English. I should have planned better."

"We had no idea what was going on or what on God's green earth could be moving in. I wasn't the least bit aware that the house had been rented so quickly. Lilly Black's only been dead a few months. Mrs. Randall, you remember her, lives around the corner yonder, told me she tried to talk to one of the Mexicans, but they just ignored her, wouldn't give her the time of day. There must've been twenty of them in all, working inside and out for five hours straight, and then they just packed it up, and left without so much as a how-do-you-do."

I put my head down in shame, and hoped she'd believe the act. "I didn't mean to make a bad impression."

"I'll tell you what, there was a run on deadbolt locks at the hardware store that week and that's no lie." She half-heartedly laughed. I laughed with her. "Hell, I got a couple for myself."

"I can't apologize enough." I'd never be able to apologize enough for the miserable stain that the women of my family had left on Sunny.

"We have a lot to discuss you and me, but I don't want to keep you. I can't even begin to imagine why you left your family in such a way or where it was you went, but you're home with your own kind as it should be. We'll go from there."

"Please stay and have a glass of iced tea with me. Just for a bit so we can talk. I can tell you my story." It was important to establish a story, and sooner was better. I could cease to be the fodder for gossip. All their stories would match, and there would be nothing more to add, allowing me freedom to go on with my life.

"No dear not today. I have an appointment with Maria at the beauty parlor." She paused to grant me a motherly look of concern. "Jim knows you're here. He saw you at the cemetery. He told Pilly, Picky told me, and when Polly found out—I don't have to tell you what happened next, the whole county knew within seconds. She practically got on the roof and shouted it. She would have if'n she could have."

"Oh?" I had convinced myself that Jim had started a new life somewhere far away, but I knew all the same he would never leave the sisters or his land. I didn't remember seeing him before I left. I couldn't recall the last words we spoke. Time takes away one's recollection of the past with slow ease, yet even with fading memories the mere mention of Jim caused a stir in my heart.

"That's right. I might be speaking out of turn, but Albee, God rest her soul, was like a sister to me, and I think she'd expect me to let you know that everyone's been waiting for this dust to settle. Your coming back has ruffled more than a few feathers."

"I didn't come back to ruffle anyone's feather," I said.

"I know that, and you know that, but folk's is just a little spooked at you showing up out of the blue is all— given the way you left. Albee and Farrest were dearly loved and your leaving tore them up pretty good. I expect people want some answers." She let out a heavy sigh. "Any who, I've rattled on long enough. I do think you should give Jim a call. He deserves a call. He's had a hard time the last few years. I'll let him tell you everything, it's better coming from him don't you think?"

"Yes I do. I plan on giving him a call soon, I just wanted to settle in first and then have him over for supper." In that moment the crew came to visit. "I know you're busy, let me help you." I pulled her up from the couch.

"I really should go now I wouldn't want to keep Maria waiting. Now don't forget to call Jim," she said as I quickly ushered her out the front door.

"Have a good evening Mrs. Davidson." The volume of the voices increased as I closed, and locked the door. Joseph was up front and boisterous.

The truth is told so seldom. What could be worse than a world full of lies? It seems that the answer is a world full of truth.

He would continue to repeat this phrase until I wrote it down. I closed the windows, and pulled the drapes as The Professor began to speak.

If one were to tell one's truth would it then become the other's truth? Just by virtue of it being one's truth?

I locked the bedroom door behind me as the other voices chimed in making it impossible for me to discern one from the other. It was ten in the morning when the session began, four hours later it had ended. This had been the fifth session of this length in the past three days. I had made a habit of checking each room after each session ended to make sure everything was the same, and the only difference this time was that the answering machine message light was blinking. It was Jim. He started by saying how it was inevitable that we would run into each other, and ended with give me a call when you're ready. His voice brought about severe pangs of guilt that I'd tried to forget. He sounded good maybe a little weathered. I didn't expect him to look the same. According to Mrs. Davidson I hadn't changed a bit. Marla said I'd softened. That was her pleasant way of saying I had gotten pale from being inside for ten years, and pudgy from the massive food supply the Todd home clinic provided. It wasn't as if I could hide from him. We would run into each other sooner or later. I took control, picked up the phone and dialed his number.

"Shit," I said out loud, "what if he's not living with his mother anymore? What if he?"

"Hello," Jim said.

"Hi. Jim? It's Shanna."

"Hey stranger, it's good to hear your voice. How the hell are you?"

"Oh, I'm good. So, how are you?"

"Good…good." His answer was followed by a painfully long pause.

"Let's not do this over the phone. Come to my house for supper, please," I begged. "I'm not a great cook but I can grill a steak and put a potato in the microwave. Maybe a salad would be good, unless you have other plans that is."

"I don't have plans," he said. "I'll be there at seven."

I rummaged through the kitchen and found everything I needed for the dinner part of the evening, but I didn't know what to do for dessert. I remembered there were at least ten cases of cookies and a freezer full of ice cream so I made ice cream sandwiches. I was bathed, dressed, coiffed, and sitting on the couch like a nervous Nelly an hour before Jim's estimated time of arrival. For the first time—in a long time—I had not thought about the crew, but this didn't mean they weren't around, and it also wasn't a guarantee that they wouldn't show themselves in the middle of dessert.

I needed to think of some sort of way to keep them from taking over. I gathered the notebooks that I'd filled since arriving from their hiding place in the sock drawer, held them in my hands and closed my eyes. I'd never communicated with them. I had screamed at them a time or two, slapped my head until my hands were sore, but I had never talked to them. That would just be another step into madness. This was not the time to worry about my mental stability. First, I tried it with thoughts and talked inside my head. It didn't work. I was half-thinking the thought and half-listening for the doorbell. Nothing I'd done made me feel as if something outside myself were paying attention. I dramatically held the notebooks above my head and spoke out loud. "I need you, all of you, to stay away. If you value me even in the least, please let me have this one night with Jim." There was no answer. "I'll take that as a yes. Thank you." And, the doorbell rang.

Jim was as punctual as ever. I walked with stoic control to the front door and turned the knob.

"Hi," I quickly said to keep my voice from quivering.

"Hi," he said, tipped his hat, removed it from his head and held it against his chest all the while keeping eye contact.

I motioned for him to come inside. The central air unit had kept the little house's climate at a steady sixty-eight degrees, yet sweat was beading on my forehead, and I could feel my armpits drip. I watched him as he sat on the couch, fumbling with his hat. The age he'd acquired made him more handsome than I had remembered. He looked the part of a typical farmer. The tension was thick and there was an uncomfortable, blaring silence. The crew was quiet, and so was Jim. Neither of us wanted to be the first to speak. He wouldn't take his eyes off me, even for a second, as I tried not to fidget.

"You got the smell out," he said.

"Mostly, but you can still smell it in the bathroom," I said.

"How have you been?" he asked sharply without smiling.

My gut was twisted up in knots. "I've been better."

"I know what you mean," he cut me off.

"You're angry," I blurted.

"No," he said.

"You sound angry."

"Do I? Do I sound angry? Huh, what could I possibly be angry about?" He was being flippant, but I knew it was just an act. He had every right to be mad at me.

"It is what it is. There's nothing I can say or do to change what I did."

"Hmm." He was breathing heavily through flared nostrils.

"Want a drink? A beer? Some wine? Whiskey? Anything that will help ease the situation?"

"You made a trip to Putnam for booze?" he asked.

Sunny had been dry since it's establishment in eighteen eighty. Putnam was due west. It had a skating rink and the only liquor store for forty miles. Pop would joke about the pastor sitting outside the liquor store on Saturday night so he'd know to whom he was preaching at come Sunday morning. I wouldn't let Jim lead me down that path.

"No, I brought it with me. Drunks like me never leave home without it. If you want to fight then let's just go at it and get it over with. Why wait? Why draw it out with insults and innuendos? Come on let's do this." I got up and walked the two steps it took to get from the chair to the couch, stood beside him with my fists raised and ready for a fight.

"What in the hell are you doing?"

"I'm fighting. It's what you want, right? You look mad enough to knock my teeth out. I'm tough I can take it. Get up boy and show me what you got, let's duke this out." He laughed, I stood my ground, and started to feel like I wanted to punch the laugh out of his mouth so I relaxed my fists, and put a hand on his shoulder, he pulled away. "I don't know what to do. How do I make it better?"

He nodded, put his hat on the table, got up and stood close enough for me to feel his breath. I leaned back not knowing what to expect. He gently pulled me close to his chest, and then wrapped his arms around me. His warmth was surreal, safe, home.

Jim ate two T-bone steaks, and I ate one. The potatoes and salad were good, and he loved the ice-cream-cookie-sandwich. It was just like old times, we gossiped about people, and laughed at their expense. He caught me up on all the scandal and news. His father had passed a few years after I'd left. He didn't want to discuss that subject. He said the sisters were doing well. His mom was active in the church, Picky was still the only RN at the hospital, and Aunt Polly had been in bad health since her stroke five years earlier. He and Jason were still living with the sisters in the Parker house. I asked him numerous times about Vicky, but he would change the subject. It was obvious he didn't want to talk about her, and that piqued my curiosity. I assumed Vicky was angry and not ready to face me. She'd probably known Jim was coming for dinner and gave him strict orders not to talk about her. He did confirm that her sister Maria was doing hair at the Salon. I would go there, get a haircut and information.

The meal had been devoured, the dishes cleared from the table, and the conversation had grown as dim as the light. It was whiskey time. "Shoot or truth?" I set an opened bottle of Johnny Walker Black on the table along with two shot glasses.

"Are you up to it?" he asked

"I am."

Jim turned up his lip in a cocky grin, and poured two shots to start. We toasted with a clink then drank. The whiskey burned from my lips all the way down to my belly. I liked the way it loosened the mood. He poured us another round. I began to lift my glass, and he put his hand between it and my lips. He looked deep into my eyes; the room spun for a second as I stared back at him. "Take your best shot," I said, and put the glass down. "Truth."

"No lies?" he asked.

"No lies, but you can't share what I tell you with anyone."

"I won't share. Where have you been?"

"I've been in a Dallas mental clinic." I'd fully intended on telling the truth, but I needed to be careful of how I went about telling the truth, and how much of that truth I told. "The day I left I went to Anson, and my car broke down—or I ran out of gas, that part I don't remember. I wasn't in a good way, I don't remember how I got where I got to, but I got there and that's where I've been." I snatched the shot glass out from under his hand, downed it without losing a drop and sat back feeling happy with myself. "That wasn't so hard. I think that went well don't you?"

"Dallas, the whole time? All ten years?" he asked.

I answered with a nod. "Ok that's enough farm boy. It's your turn for truth." He laughed, and turned a little red on the tip of his nose. "What? You think it's funny?"

"I choose to shoot," he said, and drank.

"What are you afraid of?"

"I fear nothing; I'm simply thirsty. Your turn— truth or shoot?" He filled both glasses.

"Hit me with a question, I'm feeling brave tonight."

"Why?" he asked

"Why what?"

"Why did you leave? Why did you leave without telling me? You could have told me." His eyes were filled with a deep sadness.

"That's a shot block," I said.

"It is what it is," he said.

"That conversation's going take longer than one night. There's a lot that needs to be said, it could take months to catch up on ten years. Let's keep it simple tonight and say I had no other choice. I couldn't tell anyone. I had to leave. I couldn't face Pop and make him go through it again."

"Go through what?" Jim asked.

"The same shit Zeffie and Momma put him through."

"Oh," he said. He didn't want to hear more; he knew what I was talking about. It wasn't something that needed to be rehashed. Jim started to take another shot, but this time I put my hand over his glass.

"Oh no you don't. It's your turn to tell some truths."

"I don't believe I've ever lied to you, why would I start now? Go ahead, ask me anything."

I took a shot before he had time to react. The whiskey was going down easier, and I'd felt the buzz. My mind raced to remember the questions I had asked for ten years in my fantasies of him, and now—in the flesh—I couldn't verbalize one. I looked at his strong chin, traced his jaw line down to his rugged neck. It seemed like yesterday that his face was covered in peach fuzz, and now he had a half-day's growth of hard whiskers. His white button up, cotton shirt was crisp with starch, I wanted to touch it, feel his warmth under the fabric. Jim snapped his fingers an inch from my face.

"I'm waiting for your question."

"Don't rush me," I said, and poured another shot.

Jim held my hand instead of the glass this time. "Don't overdo it," he said. We froze in that moment—for a split second—both looking down at our touching hands. He moved his, and I followed suit. It was not what I wanted, I wanted him to touch me, but it wouldn't be that easy to regain his trust. All logic was flying out the window my heart was taking over, and in that moment I would have submitted to him willfully. Was this good, or bad? I didn't know. I didn't care.

"Did you think about me?" I asked.

"Wow," he said shaking his head.

"You don't have to answer. I understand."

"What is it that you understand? Are you saying you understand what I've been through? You understand what it did to me? What it did to your Pop, to Albee? Do you understand that?" I tried to answer, but he wasn't finished. "Did I think about you? I searched the whole damned state for your ass. I spent two years of my life searching for you! I fucking thought about you every minute of every day for at least five years! I watched your actions put Pop, and then Albee in the grave. Did I think about you?" Anger pulsated through his body. He downed another shot, slammed the glass on the table, and wiped his mouth with a sleeve. He looked at me as if he could spit in my face, stood up and put his hat on. "You couldn't call, just to say you were alive? You couldn't send a note, a letter? You couldn't fucking do something so that I wouldn't think you were—we thought you were dead Shanna. Do you understand that?"

"No, I can't understand." I felt like throwing up. I wanted to run as fast and far as I could. I closed my eyes and disconnected. "I'm sorry, there are no words I can use to defend what I've done. You have no idea how sorry I am, and I know it's not enough. Saying I'm sorry can never make up for anything. I can't crawl under a rock and die, as much as I might want to. I've got to keep going forward. I had to come back. I'm sorry."

He quietly thought for a period of time, and then with a calm voice he spoke. "Now that you're here, what are you going to do? How long are you staying?"

"I'm here for good. I can't make any promises, but I'm going to try. I'm going to farm Pop's land. For now, my plans are to live right here, and farm."

"You? You're going to farm?" he asked, smirking. He was turning red, and tears were coming to his eyes as he laughed at me. "You don't know the first thing about farming."

"How hard can it be?"

"How hard can it be?" he mocked my question.

"Have you been out to the land?"

"No."

"It's a garbage dump. It's overgrown, and hasn't seen a plow in seven years or better." He poured another drink.

"Well then, it looks as though I have a lot of work ahead of me. I have to get it ready for this year's cotton season."

My statement caused him to spit out half of his drink, and stain the white cotton shirt. "You can't be serious. It'll take at least a week to get it cleaned, then you'll need a tractor and seed—you don't even have an irrigation system set up out there. You do know we're in a drought, don't you?"

"Pop didn't have irrigation. He did fine without it. I'll buy a used tractor in Abilene. Does Bradley's dad still own the Feed and Seed? I'm sure they'll sell to me."

"Woman you need to think straight. You expect these people to sell you seed? Hell, you'll be lucky if they look at you. You might have a crop by next season."

"Oh no that won't do, not at all. I need to grow and sell this year's crop to pay next years rent." Jim shook his head and groaned as he thought about my dilemma, but why? This was not his problem. I didn't need or ask for his help. Why was he assuming I needed a Knight in shining armor; I wasn't in distress. "You know it's really not your problem anyway. I'll take care of it."

"You must be crazy if you think for one second that land will be cleaned up and ready for planting without some sort of help."

"Then I'm crazy. Let's just leave it at that. I'm sure the entire town will agree with your assessment of me."

"I didn't mean it that way."

"If you didn't mean it then why would you say it?" Our eyes met. My mouth was stopped mid question by his firm kiss. His hands held my face close to his. I saw a single tear run down his cheek before I closed my eyes. He slowly pulled away and held my head firm in his hands—eye to eye.

"This is not going to be easy, it's easier to ask forgiveness than to get it," he said. "Stay tough."

"I'm tough."

"I won't lose you again," he kissed me and I could taste the salt from his tears. For a moment, the whole world disappeared as time ceased for us. "I accepted your death, and when I saw you at the cemetery I thought it was a ghost, but you're not. You're here—real—alive. I won't lose you again."

5.

*T*he crew had remained a quiet mumble throughout my evening with Jim. I slept that night with visions of Vicky the day I left. We were standing outside the school. I was pounding my ears while she yelled something I couldn't hear, and then The Poet interrupted my dreams. It was four in the morning, by six the sun was shining and the session had ended. I thought I would sleep a few hours before going to see Maria, but the doorbell rang followed by impatient knocking.

I opened the door and standing on my porch, with the rising sun behind them, was Jim, another man and a child. "Hello," I said. "Come on in."

"Hi Miss Shanna I'm Jima," the child said and elbowed past me into the living room.

"Jima?" I asked. She was no more than ten years old and looked like a miniature version of Jim, with her hair tucked up inside a baseball cap, and wearing boots, jeans, and a heavy blue cotton shirt.

"We need the weather report. Do you have a clicker for the TV?" She looked around and spied them on the table. "Found them. My daddy's told me all about you. He told me he was coming over to help you clean up that junk yard and get it ready for cotton." She plopped down on the chair, and started flipping through the channels.

I looked to Jim for an answer and mouthed the word, *Daddy*, without sound. He turned away. He hadn't said a word the night before about a daughter. The thought of what I didn't know made me nauseous. Isn't having a child something a person would bring up in the course of a conversation?

"I wanted to come help and meet you. I've wanted to meet you for a long time. I'm named after my dad. Momma got sick and died when I was a baby so now it's just me, and Daddy, and Uncle Jason, and Aunt Picky, and Aunt Polly, and Grammy Pilly, but mostly just me and big Jim. If I were a boy, I'd be a junior. Daddy said you and Momma were best friends. I don't have a best friend, least not yet." She not only had her father's looks she had his big mouth as well.

"Wait a minute," I said. My face was hot. Jim sure as hell hadn't said anything about a wife, and the only best friend I've ever had was Vicky. Was this her daughter? Jim and Vicky are married?

"Jason take Jima in the kitchen and get her a drink." Jim pleaded.

"Jason? You were just a little boy the last time I saw you," I said, my voice shaking.

"Morning Shanna," he said while carefully avoiding my eyes.

"I'm not thirsty. Besides, I need to see the weather report!" Jima argued.

"It's going to be hot, dry and windy just like yesterday, and the day before, and the day before that," Jason said. "Come on squirt let's get a drink."

"Don't call me that, weasel."

"Squirt."

"Weasel."

"Squirt!"

"Dad!"

"Get on outa here!" Jim demanded, and turned to me trying to touch my arm, but I was not having any of that. He should have told me, plain and simple.

"Don't even try to make up an excuse for this one—my best friend? Is Vicky her mother?"

"You're right, there's no excuse. I couldn't find the words, and just as you said it will take some time to catch up on your ten years, it takes time to catch up on mine."

"Just tell me if Vicky is her mother?"

"Yes she is but…"

"She said Vicky was dead. Is that true? Is she dead?"

"Yes."

The air was knocked out of me. How can that be? Vicky's married with children not the dead mother of my boyfriend's child. It was in that second that Jason and Jima came out of the kitchen, still throwing insults.

"Let's get going. The day waits for nobody. You better get your work clothes on Shanna," Jima said.

"Where are you going so early?" I forced a smile, and asked.

"Where are we going?" Jason snickered.

"Did I miss something?" I asked.

"It was supposed to be a surprise," Jim said. "I thought we could get an early start, and God willing we could get that land plowed by the end of next week."

"You screwed the pooch on this one cousin," Jason said, and the minute he did Jim slapped him across the head.

"I had planned to see Maria today, couldn't we start on Monday?" I asked.

"Beauty Parlor?" Jima asked. "You want that land ready for this season and you're worried about your hair? I'll tell you what you need to be worried about lady."

Jim cupped a hand around her mouth not letting another word escape. "Jima! Tell Shanna you're sorry. Right this second young lady!" He removed his hand. She shyly stepped forward to look me in the eyes. It was as though I'd been transported to a time long gone; she was (as Mrs. Davidson would say) the spitting image of Vicky.

"I'm sorry Shanna. I just meant," again Jim cupped her mouth.

"Learn when to leave well enough alone," he said.

"You're right Jima; this is not the time to fuss over appearances." I bent down and hugged her and whispered in her ear. "Your Momma would be so proud of you."

"You at least need to change your clothes," she said. "Those'll be in rags before noon. It's just a shame to waste good clothes."

"She's got a point there," Jason said.

When the doorbell rang, I'd grabbed the first clothes I saw; the linen pants and silk top I had worn the night before. "I'll change." I ran into my room unintentionally slamming the door. "Sorry," I yelled. I put on a sweatshirt, blue jeans, and sneakers. I could hear Jim raising his voice in the other room. I pressed my ear to the door and could clearly hear him arguing with Jason.

"She's not evil, and you best make sure she doesn't hear you say that," Jim said.

"Did you see her shaking all over? She's skinny and pale, how's she going to be able to farm? I bet she can't even change the gears on a tractor. Only a nut would want to farm that land anyhow. Besides, I ain't the only person in town that thinks she's loony tunes," Jason said. "Most people are scared shitless of her. They say not to look her in the eyes, or she'll put a curse on you."

"That's enough. You hear me?" Jim demanded.

Jim was right it was enough—enough to help me disconnect and get down to business. If Pop's land were half as bad as Jim had insinuated then I should be grateful for the help, and use it wisely. I boldly opened the door, this time intentionally slamming it against the wall, and entered the living room ready for battle. "Is this better?"

"No!" Jima laughed.

"What's wrong with this?"

"It's ok if you're going for a walk down the street in the middle of winter," she said through her laughter. "You'll die of heat stroke dressed like that."

59

"Maybe a cotton shirt and some old wranglers. Do you have any boots?" Jim asked.

"This is as grungy as it gets," I said.

"We'll take you by the house you're about Jason's size. Momma will be tickled pink to see you," Jim said.

"Really? Do you think that's a good idea? It's pretty early they might be sleeping."

"They got up before we did and had breakfast waiting on the table," Jima said.

I was reluctant to see the sisters. While Jim's mother might be tickled pink I was sure Aunt Polly would drop dead at the sight of me. Polly hated my mother and in turn saw no good in me. Jim seemed sure that I would be welcomed so off we went, all four of us crammed inside the cab of Jim's truck.

"Where'd you move from?" Jima asked before we exited the driveway.

"Dallas." I answered.

"What'd ya do there in Dallas?"

"Studied."

"What'd ya study?"

"Brains."

"Cool. Why'd you come back?"

"It was time to come back."

"I heard stuff about your Momma, and about you, but I don't think either one of y'all's evil. I just wanted you to know that."

"Good God almighty Jima!" Jim yelled.

"I'm sorry! I'm sorry! But, a girl needs to know who her allies are. Am I right Shanna?"

"You are so right Jima. You have no idea how right you are, and might I add that I am ever so grateful to have you on my side. It sounds as though I've become quite the legend."

"Something like that," Jason said.

"All right that's it. No more talking," Jim said.

After we had pulled into the driveway and emptied ourselves from the truck. Jima caught my arm. "You better wait here. We might have a triple casket event on our hands if I don't pre-announce you."

"Good thinking," I said, and walked to the back of the truck. Jason followed Jima, and Jim followed me.

"I know I owe you one hell of an explanation," Jim said. He was practically cowering. It obviously hurt him worse than it had me.

"You don't owe me a thing. You lived your life and so did I. But, if it makes you feel better then I'll take you up on your offer to help." I wanted to know what had happened to Vicky, and how they ended up together, but now was not the time. It was time to get serious about the farming. I needed to get the land ready as soon as possible. "I'd like to believe that we've outgrown games, wouldn't you?"

"Yes," he said, and walked into the house. I could smell his cheap cologne wafting behind him, as I followed. It was musky and made my head spin with a desire to be with him, to look into his eyes and see the same desire for me.

Jima was running down the hall yelling. "Better hurry ricochet rabbit's ready to bounce." Jim's mother was the first to greet me. Without saying a word she cupped my face in her hands and kissed me smack on the lips.

"How blessed we are to have you back home with us," Pilly said.

"That's very kind," I said. "It's nice to be back."

"For heaven's sake, I said I wouldn't believe it unless I saw it, and here you are." She hugged me again, and then pushed me towards the hall. "You best get going—Polly's a coming."

"What in tarnation is all that racket going on out there? Is that Jim's voice I hear? Jason, is that you?" Polly loudly asked her questions from another room. "What's

61

wrong? I know something's the matter or else you wouldn't be back home so soon after just leaving. Now, one of y'all needs to answer me. Jason come in here and help me with my walker."

"I'll get Momma; you get her clothes, get her outside and I'll meet y'all in the driveway," Jason said.

Jim ushered me into Jima's bedroom, shutting the door behind us. Jima was running in and out of the bedrooms gathering clothes, slamming doors, and talking a mile a minute. She felt inclined to tell me a story about each piece of clothing that was laid out on the bed. The wife-beater was a birthday present to Jason from Aunt Picky. He hated the color so he threw it in the top of his closet with the other rejects. The jeans also belonged to Jason, but were too small since he had a beer gut from all the drinking he did, all the time. She was starting her story about the socks when Aunt Picky poked her head through the open door. Jima bolted out in search of boots as Picky yelled after her.

"Don't run, walk!"

"Yes'm Aunt Picky," Jima said.

Her gaze turned slow and deliberate towards me.

"You're back?" she asked.

"I am," I said.

"All right then welcome home."

"Thank you. It's good to be home." She walked off without another word. Jima, waiting in the shadows, came through the door and closed it gently.

"The quiet storm," Jima said, handing me a pair of boots.

The constant hum of voices became louder, their words were taking shape, and I knew it was only a matter of seconds before they fully manifested. My ability to hear Jim and Jima was fading fast. I concentrated on what my breathing would sound like if I could hear it, and watched their mouths move, waiting for a break. I had to whisper to ensure I didn't yell. Because we were hiding from Polly, a whisper and being hurried seemed fitting. "I'll get dressed and meet you at the truck. Go ahead and get it started. I'll jump in the back. I want to ride in the back." I said. They both nodded and rushed out the door. Jim turned and said something on his way out. I gave him my most ambiguous smile. *Learn how to read lips*, I told myself.

I quickly changed and gathered my things. The room had been Jim's when we were kids, and I knew it was an easy window to climb out. I made it to the ground easily. Jim tried to make me sit in the cab with the rest of them, but I looked away and opened the tailgate. What he was saying I would never know. I smiled, waved him, and his silent admonishments away as I steadied myself in the truck bed. When we'd pulled out of the driveway I gathered the pads and pens and began writing—legs crossed with a tablet on each knee, and a pen in each hand. The sun felt warm and welcomed on my face. We drove out of town and down Farm-to-Market road 702 towards Sylvester; a town incorporated in the eighteen nineties. The post office had long since closed causing it to no longer be considered a town; which meant no running water or electricity. It did however have the largest cotton gin, Feed & Seed and Dry Goods store in the county.

I kept my eyes open and mind alert to what was going on around me. I could feel eyes on me, but I didn't look to see who of the three was watching. I kept on writing. I'd remembered riding down this road with Pop, he would tell me stories about his family coming to Texas on a boat before he was born, and how they'd docked in Galveston and rode north in a horse drawn carriage. Their small group of travelers with meager supplies didn't stop until they had arrived at government land, in the plains of west Texas, where they could stake their claim.

The row of businesses soon ended and the vast cotton fields began. I assumed I had at least another thirty minutes before we'd arrive at Pop's farm, but couldn't be sure when the crew would finish. I closed my eyes and turned my face to the sun. Suddenly I was floating above the earth. It felt as if I were thousands of feet in the air, but could see all the people below me with clarity. I saw a family at the beach. They were eating fried chicken from a picnic basket, and drinking wine from plastic glasses. At their urging, I floated down to join them in a toast. They smiled at me. I felt welcomed. The entire family liked me, and wanted me with them. The men wanted to talk to me about the weather. The women wanted to talk about their hair and fashion styles. I told a joke and everyone laughed. It was warm, breezy, and when I put my feet in the water it sent chills down my back as goose bumps rose on my arms. I was so entranced in my fantasies that I didn't realize the truck had had come to a stop.

"Teach me how to do that, please! Please teach me! I have to know how to do that," Jima said, jolting me back to reality.

My hands were limp, and the writing had ceased. I hurried to gather my papers, and didn't panic or show any fear of what she saw as I completed the task of putting my tools away. Jim opened the tailgate, picked up two rocks, threw them at me and yelled. "Think fast!" I caught one with my right hand—a split second later—I caught the second rock in my left hand.

"I still got it," I said.

Jima's jaw dropped. Jason gave me a smirk and walked to the barn.

"She's ambidextrous," Jim said. "She can do anything with one hand that she does with the other."

"What? What's that?" Jima asked.

"I'm both handed. Most people are either right handed or left handed, but I'm both handed," I explained.

"Teach me to be both handed," Jima begged.

"I'm pretty sure you have to be born that way," I said.

"Pretty sure ain't for certain though is it?" Jima countered.

I jumped out of the truck bed, and turned to face the land. To the left I saw piles of used lumber laying atop thick layers of tree limbs and brush. In the far back corner was a garbage dump. From where I stood, an eighth of a mile away, it appeared to be about five feet tall and covered a good thirty acres. There were garbage bags of all shapes and sizes, and the smell coming from that direction was stronger than a cow's afterbirth sitting in the midday sun. To the right was a wide variety of people's toss outs, from truck bodies and car parts to old mops and kitchen appliances. The only thing I didn't see was land not even a patch of dirt or weeds. I had no understanding of the foreign emotion that ran through me as I surveyed Pop's most prized possession. His land was ruined, and I was to blame for it's demise. "It smells like a fucking pig farm," I said, and headed to the barn. "Give me a second alone. I need to think."

I slammed the side barn door behind me causing it to fall off its rotted hinges. I was pissed. Everything had gone sour from the beginning. First, that damned Ceely Masters show, the dust storm, Jim, Jima, Vicky, the awful timing of the crew, and now this. I wandered around the barn in a rage bumping into tarp-covered mounds of furniture taken from Pop and Albee's house. I took a tarp off the dining room table, took another off the butcher block and that's when I saw my old VW sitting on cinder blocks. After a quick walk around, I found all that remained of her was the shell. The engine had been removed along with all four tires. My thoughts were swimming around unattached to any solution. I couldn't brush off the guilt. I was disappointed in myself. I fully understood my fault in this mess, but I couldn't understand

why people dumped their shit here. I owned what I had
done and would make amends, but the town, the people,
needed to take their share of the blame. My Pop would
have turned heaven and earth over for any of those people,
yet they allowed his property to become the county dump?
I'd seen Pop put money he could have used for his own
pleasure in the church collection plate every Sunday
morning, and they couldn't spare a dime to hire someone to
haul away the junk? Since they obviously didn't want to get
their own hands dirty. I hated that town almost as much as
I hated myself. I had spent ten years sitting around eating.
If I had to be on the run I needed to be sharp mentally, as
well as physically. The land was still there, I was still there
and together we would succeed. Fuck Sunny, fuck those
country hicks, and fuck the jerks that wish me nothing but
harm. I had myself, and that was all I needed.

"A couple of weeks after you left an eighteen
wheeler dropped it off at their house," Jim said, as he made
his way around the rubble.

"What did the truck driver tell them?"

"Nothing. He opened the truck, backed the car
out, put it in the driveway and left. Didn't say a word."

"Did you put it in here?"

"It was in their garage until Albee died. I took it
and put in here with the rest of their stuff. Your Pop had
taken the engine out and scattered it all over the garage. I
guess he thought at least it was something he could fix.
The tires were rotted out so I burned them."

"Did you put the fence around the graves?"

"Uh huh. I found it in here when I brought the car
over."

"It looks good. I'm surprised no one has tried to
steal the car."

"No one ever paid any mind."

"No one's going to steal from the devil's spawn. They're way too afraid of retribution. That's why they didn't take down the fence."

"You can't control what people think, Shanna."

"Especially not these ignorant motherfuckers."

Jim turned my head to face him gently with his hand. "Listen. You can't control what people are thinking, but you can control your reaction to their thoughts. Don't play into their games—ignore them." He kissed me gently, not a kiss of passion, a slow, lingering comforting kiss. When he pulled away I was startled at my oblivion. It was frustrating; I couldn't dare let myself react upon emotion. *I'm just a little overwhelmed*, I assured myself. Jim kept staring at me as if he wanted a response to something. I had no response to give. I looked to the side and then up, anywhere but at him.

"Good grief!" I said when I saw the track of an overhead door. "Did you do that?"

"I did that," he said. "When Pop turned eighty, I put it in. It's not automatic, but it's easy to pull. He could barely get those side doors open any more."

"You were good to them." I said. He walked around to the other side of the barn and raised the overhead door allowing the sun to flood inside. I went outside and looked at the chaotic mess before me. "Well, where do we start?"

"I'll take Jason and Jima down to the Feed & Seed. I figure Bradley's got a truck or backhoe on the lot we can use."

Bradley, the son of Bert and Betty Garner and husband of Helen, was being groomed to take over (when his father finally retired) the family's retail business in Sylvester. The Parts and Repairs Retail Warehouse carried a wide variety of car and farm equipment parts, and rented heavy equipment and haulers.

"We can burn the brush and garbage, we'll have to tow the cars and scrap the metal." Jim dug his boot down into a pile of brush and leaves until it hit hard dirt then bent down and scowled.

"What's wrong?" I asked.

"The ground is hard. There's at least a weeks worth of plowing, this soil's going to take a few turnings to get her ready. I'm not sure if we can get a tractor this late in the game. I'll have to bring mine down here."

I put on my work gloves and started piling junk, working for a good hour before Jim, Jason, and Jima came roaring down the road in Jim's Ford dually pulling a trailer with a backhoe riding on top. We worked together for eight hours and were able to clear five acres of junk into two manageable piles. One was for burning, the other for the dump. We lit the fire and then started back to the barn where it was a bit cooler, we all needed a break. We had been at it since seven that morning. The sun was relentless, and not even the slightest breeze came around to cool us off.

"That's a good start. Don't you think?" I asked, using my best optimistic tone.

"Sure," Jason mocked. "Only another few hundred acres to go. We should be able to finish that before supper!"

"Then we can go out for ice cream!" Jima chimed in.

"But not before we get our hair did!" Jason continued as he and Jima pushed each other around.

"You two take your comedy act on the road. Run over to the barn and open the overhead door, and get some oil for the backhoe," Jim said. Jason and Jima raced to the barn still laughing.

"It doesn't take much to amuse them," I said.

"Don't let it bother you. They wouldn't tease you if they didn't like you. I'll help them with the oil," he patted my butt, and ran to the barn.

I was uncomfortable with his ease. I had let this reunion with him progress too fast. Had this been a normal situation I could fall right back into life with him without complaints or concerns, but this was very far from a normal situation. I couldn't lead him on just to leave again. The problem was that I needed Jim. I would have never been able to accomplish what we did today on my own. When we kissed it felt as if I'd left one day, came back the next and Jim was kissing me hello. As good as all those emotions seemed I knew it could not last. We left with Jim's truck bed filled with the garbage that couldn't be burned.

"Do you want to stop and get a burger?" Jim asked.

"No," I said. I was ravenous, but I wanted to shower and put on comfy clothes before eating. I was not anxious to spend a tension filled evening with Jim. This had been the longest, and most emotional day I could remember. I wanted nothing more than for it to end. I was tired, sore and wanted to go to bed alone.

6.

*T*he session began before I could take a bite of my sandwich. I grabbed my bag and pulled out the notebooks and pens—found the place where the previous session in the bed of Jim's truck had ended—pushed my sandwich to the side—set the timer on my watch, and then started writing. My body was physically exhausted, and my mind overwhelmed. This was the third session in less than twenty-four hours. I closed my eyes and allowed my body to relax as I wrote.

The session lasted an hour and thirteen minutes and left me with a face and shirt that was drenched with tears. I was still heaving as if I had been bawling, yet I had no memory of crying or any of the words I had written. I closed the books, cleared my face, put on a dry shirt and ate my sandwich. Still hungry, I plunged into the refrigerated leftovers until I couldn't swallow another bite and then washed that down with two beers. Twenty minutes later I was fast asleep.

The next morning I opened my eyes. That simple act would be the easiest part of waking up. My body was not responding as it normally would. I needed to pee, but I couldn't get my legs to move and when I finally did I wished I hadn't. Every muscle I had and some I would swear never existed was screaming for mercy.

"Shanna," a female voice said, as someone knocked on the front door.

I muffled my moans, quickly got out of bed, closed the bedroom door, and stayed quiet.

"Shaaaannnnnnaaaa are you there?" It was Mrs. Davidson. I had no doubt she was stopping by for that glass of tea and a chat but today was not a good day for niceties. I remained silent, and she finally gave up and left. I walked stiff legged to the living room and fell onto the couch thankful the clicker was on the floor within reach— as long as I was lying down. I turned on CNN to catch up on some news. Cable TV is a luxury the town of Sunny had recently acquired. For a town to have cable it must house eight hundred or more residents. Sunny now boasted eight hundred and eighty. Two-thirds of them had the cable company's hand in their pockets on a monthly basis. As much as they might complain most of the customers would pay the cable bill and let the mortgage be late when times got tight. What's a house without cable?

I decided eating was more important than comfort so I used Pop's philosophy. "Hair of the dog that bit 'cha," I said and got up fast. I walked quickly to the kitchen grabbed the bottle of ibuprofen and a bowl, the cereal, milk from the fridge and made it to the table without dropping anything or screaming from the pain. Pop wasn't a drinking man, but he did believe everything came out of you the same way it got in.

I took three of the ibuprofen gel caps and ate the first bowl of cereal without chewing or tasting a bite then poured a second. I was feeling better my body was aching, but my mind was steadfast on the momentum. *Next,* I thought, *I would go visit Maria and then back to work on the farm.* First, I had to figure out what to do with the sessions. I got up again and this time it was easier. I made a pot of coffee and thought about the many spiral notebooks I'd filled since arriving and began to gather them from my bag and the sock drawer.

I sat on the couch, sipped coffee and stared at the bound books of senseless gibberish beside me. I had no curiosity about them or desire to read what was written on the pages, but I did have to do something with them. I could burn them, shred them or blow them to smithereens. I was in favor of the latter. I finally decided they should be burnt. I would have to use gas or some other kind of fuel to assure they burned completely. I was flipping channels on the TV feeling adult about having made a decision when I saw Ceely Masters' face on the screen. CNN was reporting on her interview with Doctor Marla Todd. I turned up the volume.

The show was 'Your World Today', and consisted of five highly aesthetic hosts sitting in a semi-circle with the video of Ceely behind them. It was the big reveal of the similarities between the Patient: Crew books and Wayne Perkins killing his wife. They showed Marla's close-up, she looked so frightened. I leaned forward to see her eyes were filled with fear and confusion. Her lip twitched, her eyes blinked erratically; she had lost control. Marla never lost control. Ceely had asked her a question but I didn't hear it. Marla must not have either because she didn't answer. When Ceely pushed for an answer, Marla removed the microphone from her jacket lapel and gracefully excused herself. The video stopped.

"Interesting," the blonde female host wearing the low cut shirt said.

Tim had instructed me to watch the news and read any and everything I could find concerning the books and what people were saying. He said knowledge was my most powerful weapon. I couldn't stomach this glib tabloid escapade a second longer and decided I'd grab a newspaper while I was in town. Maybe I'd pick up the Dallas Morning News or the New York Times and read them later after work.

Without another thought I put the notebooks back in the drawer under the socks, and made myself presentable for the trip to town. I wore a pair of kakis with a blue cotton top and slip-on oxfords. I was pleased (after looking in the mirror) that no one would recognize me in this preppy attire. The opposite of the jeans and t-shirts with ragged sneakers I'd worn to roam the streets ten years ago.

I locked the front door behind me, stared at the silver hybrid—by far the ugliest car I'd ever seen—and decided my legs could use a good stretch so I walked the six short blocks to Main Street. I passed the Ha-Ta-Hoe (appropriately named by the owner who hated to hoe) hamburger shack. Across the street was the only other restaurant in town, The Silver Spur. They served family style meals with a simple menu of chicken fried steak, fried okra, fried chicken, mashed potatoes with gravy, and fresh vegetables on the side seasoned with a half pound of bacon and drippings. Just as I passed by the grocerette, Jima jumped in front of me.

"Boy, I'm happy to see you!" I said.

"Really? You are?" She seemed surprised at my remark.

"I am, because I'm on my way to Maria's."

"Afraid of the blue-haired biddies?"

"You've got a mouth like Polly's," I said, showing my disapproval.

"I got that one from big Jim. Aunt Maria's not gunna let anyone say anything nasty at you...that is not to your face."

"That's all that I can ask. Let them say what they want. We're tough. Right?"

"Damn straight," she said.

I didn't enjoy hearing that sort of language coming out of her mouth, but then I remembered Jim and I cussing for the sake of cussing that started when we first met on my eighth birthday. The difference being, we would have never cussed in front of an adult. I wasn't sure if that was good or bad, but it was honest.

"Albee worked over yonder at the Post Office. Aunt Picky says your Pop was a good man and that he helped everyone around this town with whatever they needed. She said he had an angel on his shoulder because he never did a bad deed only good ones. Daddy says he was the plumber, a mechanic, and the mayor all at the same time. He said Sunny would have been dead and buried a long time ago if it hadn't been for your Pop contracting the electric co-op the way he did."

"How do you know so much?" I asked.

"I listen," she said. "I know more than most people think I do probably more than I should. People around here talk a lot especially about other people, and I listen a lot. What else is there to do around here? It's not exactly a cultural Mecca you know. Come on we're here." She pulled me through the front door of Maria's Style Emporium. The spring-loaded door slammed behind us as if to announce our presence. Maria was at her chair combing out the blue tinted hair of an elderly customer who looked like Mrs. Garner—one of Polly's friends. When Maria saw me, her eyes lit up with recognition. She was beautiful like her sister and didn't hesitate even a second as she put her comb in the pocket of her floral smock, and skipped over to where I was standing.

She looked at Jima. "Vicky Lynn and James are in the house go check on them for me. There's soda pop in the fridge you can each have a bottle."

Jima looked at me for approval. I am positive that if I would have given her a desperate look she would have stayed, but I thought it was best if she didn't hang around to hear the stories I wanted told. I smiled and nodded my approval.

"Holler if you need me," she said, ran past the styling chairs, and Maria.

"Stop!" Maria demanded. Jima stopped. "Walk."

"Yes ma'am," Jima responded and walked quickly through the door that led to the house.

"Look at you standing right here in my shop as pretty as you please." Maria grabbed my shoulders and gave me a fierce hug.

"Is that Mayor Green's daughter? I thought she was dead," an older woman with her curled head under the dryer asked.

"She is dead, stupid old woman. Dead and gone to hell," the old woman in Maria's chair said. That was Mrs. Betty Garner all right. I would know that sharp tongue anywhere. The lady under the dryer was Mrs. Ethyl Summers.

"This is Shanna, Albee's granddaughter. You remember Shanna don't you ladies?" Maria asked sweetly.

"She should've stayed gone," Betty Garner said, as she got out of the chair and gathered her belongings. "My only hope is that you join your mother soon, and burn for what you've put your family through. Bad seed the whole lot of them." She pulled some money from her purse and handed it to Maria, and then helped Mrs. Summers out from under the dryer hood.

"What did you say her name is?" Mrs. Summers asked.

"Deaf as doorknobs, both of them. Ethyl's done lost her last marble," Maria said quietly, and helped Mrs. Garner get Mrs. Summers to her feet.

"I can give her a quick comb out," Maria said.

"No." Mrs. Garner snapped. "We are settled up here. I'll do the rest at home and bring your rollers back next week. If you need them before that well, you can come by the house. As long as you're trading with the likes of that then you won't be trading with me." They moved at a snail's pace, Mrs. Summers behind a walker and Mrs. Garner with a cane, out the door. Maria hugged me again, this time with sobs.

"It's just so good to see you," she said through her tears. "When Jim said you were back I couldn't believe it. I just couldn't. Come on over here and sit next to me let me soak you in a little." She led me to the chair where Mrs. Garner had been sitting, dusted the hair from the seat and sat beside me. Maria continued to cry and wipe her eyes. When I thought she was all cried out she'd start up again. The awkward moment built with every nose blow.

"I'm so sorry. I didn't mean to run off your customers. The town's not exactly rolling out the welcome mat for me. I didn't expect it to be easy," I said.

"Nothing worth it ever is," she said and blew her nose again. She took in a breath that made her sit at least a foot taller in the chair. "Now don't you worry yourself one little bit with those old biddies. They'll be back as soon as their hair gets dirty. Where else are they going to go? And don't you worry about Sunny and you fitting in or anything like that. It's just the old folks who carry the past in their handbags you'll see soon enough that everyone else, all your old friends, they're fine and can't wait to welcome you." Maria was just a kid when I left, and now she was a full-fledged woman. Time had gone on without me.

"You're married?" I asked.

"Yes I am, and with two precious babies."

"Who did you marry?"

"Billy Price, four years ago next month. Vicky Lynn was born nine months and fifteen minutes later. Eleven months after that, William James Price Junior came along. My hands have been busy since. When we went through the drought in o-four, the whole town durn near died off. It was a blessing for me and Billy because Molly Winston, you remember her don't you?"

Molly Winston moved to Sunny in the summer of nineteen ninety-nine, I was thirteen years old. Pop brought me to the salon, and I sat in the same chair Mrs. Summers had just left. It was my birthday.

"Give her the works," Pop told Molly.

Molly gave me a haircut, manicure and pedicure. I
flipped through a Teen People magazine—a publication
Albee frowned upon— that she had on the counter as
Molly and Pop talked about subjects I shouldn't have heard.
You see Molly was a Catholic (there were no Catholics in
Sunny), and people had refused to do business with her
until she saw the error of her ways and converted. In the
case of Catholics and Jews the town would agree, it didn't
matter which you chose, The Church of Christ or the
Baptist, as long as you choose one. Molly cried as she
talked about going bankrupt. She had spent all of her
money on renovating the building so that she could do hair
in the front and live in the back. She was sure to have
more than enough customers since she was the only
hairdresser in town. Nothing went as planned. She'd only
had one customer in the previous six months, and the bank
was threatening foreclosure. Pop told her he'd poke
around and see if anyone wanted to buy the business. She
moved out a month later, and the store was still vacant
when I left.

"Of course you remember. She left in ninety-nine.
I'm sure you know all that, but no one knew how nice the
shop and apartment was. Billy's daddy is the bank
president, and he said he'd give us a loan—if I was willing
to get my license. I went to school in Sweetwater, took me
about a year, passed the test in Austin, and here I am. I
took over the shop, and Billy rented a hauler and pumped
the water from his daddy's well to save on bills. I started
making money. We made it through by the skin of our
teeth, but we made it all the same. The shop all but pays
for itself…and the attached house, it's got two bedrooms.
With Billy still working the land we'll make out fine. Might
even be able to sock a few bucks away at some point."

"You're happy and that's good," I said.
"What brought you back?" Maria asked.
"I'm farming Pop's land."

"I heard about that this morning. I haven't been out there, but I've heard it's in pretty bad shape. Your neighbor Burton Evens put up a big wooden fence to keep the junk from falling on to his land. It would have cost the old sanctimonious bastard less had he just paid someone to clean it up."

"He was Pop's friend," I said as memories flooded my head. "Pop plowed his field for him when he had back surgery. I don't understand why he or anyone else in this town for that matter let this happen."

"I guess they weren't doing it to him so much as they were punishing you. Everyone knew you inherited it all. I think in their simple minds they wanted you to suffer and that was the best way to make it happen. Now that they know you're cleaning it up they won't dare lift a finger to help out. Hell no they'll sit back and laugh at you having to do all that work all the while saying you deserve what you got. Gossip flows at a fast pace through these streets," she said. "Nothing ever changes in a small town, but let's not dwell on the negative. I want to know everything that's happened to you in the last ten years. You shocked us all when you left without a word. I suppose most people thought you'd died I mean after six, or seven years passed without a peep out of you."

Maria was fishing for fresh fodder, but I didn't take the bait. "What happened to Vicky?" I asked. "How did she die?"

"Don't you just love that Jima she's a pistol all right has her daddy's eyes and her momma's smile. She's also been cursed with Picky's temperament. She says what she wants when she wants. Oh lord sweet Vicky—I guess I should start at the beginning."

"That's as good a place as any," I encouraged.

"Promise me you won't get too upset or take on the blame," she said.

"I'll do my best."

"When you left, it hurt Vicky most of all because she was the last one to see you. She cried and cried, day and night. She felt so guilty because she didn't stop you. She went to Abilene after that trucker brought your car back. She was convinced you had been kidnapped she said you'd never leave that car willingly." Maria lowered her head. "She went to some seedy places and ended up getting herself raped. Vicky had to stay in the hospital for a couple days and when she came home, well she was just a mess." She cocked her head and looked at me. "Are you ok sweetie?"

I nodded. I didn't want her stop.

"About that same time Jim's daddy was eat up by the combine while Jim was in Sweetwater filling out an application at the community college. He went out to the land before going home and found chunks of his daddy lying in the middle of the field. Jim took charge. He planned the funeral, took over the bills and started running the farm. He forgot all about college from that point on."

"Vicky found out she was pregnant a month later and told Jim. Being the man he is Jim told Vicky they would get married, and he would raise the baby as his own. To cement the story he went forward and confessed to the sin of fornication the very next Sunday morning. He stood up before the whole church and proclaimed himself the father of Vicky's baby and asked for forgiveness," she said proudly nodding her head.

I was in a shocked daze as Maria talked. Jim's father ate up by a combine—I couldn't imagine what he'd been through. Jim and Vicky helped each other get over one of the hardest times in their lives. I had to bring some goodness out of this horror story and that would be it. They had each other.

"A few months later Jima was born, and for a while they were a happy little family. They moved into the little guest house behind the sisters. Anyway they seemed happy, but I was wrong we were all wrong. Jim loves you always did always will, and Vicky knew it. He never said a word to her about you, but it didn't matter because Vicky knew. He was always running around here and there looking for you. He never stopped looking for you. One day when Jima was only four months old she took her to Pilly and asked if she d watch her for a spell, said she needed to go shopping. Vicky didn't go shopping. She went to the back of the garage with Jim's twenty-two and shot herself in the head."

My gasp startled Maria and she held on tight to my shaking hand.

"I know it's shocking take a deep breath and remember it is not your fault."

"How can you say that?" I asked, my heart racing. She shot herself because Jim loved me and not her. *Disconnect*, I told myself, *disconnect*. "If I had stayed, she would have never gone looking for me and none of this would have happened."

"You could have stayed and she would have died anyway. I believe when it's your time to go it's your time to go. Nothing can change when your life is meant to end."

"I don't share your belief," I said. "I refuse to believe blowing your brains out could ever be what's meant to happen. What happened after that?"

"Jim moved back in with the sisters, and they all raised Jima together. I help when I'm able, but as I said I got my hands full with my own. That little girl is lucky to have so many people loving her. Jim, the sisters and I are the only ones who know the real truth, and now you. Our aim is to keep it secret. Jima need never know."

That's the way the good people in some small towns go about living their good lives. Secrets. Awful as it may be Jima would some day want to know the truth, and would deserve to know. I'm one of those secrets; the kind you wish would stay away. My Momma was seeded by one of these good people and that secret has never been told. Instead they burned Momma's house to the ground killing her in the process, but one little secret survived their justice—me. My existence alone was the reason for their hatred of me. No one wants to be reminded of his or her evil deeds on a daily basis. Their hatred was taught to their children, and no doubt their children's offspring as well.

A horn honked once outside on the street, and a whistle followed—the kind that is meant to get attention—causing Jima to run from the house and into the salon slamming every door in her path. "Dad's here! Dad's here!" Jima said while rounding the corner and heading to the door. I was ready to run with her. It was time for this visit to end.

"Stop!" Maria yelled, Jima stopped.

"Dad's here," she pleaded, "please."

"Walk," Maria demanded.

I wanted to hold on to Jima's shirt tale and follow as she walked out the door but Maria started crying again. Her whole body was shaking as she dried her tears with the flowered smock. She needed something from me that I couldn't give.

"I don't know what's got into me," she said. "I suppose it's all the memories pouring in."

I was racking my brain trying to conjure up some words that would help this poor woman move on with her life when Jima ran back inside letting the spring loaded door slam behind her. She reopened the door and shut it quietly while looking for Maria's approval. "Shanna, Daddy says you need to come with us right now," she demanded. "Please." A horn honked once outside followed by another whistle. "That's him and he's not a patient man," Jima said.

Maria became distracted by a commotion outside the shop's door and stopped crying. "Well for heaven's sake half of Sunny is outside my door." She went outside. Jima and I followed behind her and quickly got in the truck.

"What are you people doing out here?" Maria asked.

There were about fifteen people standing in groups of four or five whispering their opinions on the latest gossip—which obviously concerned me—in front of the salon. They glanced, not all at the same time, but never made direct eye contact and certainly didn't speak to me. Jim drove away without saying a word; he turned up the radio and listened to the sorghum and grain prices on the farm report.

"What was that all about?" I asked. Jima looked down shamefully as if to let me know she had been forbidden to tell.

"Did you and Maria have a pleasant talk?" Jim asked.

"I'm sorry, I must have forgotten the proper protocol when in Sunny. I should have known better than to ask about that which will not be spoken of." Jima giggled. Jim quieted her with a squeeze of a knee. I decided not to ruffle his feathers, at least not in front of Jima. "It was a good talk. Learned a lot about what's been going on since I left," I said. He must've known about Maria's open mouth policy when it came to gossip and therefore aware that I now knew everything.

"Uh-huh, well if you need any more talking we can do that later," he said. Jim turned off the radio and within ten minutes Jima was asleep on his shoulder. He carefully pulled his arm up and snuggled her close to his chest. *She's got Jim's eyes*, I remembered thinking those words and Maria saying them, but it wasn't true she didn't have a drop of Long blood in her. Still the love I saw between Jim and Jima was more than blood could encompass.

I leaned my head out the window and let the wind blow the worries out of it. This was something I would do on the day trips with Marla. The hum of the crew was omnipresent inside me but when the wind blew on my face at a high speed it would muffle the sounds, and I could hear my heart beating with the rhythm of my breath. I missed Marla. I was curious about the scuttlebutt in town and what all those people were whispering about, but at the same time I didn't give a rat's ass what got their panties in a wad. I had no feelings about it whatsoever. I had one thing and one thing only on my mind, farming. They would eventually tire of me and focus their attentions on some other poor soul.

We pulled up to the land, and my eyes could not open wide enough. I blinked and rubbed them, but the scenery remained the same. The land had been completely cleared and cleaned. Only a few smoldering embers from where the fires had burnt were left on the dirt. The garbage, car parts and thrown out kitchen appliances had all been taken away leaving hundreds of acres of clean farmland.

"How did you do this?" I was yelling with excitement as I ran into the field to get a closer look. "When did you do this? This is what's got those busybodies going?"

"It wasn't me," Jim quietly said. He was not sharing my gleeful response.

"Who in the hell did?" Jima said as she rubbed her sleepy eyes, and stretched her legs.

"Watch your mouth girl," Jim said. "I don't know. Shanna?" he looked at me for an answer.

"Me?" I asked. "I don't know who did this. You must have done it." I ran around the field. I was so happy I wanted to roll in the dirt like a pig in mud.

"I had nothing to do with this," Jim said sharply. "I didn't know about it until Bradley called this morning."

"It had to be someone from the church I'd bet," Jima said.

"Yeah," I laughed. "That must be it."

"God must'a pinched someone's ass but good," Jima said. We both laughed.

"You need to start talking," Jim said glaring at me.

"I've got nothing to say. I told you a second ago and I'll tell you again right now I had nothing to do with this. But I'm not complaining about it either. A week worth of work did in less than twenty-four hours is nothing to complain about. I'm pleased as punch and so should you be."

"I'm sorry if your having a bad reputation doesn't please me," he said.

"Me having a bad reputation? What do you mean by that?" I couldn't believe this was coming from his mouth. "What are they saying Jim? Are they saying I cast a spell? Slaughtered an animal and sacrificed it to Satan? I bet they think I saved some of the blood for you to drink. Come on Jim you know better."

"I don't know what they're saying, but you've got to admit it's a bit strange," he said. "I'm sorry but I'm stuck between two mountains without a way out."

"I can't believe I'm hearing this out of you, of all people. You're worried about your own reputation not mine." I walked away furious. He was making it easy for me to disconnect I should've thanked him.

"You shouldn't fight when something good happens," Jima said. 'I'll never understand you old people."

Jim heatedly kicked up some dirt and walked around in circles convinced I was hiding something from him. I kept my back to him as he walked to the barn, opened the overhead door, and went inside. Jima was staring at the tree line just beyond the field as if she were looking for something.

"What do you think about all this stuff going on here?" I asked her.

"I don't know."

"You don't?"

She looked down avoiding my eyes. "Maybe we could talk alone for a little bit. You think we can get rid of big Jim?"

"Your daddy's madder than hell. He's not going anywhere anytime soon. Maybe you could come to my house later?"

"No. It's better if I show you what I'm talking about," she said and then winked at me, slumped over, hugged her belly and started to limp.

7.

"*D*addy my tummy hurts. I need some Midol. Maybe some tampons too," she moaned. Jima held her mid section tight, and Jim all but ran from the barn to his truck.

Jim rolled down the window and asked if I had anything she could use "You know for that woman stuff." I played along with Jima and assured him I had nothing that would help. He rolled up the window and sped down the road to the Dry Goods where they sell any and everything that will not perish.

Jima and I both had a little laugh at his urgency. "I haven't even started having my periods yet," she said.

"What is it you know about all this?" I asked. "Do you know who cleaned the land?"

"I think I do but I don't know anyone personal like, it's just I think I know something else they might have done," she said.

"That makes no sense. You either know, or you don't." I was firm. All loving feelings had faded hours ago. I was sick to death of this town, and I'd only been here two weeks and a day. If whoever cleaned up the land would be a problem I wanted to know from the get go.

"I know," she said. "That's why I said I'd have to show you, and tell you. Then, you'll understand."

"Then show me."

"We have to go back there," she pointed to the tree line she had been staring at earlier. "It's behind the brush."

"What is?"

"It's better if I show you, besides it's something you should know about now that it's yours."

We walked across the cleared field. I was amazed at how smooth it was. All that was left to do was plow and plant. Jima was silent throughout the journey from the field to the brush line. She talked when we got to the trees that led into the hills and only then to let me know when I should be careful. I had only known her for a couple of days, but I thought silence was probably unusual for her.

Beyond the trees, we crossed a thicket of limbs and thorn bushes. The brush lasted for a good twenty yards before it let out into a small clearing canopied by the trees. Jima stopped in the middle of the clearing, and pointed to an area of wild rosemary bushes that had grown to at least six feet tall and round. I could smell their fragrance from where I stood. Behind the rosemary was another row of trees none of which were very tall. Every tree had clusters of climbing roses that went from the ground to the tops. Red, yellow, white and pink roses covered the trunks, branches and limbs. The beautiful garden of roses and rosemary was far from a natural occurrence this close to the cotton fields, or anywhere else for that matter. This garden was not accidental it was planted and regularly attended. The temperature seemed to have dropped ten degrees under the tree canopy, and the smell was hypnotic.

"It's beautiful Jima but what does this garden have to do with the field? Do you think the same people who planted these flowers also cleaned the land?"

Jima still silent walked to the middle of the rose covered trees, and stuck her hand between two of them opening a hidden door. Slowly I could see the outline of a house that was uniquely camouflaged within it's own surroundings. I walked closer and saw the wood slats that had been cloaked by trees and roses. The smell was intense and sweet. I couldn't stop filling my lungs with it.

"You should come inside and see this," Jima broke her silence.

"What is this place? Is this? No it can't be—can it?" I asked questions that my mind had already answered. This was the house Pop built for Momma when she turned seventeen. He moved her out to the land where he could keep an eye on her and she could live in peace and so could he—this was the house where I was born. "It's not possible that it's the same house. They burned it down. Everyone in the county knows they burned it down." I was frozen where I stood completely bewildered. Jima pulled me inside.

"It's your Momma's house all right, come in here there's more."

The house was no bigger than the one I'd rented in town. The front door opened to a small living space fully furnished with two chairs, a table and an oil lamp. There was a small wood pellet stove standing on top of a chiseled stone for heating. A small dining table (with four chairs) sat in the kitchen, which was open to the living area. A couple of open doors led to a bedroom and bathroom. A charcoal sketch of a woman sitting on one of the wooden chairs hung on the wall above the pellet stove.

"That's your Momma," Jima said.

"I know," I said.

"Over there in the corner in those boxes are her diaries."

I saw the boxes lined up against the back wall of the living area behind the chairs. There were twelve boxes all numbered and stacked in order. "How did you find this house and these boxes?"

"I found the house about a year ago. I was just wandering around, and here it was. It wasn't locked. I didn't bust the door down or anything like that I just walked in through the unlocked door."

"Don't worry I'm not mad at you. I want to know what's going on around here," I said. The last thing I needed right now was for her to clam up again.

"Like I said, I was wandering around out here while Dad and Jason were working in the barn. I thought I saw someone running and I followed them."

"Who did you see?" I asked.

"I don't know. I never saw them again, and it could have been anything I guess like a deer or rabbit or something but it sure did look like a regular old person. So...anyway I sort of ran into the side of the house and found the door and just went in. This is what I found. I come here sometimes when Dad or Jason is on the land and one time I rode my bike from our farm it's only a few miles. The place always looks the same. Nothing is ever out of place. I even left a couple of leaves on the floor you know like on purpose just to test and see if it was cleaned up and the next time I came back it was clean."

As Jima was telling me about her discovery I was looking at everything. The kitchen was small and efficient with a back door. The bare wood walls gave the cabin a rustic smell. The chairs were carved out of pecan wood, which is plentiful in this area, and the cushions looked handmade. The shelves and tables were made from mesquite, but it was those boxes numbered one through twelve that I really wanted to see. Every box was full of neatly stacked black and white composition notebooks. Every page front and back of the first book was covered in handwriting. I grabbed another, and it was the same. I looked through another and another; all of them were filled with her writings.

"Have these boxes always been here?" I asked. "You said they were diaries? How do you know that?"

Jima looked down with shame. "I read some of them. I know I shouldn't have read them, but I was curious. When I opened one of the books and saw your Momma's name in the cover it made me even more curious."

"No. You shouldn't have read these. They don't belong to you. Does anyone else know about this place? Your friends?"

"I haven't told another soul. I swear to it," she said and held up her right hand.

"Are you absolutely sure?"

"I had no reason to tell anyone besides if I did it wouldn't be my secret place anymore, but now that they did that to the field I suppose everyone will know," she said. Jima was a child yet still fully aware of the seriousness of this situation. "I think the same people who take care of this house cleaned up the fields. That picture is your Momma. I think they loved your Momma. They saw you in the field and thought it was her."

"It must be the hill people," I said.

"I don't know. I've never seen even one of them. Not even Aunt Polly'll talk about them, and she talks about everyone." She cupped her hand to her ear in an effort to hear something from a distance. "Dad's here that's his whistle. We better go." Jima was up and running out the door within a split second.

"Wait," I said as I gathered a few of the notebooks, shoved them under my shirt and ran to catch up with her. We ran around the trees and down the path to the sticker patch up and around the massive tree limbs and brush back to the field. We could see Jim at the barn so we pretended to race back to where he was standing.

"I win," Jima proclaimed as she slapped Jim smack in the belly.

"Looks like you're feeling better," Jim said suspiciously.

"I guess it was just a passing thing," Jima shrugged.

"What were y'all doing back there?" Jim asked.

Jima explained that we were racing back and forth across the field looking at different bugs, and making plans for the crop. I snuck back to the truck where my bag still sat in the passenger side seat, slid Momma's notebooks inside, and then went back over to join Jim and Jima. Jim was obviously still put out with me and didn't have much to say to Jima either. He handed her the pain relievers and tampons, she proceeded to throw them in the truck bed without so much as a thank you.

"Can you take me home?" I asked.

"What are you going to do about this?" Jim asked.

"I'm going home to think about it."

"You best do more than think. There was a crowd at the Dry Goods. Looks as if you've succeeded in irritating the town."

"I didn't do anything. It wasn't me," I said. I got in the truck and waited, as Jim looked around the clean field kicking up the dust a few more times. Jima got in the truck beside me.

"He won't settle down until he knows the truth," Jima said.

"I know," I said.

An hour later I was sitting on the couch with a cup of coffee and the first page of Momma's diaries.

****

Anna Ruth Green

January 10, 1983

Daddy gave me a diary today for my birthday. What a wonderful day this has been and now, since you are my gift, I have someone special to share it with. Today, I turn sixteen years old and I have been kissed. It was only once and just a little peck, but it counts just the same because it was from my boyfriend Bobby Garner. He came by the school to pick me up and kissed me smack on the lips right in front of everyone even the teachers. It was delicious to watch everyone's eyes go all wide and buggy. He's only three years older, but you would think he was thirty the way everyone in town carries on about it. Daddy hates him and says he'll amount to no good. He said Bobby's after two things, a wife and a free ride. I think he's cute, and now I know how good he kisses.

****

Most of the first journal was about her sixteenth year and the ups and downs of her and Bobby's relationship. The Garners were the largest family in Sunny. Most people claim to be related to the family in one way or another. Buford Garner was the first mayor of Sunny and the second largest landowner—next to Pop. Bobby and Burt Garner (Buford's great-grand sons) built and owned most of the businesses in town including the veterinary clinic and the only Laundromat.

I flipped through the pages reading her personal thoughts. She wrote lines and lines about Bobby, and the girls who were mean to her. She went on about having to help with the housework, and she seemed to utterly hate church. She made many comments about the Preacher and how she disagreed with almost everything he said. She seemed like a typical teenager until I turned to the page dated January 3, 1984 on that day she wrote:

****

Daddy took me to Sweetwater today to see Doctor Peters. He checked my ears and said everything looked like it should. He gave me some antibiotics because he thinks I could have burst an eardrum or something. He didn't want me to get an infection and said the pills would help. My ears were roaring so loud I could barely hear what he was saying. I didn't even want to eat supper because Daddy kept asking me what was wrong and couldn't tell him, I don't know. I acted as if I were sick to my stomach and waited until he had gone to bed, and then I went into the kitchen and ate the leftovers. I can't sleep because of the freight train running through my body. The noise is unbearable it never stops.

****

January 5, 1984

I scream out loud and hear nothing. I can't hear my heartbeat I can't hear my breathing. I hear nothing but the roar and my head pounds. I cry all day and all night. I don't know what to do. Daddy writes notes to me, and I try to answer without yelling. I have no way of knowing how loud or quiet I am. My life is over. Bobby came by to see me, and Daddy sent him away. He told him I wasn't good. I believe that to be a huge understatement. I missed the first day back at school after Christmas break. I was supposed to turn in a book report, but reading has become impossible.

****

January 9, 1984

Tomorrow is my seventeenth birthday, and yesterday I received an early birthday gift—the roaring stopped and the talking began. The talking goes on in my head for hours on end and when it stops I hear rumbles of voices in the background. I know when the talking will start because the mumble grows louder and louder and then out of nowhere I'll hear a voice. That voice repeats itself relentlessly while other voices begin talking over each other each voice saying something different. I told Daddy what was happening and he set up an appointment with another Doctor. This one is in Abilene. She wrote a book. I heard Daddy on the phone with the Doctor, and he said my mother was mentally ill before she killed herself. I've heard the gossip and people have always given me a look of pity when they talk about my mother—but I've never heard Daddy talk about her that way.

****

I was brought back to reality by the doorbell, not one but multiple rings followed by knocking. I opened the door, and Jim stood there with a look of worry on his face. I let him in; neither of us said a word not even a simple greeting. I hadn't noticed the sun going down, and the room was almost dark. I scrambled around him to turn on a light and picked up the journals that were strewn across the couch. He sat for all of a second and then stood up and started to pace around the small room.

"Something wrong?" I asked. "Obviously there's something wrong or you wouldn't be here past nine on a Saturday. Got to get to bed early so you can get up for church in the morning isn't that what Polly used to always say?" I laughed, Jim didn't.

"Sit down I need to talk to you," he said.

I sat, continued to neaten the journals then placed them under the coffee table out of sight. "What's up chuck?" I laughed again—nervously waiting for the shoe to drop.

"Jima told me about the house, and the journals."

"Ok. Do you want an explanation?"

"Let me finish what I want to say. I know all about it, and I'm fixing to tell you right now how this situation's going to pan out. I'm going to lock up that house, and we're going to forget it ever existed. Do you understand me? We will not let anyone know that house is there. Better yet we need to tear it down."

"Excuse me? You're kidding right? I'm not tearing my house down. It's a miracle it's still there I'm not going to destroy it."

"You don't have a choice. That house has to go. This is serious. You told me you came here to mend what you had broken. You said you wanted to farm and be one of us again."

"I said I wanted to farm, but I never said I wanted to be a part of the town again. I never said that not once."

"How is it that you plan to farm here without being accepted by the very people who will sell you seed and buy your crop? Do you think these people will help you of their own free will? Is that what you think? Jason had to tell Bradley that he wouldn't sell him this year's seed crop if he didn't let us use that backhoe. Hell I even had to bribe Miss Black's son so he wouldn't kick your ass out of this house once he found out you was signing the lease. Don't kid yourself into thinking anyone in this town is happy you came back. The field being cleaned so fast has already got them all up in arms. They're just waiting for the next thing to happen, and uncovering that house would be it. That house doesn't exist. Not to you, me or anyone."

"You're wrong. You're all wrong, every one of you. That house does exist and it exists for me and only me. Do you think I give a flying fuck what anyone thinks or says about me? I don't. I didn't come here to make friends. This is hardly what I'd be doing if I had a choice. I came here because I couldn't stay in Dallas any longer and this is my home. I was born in that house. It's the only place I have, and the land is mine. I will farm the land, and I will live in that house. It's the only thing I have that was my mother's. I will keep it and I will defend it till I breathe my last."

"I hope that's not what it takes. No one's going to make this easy for you."

"Not even you?"

"I don't know. I can't follow you blindly into some abyss. I have to think about it and how it will affect my family especially Jima. God woman you get on my last nerve. That house has to go."

"The house stays. It's my land. I have the deed. The house is on that land and what I say goes. The house stays," I stood my ground. "How many acres do I have? I thought Pop had a little over six hundred?"

"There is but he never plowed the back two hundred," Jim said.

"Why?"

"Hell I don't know. What does it matter?"

"So the land goes deep into the hills, right?"

"Don't get those wheels turning again. You're not going to clear that land. I thought you wanted people to think you were different than your mother, but you're acting," he stopped short.

"Crazy? That's the second time you've called me that word. I think it's all y'all that's crazy. I think any town that would burn a woman's house to the ground with her and a baby inside are the crazy people. Why did they burn it Jim? Don't you remember that part of the story? Why'd they do it?" I asked.

"Let's not do this," he said.

"Why are you backing down now? Let's find out who the crazies are here."

"I didn't mean it that way it's just a figure of speech. You need to calm down and talk about this in a reasonable fashion."

"So now I'm unreasonable? Well I think it was unreasonable what they did to her. Why did they do it? I don't think I heard you," I said, every word louder than the one before.

"Fine. You want to do this then we we'll do this. They burned her house down because she had sex with almost every man in town and then told them their futures. Is that what you want to hear? They burned her house to stop her from doing the things she did They thought what she did was evil. They thought she was evil. Is that what you want me to say? I'm not saying they were right. I think they had their reasons for doing what they did. For God's sake Shanna, she predicted Bobby Garner would die and he did—the time and date every detail. Most people still believe she caused that accident. Emotions got too high and rowdy. I don't think anyone really meant for it to end the way it did," Jim was exhausted. He was talking himself into a corner and knew it.

"You can't be serious. He died in Houston Jim—Houston. How did she get to Houston and back before the next day when they killed her?" Then, I understood what he was saying. He wasn't accusing her of causing the accident. "She didn't curse anyone. She was sick not evil. She was sick and needed someone to help her. Who helped her? Did she walk down Main Street and beg those men to follow her home? She didn't do anything they didn't want her to do. They knew she wouldn't fight them off, she couldn't. I believe they burned the house and her because they wanted me dead. I was proof of one man's sin and that man wanted to get rid of me."

"Oh come on. You know that's not true," he said.

"I know nothing of the sort. I know it's the truth I accept. You can accept whatever truth you want but that is mine."

"You're angry. You've been angry since you heard that story. You're doing this out of vengeance to get some sort of retribution."

"So what if I am. I have every right to be angry."

"Don't you ever get tired of it? Don't you ever want to live a quiet peaceful life? Isn't all that anger tiresome?"

"No," I lied.

"Well it is for me. I may not be the most important man in the world, but I live my life with peace and dignity, and I try to make wise decisions that won't harm other people."

"You lied to everyone about Jima. Is that peaceful for you? Was it a wise decision that she should never know the truth?"

Jim's eyes relaxed as they blankly stared at me. We stood in the silent house face to face. I wanted him to see my side of the story. Maybe it would be different if he put himself in my shoes.

"Why did you feel like you had to lie about Vicky being raped?"

"I didn't. It's what Vicky wanted. She didn't want pity."

"You went along with her lie, and silence equals approval."

"I won't hurt Jima, blood or not she's mine. I won't hurt her and swear if you," he pointed at me.

I grabbed his hand. I couldn't be this mean to him. "I won't say a word to Jima. I wouldn't do that please believe me. I shouldn't have implied. I just wanted you to see my side."

Jim pulled his body away from my touch. "There are no sides. That's what I'm trying to get you to see. There is no battle. It's all in the past and that's where it should stay but letting people know about that house or see it... well that's just dredging up the past and everything the past brings with it."

"I'm tired Jim. My head hurts my heart hurts, and I'm tired."

I leaned forward to lay my head on his chest, and it was like hugging a stone statue. "Don't be mad. We can be mad again tomorrow but right now let's just be nothing." He lifted me off his chest made sure I was steady on my feet and backed away.

"We can't do this anymore. I take the blame for what has happened up to now, but we have to stop this now. I'll be your friend and I'll help with your crop as much as I'm able but no more of this." He pointed to himself and then me. Indicating no more us, no more kissing, no more hugging.

This was painful. No one had rejected my hugs— or me—for ten years while I lived in the bubble of safety and comfort created by Tim and Marla. Who was he to say those words? I was the one who couldn't connect to him. Did he think I wanted more? It was just a hug between friends for Christ's sake who the hell does he think he is? "That'll make it easier for both of us in the long run," I said.

"Tomorrow's Sunday and church," he said. "Let's take some time to think this over. You know how superstition runs wild around here during planting season. Anything you might decide to do could bring a dark cloud over this town. It's not the right time to stir the pot."

"Ultimately Jim it's my decision not yours. You have no control and get no blame so don't worry about it."

"Easier said than done," he said.

8.

I didn't sleep well that Saturday night. My thoughts were consumed with questions. Marla taught me to buck the system and never follow the crowd. Inevitably they would be headed in the wrong direction. Tim's favorite phrase was, show me a man without an ego and I'll show you a loser every time. I decided I'd move into Momma's house, and be damn proud of it. A house lit up and not hidden isn't easily destroyed.

The sun rose and drove the temperature up to ninety degrees by nine AM. The crew had remained a mumble, and I (briefly) thought about going to church, but decided I'd rather not so I turned the thermostat down to sixty, wrapped myself in a blanket, and sat on the couch with a soda and bag of cheesy puffs. I turned on the TV with my trusty clicker and flipped through the thirteen channels provided by the local cable company for a fee of twenty-nine ninety five—and decided I needed an upgrade. More than half of the channels were airing Sunday services at various religious denominations throughout the area the other half were news channels. I tuned in to a national news station, and was alarmed to see another story about Doctor Marla Todd and her book. I was beginning to wonder if it would ever go away.

"Good Sunday morning!" Mack the show host said as he turned into his close-up. The background screen showed a mangled pile of metal and cement. He held up the book with its familiar red cover. The title Patient: Crew was in black block letters across the front. "Was this yet another avoidable tragedy predicted in the now known as prophetic book Patient: Crew? Where is Doctor Marla Todd the author of these books? Has she vanished or will she come forward and give us some well-deserved answers to our many questions? The most important of those questions being who is Patient Crew? This is our focus today on Showbiz Showcase. I'm Mack Trenton your host." The network cut to a commercial and I made some microwave popcorn.

After the commercial break, Mack introduced his guests. A cute, tiny girly girl appropriately named Barbie was first. She represented the common reader and was convinced the first book had saved her life. The other guest was a dark haired skinny man. He was a psychiatrist from New York. He called the reaction to the books nothing more than psychotic mass-hysteria and was peddling a book using said phrase.

"Let's begin with you Barbie," Mack said.

Barbie sat up straight in her seat and was ready to take the floor. "This is a quote from the first book entitled Patient: Crew," she cleared her throat. "On January third, two thousand and three Joseph says: *Eight years time plus eight days Thomas P. and Bagley will fall at midday. Go not near him.*" She closed her eyes and the smile left her face. "On January eleventh, two thousand and eleven at three o'clock in the afternoon The Bagley Building which was built by Thomas Peters, and formerly known as the Thomas P. Building literally fell, killing thirty-six people. I was one of the over two thousand people who survived because of the book. We all read it in the book. We all knew what it meant."

"You have fallen prey to typical psychotic mass-hysteria," the Doctor said in a matter-of-fact tone.

"George Phillips is our other guest today. He is the head of Psychiatry at New York Hospital in Manhattan. Welcome George." The men shared a head nod.

"Now, you say it's all just coincidental but I have to tell you I've read the books and I'm becoming a believer. Does this mean I'm following the pack into psychosis?"

"Don't beat yourself up Mack. We all fall for snake oil occasionally." They laughed together.

My anger was rising as I listened. I felt cold. I wanted those books to disappear. I wanted to be in Dallas with Tim and Marla. I missed them more every day. I would have given my life for one more day with them.

"It's a simple case of psychotic mass-hysteria. This was one prediction out of thousands that actually if I might," he held his hands up and used his fingers to create air quotation marks. "'Came true'. No one wants to discuss the so-called prophecies that didn't come true. Even a broken clock tells the right time twice daily," George smirked.

Barbie was frustrated. "The only reason the others didn't as you say come true is because the people interpreting the books are wrong. It doesn't mean the book is wrong it means we are wrong. But, there are people who are smart and they are cracking the code." I growled at the set, turned it off, grabbed my bag and Momma's notebooks from under the coffee table and found an oil lamp and matches in the kitchen. I poured coffee in my travel mug and locked the door behind me.

I drove down the dirt road—which serves as a property line between my land and Burton Evens'—that led to the acreage behind the field. I parked as close to the tree line as the little car would go without getting stuck. After getting a flashlight from the glove box, and with the bag on my arm—now stuffed with notebooks both Momma's and mine—the oil lamp and coffee in one hand, and flashlight in the other I started for the trail. I laughed out loud at my clumsiness while trying to carry so much and find my way through the brush. I searched for the path Jima had taken me down and saw a single rose on the ground that looked so oddly out of place among the weeds and brush that I went to it. My instincts were right. The out of place rose was followed by others and laid out a path through the brush and prickle bushes straight to the house. I found the door easily and as expected it opened. The trees blocked all the natural light and heat. I lit the oil lamp, set it on the table between the two wooden chairs and turned up its wick. The light from the lamp caused the walls to emit a golden glow that filled the house. Little vases full of cut roses were placed on the table. Their sweet fragrance filled my body with warmth.

"You were expecting me," I said to the sketched picture of Momma that hung above the pellet stove. I felt safe. I didn't feel threatened by whoever was doing these things, marking the path, cleaning the land and giving me flowers. I felt welcomed and wanted. I sat in the chair and sank into the down cushions. It was like sitting on a cloud. The cushions were made from heavy burlap that someone had finger-painted with die using all the colors of the rainbow. They looked like an Art Deco painting stuffed with feathers. I was sure Marla would love them.

I started reading Momma's journals where I had stopped when Jim came over. The entry on January 9, 1984, one day before her seventeenth birthday, was the last entry for two months:

****

March 13, 1984

I came home yesterday so happy to be home. I never want to go back to that house. NEVER! NEVER! Supper was good.

****

March 30, 1984

I went into town with Daddy, but people stared at me. I started screaming. Daddy said I should stay home from now on.

****

April 15, 1984

Daddy is moving me to Gram's house on the land.

****

"Gram's house?" I questioned. This is her Grandmothers house? Pop didn't build it for Momma. Who built it for her Grandmother and which Grandmother, Zeffie's mother? The pages from that point on were filled with what some might see as the ramblings of a maniac, but I knew better. Momma had her own crew. She must have realized on her own that writing helped silence them.

****

Sarah Michelle was hit with a rock her blood was splattered around three blocks the man with the hole in his hand did the deed if you understand. Jeremy Rockets said there were stones in his pockets and threw one directly to the head before he cocked it. Night comes before day, and then day before night the confusion sets in and we know not one from the other. 612398756473890576483023-04955677893-02847-58493049875-2417 south of 35 north of 20 east of 80.

****

There were hundreds of pages in the notebooks just like this. They would have made no sense to her or anyone else. I opened another box and flipped through the books it housed. They were also filled with ramblings of words and numbers. I picked one from the box marked eleven and noticed a small penciled star next to some of the writings. I flipped through the books in box number ten and saw the same star. I thumbed through the first book I'd read and found just one star, next to a two-sentence phrase, and this one was dated:

****

April 13, 1985

Bobby G it seems is a very bad boy. He drank his Sunday whiskey and then at one, two, three he bashed his head into a tree. Drunken

in a city on the shore and nowhere to go but home to the only one he
adores. She left his heart broken without so much as a token of the
love he thought was evermore.

Written below the star in different color ink was:

Bobby Garner died Sunday May 1, 1985 at 1:23 AM.
****

    She did know Bobby Garner would die. She'd
written it before he died, and her voices had predicted it.
Believing Momma's voices told the future meant mine did
too. Believing was like jumping off a cliff; you're never able
to turn back. I looked through the notebooks until the sun
went down, and my stomach was growling to be fed. The
coffee I'd brought with me had long since gone cold and I
was wishing for a hot cup. My head ached from reading
the journals and lack of nutrition. I put the notebooks back
in the order I had found them, and closed the boxes. I
thought about going back to the house in town and making
something to eat but every time my body moved my head
throbbed so I took the cushions from the chairs, laid them
on the floor and cuddled myself on them.

    The smell of coffee and the ranting of The
Preacher (serenaded by The Singer) abruptly woke me the
next morning. The sun was breaking over the horizon,
beaming in through the tree trunks and into the house. I
saw a shadow of someone and got to my feet quickly. As I
turned towards the kitchen, I saw the backdoor close. I ran
to the door, opened it and stood on the back porch. A man
wearing blue jeans with a blue cotton shirt turned to look at
me. He tipped his brown hat and smiled. It looked as if he
mouthed a few words, but the voices had taken over my
hearing. It was the same man who had come to town
seeking Pop's help with his sick wife, I had no doubt; it was
the way he tipped his hat.

The crew was demanding attention. I went back inside to get my tablets and noticed that on the little dinette table was a plate of eggs and toast. Sitting in front of the plate was a glass of orange juice and a steaming hot cup of coffee. I took the coffee into the living room to search for my bag where I'd put my notebooks. On the table, next to the chairs were two new composition notebooks identical to Momma's, and two pens. I had neither the time nor need to wonder who had made the breakfast and set out the notebooks, it was the man who tipped his hat. He was paying his debt to Pop. I set the coffee down and began to write.

I was famished when the session ended. The breakfast had gone cold but was still delicious, and I ate every bit. After washing the plate and juice glass in the sink, I put them back on the table in the same way I had found them. I stepped outside the front door. The rose covered trees bathed the house with fragrance. I heard a tractor plowing the land and thought it must be Jim and he'd almost certainly seen my car. The sun told me it was still early morning. I must have written for at least an hour. The stiffness of my body as I bent down to sweep away the leaves from the entry confirmed it. I stretched, closed the front door and counted my steps to the backdoor. There were fifteen steps. From there to where the tree line thickens and the hills began was another sixty feet.

The hills between Sunny and Sweetwater are more like a series of humps above the earth and are made up of dirt, caliche and trees that lay on a forty-mile stretch of land. Between the house and tree line, was a small yard of overgrown grass and a fenced off area that looked as if it had once housed a vegetable garden. A chair made from braided vines and tree limbs sat next to it. I sat in the chair and listened to the birds as they sang and flew from tree to tree. I felt a sense of belonging on the land, in my mother's house. I had heard stories about the hill people and how they lived in little communities of dugouts and how they played with snakes and drank poison. The two I had seen didn't seem any different from the people in Sunny. I remembered Albee pointing at some family in town and telling me to stay clear of them because the hill people were inbred. I didn't know what that meant, but it didn't sound good. As kids we would chalk it up to old people's delusion. The hill people knew Momma and that was not a delusion. It was also not a misconception that they knew me. There was an obvious connection, but I had no idea what it was. I couldn't help think the voices played a part in it all.

I heard leaves rustle behind the trees. I could feel eyes on me, but saw nothing. Perhaps it was a squirrel burying an acorn. Just in case I said out loud "Thank you, for everything."

I'd decided to spend the rest of the day in my new house and maybe even the night. I needed supplies. I went back inside and made a list of the things I would need so that it would be a quick in and out. At that moment I realized that I hadn't seen my cell phone since dinner with Jim on Friday. This was Monday; four days had passed without a thought of that phone. During the dust storm I checked it every hour in hopes Marla would call, but she never did. I didn't have a computer, which made my phone the only Internet resource—to imply I had proper access to Internet is laughable.

I was able to get in the car and start the motor before Jim saw me. He stopped plowing without killing the engine, took off his hat, and wiped his brow before bending to rest his hands on his knees and stare at me. He looked older on the tractor with his skin tanned from dirt and sweat. I stared back wishing he could read my mind and realize that more than anything I wanted to be able to share my life with him. I couldn't share what wasn't mine. He deserved much better than what the fates had given him. I started the car, backed out onto the road and headed to town. Within an hour, I had gathered my supplies and was back settled into the living area in my home, and my new favorite chair. I'd found the cell phone on the charger and tried to get online to no avail. There were no missed calls. I did however have music, which was a welcome relief from the mumblings.

I thought it was time to get to know my house better since I had only been in the kitchen, Marla would call it an eat-in, and living room. Between those two rooms was a short hallway with two doors. One of the doors I'd already opened—the bathroom. It was a small but complete room with a toilet, shower and sink. Sufficient and efficient Tim would say. Across the hall from the bathroom was the bedroom. It was an empty square room with a window and only big enough for a bed and dresser. There was a corner closet meant for no more than a week's worth of clothing. Both rooms had been cleaned thoroughly.

I took the two bags of supplies I'd brought from town into the kitchen. It was a small space but would suffice. On the back wall was a door that opened up to a walk-in cupboard. Standing against the shelves was a shovel, spade and packets of vegetable seeds. I put the snacks and bottles of water on one of the lined shelves and took the tools and seeds outside to the garden.

I pulled up weeds and spade the hard dirt, turning it over to the rhythm of the plow with a mumbling voice background. I didn't think about the crew, Momma, Marla or even Jim, my mind was on the garden and my home. I was planning the move and how exactly to manage it. I needed my bed and linens, bathroom sundries and kitchen supplies. The living room was perfect the way it was. Most everything could be carried in the car, but the mattress would need a truck and that meant I needed Jim, again.

The plow stopped, and the tractor engine ceased. The sun was dead center in the sky, lunchtime. I went inside and washed my hands and face in the sink. I had nothing but my shirt to dry myself. I got the bread and bologna I'd brought and made a couple of sandwiches, grabbed a couple of bottles of tea and went outside to the field. I was bringing the best peace offering I had. The tractor was in the middle of the field, and Jim was nowhere in sight. I could see his truck by the barn and thought he must have gone inside for his lunch. He knew where I was but had no intentions of coming to me. I sat on the dirt, ate my lunch, and the one I'd made for Jim. I was back at work in the garden for less than five minutes before I heard the tractor engine begrudgingly turn over. Jim and I worked until the sun was in its final decline. When the tractor stopped so did I. Jim had finished the field and I had planted two rows of green beans, okra and tomatoes. The next day I'd plant the peas and carrots.

After drinking two glasses of water, I took a shower and put on the same dirty shirt I'd worn while working outside. I'd brought food enough for a week, but not one change of clothing. I hadn't planned on planting a garden. I hadn't planned anything. My phone still had some power left so I listened to Alison Krause, lit the oil lamps and opened another box of Momma's notebooks. I flipped through the pages but became bored with reading the ranting that meant nothing to me. I didn't read my own sessions for the same reason. If these writings told of future events why doesn't something stand out, anything? I read through the session I'd written earlier in the day to compare it with her writings. I started with what the left hand had written.

The Singer sings: It could have been heaven for everyone.

The Poet says: *The Earth remains stoic. Her boarders lament themselves only for the end homesick. Never in living do they delve. Their arrogance shines bright the credit they take away its truly Floras limelight from creation to this day. She asks not for permission from those who lease her land, or a time to change a season a notion they can't understand. Must there always be one right and always many wrong? Akin dogma unchanged plight. Succeeding verse of matching song. They were created with bless'd choice then go about devising destruction. They extinguished their own voice. Proving themselves the laymen. Hopes turn into bygone dust reclaims its matter as time for fresh tenure dawns the foreman now the latter the earth remains stoic. Her boarders lament themselves only for the end homesick. Never in living do they delve.*

I read the right hand tablet.

The Singer sings: *They created an abyss made from their own undoing.*

The Preacher says: *Make no mistake his will is done. All are judged with wise love. Created by the same maker are those who scorn life. With plans crafted in prevenient grace the blood of their brothers they spill in that month of a thousand deaths.*

The Hippy says: *Man, bitching wild ride. Finneaus Albert the groove to move, with big brother programming how to fight the rap machine? When the wicked becomes the one there is no motto left to trust.*

The Professor says: *Nations hold to an invisible faith not adequate explanation of fact. Even if human mass is constant each with unique will and destiny the silence is resounding. They are destroyed from within.*

Joseph says: *With rhymes and riddles irresolute we must now speak the truth. The thousand will perish within a moon while 4X4 are all destroyed through faith for Finns success. Through the comrade no resistance will this grave provide. She did it all for him and the children lost. They weep out of ignorance for the house on Jacob lane. Their plans were displayed for the world to know. When will their lives end?*

Mother says: *She liked to draw pictures on the wellspring of knowledge.*

Ok now what? What did it all mean? Were they trying to say something? Not to me, it meant nothing to me. Should I tell someone? Who should I tell? If these writings were predicting death was I at fault if I burned the books and did nothing? I blamed my sudden need to scream on reading the session. It caused more confusion and more questions without answers.

"I need some help here," I begged the universe. "I wish I didn't know this any of this. Make it go away. Give it to someone smarter. Someone who knows what to do with these writings, I don't want this. I can't do this." That was it. If the voices wouldn't go away on their own, I'd make them go away. I would burn them. A knock at the door almost made me jump through the ceiling. *It must be Jim no one else knows I'm here but what if it's not Jim,* my thoughts raced. I walked stealthily to the door.

"I've got a gun," I threatened.

"Good. Give it to me so I can blow my brains out. I told myself while I was plowing your field I should just hold a gun to my head and get it over with. It'd be a lot easier than turning this hard ass dirt," Jim said from the other side of the door.

I opened the door—relieved—and there he stood dusty from the land. He smelled like fresh turned earth, pure and masculine.

"What are you doing here?" I asked.

"I'm doing charity, he said. What are you doing here?"

"I was just hanging out, and it got late so I thought I'd...you know...camp out a while that's all." I felt like a kid caught with her hand in the cookie jar. "I planted a garden. Want to see?"

He stepped inside and shined his flashlight around the room that had become quite a mess. Dinner sandwich crusts lay on the floor alongside some coffee cups and bags of chips. Notebooks were opened and scattered around the chairs. He let the light linger on the sketch of Momma. It was his first time in the house. "Hang out? It looks as though you moved in," as the words escaped his mouth he lit up my face with the light. "Are you all right? I thought I heard someone yelling."

I shook my head to avoid his questions. He took the light off my face and stood silently. Neither of us knew what to say.

"Come over here," he said. He wrapped me in his arms and swayed while humming lightly in my ear. "Everything's going to be fine," He whispered in my ear.

Would anything ever be fine again? I let myself feel the sway of his body. I breathed in his smell, allowing only the melody of his hum to enter my mind. No more questions no more thinking. This could have lasted an eternity and it wouldn't have been long enough for me. He raised his head and I followed with mine. Our lips joined with animalistic want and need. I pulled away for a breath but he wasn't allowing it—not this time. I pushed harder. He pulled me back with control. I gave in to him.

"I don't want to stop," the breath from his words embraced my ear.

"Then don't."

9.

I fumbled around in my bag and finally found what I was looking for. "See I told you I brought candles." When the room was lit up, I could see regret in his eyes. We both knew what just happened should not have. I sat on the chair next to the bed of cushions we had just tainted with our questionable act. It was so easy to be with him that it had to be wrong. Anything this good was doomed from the start.

"I love you," he said. "I will always love you. There's not a damn thing I can do about it—it's just a fact. I need to figure out how to deal with it because I sure as hell can't change it."

"You don't love me," I said. "You love the memory of us ten years ago. As soon as the sun comes up and burns off the smell of love reality will set in and you'll remember that I'm the worst thing that ever happened to you."

"Let's go," he said abruptly, got up and started dressing.

"I'm not going anywhere."

"You're going home."

"I am home," I said, standing my ground.

"Not without a lock on the door and not fully exposed the way you are now. Come on let's go. We can leave your car here, and I'll bring you back in the morning."

"I don't want to go. No one knows this house exists. There is no need for a lock trust me on that."

"How do you think I knew you were here? I saw your car."

"If I go back, it's only to get my stuff. I'll need your truck to move the mattress tomorrow."

"What's wrong with you?" he asked.

"I don't know, what's wrong with me?" I answered and asked.

"You're so damn cocky. Why do you feel the need to move out here in the boonies?"

"This house feels like home. It was my Momma's house, and now it's mine," I said and got dressed. "Why should I waste my money renting in town? I hate those people. I can get supplies in Rotan and never have to see any of them again."

"You don't hate them," he said. "You're mad at them. It's the older people who care about that stuff with your mother. Maria, Bradley, Bobby, me...we don't care about that stuff. Just the other day Helen asked about you."

"I'm moving into this house with or without your help," I said.

"Look," he said and pulled me onto the cushion bed, cuddled me to his chest and ran his fingers through my hair. "I'm not trying to hurt you that's the last thing I want to do, but my situation has changed. I have a child to consider. Jason's pretty much useless around the farm. We aren't kids anymore, and if farming is what you want and you want to do it here then you've got to be more pliable. You've got to let go of that grudge and give them a break even if they don't deserve one. You'll need seed and a contract with the gin you can't avoid them." He saw the concern across my brow. "Stay tough."

"I'm tough," I said, and closed my eyes.

Exhaustion overcame me. My mind drifted, and I saw Jim and me on a boat sailing across a wide ocean of calm water with no land in sight. There were no secrets, lies or baggage. We were locked in an eternal kiss as the ocean breeze cooled us. Jim jumped off the boat and begged me to follow. He swam under water until I couldn't see him anymore and then bobbed his head above the surface and pleaded with me to jump, but I wouldn't. I was trembling from fear, and my feet were frozen to the deck of the boat. I clutched the life jacket around my neck and saw that Jim wasn't wearing one. I yelled and cried for him to put on a life jacket. I screamed to him "You're going to drown." He didn't listen and continued to plead with me, beg me to join him under the water. He wanted me to go under with him because something was there. What was there? I couldn't trust him. Every time I tried to jump I was held back because I couldn't trust him. I wouldn't trust him. He went under again and this time his head didn't resurface for a long time. When his head did finally come above the water he smiled. "This is your last chance Shanna."

"No" I yelled and sat up. Jim was sitting on the chair beside me tying his shoes.

"We have to," Jim said. "It's late, and I have to take Jima to school in the morning."

"Oh shit how long did I sleep? You go on home. I'm fine here."

"No," he said loudly. "I'm not leaving you here. Now get your ass up and in the truck we're going home."

"Will you sleep over?" I asked.

"Yes but only if we leave now."

It was well past midnight when we left, and the full moon was high in the sky. Millions of stars lit our way into town.

"You know?" Jim asked.

"No. I don't know," I said.

"As I was saying earlier, you know a lot of people were asking about you at church yesterday. They would like to reacquaint. You remember Helen Garner, Bradley's wife. She used to be Helen, um," he said.

"Helen Hopper. I remember Hells Bells. Is she still the bitch she was in high school?"

"Now see there you go again. She's actually a very pleasant young lady. She and Bradley have been married going on ten years now, got married right out of high school. They make a fine couple."

"That's sweet."

"Yes it is. She asked about you, and then Carla White said she wanted to have you over for lunch. Betsy Miller said she'd love to have lunch with you and thought they might have a welcome home party for you over at the church."

"Why would they want me back in that church? I'm not comfortable going there. I don't see that happening," I insisted.

"Calm down it's just a thought that's all." He patted my leg the same way Pop used to. A pat that told me that I was allowed to think whatever I wanted to think, but we would still do everything his way. I pushed his hand away from my leg.

"No church. Got it?"

"I got it," he said, and turned up the radio volume.

When we arrived, the little rented house felt cold and sterile. I was already homesick. "You hungry?" I asked.

"I could eat," Jim said.

"I'll make some eggs."

We ate eggs with toast and washed it down with a fresh cup of coffee while listening to the radio weatherman give the grim prospects for rain. He said that thirty-five percent of the entire United States was now considered to be in the worst drought since the fifties. Jim's face aged with worry as he listened, deeply concerned about his crops.

"Run off with me. There's always going to be a drought or hail storm or tornado. There's always going to be hardship here and never a break," I said. I was, for the most part, fantasizing.

"Where would we go?"

"Anywhere but here."

"What would we do?"

"Anything but farm."

With full stomachs, we collapsed into the bed. My sleep was peaceful and dream free. I was up before the chickens the next morning. I had three boxes packed, and in the truck when Jim walked out of the bedroom, rubbing his eyes and wondering what all the noise was.

"What's going on?" he asked.

"There's some cereal on the counter and milk in the fridge. Help yourself. I've put a couple of boxes in the truck." I went to the bedroom and stared at the bed. "Jim," I yelled. "I want to take the mattress and bed over today. Do you think Mrs. Black's son would like to keep the rest of the furniture or should we just give it to charity?"

Jim came into the bedroom with his cereal. "Sure—I guess," he said. "I still think we should talk about this first."

"There's nothing to discuss. I've made up my mind," I said.

"You will have locks on the doors, and we won't discuss that subject either. We can stop at the hardware store on the way out."

"No need. There's some spare locks in the kitchen under the sink," before I could even finish my sentence he was in the kitchen inspecting the locks.

"Why does anyone have ten spare doorknobs and deadbolts?" he asked.

"They were on sale," I said and carried another box to the truck.

The sun was hot, and we were headed for a one hundred degree day. It was late April and that meant nothing but dry heat. Perfect for cotton growth but hard on the farmers. I packed more boxes of food, pots and pans to cook the food in, books to read and candles to light. I stacked the boxes of spiral notebooks on a dolly and tried to rush it past Jim, but he stopped me at the door.

"Do you need that many notebooks? There must a hundred of them."

"Two-hundred and fifty. They were on sale," I said.

"You're going to go broke saving money at this pace," he said.

"Are you ready?" I asked.

"Do you want the mattress now or later?" he asked.

"You probably needed to plow or work on your own place so I thought you could help me unload this stuff and take my car. I'll come back with the truck. That mattress is small I can get it."

"I don't know if that's a good idea. Maybe we should drop off this load and come on back for the rest before I start on the farm," he said and looked at his watch. "I've got to take Jima to school."

"We can accomplish twice as much in half the time by doing it my way," I insisted. This was an argument I would win. I wanted to take his truck merely because it was easier, but I would have used my car if he had protested. Either way I was moving that day.

"You'll take Jima to school in my car, and we'll meet up here in two hours."

"Where?" He asked.

"There," I said.

I was hauling the last load of bed and mattress to the farm by noon. Jim had finished working on his land and was there to help me unload. I hinted that burgers would be good and showed him the old grill in the back yard. He had it cleaned and burgers sizzling within an hour. We ate and Jim kissed me goodbye when he left for the fields. Within seconds of his leaving the crew took over.

The session was long and tiresome. I still had boxes to unpack and a bed to assemble.

I was on my way to the bedroom to start working when there was a knock on the door. "You could not have possibly finished that field already," I said, and opened the door thinking it was Jim.

"Hidy-do," Jima said and let herself in.

"Well, Hidy-do to you too," I said and we both giggled. "What are you up to?"

"Nothing much but it looks like you've been up to hella lot," she said. "You've gone and moved yourself in. It's nice in here isn't it? I like the way the wood smells. You got the genny going yet?"

"The genny?"

"Sure, you know the generator."

"There's a generator?"

"Well of course there is. Why would they have all the plugs if there weren't nothing to power what's plugged in?" She moved the chair to the side and sure enough there was a plug cover over two outlets. "You can bring in a fridge and stove too. There's space in the kitchen for them. I think there's some stuff like that out in the barn. I'll go and get dad to open it up for us," she said and ran out the door.

I felt a sudden rush of foolish embarrassment for not knowing. It made a lot of common sense that Pop would have powered the house in some way. It's not as if you could stay cool all summer in here. Now, I could live here forever. My ability to hide the crew had been proven, and I would burn the sessions; no one need ever know.

Jim and Jima brought in an old, but usable, refrigerator and stove they found in the barn. Jima found two lamps that I remembered being in Pop's office. They were in mint condition, which didn't surprise me seeing as I wasn't allowed to touch anything in that room. I plugged in one of the lamps, turned the switch and it was good. The room was now brightly lit and in need of curtains. We all cheered the success and then Jim asked. "Did you start the generator?"

"No, I thought you did," I said.

"Well who the hell cares at this point, it works," Jima said.

"Hell yeah!" I said.

"Watch your mouth little girl," Jim said.

"Yeah Shanna," Jima laughed. "Watch your mouth."

Jima found a light switch behind the kitchen cupboard door and flipped it on revealing a hidden light above the sink. I didn't take time to be embarrassed for not finding it on my own and Jima couldn't care less. Jim busied himself outside with questions of how we could possibly have power without a line or pole. He was convinced that it must run underground but where was the transformer?

"I don't profess to know much about electricity, but I do know it's not a normal setup out there. I found an underground line and it's connected to the house but there's not a meter box or anything else that would tell me which power company it comes from," Jim said. Jima and I were busy cooking our first meal in the house, and I wanted to enjoy the moment, but Jim was spooked.

"I just don't understand where it leads. It seems to go in the direction of the hills but there's not a power station in the hills, is there?" he asked.

"Don't ask me," I said.

"It's not a power plant it's a windmill," Jima said.

"How would you know that?" Jim asked.

"I don't. I'm just guessing," she said.

"I just don't get it," Jim was not leaving this alone. "The field, the house, the power. I just don't get it."

"Maybe there's nothing to get," I said. "Maybe we should take the gift and not ask why."

"No," Jim said. "I would at least want to know who gave me the gift if not just to say a proper thank you."

"I can't argue with that," I said.

Jima quickly changed the subject over to school and what she'd experienced that day. I could tell Jim was enjoying the evening and our time together. We could have been mistaken for a real family that night.

Jim continued to work both his and my farms during the day while I tended the garden. By the end of the week, it was time to sow my fields and with that came the discussion of buying seed. Jim was concerned we would have a problem buying at the Feed and Seed because of Bradley Garner. Needless to say, Bradley's reaction would be far worse than his mother's was at Maria's salon. If his Daddy were at the store, we wouldn't have a chance in hell of walking out with anything except the money we expected to spend. I suggested we go to Sweetwater, but Jim said Bradley's brother Tommy owned that Feed and Seed.

"As much as I don't want to, we might have to trek on out to Abilene. Seems a waste to pay those kind of prices," Jim said.

"Maybe there's another way," I encouraged. "There's always more than one way to skin a cat."

"Well, when you find that way let me know. I hope it's soon because we're already two weeks late," he said.

The next day I stopped in at the Dry Goods to pick up some Wranglers, work shirts, boots, and a different way of skinning that cat. Hells Bells had managed the store since high school. The Feed and Seed was next door. I received what I thought to be a fair-to-midland reception. I smiled at faces I should have remembered, but none of the names came to mind. Maria was there with her children, Vicky Lynn and James. I told her I had moved into Momma's house on the farm, and a hush crept over the entire store. It was probably my imagination, but I swear you could hear crickets.

"Do you think that's a good idea?" she asked quietly while looking around as if to say it wasn't.

"It's the best thing to do," I said. "In this economy I can't be throwing money away on rent when I own a perfectly good house. I'm sure you understand what I'm talking about."

"Of course I do," she exhaled deeply and her judgment left with her breath. "I think it's wonderful and I hope you have us over for dinner as soon as you're ready for visitors." Maria seemed genuinely happy for me, and the busy bodies continued on with their shopping. Maybe Jim was right maybe these people didn't care about the past.

"I'll do that," I said with a smile.

I found the clothes and boots while people shopped around me trying to be inconspicuous with their stares. A young girl with braces was at the checkout counter, and I paid cash. I could see Helen in the office about ten feet from where I stood, but she kept her focus away from me. *It's now or never*, I thought. "Helen is that you?" I asked loud enough for half the store to hear.

Helen turned to look at me and displayed a well performed act of surprise, "Shanna Green is that you?" She came out from her small office with arms opened for a hug. "Just look at you why you've not changed one little bit. I think you're even wearing the same hair style, still."

"Oh, I've changed," I said, and gave her a brief back patting hug while ignoring her jab. "You look beautiful," I said but thought she looked like the super sized version of her high school self.

"Did you find everything you were looking for?" she asked.

"I did," I said. "I needed some good old work duds. I also need to buy some cottonseed."

"Well, I don't, Bradley," Helen said, trying to find the best way to end this conversation immediately.

"I heard Bradley ran out of seed a few weeks ago so I went to Abilene, and they're willing to sell it to me, but it'll cost twice the amount the Feed and Seed would charge and I was just thinking that," I said.

Helen and I were never what you'd call close friends nor did we share any deep dark secrets but what I did know about Helen Hopper is she grew up poorer than dirt. The only reason she married that shit for brains Bradley is because his family is the richest people in Sunny. Helen wouldn't dare miss an opportunity for extra cash at my expense.

"I was thinking I would much rather pay Bradley the extra money. That is if he thinks there might be a little cottonseed left."

"Don't you worry about a thing," Helen said. "I'll call over to Brad, and he'll fix you right up." She had the phone to her ear, and was dialing the number before she could finish the sentence.

"Thanks Helen," I said and walked next door to the Feed and Seed. I could see Bradley on the phone, still saying yes'm to Helen, through the front glass. Billy Price was sitting in his truck waiting for Maria and the kids to finish their shopping. He tipped his hat as I walked by, *a good sign* I thought. I ended up paying a third more than I should have for the cottonseed, but Jim was proud of my accomplishment and happy to get the fields planted.

"Now it's up to God," Jim said. The three of us— Jim, Jima and myself—admired the straight plow lines in the field while on our way to town for a celebratory burger and shake.

"We do the work, and he gets the credit," I said. Jim stared at the road not wanting to give my statement any credence.

"That's a good one," Jima said.

"Don't encourage her," Jim smiled.

We stuffed ourselves on burgers, fries and chocolate milk shakes while basking in the glow of our accomplishment. Jima fell asleep on Jim's shoulder as he drove me home listening to country music on the radio.

"You're a good father," I said.

"You think?"

"I know."

"Thanks." We listened to Willy, Waylan and the Boys sing a song about Luckenbach, Texas. When Alison Krauss started singing, Let Me Touch You For A While, Jim reached around Jima, and put his hand on my shoulder. When Trace Adkins started singing about the young love he couldn't forget, Jim started to stare at me.

"What?" I asked with a chuckle.

"Nothing," he said with a sly, half-cocked grin. He turned his eyes towards the road and quietly added, "You're beautiful." After dropping me off at home, Jim drove Jima back to town, tucked her in and drove back out to the farm to stay the night with me.

For the next month while the cottonseed grew into plants, the three of us became a family during the days. At night Jim would always find his way back into my bed after Jima was taken home. We became secret lovers. I ran into Picky and Pilly a time or two when I'd go into town for groceries. They were always cordial but retained a certain level of suspicion in their eyes. Polly was bed ridden and Jason spent most of his time tending to her needs.

My vegetable garden had produced more than I could handle. In the mornings, when Jim took Jima to school or tended to his own fields I would gather the vegetables in a big basket and put them inside the back tree line. By noon the vegetables would be replaced by a bundle of wild flowers, or spices, and on occasion freshly baked bread and churned butter. For a second here and there I allowed myself to believe the fantasies had come true. But, inevitably the crew would be around to remind me that happiness should never be trusted.

By the middle of June, the heat was vicious, and not an ounce of moisture had hit the earth for two months. Cotton farming is basic; the plants thrive off minimal amounts of water or care but there are times when water is important. My plants, having been planted three weeks late, were still healthy. Jim's plants were a month older, and the drought had left the leaves dry. If they didn't get a good amount of water soon the bolls wouldn't have time to develop, and that would mean no cotton. Jim had irrigation but the well was running low. He only watered the plants during the dead of night giving the plants time to soak up the moisture and Jim a good reason for not being home. We weren't fooling anyone other than ourselves. The looks I got in town told me everyone knew our little secret and few, if any, approved.

10.

*I*t was the twenty-ninth of July, two thousand and twelve. The moon was full, and Jim was sitting outside on a lawn chair (hidden between two trees) with a shotgun across his lap. During the previous few days we'd woken up to puddles of water in the fields without clouds, rain, or irrigation to create them. I didn't know how, but I knew who was watering the fields. It was the final straw for Jim. He had become obsessed with the need for facts. This would be the third night he'd spent outside daring the perpetrators of goodness to show themselves. I tired of his stakeout within minutes of the first night and now found myself bored and alone without anything other than my mumbling mind to keep me occupied. I had tried multiple times to get the TV to work, but without cable all I received was white noise.

I turned on the radio and listened to the only FM station with a strong enough signal to reach the west Texas plains. The droning country music gave me a better understanding of the slow nature of people who listened to it hours on end. I flipped the switch to AM and listened to the last farm report of the day and was pleasantly surprised to hear a promo for Texas Today, an insightful discussion of statewide issues.

The first story was about the Texas Rangers vs. Red Sox baseball game. Texas took that game nine to one. The second story was about politics, and the run off election held that day. Texas always did know the proper priority of events. I looked around the kitchen for a snack while the political pundits speculated their party's win. The fourth story caught my attention.

"It's nine thirty-eight, and next we have a follow-up to Wednesday's car bombing death of CIA agent Frank Argot. Former Agent Timothy Todd, Argot's partner, along with his wife Doctor Marla Todd are still missing and wanted for questioning by the CIA. The FBI along with the CIA and all local law enforcement are not commenting on the tragedy. Agent Argot was a single father of two young girls. In other news, today was the one-hundredth day without rain and the twelfth day with temperatures above the century mark."

The shock to my system was immeasurable. I was frozen with fear as the room, and my thoughts spun. I started to search for more information, turning the dial and stopping for any signal I could hear in hopes there was a rogue station breaking through the radio waves with nothing but news to tell. I fumbled through the newspaper Jim had brought inside for his daily sit on the toilet, but it was from the previous Sunday. The reporter had said it happened on Wednesday.

"It happened on Wednesday, yesterday," I said. "Facts—Tim and Marla are still alive, on the run. It happened yesterday and what were you doing yesterday while all this mayhem was taking place? That's right you were playing house. The dutiful wife and sex slave skank all rolled into one." I wanted to hurt myself as my mind visualized Tim and Marla being tortured by the government to give up their fortune telling freak.

I turned on my cell phone and attempted to open the Internet, but it wouldn't connect. I gathered Jim's clothes, wallet, and keys then headed outside. He jumped to his feet waving the shotgun around when I slammed the door behind me. "Point that thing down before you hurt someone," I said, and handed him his belongings.

"What's this?" he asked.

"You're going home."

"What?" he asked and scrambled to hold onto the clothes and gun without dropping either.

"I said you're going home."

"I know but why?" he asked.

"You need to spend time with your family."

"It's ten o'clock at night they're all in bed by now."

"Then, you'll be there for breakfast in the morning," I said walking back to the house.

"Did I do something?" he asked.

"No I did," I said.

I lay in bed that night making mental lists of what I'd do the next day. I needed some national newspapers and a source of constant information, which meant cable TV and Internet. I was worried sick about Tim and Marla, and as much as I wanted to know I didn't want to leave again. Tim said if the shit hit the fan (and it had) I should wait for them to contact me, and that's exactly what I'd planned on doing. Act normal and wait, but in the mean time I needed information.

By nine the next morning I had eaten breakfast, harvested the garden, and was driving east on I-20, thirty miles west of Abilene. I'd picked up an Abilene newspaper at a gas station in Anson. There were no articles about the CIA bombing or Tim and Marla, but there was an ad for Total Electronics; everything you need to keep you technically up to snuff. I liked the tag line but what attracted me the most was the twenty percent discount I'd get for presenting the ad to my cashier when checking out.

The store was small, and at the end of a strip mall situated on College Street in north Abilene. The sign on the door said they opened at ten. It was a quarter past, and I was the only customer. I looked around at computers and realized I hadn't the first notion of what I would need. I went up to the cash register where a zit-faced nerd was playing games on his cell phone.

"Hi, I wonder if you could help me with something?" I asked.

Without looking up or skipping a note of the beat his thumbs were tapping out on the phone he asked, "purchase, repair or tutorial?"

"A little of each."

He pointed to a desk in the back of the store where an extremely large black man was sitting behind a trio of computer monitors. "Fat Boy's the know it all."

I walked to the back of the store and stood in front of Fat Boy's desk. "Hi, I'm Shanna. The kid at the register said you could help me."

"I'll be right with you," he said with a quick look and grin. "Give me one second. There, all done. If I can't help you, you can't be helped," he extended his hand and I accepted the gesture with a firm handshake. "What'll be?"

"I live in the country," I said.

"No cable, no cell, didley squat?" he asked.

I confirmed and he shut off his monitors with a master switch. "Lets look at a sat dish, you could probably pick up some FTA, won't give you much—won't give you Internet—you'll need a provider for that. What do you like to watch?"

"I need news stations," I said.

"God knows there's plenty of them out there," he said. "What are you using? PC? Mac?"

"Neither. I've been trying to get a signal on my cell, but I can't even get enough bars to carry on a complete conversation," I said.

"I hear you sister, and I can hook you up. You don't need one of those high priced me pads we've got a netbook that does the same thing at a fraction of the price."

"Ok," I said. "Hook me up."

I watched Fat Boy walk in circles around the store grabbing items from the shelves and bringing them to a counter next to his desk. He had a light step considering his overwhelming size and moved with smooth precision. The choices were made, and the counter was filled with boxes and cables to connect what was in the boxes in order to give the devices an ability to capture invisible signals that gave me access to the rest of the world and most importantly knowledge.

"How hard will this be to install?" I asked. "Does it come with instructions?"

"We install," he said.

"Can you do it today?"

"Where do you live? Tomorrow's Saturday, I can grab a ride over in the morning and have you fixed up by noon." He handed me a pad and pencil. "Write down your address and phone number. I'll call you when I'm five minutes out."

"I live in Sunny."

"Where's that? Is that out near Lytle Lake?" he asked. "I know that area."

"No it's a town. Sunny, Texas. It's west of here."

"A town? How far west?"

"About forty miles."

"I don't have a car. Isn't there someone in town that could help you? Your husband, or a boyfriend could probably figure it out."

"I don't have either, and I can't trust anyone in town to do a good job. It's a farming community," I said.

"I can't," he said. "I don't have a car, how would I get home?"

"I'll drive you both ways. I can pay extra for your trouble. I'll even make you lunch."

"Lunch?" his brows rose with interest.

"Whatever you want," I said.

"Agreed," he said. We shook on it, and I paid using my twenty percent off ad, while Fat Boy loaded the car.

The drive back to Sunny took us a little under an hour. He told me more about my car than I cared to know and even more about the stereo. Who knew it took over twenty connections using forty wires with three different colors—four if you're using tweeters—to install properly.

"What's your name?" I asked.

"Fat Boy," he answered.

"You're big, but you're not fat. What does your Momma call you?"

"Kevin. My name is Kevin Stewart but Ma's the only one who calls me Kevin, my friends call me Fat Boy."

"Did you go to school in Abilene? Where's home?" I asked.

"I grew up in Houston. My mother works as a social worker for the state. When I graduated from high school, she got a job in Abilene so I moved with her."

"Do you have any brothers or sisters?"

"Nope, my dad died when I was a baby. He was a cop. It's just Mom and me. I graduated from Hardin Simmons, got my masters from McMurry, and now I'm going to apply for the Doctorates program at Abilene Christian."

"You must really like Abilene."

"Not really but I like Ma and this way I can get my education and look after her. Besides, I don't have to pay my loans back until I stop going to school." He turned on the radio and searched to find a station.

"The country station's all I've been able to get so far," I said.

"You have OnStar. See this red button?" He put his finger on a little red button next to the radio and pushed it. "I'm going to get you some free time."

I heard static through the speakers and then a female voice. "OnStar this is Debbie, how can I help you?"

"Yes Debbie, can you direct me to your sales department?" he asked. More static ran through the speakers.

"This is Michael would you like to start your thirty day free trial."

"Yes we would thank you Michael," Fat Boy answered.

"No problem, give me a second to pull up your records. Here we go. Am I speaking with Timothy Todd?" he asked.

Kevin turned and gave me a look of confusion mixed with suspicion. I panicked, pulled off the road and killed the engine as Michael spoke. "Mister Todd, are you there?"

"Hey," Kevin protested grabbing onto to anything that would stop his foreword momentum into the dash. "What was that?"

"Look," I said. My hands were shaking on the steering wheel. I pressed them on my legs, which were also shaking. "Don't mess with my shit ok? Let's keep this simple we're not friends. You're doing a job for me. Got it Kevin?"

"Got it," he said. "Who's Timothy Todd?"

"I don't know," I lied. "The car's used maybe it was the previous owner. Does it matter?"

"It doesn't matter to me," he said.

You've got to stop making stupid mistakes; I admonished myself. I should have read the owner's manual and known every detail of this car so that something like what just happened wouldn't have. The only part of the debacle that made me feel better was that Tim had made a mistake by keeping his named attached to the car. It was not like Tim to overlook even the most minor detail, but at least I wasn't worthy of complete blame. Kevin was curious about Tim's name. He didn't want to appear curious, but he was. Maybe he'd heard the story on the news. Maybe there was a public manhunt for him. My regret was mounting, and now I was taking a stranger to my house. I felt as though I were at a point of no return. I had to go forward and deal with whatever consequence Kevin's inclusion caused.

We pulled onto the path that led to the house, which was now considered my driveway and stopped in front of the tree line. Kevin got out of the car and walked to the fields.

"Is all this yours?"

"It is. With the house, and the hills it's a good amount of land."

"Is it all cotton?"

"Nothing else will grow out here."

"Show me inside and we'll get busy," he said and followed me to the house. "Farmers eat a lot of beef don't they?"

"I'll set out some steaks and cook them on the grill while you're working," I said acknowledging his hint. "I'll make some hash browns and beans on the side."

"Sounds good," Kevin said. He seemed more interested in the house than he did the food. "Is this a family homestead? When was it built? I love the wood, and the craftsmanship is remarkable. The front garden is perfect and the smell of the roses mixed with rosemary is brilliant. Did someone in your family build it?"

"My Grandfather's family came to Sunny in the mid eighteen hundreds. I'm not sure who built the house or how long it's been here. It's just an old farmhouse without much history, but it beats pissing my money away on a rental."

"Seen any ghosts?" he asked with a snicker.

"Nothing like that," I said. Not wanting more chitchat I added, "the TV's right here as you can see."

"I'll get the stuff." Kevin unloaded the car, and I wandered around to the back yard trying to get phone reception. I needed to call Jim. I didn't want to apologize for sending him home the previous night. I needed to ensure he'd stay away for the day and the only way to accomplish that was eating crow.

"Hello," Jim said.

"Jim? Can you hear me?" I had him, but the line was scratchy. "I'm sorry about yesterday. I needed some time alone, to think about things. I guess things are just going too fast for me." I sounded like one of those whiney bitches on a mushy primetime soap opera.

"What?" Jim asked.

"Can you hear me Jim?"

"A little. Did you say something?"

"Just that I needed some time," I said.

"I can't hear you. Polly's in the hospital we brought her to Sweetwater Memorial last night. Are you there?"

"I'm here. Is she ok?"

"She had a pretty nasty fall, hit her head on the floor and knocked herself out. You there?"

"Yes, I'm here."

"If you hadn't sent me home, she would've died on that bathroom floor. Not one person woke up. Hell if it weren't for her fuzzy pink slippers sticking out of the bathroom door, I probably wouldn't have found her myself."

"Thank the lord and pink slippers," I said.

"What? I can't hear you."

"Nothing."

"I'm going to be here for the day, and probably through tomorrow. We're waiting on the Doctor."

"Of course," I said.

"I'll call you tomorrow," he said.

"Jim," I said with hesitation.

"Yeah Shanna what is it?"

"Stay tough," I said. I wanted to say I love you. I wanted to say stay with me forever. I couldn't say any of the things I was feeling. This was just another bridge I was being forced to burn.

"I'm tough," he said and the phone disconnected.

Jim loved his family. He had always felt a deep loyalty and responsibility for their wellbeing. I felt sad for him and—to a certain extent—Polly. I also felt a great wave of relief. I wouldn't have to explain Kevin, and with that accomplishment came hunger. I started the charcoal in the grill with some mesquite twigs.

The steaks sizzled while my mind occupied itself with thoughts of running. I would wait a few days for Tim to contact me and if he didn't, I'd leave. Meanwhile, I'd at least be able to follow the news. I would have to ease out of Jim's life swiftly; there was no time to waste. It wouldn't be easy for him. I was confident the people in town would make it harder for him with their I told you so's. Sunny would never be my home again. I heard the backdoor slam, but I didn't hear Kevin's footsteps coming to me. I looked down at the steaks and could no longer hear them sizzle. I saw Kevin's lips moving yet all I heard were Joseph and The Preacher fighting for attention. This session was different. As usual, the crew took over my hearing but this time my vision was fading. I was dizzy and felt as if I were being robotically driven to find the notebooks and pens. I bumped into the empty boxes Kevin had left on the floor. He followed me, tapping my shoulder to get my attention. I went into my room and sat on the bed.

All concept of time had been lost, and I felt as if I had simply been asleep. There were no visions, dreams or feel-good fantasies. I hoped I'd done just that, fallen asleep and merely had a nightmare. I stretched my legs and fingers dropping the tablets and pens on the floor at Kevin's feet.

"I must have fallen asleep," I said, and quickly gathered the tablets and stuffed them under the bed sheets. That's when I noticed the empty bags of chips, and cans of soda that littered the bed and floor. "Are you finished? Everything working?"

"You were cooking steaks on the grill and then," he said while air writing with both hands. He had what Pop would call a shit-eating grin on his face.

"Don't jump to conclusions," I interrupted.

"I've long since passed conclusions." He picked up his garbage and dusted the crumbs off the bed. "When I saw it, I was…I was…fuck I don't know what I was but it blew my fucking mind."

I laughed to diffuse him. "I don't know what you think you saw but."

"No. Don't make up a lie. I know what I saw. I know you're Patient Crew," he said. "I've studied both books."

"I'm not a crew or a patient. What do I owe you?"

"Owe me? You don't owe me anything."

"I owe you for the work you've done. I intend to pay you and take you home. Now what do I owe you?"

"Wait here."

He went into the living room and came back with his backpack. He took out an all too familiar book and thumbed through the pages. "Here it is," he sat next to me on the bed and held my hand as he read. "The Poet says: *Someone to help the water bearer. Her time will soon run short. A portly man is he who sees her. Now welcomed to our court. Noble he will become. As he sees what she has done.* There's more, should I continue?"

I pulled my hand away from his grasp, and stood up taking the book from him to look at the page he was reading. What Kevin failed to mention but pointed out with a chubby finger was how the poem created an anagram. He had circled the first letter to each new line, and it spelled Shanna. I handed him the book and said the first thought that came to mind. "Get out of my house."

"Oh hell no, I'm not going anywhere besides what am I supposed to do, walk?" His laugh shook the bed making the old wood frame groan.

"I don't care if you have to crawl just get out. You don't want to be a part of this and I don't need you." I went to the living room, and he followed. "If you don't leave, I'll call the cops."

"Go ahead call them I'm not leaving," he said and sat on the chair with arms crossed. "Looks as though we've got ourselves a standoff."

I stood next to the chair pulling his arm. "Look at you, little white girl," he laughed. "I bet you don't tip the scales above a hundred."

"I'm stronger than I look," I said. Who was I kidding? He could lay me out before I saw it coming.

"You don't have to be tough around me. I'm not going to hurt you," he said.

I leaned against the wall facing him. "What time is it?"

"Nine-forty," he said looking at his watch.

"Can't be," I argued. "It's light out the sun's not even down. Wait a minute what day is it?"

"You've been out for while," he explained. "You were cooking the steaks I ate yours...hope you don't mind. But, then all the sudden you were on the bed writing with both hands and turning the pages and writing again...fucking awesome."

"You already said that, and I'm not amused by your amorousness. So it was around noon when I started, how long did I write?" Kevin sat up straight and stared at the wall beside me. He looked like an android dialing into his memory banks.

"You wrote for approximately six hours without stopping. You then laid yourself out on the bed and slept until three thirty-six AM then sat up and started writing again. Your eyes were closed, and you appeared to be in a state of sleep. That lasted until six eighteen AM at which point you lay back on the bed and slept until nine thirty-seven AM. You woke up and that brings us to the present," he looked in my eyes. "Is that what you wanted?"

"None of this is what I wanted. I shouldn't have brought you here. This is a huge mistake." I slid down the wall and sat on the floor holding my head in my hands. "I've fucked up everything."

"You did what you were supposed to do. You need me and I can prove it." Kevin started to sway with eyes closed while humming, and sang: *"Maybe she won't suffer if she listens to her mother. Maybe a dark warrior will break down the barrier. Listen listen to me. Hear me hear me say this. Both bear the others need. One is the code the other the key.* I think this next part is the chorus," he said, and began to sing again. *"Warrior oh warrior. Warrior dark warrior guide guard, direct her.* There's a second verse," Kevin said. "Do you want to hear it?"

With my head still resting in the palm of my hands I gave no response, which didn't seem to matter. He would continue whether I liked it or not. I thought it best to let him get this out of his system.

"Dark warrior see the calling pipe and vessel as it should be. Right to left, left to right read it rite day and night."

"That's enough," I said quietly.

"What?"

I raised my head, "I said that's enough. I've heard enough. I've had enough."

"So you understand what The Singer's saying? You know it's about me and you."

"No I don't see that. That's just your own imagination taking over."

"No it's not," he said.

"Did you memorize both books?" I asked.

"If it's something important I remember," he said.

"Important? What does it matter? It's just a song written by some crazy person who hears voices. What the fuck does it matter?"

"Have you read it?"

"Read what?"

"The things you write."

"No." I let my head fall into my palms again. The crew was coming back. My choices in that moment were limited. I could pretend I wasn't the person Kevin knew I was, or I could let him in. I went to the bedroom leaving the door open, sat on the bad and started to write.

11.

Kevin shook my shoulder, and repeated my name a few times before I was able to open my eyes and focus on his face—*When I consider now the way in which I met Kevin and how I befriended him, I have no excuses. Nothing was whispering in my ear that this guy was good. I liked his kind smile and trusting eyes.

"Listen to this," he cleared his throat. "The Preacher says in Patient: Crew, book two, page ninety-six." He started talking like a southern preacher. *"And I tell you this day as the snow falls upon Edom... ah...the meeting will be held on that day of discovery...ah...and when the gates close on that time and that place they will never open again...ah. And I quote to you today the first good book of Patient: Crew in the page...ah...of sixty-six and the line of four, 'It is a groovy cool one who helps the flower child. His name rhymes with heaven', thus says the Hippy."* Kevin sat on the bed making it bounce. "I know it's me they're talking about. I have no doubts."

Still dazed from the last session I was by no means ready for this conversation. "How long this time?"

"You wrote for three hours and slept for two," he said. "Come on in the kitchen you need some food. I'll make you some coffee and eggs. I had a snack earlier, but I could eat." I followed him to the kitchen. "Sit down and take a load off." He made me a plate of scrambled eggs with toast and butter and twice as much for himself.

"Thanks, this is good. I guess I was hungry," I said.

"Can I ask some questions?"

"One," I said.

"Do your hands hurt? You were writing nonstop in there they must be screaming."

"Do my hands hurt?" I was amused. "That's what you want to know?"

"I want to know everything you're willing to tell but if you're putting a limit on me…yes that's what I want to know."

"No they don't hurt."

"Got it," he said.

"The book wasn't my idea and it's done me nothing but harm."

"I'm here to help and protect you. Anything you need you've got," he said, eyes fixed on mine. "I'm making a commitment to you and I don't take that lightly. I won't say it wouldn't help if I had a little background knowledge. Can you tell me when you started hearing the crew?"

"First, you have to give me something. How old are you?"

"I'm thirty eight, six feet five, three hundred twenty-five pounds. When did it start?"

"It started when I turned seventeen."

"Did anyone else in your family do this kind of thing?"

"What's your mother's name?"

"Jade Stewart," he said.

"Momma heard them at seventeen too. I think her mother Zeffie was the same age, but she didn't write anything down at least not that I know of."

"Did your Momma write?"

"What's your favorite color?"

"Red."

"Momma wrote too."

"What happened to Zeffie and your Momma?"

"Zeffie killed herself and the good people of Sunny killed Momma."

"How'd they kill her?"

"What's your degree in?"

"Law. I want to be a lawyer."

"They burned this house down. She was able to get me out before she collapsed."

"Did anyone get arrested or go to prison?"

His question made me chuckle. "No."

"Small town justice. Who rebuilt the house?"

"Why a lawyer?"

"Have you seen what those guys make?"

"I don't know who rebuilt it."

"How'd you meet the Todd's?"

"Oh God I need to check the news. Where's my computer? TV?" The house was cluttered with boxes, packing foam, and instructions from Kevin's installations making it difficult to find the floor, much less the TV.

"Nothing new has been reported since the day it happened," Kevin said. "The FBI and CIA are both silent on the issue. They don't inform the public until they need the public."

"You figured out the Timothy Todd stuff?" I asked.

"A little, but I'd like to know more."

"I don't understand why they haven't called me."

"How did you meet Doctor Todd?" Kevin asked again.

"I left when I started to hear them and ended up at Marla's clinic. She took me home, and I lived with her and Tim for ten years. During that time, I was Marla's patient. She's responsible for my being able to retain a little piece of normalcy. She's the one who discovered that if I write everything they say, they would leave me alone. Sometimes days—sometimes hours—sometimes minutes. Have you checked the Internet?"

"Yes nothing new. She knows the writings are prophetic?"

"Nobody knew before the Ceely Masters show."

"I see," he said.

"You see what?"

"Nothing. Why'd you come back here?"

"The books and Ceely Masters," I said.

"Why would you come back here after what they did to your mother?" Kevin asked.

"That's enough for now."

"Can I read your writings?"

"Sessions," I said. "I call them sessions."

"Can I read the sessions?"

I gathered the notebooks from the bedroom and handed them to Kevin. "Knock yourself out, read between the lines and have a blast."

"Read between the lines? Not with the crew, no need to. We go down the paths the crew leads us. It's all there in its simplicity."

"We?" I asked.

"There's a few of us who take the crew seriously and realize the change they will affect."

"This is not a good idea. I shouldn't let you read these," I held out my hands for Kevin to return the books and he held them away from me.

"I'm not going to hurt you. I'm trying to help you."

"I found you, not the other way around," I said.

"We found each other its fate."

"There is no such thing as fate. We create our own destiny."

"That's very psychologist of you. Call it what you want but the facts remain," he said. "You are Patient Crew and I am the dark warrior they foretold." I again reached for the sessions, and his reaction was to sit on them.

"Don't be childish," I scolded.

"Don't be selfish," he retorted.

"How am I being selfish? You're the one sitting on them."

"You could have written about someone's death you could save lives. I call that selfish."

143

"Low blow," I said and hung my head. If his intent with that statement was to guilt me into letting him read the sessions in peace it worked. We sat across from each other in the living room chairs. I watched him read through the notebooks while flipping through the news channels on the TV. There wasn't one report or story on the bombing. My eyes became heavy, and I drifted into a light sleep. I heard Kevin when he stood up, felt him touch my arm and shake me gently. It felt like only minutes had passed but when I woke up it was late afternoon.

"Shanna can you hear me?"

"What is it Kevin?"

"It's your cell phone. It was vibrating, and I saw you had eight messages. I thought it might be important."

"Tim. Marla. It's got to be them." I rubbed my eyes and tried to focus on the phone screen. "It's Jim." I walked outside the front door where the service was better to return his call, Kevin followed.

"Who's Jim?"

"He's just Jim," I said and called. It took him three rings before he answered. "Jim? Is everything ok?"

"Polly died last night," Jim said.

"Oh poor Polly I'm so sorry." I listened for Jim's response. Kevin started humming to himself and ran inside the house.

"She never regained consciousness, and passed this morning."

"What can I do?"

"Nothing at the moment. I just wanted you to know. I'll call you later I need to get back to the family."

"I'm very sorry for your loss," I said.

Kevin came outside with my notebooks, flipping through the sessions and started to sing. *"In two weeks plus a day, she'll be going away, Polly wolly's dead that day. She took a great fall near the bathroom hall, Polly wolly's dead that day. Yes she is, yes she is, she is surely dead that day. Now, her pain will be over and in heaven she'll see Peter singing Polly wolly's dead that day."*

He showed me The Singer's song I'd written two weeks earlier. I pushed him aside. I couldn't stomach knowing. "Leave me alone for a second ok?"

"I don't think that's a good idea let's talk it out," he said following close behind.

"I'm worried about Tim and Marla. I'm worried about Jim and how I'm going to leave again, and he just lost his Aunt Polly. I must have known it would happen and didn't do anything to stop it."

"Is Jim your boyfriend?"

"No." I didn't want to explain. "And you. What am I going to do about you? I don't know what move to make next. I'm all over the place with this." I walked past the tree line and looked out into the field. The cotton was knee-high and a deep healthy green far greener than the neighboring fields. I could see the ground was damp with water. I was furious. "Who is fucking with me? It's the worst fucking drought in forty years, and my fields are soaked. Why? I hear voices that presumably tell the future? Then tell me what to do. Tell me or leave me alone. What good is it if I can't use it for my own benefit? I do all the work and don't even get a hint? Tell me without riddles, rhymes or songs. Do you hear me? Does anyone hear me?" I yelled.

"Calm down Shanna," Kevin said. "Breathe."

"I can't do this anymore. I don't want this can't you see that? I just want to be left alone. Just let me live, please just let me live in peace." I couldn't hold back the anger that was welling in my body. I ran into the field, Kevin trying to keep up, and started pulling up the cotton plants. "I want this to stop. Do you hear me? Do you hear me? Show yourself or stop this now."

"Shanna please stop. Breathe," Kevin was panting trying to catch his own breath. "See like this—in through your nose and out through your mouth."

"I swear Fat Boy if you tell me to calm down, and breathe one more time I'll slap the shit out of you! It's not that simple. Nothing about this is simple. I didn't put in irrigation, but my fields are constantly damp. I didn't clean the field; I haven't dug out a path to the house that is magically widened daily. I don't pay for electricity, but I could light up the whole damn town. This house, my Momma's house, the town burned it to the ground yet here it stands sturdy like a shrine. I didn't ask for this do you understand me Kevin? I didn't ask for any of this."

"It's not your fault," he said.

"It's not about fault it's about being able to help Tim and Marla the way they helped me. I've already hurt so many people…truly damaged people…I don't want to hurt anyone else. I already started down the path to pain with Jim. But tell me what am I supposed to do? I can't do anything because I can't even control what happens in my own body. I have no choice or control over anything."

"You can control the crew. Don't you see? It's brilliant," he said. "You need to listen what they say. You can control everything. You have total control at your fingertips. You can help many more people than you've hurt."

"Have you heard a word I've said?" I fumed back to the house, and Kevin followed. "Stop breathing down my back."

"Then stand still and talk to me," he shot back.

"What do you want to talk about Kevin?"

"You need to calm down."

"And you need to shut up."

"Calm down."

"Shut the fuck up!" I yelled and went into the bathroom, slammed the door and started the shower. Why did Kevin have to sing that song? Why was Tim's partner blown up? Why does it all have to be like this? I got in the shower, and let the water run over my body hoping it would somehow wash all the bad down the drain. I never wanted to leave that shower. I sounded like the baby I'd accused Kevin of being. *Keep moving forward*, Tim had said. I finished my shower got dressed, put on my makeup and went into the living room. Kevin was sitting on the floor with the session notebooks scattered around him.

"I'm going over to Jim's house and pay my respects to his family," I said.

"He's your boyfriend."

"No, it's just the right thing to do."

"I guess most of the town will be there."

"Probably. Polly's lived here all her life. Everyone knows her, and most don't like her but they know her."

"Everyone loves the dead."

"That's it then. I'll go over there now. I should take some food. I have a cake mix," I said. The thought of baking caused me to cringe with disgust. Kevin laughed and went into the kitchen and started pulling out bowls and pan's as if he owned the place.

"I'll have a fine—from scratch—apple crisp ready in twenty-five minutes. If anyone asks, and trust me they will just tell them it's a family recipe."

I sat in the living room and watched the news. Kevin had left the sessions on the floor, and I glanced at a few sentences here and there but nothing stuck out as interesting to me. It wasn't long before I could smell something sweet baking in the oven. "That smells good. Jim will never believe I baked it."

"He's lost family he won't be concerned with your cooking."

Twenty minutes later I was in the car with a steaming pan of apple crisp sitting on the back seat, and headed to town. As I pulled in the driveway and walked up the walk to the Parker house it dawned on me that I was about to be thrown into a den of vipers. There were at least seven cars parked around the house. *Should be interesting*, I told myself and rang the doorbell. Jim answered and stepped outside closing the door behind him.

"Thanks for coming," he said and pulled me in for a kiss.

"I wanted to pay my respects," I said. Jim, distracted, pulled away from me.

"Who's that?" he asked.

"Who?" I asked and followed his glare. A man wearing a dark suit was closing the door to a black sports car. "I don't know, but he's dressed like an undertaker. Probably works at the funeral home."

"I guess. But, why's he taking pictures?"

We watched as the black car pulled onto the street and slowly drove away. My body trembled, and the mumbling voices became louder and, much to my relief, quieted.

"You're right he's probably with the funeral home," Jim said and turned his attention back to me. "Before you go in you best beware all of Polly's friends are inside. You don't have to do this."

"I appreciate your attempt to protect me, but I can't avoid them forever, and besides it's a day of mourning. They won't lay into me while they're in a dead woman's house."

"I guess we're about see."

"I brought an apple crisp."

"You baked?"

"Don't look so shocked."

We walked in the front door and all talking ceased. You could've heard a pin drop if the floors weren't covered wall to wall in nineteen seventies shag carpet. The living room was filled with people standing, sitting, and eating. All eyes were on me as I walked down the middle of the room and into the kitchen. Jim, snagged by an older man, was left behind. The kitchen was warm and smelled of pot roast, mashed potatoes and chocolate cake. Pilly was the first to see me.

"Oh now aren't you the sweet child. I swear on the good book if any of them busybodies would stop and see you for you...well I think you're an angel in disguise. And what is this? Homemade?" she asked pointing at the apple crisp.

"Just out of the oven," I said. I didn't lie it was. "It's an apple crisp and it goes well with coffee."

"I can't wait for a taste. Picky could you serve up this beautiful apple crisp little Shanna brought over."

Picky, busy with washing dishes, jumped to her orders. The sisters each had their own special duty in the house. Pilly was the cook and domestic engineer. Picky was a nurse and because of her education was the head over all that must be thought out or decided upon. Polly was in charge of information. Albee used to say, "Tell a graph— tell a phone—tell a Polly, all the same thing."

"Thank you for your kindness," Picky said sharply and took the apple crisp.

Jima rounded the corner into the kitchen and only slowed when Pilly grabbed her arm. "Shanna! I knew you wouldn't leave me here in this mentholated blue-headed pasture of grief alone. I can't get my friends to come within a block." She pulled away from Pilly and led me into her bedroom shutting the door behind us. We sat on her bed across from each other.

"Are you ok?"

"Sure I guess, it's sad and all and I'll miss her. She was old and bitter so I think she'll be happier elsewhere," she said.

"You know if you need to talk or anything, I'm here for you anytime."

"I know you are. We're best friends just like you and my mother were," she laid her head on my chest and began to cry. I didn't know what to say. I was not the comforting type of person by any stretch of the imagination. I didn't (and still don't) have a sympathetic bone in my body. My philosophy has always been; pick yourself up, dust off your knees and get on with it. But, this was different—I owed Vicky. I was as much to blame as her rapist.

"It's ok to be sad. It's hard to lose someone you love." I wished there was something after this life and that Vicky was present in that something watching me with her Jima. Our Jima. I wanted her to know I'd move heaven and earth for this child. This wasn't the first and far from the last time I would envy the one who had died. "I'll never leave you," I said holding Jima's face in my hands. "I promise." And suddenly as if all cried out she sat up and dried her eyes on the sleeve of her top.

"They've been going on and on about you and the farmhouse. Miss Edwards mostly but it's like a pack of possessed chickens. They said you had those Mexicans build it. Then, they said you cast a spell and brought it back to life and your Momma's rotted body is stashed inside. Most of the old ones are in shock and won't even talk about it because of the curse. It's just awful, awful and terrible, the things they say."

"Oh my God," I was appalled. "They didn't really say that about her body did they?"

"Well maybe not that part, Aunt Picky says I'm good with embellishments. But, I say what's cake without icing? They did say they thought you made a deal with the devil and that's why your crops are so green. Your healthy plants have gotten them all in a tizzy."

"Let them tizzy. I really don't care what they think and I'll cry about it when I cash my check after harvest," I said, and thought twice. "That's not a nice thing to say.

You shouldn't talk that way and I shouldn't either. It makes us no different from them. We will rise above it all, we will not become the things we despise."

"Yes Miss Shanna." She rolled on the bed laughing and then jumped off and went under the frame to retrieve a box. "I want to show you something and get your advice. First, you have to swear an oath that you won't tell anyone the secret I'm about to reveal. I need your most awesome promise. The sisters will hang me upside down by my toes if they catch wind of this." Jima held the box lid closed while waiting for my oath.

"How bad is it? I can't promise without knowing what it is."

"It's not about me, but it is about someone we all know," she said and opened the box. "I have to show you. You're the only one that can help me. Everyone else would just yell at me. We're allies on the same side. I got no other choice."

"I know the feeling."

She slowly opened the box and took out a book covered in newspaper. "I read this book of prophecy, and there's one about Helen, I mean Mrs. Garner." She thumbed through the pages, landed on one and started reading. *"Only once in a blue moon just as you turn to leave, the sick hell swells from desired life."* She closed the book and looked at me with dramatic seriousness. My heart sank, *you too Jima?* "When I was leaving for school last Tuesday, the day of the blue moon. I picked up this very book. I was going to take it to school because I promised Becky she could read it. But, I dropped it and it fell open to this very page. I read it and in that instant I heard her barfing in the back yard. I mean she was hurling chunks big time so I looked. She was spewing something awful but then, when she stood up I saw like vision or something. I swear her belly was swollen bigger than if she'd swallowed four whole watermelons—whole! Then the sun hit her and I could see through her dress. I swear on everything holy I saw a baby in her belly."

"Who?"

"Helen, Mrs. Garner, Bradley's wife for Christ's sake. Everyone calls her Hells Bells because she's so mean, and everyone knows she's so mean because she never got the baby she prayed for—the desired life," she pointed at the phrase in the book. "I heard Aunt Picky saying that she has a tumor in her belly and tomorrow they're going to remove it but it's not a tumor. It's a baby. I know it is because I saw it right out that window right there. You have to stop them."

"Jima be rational. You can't expect me to tell Bradley and Helen they're going to have a baby because you read it in that book. I can't do that."

"We have to do something. We can't let them kill that baby. Patient Crew said it would happen and that means it will happen."

"Where did you get that book?"

"Sweetwater but what does that matter?"

"How do you know about that book? You shouldn't be reading this stuff not at your age."

"Who doesn't know about Patient: Crew and what does age have to do with anything? What does any of it matter now? We have to do something and if you won't, then I'll have to. I could talk to Aunt Picky, but she won't believe me, that is not until they take that baby out and kill it." Jima was pleading. She got up and put the book inside the box and slid it under the bed. "I'll tell them myself right now."

I almost fell off the bed grabbing for her arm. "Don't you dare go out there and make a scene not today. I'll talk to Bradley."

Picky, with a scowl across her face, opened the door. "You need to be out there with the family," she said to Jima. "You aren't getting any points holding up in a kid's room," she said to me.

"Yes ma'am," Jima and I said in unison. I walked into the living room with Jima and saw Helen standing next to her mother, Bertha Hopper. I figured it was as good a place as any to start.

"Hi Helen. It's nice to see you again," I said and extended a hand. Helen shook my hand and then gave me a forced and quick hug. "I hear you're going in for surgery tomorrow. I hope all goes well for you."

"Thank you Shanna. It's nothing really just a little fibroid tumor. Doc says it's nothing to worry over."

"Doc's getting old and his equipment is even older. Do you think you should get a second opinion?"

"I believe Doc's still sharp minded. He's a good man, and we trust him. It's not something you or anyone, should worry about." The room quieted. Every ear was straining to hear our conversation.

"Did Doc give you a pregnancy test?"

Helen nervously laughed. "I'm not pregnant Shanna. Now that's enough of that. Mother," she spoke loudly to Bertha who looked as though she was next in line to be mourned. "You remember Shanna Green she's come home after ten years." Helen hadn't lost her touch in all those years. She had wittingly and with a loud voice alerted her mother to my presence.

"Who?" Bertha said loudly. "Speak up if you want to be heard child stop being so cowardly." She gave me a rigid look and her eyes grew wide. "Get thee behind me Satan. That's Ruth Ann Green. The bowels of hell have spit out Jezebel herself. That's what kilt Polly. Don't look at her or you'll be in the grave right next to her."

"Mother please," Helen pleaded but it was bit late as everyone in the room had already heard. "It's not Ruth Ann it's her daughter Shanna."

153

"Even worse the witch's bastard child. What's she doing here? Polly wouldn't like this, not one iota."

"I'll just step outside," I said. "Let her calm down a bit."

Helen had succeeded. Walking through that room felt like swimming in pea soup. I couldn't get out of there fast enough. Every eye was forced downward and away from mine. I felt a wave of relief shower the room as I closed the door behind me. I stood on the porch for a second to catch my breath and saw Bradley sitting in his truck waiting for his wife to finish her Christian duty. I thought about what Jima was asking me to do. She had no understanding of the situation she had created. However innocent her request seemed it would start a shit storm. I was well aware of the implications and even more determined to continue. I walked over to Bradley's truck. He stared straight ahead and acted as if he hadn't seen me as he began to raise the door window.

"Give me a second, please Bradley?" I asked, and he begrudgingly lowered the window.

"What is it you want woman? I already got my name being dragged through the mud for selling you that seed for twice the price. They all think I'm consorting. You ain't nothing but trouble," he said.

"It's about Helen."

"What about Helen?" he scowled. His hands were shaking. He wasn't a young man, but he wasn't old either (at least not old enough to have the shakes). I frightened him; this was not something I enjoyed.

"You need to make sure they give her a pregnancy test. Make sure she's not pregnant."

"That's it?" he laughed. "Hell's not pregnant and Doc Williams said if we don't get that tumor out of her," he was frustrated. "Don't you think we've already done tests on her? What business is this of yours?"

"If you let the doctor operate on her, he'll be removing your baby."

"You're the spitting image of your Momma," he said.

"So I've heard."

"The fruit don't rot far from the tree. Your Momma cursed my uncle and it took his life. I am not my uncle so you go on now and get out of here witch. I can't figure out why the hell you came back in the first place. Can't you see you're not welcome here?"

"Shut the fuck up and listen to me you stupid hick. There's a baby in there. Get a sonogram and you will be able to see it. What have you got to lose? If I'm wrong you can tell your buddies and have a good laugh at my expense and at the same time let Helen be the horse's mouth of the latest gossip. But, if you let them operate—mark my words Bradley Garner, you'll be burying your unborn child." I turned to leave, and Jim was standing behind me.

"See what you've gotten yourself involved with boy," Bradley said. "Is this what you want for your own daughter?"

I walked around Jim and got in my car. He followed and got in the passenger side. "What was that all about?" he asked.

"Nothing. I was just trying to help. I think they should at least know for sure that's all," I said.

"Sounded to me like you knew for sure," Jim said. "How do you know those things?"

"I need to go. I have to go do something."

"Ok, you go do something but soon, real soon, we need to talk," he said. I hate those words—we need to talk—they always make my stomach hurt. I distinctly remember every time someone has said those words to me, and it was never good.

My stomach was churning, and I felt sick as I tried to recall the words I had spoken with Bradley. I wondered how much Jim had heard. He looked shocked. My best guess was he'd heard it all. I drove home at a snail's pace and was certain Kevin would greet me with a big grin and a plate of food. I wasn't hungry and wasn't ready for more human interactions. I missed the long boring days with Marla in Dallas. We'd talk about everything from eternal existence to the best brownie recipe. She had collections of works by all the great authors: Virginia Woolf, Shakespeare, Tolstoy and Hemingway. She liked a well-worn soldier type of story. I could never get into Hemingway, but he was Marla's favorite. When I finally made my way home Kevin was sitting on the floor against a wall. Momma's journals were strewn around him along with two dirty dinner plates and a couple of soda cans. His eyes were red and puffy, he had been crying.

"Its all here—everything—right here," Kevin said. "Most of this was written twenty years before any of it happened. This one book here could have saved hundreds of thousands of lives." he held up the notebook and waved it at me.

I ripped it from his hands, and picked up the other books, shoving his leg aside to get the ones underneath and then put them back in the box. I could feel my blood getting hot as I stood over him with raging anger. "Who in the hell do you think you are? Who gave you permission to read these? This is my personal property. You had no right to read them."

"Do you realize your mother predicted 9/11, the Sri Lanka tsunami, the earthquake in Haiti, and all the market crashes for the last ten years? And that's after reading two notebooks. Do you know how many lives would have been saved if we had these writings at the time she wrote them?"

"Do you know how many doctors she had to see and the medications they forced her to take? Do you have any idea how people tortured her and her family? It ruined her life. The voices took her life they took everything away from her."

"Those voices didn't take her life. This town may have but not the voices."

"May have? You don't know what the hell you're talking about. I suggest you mind your own business. This stuff, these diaries they're mine. You are not allowed."

"These writings belong to the world. These are not her personal thoughts they are prophesy the same as your writings. It's not for you it's for us."

"All that matters to me is my own well being. I'm no different from anyone else. We're all selfish at our base. No one fights for me, and I fight for no one."

"Who filled your head with that bullshit?" he asked. "If you'd read what you've written you'd know the truth. Hell, book one is all about the parts of the whole, the pipe and the vessel. We are nothing without the other, and I'll tell you something else—we are not selfish at heart."

"I don't write those things I take dictation. Marla and Tim both told me it's better to disconnect from it. They warned me about people like you. The crazies that look at this like some sort of religious awakening. God isn't talking to you anymore than he talks to me. You're acting like one of the crazies."

"Disconnecting does not negate its existence. Listen to this and if you think I'm reading between the lines or making something out of nothing then I'll concede, and we won't talk about it again." He looked through a box of Momma's notebooks until he found the one he wanted.

"And you'll go back to Abilene?" I asked.

"No," he said. "This one is dated July twenty six, nineteen seventy nine. That's before you were born, right?"

"You're right."

"She writes: *I had a dream last night. I dreamt that I was inside the house baking cookies. The sun was pouring inside through the windows making the wood glisten. I was happy, singing and right there on the table in the living room was a little blonde headed baby. I know it was a girl because she looked pink and precious. I walked over to the little baby girl, and she started talking to me as if she were an adult. She said to me, "My name is Shanna and you're my Momma." That was all there was to it. Then I woke up."* He closed the notebook and placed it gently in the box. "Did she put a date on everything she wrote?"

"I don't know," I said.

"You need to read these," he said. "Everyone needs to read these."

"No."

"Why?"

"Just no."

Kevin stood up and did something I hadn't expected. He hugged me long and hard, held me close, patted my head and then finally let my body loose, but continued to hold my hands. He then took my hands and gently kissed them one at a time. "Trust me," he pleaded. "I know you're confused, and you don't know what to do but you can trust me. Whatever choices you make" he said putting my hands on his heart, "I won't disappoint."

"What's up with you and all this loyalty crap? You don't know me. I don't know you. For future reference I don't do hugs," I said. I took a couple of steps back and regained control of my hands. "I don't have choices, never have."

"Who told you that? Tim and Marla?" he asked.

"No one had to tell me that. I learned it on my own. Don't talk shit about them. You don't even know them. They are good people. Without Marla I would be locked in an institution."

"You always have a choice." As he spoke the crew came forward proving him wrong.

"What choice do I have now?" I went in the bedroom and sat on the bed with pads and pens and began writing—this was not a choice. There was no need or time to hide it from Kevin. I was aware of my actions and didn't allow myself to escape. I could hear the choir of voices in my head as I watched my hands move with swift precision. Every word was written with my hands controlled by the crew. I could feel Kevin hovering over me and breathing on my shoulder. His face was inches from mine. I dropped the left pen, and my hand flew to his face stopping within an inch of hitting him. He moved back and only then did I pick up the pen and continue writing. As the session ended I heard a faint rapping at the front door. I turned to look at Kevin who was standing a safe distance behind me.

"What's wrong with you?" I asked. "You look sick."

"I think its Jim. He's outside knocking has been for the last ten minutes."

"Why didn't you answer the door?"

"I'm a big black man answering his girlfriend's door and he's a big strong cowboy looking for something to hog tie."

"He's not my boyfriend."

"Should I hide in the closet?" he asked. "This guy is relentless. He walked around the house and knocked on the back door and went back around to the front. I got a glimpse of him, and he's not happy." I laughed at the thought of Kevin nervously crouching as Jim made his way around the house, and then at the thought of him trying to shove his huge body into the small closet.

"No I don't think you'd fit. Just sit here and wait for me and don't read these." I picked up the notebooks, shoved them under the mattress and went to answer the door. Jim stood on the porch and stared at me. Jima ran past me into the house.

"Jesus H. Christ we've been banging on that door forever. Where you been?" Jima asked.

Jim took his glare off me and came inside. "You left everything in quite a mire."

"I was sleeping. It's been a very stressful day. I don't believe I did anything to cause a stir. I simply made a suggestion to an old friend."

"You're a piece of work you know that? You've got a chip on your shoulder, and you'll do anything to get someone to knock it off, anything to start trouble and make them think you're a," he said, catching himself before he said too much.

"What reason do you have to be mad at me?" I asked and turned to look at Jima. She wouldn't take her eyes off the floor. "It was a suggestion. I read a medical article about her condition. I was just trying to help, to be friendly, like you wanted me to be. What happened when I left?"

"Mr. Garner came barreling into the house and grabbed Mrs. Garner's hand." Jima lowered her voice. "He said, come on we're going to Sweetwater and get you a sonogram. That's when Gramma Pilly sent me to my room, that's all I know." She gave me a grateful smile and wink.

"What happened next?" I asked.

"The short story is—Aunt Picky followed them outside and got into it with Bradley," Jim said. "Let's just say your name was thrown around a few times and everyone inside heard it although they pretended not to." They were pretending not to hear it for Jim's sake. I'd embarrassed him and that's why he was angry.

"I'm sorry," I said.

"Seems like you're saying that often these days," Jim said.

Jima was roaming through the house from the living room to the kitchen and then the bathroom and back into the living room. "Who's visiting you?" she asked.

"No one," I lied.

"There's two of everything," she said. "Two plates on the floor, two glasses and two more plates in the sink, and two forks. In the bathroom, there's a pair of boy socks on the floor and a razor left on the sink just like Dad does after he shaves."

"Aren't you the junior detective," I said. Jim was looking at me with suspicious eyes. "Actually I ate an early breakfast. I shaved my legs at the bathroom sink and rushed to your house, after the cake was baked. When I got home I was hungry so I had lunch and took a nap. I've been in a rush most of day and haven't had a chance to pick up after myself." Jima knew I was lying but Jim didn't. The only thing on his mind was what to do with me. I was causing trouble for him, and now he had become the star in the latest gossip saga.

"We can't stay," Jim walked to the door. "Momma wanted me to check on you and make sure you were ok. I see you are. She also wanted you to come by for supper tomorrow night after the funeral. She said you wouldn't need to come to the burial but to come by for supper."

"Is that what you want?" I asked.

"It's what I want," Jima said. Jim was silent.

"Really it's ok if you'd rather I stayed away. I'd understand."

"No," he said. "I want you to come over. I don't want any tension. I want a pleasant family meal with them, and you. All I ask is for is a little peace and harmony."

"I'll stay clear of the cemetery and be there for supper, and I'll be on my best behavior." Jima jumped for joy while clapping her hands and Jim smiled. I couldn't bare the thought of leaving them and wouldn't let myself think about it—not yet at least—but I knew the time would come when (again) I'd have no other choice.

Jim and Jima left, and I went back to the bedroom to open the door for Kevin.

"So?" he asked.

"What?" I asked.

"What did you do at their house? What were they talking about?"

"Jima has a crew book and talked me into thinking Helen, an old friend, was pregnant. Doc—who is older than God—gave her a pregnancy test and it was negative. They scheduled a surgery to remove what they think is a tumor, but because of what the book says Jima thinks they'll inadvertently kill the baby when they cut her open. I fell right into the mob mentality with Jima and that stupid book. How she got her hands on it I don't know, but I do know she shouldn't be reading that junk." I realized I was ranting and throwing stuff around in a failed attempt to neaten. "You need to get out of my sight for a while. I need to think and I can't think with all of you people around me."

Kevin left without another word. I wondered where he'd go without having a car, but I didn't care enough to find out. I didn't care about anything at that moment. I was happy to have enough space to think about my next move.

12.

*T*he hour I had to myself was not enough time for an inner debate. I made swift firm decisions. My desire was to leave (this time) with dignity. First, I'd close my account and secure the cash. Next, I'd go to Jim's house for dinner and smooth things over between him and his family. I'd be a quiet and perfect angel. I would talk to Jim about the book Jima was hiding, it was the right thing to do. I still hadn't heard a word from Tim, but I'd only wait a week longer for him or Marla to contact me, and I would keep Kevin around for maybe a night or two longer.

"The sick hell swells from desired life," Kevin said when I opened the front door. "You warned him about the baby because you know it's true." Kevin was standing against a tree in front of the house reading from the book.

"Do you take that thing everywhere you go?" I asked. "You're one of the crazies Kevin."

"What are you going to do when Helen finds out you're right? When she finds out she is pregnant. They'll come looking for you."

"Probably," I said.

"You're not waiting around for that to happen you're making plans to leave. I can see it in your eyes. You're running."

"It's none of your concern," I said.

"Like hell it isn't. I'm the dark warrior protector of the flower child—that's you—where do you plan on going? You can't go at this alone. You need help. You need me."

"It's none of your concern," I said again. "Are you hungry?"

"I could eat."

We pulled together a chicken salad on toast. It tasted wonderful with a big glass of iced tea. Kevin told me about life with his mother in Abilene and his job at the computer shop.

"You've been here a couple of days, do you need to contact her or your job? Do you need a change of clothes?" I asked.

"I'm good. You have a huge supply of toothpaste and shampoo, and I always have a change of clothes in my pack," he said.

"You're a good boy scout," I said.

"You could say that. Tell me about Jim."

"There's not much to tell. We've known each other since we were kids."

"It's more than a friendship," Kevin said.

"It can't be more," I said and took the dishes to the sink.

I cleaned the kitchen while Kevin turned on the news. Within seconds of turning the set on he was opening the front door to watch a commotion outside. "Shanna you better come see this," he said.

I heard what sounded like animals growling. As I got closer I could see that Jim was on the ground struggling with a man. When they'd scrambled to their feet, Jim was holding a camera and the man's suit collar. The man took one look at me and ran, ripping off his collar where Jim had held it. Jim turned to Kevin who backed his way into the house. I stood between Jim and the doorway not letting him enter until I'd had a chance to explain.

"Who was that man?" I asked.

"Who is that man?" Jim asked.

"Kevin come out here please," I kept my eyes on Jim and could feel the tension rise as he saw Kevin walking to the door. "Kevin this is Jim. Jim this Kevin."

"My friends call me Fat Boy," Kevin said and extended his hand.

"My friends call me dangerous," Jim said, keeping his fists up and ready for battle.

"Kevin is a friend of mine from Dallas," I said.

"A friend?" Jim asked. Kevin backed up, Jim's breathing became heavy.

"Yes a friend," I said. "Who was that man? Where's Jima?"

"Same guy that was on the street at my house. He's following you and taking pictures," Jim said and handed me the camera.

"You smashed it good. Lets check the card." Kevin took the camera and pulled out a small digital card from the base and inserted it into the computer slot.

"Where's Jima?" I asked.

"She's home. We passed the picture man's car on the road. I doubled back after taking her home and found him looking in the front windows."

"Look what we have here," Kevin said. We watched as he scrolled through the pictures. The series of pictures began when Jim was helping me move out of Mrs. Black's house in town. The last picture was of me coming home from Jim's house earlier that evening. There were pictures of Jim and Jima at the Dry Goods, and one of Picky and Pilly standing outside their house. There was a picture of Kevin leaning against the tree a few hours earlier.

"How many are there?" I asked Kevin.

"Hundred and twenty six," he said and gave me a look of understanding that Jim quickly caught.

"Who's watching you?" Jim asked.

"I don't know," I said.

"You don't know? Then who does?" Jim asked. "Does Kevin here know because he sure acts like he knows something?"

"I know nothing. Nothing at all," Kevin said.

"Jim why don't you meet me outside. Give me a second and I'll be right out," I said.

"I'm fine right here," he said never taking his eyes off Kevin.

"Go outside," I insisted. "Leave the door open if it makes you feel better." Jim begrudgingly left, and stood just outside the open front door.

"It'll be ok," I whispered. "It has to be Tim looking for me I'm sure it is. He doesn't know about this house. He doesn't know I've moved. It's a good sign that he's alive and looking for me. He'll call soon." I had a fleeting thought that Tim and Marla could have turned me over to the CIA, but quickly shoved it aside. If their intentions were to sell me out they would have done it during the ten years I was with them.

"We have to talk about the last session," Kevin said. "It's urgent."

I went outside to join Jim knowing I would need to be extremely careful with my words. He wanted commitment and honesty. I couldn't give him either. He leaned against his truck with his arms crossed and head down. I stood in front of him.

"We were happy for a few weeks," he said.

"We were," I said. "I take the blame.

"I'm not finished." He raised his head, looked at me and smiled. Not a big smile, not a happy smile, but a crooked little smile of concession. "I've done everything I know to help you. I plowed, sowed, and treated this land as if it were my own. I've had to explain every strange thing that happens around you to the people in town just to keep them at bay. Everyone, even my own family has been telling me to stay away from you. I went against every last one of them, and I'm going to tell you why." He slid his boot next to my sneakered foot. "You turned the switch on in my heart when we were ten and you beat up Bradley for pushing me off the slide. Do you remember that?"

"I remember. He's always been a little bastard," I laughed.

"Since that moment, it was never you without me. It's always us. It always has been. Even when you left I knew you'd be back, knew you would come home to me. You've been the only thing I've done that's right. I'm not letting you go again." His words made my heart ache. I wasn't worthy of him. I should have stopped him from saying those words to me. It was easier to not hear those words. "I'm an open book, no skeletons no past and not much of a future. You, on the other hand are one big unknown. I'm not getting the full story here. Today, I beat up a man I don't even know for taking pictures of you, and then I meet a rather large black man named Kevin who looks more like a bodyguard than a friend. What is it you're hiding from me?"

I didn't speak. Even if I knew where to start I wouldn't know when to stop. Jim knowing anything now would be of no good to him or me. It would only serve to put him and Jima in harms way. I shrugged my shoulders and kept my mouth shut.

"You think on it tonight, and then tomorrow you come on over the house for supper. After that we're going to have a talk and I'm going to get some answers to my questions," he said and got in his truck. "Honest answers. Come here," he said and leaned through the window to kiss my forehead. "I love you." I watched as he turned the truck onto the road. *Disconnect*, I told myself as I went inside.

The TV was blaring, and Kevin was standing inches from the screen. The session notebooks were on the floor at his feet. I could hear the reporter state with a grim tone that the confirmed dead are now two hundred and forty. "What's happened?" I asked.

"It's started. A bomb at an elementary school," he said.

"What's started?"

"The month of a thousand deaths. You wrote about it."

"When? I don't understand."

Kevin fumbled with the notebooks, picked one up and pointed at a phrase. "Right here—in that month of a thousand deaths. It's started."

"I don't understand."

"If I am right there'll be more deaths after this. They'll be more bombs and more deaths. I need to study the sessions."

"This doesn't say anything about bombs."

"It's in the earlier sessions. It's in both books and the recent sessions are filled with it. I need to research," Kevin said. He sat on the floor in front of the TV and started flipping through the notebooks.

Four bombs had caused the elementary school in Forman, Oklahoma to implode. The school had full attendance that day for the fifth grade graduation. Three hundred and ninety-four people died. One hundred and eighteen parents, grandparents, siblings, and friends attending the graduation, and the rest were children, teachers and staff. If there were a hell, a special place is reserved for me if I didn't do whatever it took to make this stop.

The next crew session started an hour into our marathon news search for information about the school bombing. Kevin would write notes, research the Patient: Crew books and the writings since I had returned to Sunny. Thirty minutes after the first session ended another began. The crew and I had four sessions that night. I collapsed into a deep sleep within minutes after the fourth session ended. I slept through to the next afternoon and woke up to Kevin standing over me with a plate of eggs, toast and a big smile.

"We have another visitor," he said.

I got out of bed and quickly dressed in the clothes from the previous night. "Who is it?" I asked.

"Tim," he said.

I stopped and sat on the bed. I was afraid but why? I couldn't understand what my hesitation was telling me. Why wasn't I running to him with pure delight?

"What should I do?" I asked.

"You should hear what he has to say. You don't have to follow his orders. You are capable of making your own decisions and I will keep you safe." Kevin was trying to get me to stay with him. He wouldn't admit it but that's what he was doing.

"I can keep myself safe," I said. "You keep your eyes open."

Tim was sitting in a chair going through the sessions that I had written the night before. He instantly jumped up to hug me. "What's going on here Shanna? Who's that thug and why are you living in this house? Are we safe?"

"Yes," I said. "We're safe. This is was my mother's house. That's Kevin he's a friend who doesn't know anything. He's just here to help me with the cable TV. No one has come to look for me."

"Is this the house they burned?" Tim asked. His tone was filled with suspicion. His forehead was beaded with sweat and his eyes darted around the room.

"It was, maybe Pop rebuilt it. What happened?" I asked. "Where's Marla?"

"Who beat up my man? I sent him to find you, and now he's in the hospital with broken ribs." Tim stood up and closed the notebooks but didn't set them down. "Who beat him up your cable friend?"

"No," I said. "That was Jim."

"You've established yourself."

"You told me to."

"So I did. Where are the rest of your sessions? Did you destroy them?"

"No I have them in a safe place."

"Have you been reading them?"

"No nothing's changed with me. Where's Marla? Is she ok?"

"None of us are ok," he said. He looked sad and I couldn't think of a time in ten years he had ever looked sad.

"Why?"

"After you left, the Agency hit us hard. We were under constant surveillance and I was put on leave. I had to sweep the house for bugs. We didn't even discuss the grocery list without turning up the radio. Two weeks later they arrested me. I was treated like a civilian. They held me for three days relentlessly throwing questions at me."

"Why?" I asked.

"They want the source. They want you."

"The sessions, ten years of them?" I asked.

"They have them, but it's not enough. They want you. When I went home I tried to contact you. I thought they'd found you."

"I was moving into this house. It's safer for me here. No one even knows it exists," I said. I felt an immense guilt run through me. "Who killed your partner?"

"The Agency. The CIA orchestrated the damn thing. It was supposed to be me in that car, but I saw him. I saw him take Marla, and I got out. The car blew and took Frank with it. They didn't kill me so now they blame me. I ran and have been running since, running and searching for Marla. I need your sessions. They'll tell me where to find her."

"So you believe what they say? You believe they tell the future?" I asked.

"I've got nothing else. I have to believe."

"Who took her?"

"I don't know. I didn't get a good look at him."

"Was it CIA?"

"I don't know," he said. "I need to read your sessions. She needs our help Shanna." His eyes fixed on mine as he held my hand with a tight grip. "If it's the Agency, they won't stop until they have us both. It's just a matter of time before they get the ace of spades."

"The only way they'll know who I am is if Marla tells them," I said.

"You can't stay here and hide your affliction from everyone," he said. "Do you really think these hicks will protect you? They'll figure it out. You can't hide forever. Even if Marla dies with your identity someone else will find out and give you up in a heartbeat." He was right. If the CIA came to Sunny with a picture of me, people would stand in line to tell their stories. If they were offering a reward, they would kill each other to be first in that line.

"What's your plan?"

"Mexico. Marla and I have an understanding. We have a house and she'll know to go there when she's freed. They can't keep her forever. If they try, we'll go public."

"What do you mean go public?"

"We'll tell the media she's being unlawfully held," he said. "The whole damn country believes she's a holy messenger. They want Marla to write more books, and she can't do it locked up. It's become a religion to some people. Everyone wants to know who patient crew is. The only safe place for you is with us. We are the only ones you can trust."

"What will stop the CIA from following Marla to Mexico?"

"Nothing, that's why we have to do this right. I know how these guys work I can make it happen but not without you."

"When do we leave?" I asked.

"Good girl," he seemed relieved. "Tomorrow. I'll go back to Abilene tonight, and we will meet at the airport tomorrow at seven PM it's the last flight out. It would be easier for you to come with me now, but it's not safe." He pulled a piece of paper out of his pocket. "This is your confirmation for the ticket. You'll need your license and passport. Do you have them?"

"I've got them."

"You'll be there?"

"I'll be there."

He handed me the notebooks. "Bring them with you, everything since you've been here. Don't forget them," he said and left.

I heard a loud diesel engine.

"Eighteen wheeler," Kevin said.

"Doesn't surprise me," I said.

"Are you leaving with him tomorrow?"

"I have to go to out," I said and grabbed my bag. "I'll be home in time to clean up for dinner at Jim's."

The folks on the street turned away as I drove down Main Street. I was sure they'd heard all about the Bradley fiasco. I parked in front of the bank and went inside. It was a tiny room with one teller and a table off to the side for people to prepare their transactions. I filled out a withdrawal slip at the table. Not wanting to cause suspicion I left a few dollars in the account. A man joined me at the table, but he wasn't filling out any slips.

"Good afternoon Shanna," he said.

"Good afternoon," I said. I turned to greet the teller. She kindly gave me the money and I left.

"Excuse me Shanna," the man was following me, but I didn't recognize him.

"Do I know you? What's your name? Do you live in town?" I rattled off the questions.

"No I don't believe we've been formally introduced. I'm a Caleb," he extended his hand. "Joshua Caleb."

I didn't want to appear paranoid so I accepted his hand. "How do you know my name?"

"I knew you when you were just a tiny baby," he said, and looked at me as if I were a dream that could quickly vanish. "I knew your Momma. I knew her very well, and you are the spitting image of her."

"That's what people keep telling me," I said. "Unfortunately the only thing I know about you is your name."

"If you would be so kind as to give me a ride home I'd be happy to tell you all about me and my people," he said.

"Your people wouldn't happen to be government people would they?" I asked.

"The government don't give a hoot nor holler about us, and we in turn don't have anything to do with the government. I think you know us as those people who keep doing shit to you," he smiled. "Most everyone in town calls us the hill people."

"You brought me breakfast, and notebooks. Did my Momma trust you?"

"Ruth Ann didn't trust anyone after those townies got ahold of her. She relied upon us though, and I like to think she held a certain amount of affection for us in her soul. She helped us, and now we're here to help you. It's the least we can do." On our way out of town, Joshua Caleb told me things I'd never heard about Momma, and not one of his stories was vaguely similar to the gossip. He said she was full of sweet kindness and forbearance.

"I was told she was possessed by evil and that she told men their futures to get them to sleep with her."

"That couldn't be further from the truth. She was shunned by the town but continued to help them the best way she knew how. She was convinced her writings could help people. She hoped that in return they would accept her and welcome her into their fold. Her father," he said.

"Pop?" I cut him off.

"Yes. He got enough of the situation. He moved her to the house hoping everyone would leave her alone but that didn't stop Ruth Ann. She fought back even harder. She would sneak into town in the middle of the night leaving notes on people's doors, giving them solutions to problems that were private. She was trying to help these people. Her writings revealed too much of their secret lives. They couldn't figure out who was telling this girl their private business. They accused her of spying on them, peering in their windows while they slept. I'm not sure how they thought she could do that so often without a single soul catching her in the act."

"Is that why they burned the house?" I asked.

"They were trying to silence her, and they succeeded. She didn't deserve what they did to her. She wanted their acceptance and would have done anything to gain it. The people she had left notes for started the rumors about her being a witch and consorting with the dead. They set up a meeting with her father and demanded a solution. They wanted him to take her to a sanitarium and have her locked up."

"Pop refused?" I asked.

"Two days later they showed up with torches and fuel, burned the fields. It had been a dry year so the fire quickly spread to the house. It didn't take long for the mesquites to go up in flames. Ruth Ann tried to put out the fires in the field. When she noticed the house had caught she panicked and went inside to save you. No one in town knew you existed until that fire. She was able to get you out the door before she collapsed from the smoke in her lungs. No one lifted a finger to help her. They saw her on the ground and left satisfied with their justice. By the time we got to her she was gone."

"Why did she hide me?"

"She was fearful they would take you away from her. Your grandfather cried over your Momma. He came to my father asking that we respect his decision to take you and raise you as his own. My father agreed."

The question was burning in my gut. The words were hard to form in my mind and even harder to say out loud. "Do you know who my father is?" Joshua Caleb was silent, but I could tell the answer was a resounding yes.

"Ruth Ann was a beautiful woman. Any man in his right mind could see it. She was a quiet girl, but her beauty was loud. My brother was the moth to her flame. He protected her from the goons that came from town, banging on her door, demanding to be told their futures. The funny thing was when she told them what they wanted to know, and even when she put the notes on their doors as warnings it all came back on her. They blamed her for everything right down to the drought. If someone got hurt, sick or died they'd say she did it, manipulated it, or put a curse on them to make it happen. Any and everything she predicted came back on her in the most negative way."

"I'm just like her," I said.

"Spitting image," he said. "There're a lot of people out to get you—same as it was with her."

"I know."

"There's a lot of people you can trust just the same," he said.

"Can I trust you?" I parked the car a few feet from the house and shut off the engine. "The problem is I owe the people who helped me in Dallas, but I'm not sure loyalty is the best course of action."

"Doing what's right isn't always the easiest path to follow. Your Momma learned that the hard way," he said and got out of the car. He walked to the side of the house, and I went to the front door.

"Where do you live?" I asked.

"In the hills," he said. "If you need us just follow the path and call out my name. There's a good bunch of Calebs, someone will be sure to respond."

"Thank you, Uncle Joshua Caleb."

"You're mighty welcome Niece Shanna."

13.

*F*ive cars were in and around Jim's driveway, and the owners were saying their final goodbyes to fellow mourners as I turned onto his street. I stayed at the curb and waited until I saw the last of the visitors leave. I wasn't in the mood for confrontation. A newfound confidence brought about by meeting family had given me strength. I wanted to know more about them more about my father. I wanted to meet the other Calebs to become one of them, one of the hill people. I faded into the memories of Albee tending the garden behind the fields. I must have been five or six years old. She tended that garden daily, but I never once saw her pick or use any of the foods it produced yet the ripe vegetables were always gone the next day. I gained an ounce of respect for her that day.

The sister's house was filled with the aromas of food. Pilly was in the kitchen up to her elbows in dishwater suds. I gave her a quick hug and offered to help. She had me fill the tea glasses while she put the food in the center of the table that was beautifully adorned with antique china, Granny Parker's Sunday best crystal tea goblets and freshly polished silver. The centerpiece was a platter stacked high with fried chicken. The usual sides of black-eyed peas, fried okra and mashed potatoes with gravy were placed around it. We all sat around the table, held hands and Jim said the blessing. He had become the head of the house and recited his father's prayer word for word.

"God our heavenly father bless this food which we are about to partake to the nourishment of our bodies. Forgive our sins. Guide, guard and direct us until in heaven we see your face. In Jesus name we pray, amen."

Oh warrior dark warrior guide, guard and direct her. It was Kevin's song; it was also the prayer Jim's father said before every meal. I'd heard that phrase more times than I could count in my life, yet it didn't impress me in the least when Kevin sang his song. Chills ran down my spine. My brain searched for a purpose or meaning and came up with nothing. Pushing the thought aside I filled my plate and started eating while the others discussed the funeral and how good Polly looked. Jason was more than a little sick of the light conversation about his mother and her demise. He was distant and no one seemed to notice—if anyone did they didn't show it. He picked at his chicken for a few seconds and then got up to put his plate in the sink.

"Where are you going to Jason?" Pilly asked. "You hardly touched your supper."

"I'm not hungry," Jason said. "I'm going outside for some fresh air."

"I don't see how smoking a cigarette is getting fresh air but go on," Pilly responded.

"Leave him alone Ma," Jim said.

"I suppose you're right. We all have to grieve in our own way."

"He's planning his escape," Jima said and everyone's eyes went to her. "That's the way I hear it at least." She continued to eat and the rest of us waited until she had swallowed. She was getting ready to take another bite when Pilly slapped her hand down.

"You can't say something like that without further explanation young lady now tell us exactly what you know," Pilly said.

"He was talking to Mike Murrow and said now that his Momma was gone he's going to join up with the air force," she said and took a drink of tea. "He said there was nothing for him here and he might as well cut his losses and move on. He said nobody needs him for nothing anyhow."

"Oh Jim oh no Jim," Pilly cried. "You have to talk to him he can't just go off and leave us like that. You must talk to him."

"I will, but right now I'm eating my supper. Let him cool off a bit. It's good for a man to be alone with himself to get his thoughts straight."

"You know best," Pilly said. "Don't you let him leave and for heaven's sake don't let him join up with the military. Lord help us. Where's Picky when you need her? She'll slap some sense into that boy."

"God almighty something smells good. I hope that's your fried chicken I smell Pill. I'm about to starve to death," Picky yelled from the living room after slamming the front door.

Pilly yelled back, "It sure is and it's still hot. Come in here, fix yourself a plate and sit down. Was the hospital busy tonight?" She used her hand to fan herself and looked up to whisper a *"thank you"* to Jesus.

"Just let me get my shoes off," Picky continued to yell from the living room. "I dealt with Bradley Garner all day. He took Helen to Sweetwater yesterday and ended up having to bring her to Doc this morning. She was vomiting up her breakfast. The stink was miserable. Bradley gave Doc a DVD of the sonogram and Doc just looked at him all confused. Like he would know what to do with that thing. He couldn't understand, and frankly neither can I why in the name of Jesus Bradley's spending all this time running back and forth to Sweetwater just because of what that psychotic little twit said to him." Just as the word twit came out of her mouth she rounded the corner, and my eyes were the first pair hers met.

"I'm going to join Jason for a little of that fresh air," I said.

"No!" Jima yelled. "No! Dad, don't let her go!" She looked at Picky. "Don't run her off like that. Apologize for what you said. Apologize right now."

"I'll do no such thing young lady," Picky scolded. "And you will not raise your voice at me."

"Let's all just calm down now," Pilly pleaded. "Let's not ruin our pleasant supper here."

"Mine has already been ruined," Picky said. "Excuse me."

"No," I said. "This is your house I'll leave. Pilly, Jim thank you for having me for supper. It's ok Jima everything is ok."

"No it's not ok!" Jima said. "It's not her fault don't you see it's not her fault." Jima started to cry and then bolted from the table running down the hall to her room, and back to the table within a few seconds. She had the Patient: Crew book in her hand. "I told her to do it. It's my fault. I told her she had to tell Bradley the truth about Helen, I mean Mrs. Garner, being pregnant. It's all here in the book. The crew told me. Shanna only did what I asked her to do."

I sat down in the chair before my knees buckled. Silence was my best option. Picky took the book from Jima and thumbed through some of the pages and then concentrated on the cover.

"I can show you the passage that talks about Helen, I mean Mrs. Garner, being pregnant," Jima said and tried to touch the book. Picky slapped her hand away and shook the book in my face.

"You knew she was reading this trash this devil scripture and did nothing to stop it? Not only that, you didn't let us know. You were talked into making a fool out of yourself, Bradley, Helen, Doc and me. She's a child. Are you crazy?"

That did it, that one little word. "I'm crazy? I'm crazy? I'll tell you what's crazy lady."

"Ok that's enough," Jim said and held my shoulders. "Aunt Picky, you should apologize to Shanna. Shanna, Aunt Picky's had a hard day. Her sister was put in the ground this morning, and you have to admit that pregnant stuff did come out of left field."

"What is it with you people," I said. "You've had a hard day, something bad has happened to you so you're allowed to take it out on the local twit, crazy woman. Were you having a bad day when you killed my mother?" I walked out the door ignoring the pleas from Jima. It was better that I left than say any more of the words that were flooding my mind. I stood on the porch steps, closed my eyes and took a few deep breaths. I smelled the smoke from Jason's cigarette, and followed the trail.

"What's got them going?" Jason asked as he saw me coming towards him. "Ah never mind I don't want to know."

"You can figure it out, and if not then I'm sure you'll hear about it tomorrow," I said. Jason took a long drink from a bottle of whiskey that he held between his knees and offered it to me. "What the hell," I said and took a swig. It went down like liquid fire and quickly calmed my body.

"I don't see what the big fuss is," Jason said. "I mean since they know she's pregnant isn't it better? I would think they would be happy they found out in time."

"She's pregnant? They know that for sure?"

"Bradley told me the doctors in Sweetwater said she was about eighteen weeks. Like I said what's the big fuss? The crisis has been averted."

"I don't know Jason maybe it's because it came from me. I don't think my coming back was good."

"Why in the hell did you come back anyway?" he asked. "That's the only reason I think you're crazy."

"Enough with that word ok?"

"But it is crazy that you got out of this town and then voluntarily came back," he said. "You were out clean. People didn't even talk about you anymore. You were dead and good riddance." I was taken aback at his statement, and he noticed. "I...I mean that's what they said," he said. "I mean I...I...I don't really remember you that much I was only ten."

"It's ok Jason."

"Do me favor?"

"I'll try."

"If you leave again," he said. "When you leave again," he corrected himself. "Take Jim with you, and the squirt. Get them out of here before this town ruins them both."

"Jim's never going to leave Sunny," I said. "He'll never leave his land."

"He has to. He has to do it for all of us," he said. "Did he tell you old man Randall offered him close to a quarter million for it?"

"Why? It's not worth half that."

"Mineral rights. His daddy had that land prospected in the seventies when everyone was doing it. They found oil but he decided not to drill. He said it would taint the land. He said your Momma told him that."

"Jim's not going to sell it is he?" I thought better of giving his statement about Momma any credence.

"Nope, not a chance in hell."

"You want him to sell?"

"Yes."

"What about Picky and Pilly? Do they want to sell?"

"I don't think Picky really gives a flying fuck what we do with the land she never had anything to do with it anyway. Pilly don't care a bit neither."

"What about you? What would you or Jim do? All you know is farming."

"I'd like to go to school somewhere. Maybe a trade school to learn a trade. Jim could do whatever he wanted seeing as he's good at everything. He could get Jima out of here and into a better school system. She's a smart girl but if she stays here she'll be married and pregnant by the time she's sixteen. She's too smart for that."

Jim walked out the front door and whistled; Jason whistled back. "What are y'all doing out here?" Jim asked.

"Having our own private party away from the drama," Jason said.

"Hand over the bottle," Jim said. He took the bottle from Jason, downed two big gulps and growled.

"Still pretty rough in there?" I asked.

"Rough as hell. Bradley went to the elders," Jim said. "Most of the church are meeting with them now, which I think is ridiculous now that we know you got it out of a book. You should've told me about that book."

The ever-present mumbles became loud. A cold rush of foreboding ran through my body as the crew came forward. I was overcome by a dizzy sickness. I got up, ran to my car, started it and left. I wasn't aware of my surroundings only of the road in front of me. The Preacher was loud and very much up front. He was on a roll and most of it was nothing more than jumbled up words except for the names, Tim, Marla and Finneaus Albert. The Singer was singing a song that consisted of one phrase. *The death begins and will not end until a thousand souls are released.* I pulled onto the dirt road, and I could see the silhouette of Jim in the moonlight. He must have followed me and even passed me at some point without my knowing. He was standing in the road making it impossible for me to go around.

The west Texas winds were blowing hot and hard. The few small mesquite trees that lined the house were bending with each gust. I left my car with the motor still running and the headlights on. Kevin came out of the house, but Jim didn't notice. His eyes were fixed on me. He gently held my arms, his mouth was moving quickly, but I couldn't hear him.

I took Jim by the hand, led him past Kevin and into the house. Never letting go of his hand I rummaged through the piles of notebooks, food and garbage on the floor but I couldn't find them. My head began to pound. It felt as if it might explode from the increasing level of urgency from the crew. *Kevin*, I thought, *Kevin has them*. I pulled Jim to the door as Kevin came in the house. Just as I thought he had both books in his hands. I took the books from Kevin and put them in front of Jim's eyes so he could plainly see the title, Patient: Crew, across the front. I forced him to hold them in his hands, and led him by the arm into my bedroom. I sat on the bed, took two notebooks and two pens from the nightstand and began to write. I looked up at Jim, and Kevin kept him from coming closer.

"This is who I am," I said.

It was three hours later when the voices calmed, and I'd regained control. I was sitting in the passenger seat of Jim's truck. Joshua Caleb was behind the wheel. I saw through the front windshield dozens of people—men, women and children. Some of them were carrying buckets of water; others were throwing that water on the house. Smoke was rising from the mesquites and billowing towards us. It didn't take long for me to understand what was happening.

"We got to get you out of here," Joshua Caleb said and put the truck in gear. He drove in the opposite direction of the house and smoke. I struggled to watch as my house, and the people surrounding it faded into the distance. Neither one of us spoke as the truck came to a stop in front of my car. Kevin was in the driver's seat. The back seat was packed with boxes. Jim and Jima were standing next to the open passenger side door.

I hugged Joshua Caleb and whispered in his ear. "Thank you Uncle Joshua."

"If you remember nothing else remember you have family and we will always be here for you," he said.

"Can you hear me?" Jim asked.

"Yes," I said.

"You promised you wouldn't leave me," Jima cried as she wrapped her arms around my waist. "You promised."

I bent down and forced her to look me in the eyes. "I'm not leaving you Jima, I'm leaving this town."

"Then take me with you! Please, don't leave me here with them!"

"I can't take you. I don't know where I'm going. As soon a I know," I said. Jim gave me a look of disapproval. "I will be back. I'll never stop trying to come back. We will be together again." I could feel Jim's cringe, and I looked into his eyes. "I promise both of you. I will come back."

"Take this," Jima said. She removed a ring from the necklace that was hidden under her shirt. "It was my mother's."

"No Jima, don't give that to me."

"Take it. It's my only guarantee that you'll come back." Jima held my hand and slipped the ring on my finger. "Don't ever take it off."

"I won't take it off until I can give it back to you," I promised.

"I'm so sorry Jim," I said.

"We don't have time for sorry. I understand the things you can't say. I would have sworn we could make it anywhere as long as we were together. I was wrong; we can't make it here." He pulled me close and lowered his mouth to my ear. "Stay tough."

14.

Kevin drove twenty miles to the Anson town center before either of us spoke a word. He pulled the car to a stop at the gas station and gave me a sympathetic smile. "Are you ok?"

"Where are we going?"

"Abilene," he said.

We got out of the car. Kevin started to pump the gas. "Abilene, that's the plan. We'll go to Abilene. I'll drop you off, go to the airport, get my ticket and fly to Mexico with Tim."

"Are you hungry? I'll get some snacks inside. Want anything special?" Kevin asked.

"My bag. Where's my bag?" He held up his index finger to say one minute and walked around to the trunk of the car, opened it and brought back my bag.

"A woman and her bag are not easily parted," he laughed. "Sit tight, I'll be right back."

I looked inside for the ticket confirmation Tim had given me, and there it was folded and tucked inside along with my passport just as I'd left it. *Abilene, that's the plan.* Kevin returned with chips, soda and a variety of convenience store junk food. It was almost midnight, and my last meal had been hours earlier. I ate half a bag of chips and chugged a Dr. Pepper.

"Feel better?" Kevin asked.

I let out a long deep belch. "Now I do."

"I'm glad you didn't lose your sense of humor. My Momma says laughter keeps you sane."

"She hasn't met me."

"No," he laughed. "She hasn't met you, yet. Are you ready to hear what happened?"

"I know what happened. They tried to burn me, they won't be happy until I'm dead."

"It's not that simple."

"It's not that complicated either."

"You should know what happened."

"If it will make you happy then by all means give me all the gory details. Don't leave out the inspirational—don't suffer a witch to live—chants."

"You know about Jim and bringing him in your room. You showed him. You let him in," he said.

"It was a push. I didn't have a choice."

"It was a good thing to do."

"Time will tell," I said.

"You went deep inside. We tried to wake you. You wouldn't snap out of it. Jim opened the front door, and the smoke billowed in we couldn't see any flames, but the wind was whipping tonight. It carried the smoke for miles." He looked over at me and raised his brows, "You ok?"

"I'm ok, go on."

"Jim drove his truck around to the back of the house, carried you out and put you in it. Your hands kept writing—in the air. I put the pens in your hands, and the tablets on your lap when we got you in the truck. You just kept writing. You didn't miss a beat."

"Did Jim talk to you, about me?"

"That man does not have the gift of gab. I guess you know that."

I smiled. I loved that about him. "He's not a chatter box, at least not now."

"He loves you," he said and looked to see my reaction.

"Go on finish your story," I said.

"When we got around to the front of the house, the entire field was in flames. About that time, people came out of the hills. There had to be a hundred of them

187

carrying buckets of water. They formed a line into the woods and as soon as they emptied a bucket of water there was another to take its place. They kept the house from burning."

"The cotton?"

"Hard to see in the dark but I'd say its nothing but an insurance claim," he said. "The kids started the fire."

"What kids?"

"It seems the adults were having a bitch fest at the church with some of the leaders, and they started talking about your Momma. Some of their kids, the ones in high school, heard the part about them burning the house down and the devil raising it. The kids decided that if they burned your field as a sacrifice their daddy's crops would not only survive, but also thrive since they'd done what God commanded of them. The witch stuff came in at that point. A couple of the kids hung back because they feared the whipping they would get when caught. I guess they ratted out their friends to assure immunity."

"Who told you all of this?"

"Jima," he said. "She heard it from Trenton Lee whose sister Tammy was one of the whistle blowers. Two of the men rode out with the fire truck and about ten others came in cars, but it was too late. The field was just a smolder by then, and the hill people were tending to the house. There was nothing else to do but take their kids home and commence the punishments. Jim told me to pack the car with anything important and drive at least two miles down the road. He told Joshua Caleb to wait until you woke up, and then drive out to meet us."

"Is that it?" I asked.

"No, that's the good news. There were government agents on the road talking to the guys in the fire truck."

"How do you know they were government?"

"Jim told me."

"Jim talked to them?"

"He ran them off and told them they couldn't go on private land without a warrant. They didn't want trouble. Central Ignorance Agency never does." He laughed at his own joke. "The FBI now that's a cool group of guys—and gals of course. Those FBI agents, they got it going on."

"What did the agents want?"

"They were looking for Tim," Kevin said. "Must've followed him to the house. They showed the guys in the fire truck a picture of Tim, and when no one recognized him they asked who lived in the house. Jim said one of the guys, don't remember his name, told the agents your name but that's about it."

"I don't want to become one of their weapons."

"Understood."

The rest of the drive to Abilene was silent. I rolled down my window to feel the air. The crew had been intense over the previous days. It was nice to have nothing but the sound of the wheels on the road and the distant mumblings. We drove past Clyde, a small community next to the airport, and Kevin changed lanes heading for downtown Abilene.

"Where are you going?" I asked. "You need to take me to an airport hotel. I have to catch a flight."

"I thought we'd go to my house. My mother's probably worried stiff. We can get some rest and decide our next move."

"No. Take me to a hotel," I said. He pulled the car into the breakdown lane and put on the emergency flashers.

"You wrote at least thirty pages tonight with each hand so that's sixty pages in all and I haven't had a chance to look at any of it yet. Hell girl, I've not even been able to go through half of your marathon session from the night before. Give me a break, I need some time to make sure it's safe for you."

"You're the one who said I have choices. Now that I'm making a choice you want to talk me into something different."

"You're not making a choice you're obeying Tim. The choice he made."

"No I'm not," I said and opened my door, "and if you won't drive me I'll walk, but I'm staying in a hotel near the airport tonight, and I'm getting on a plane with Tim tomorrow." I started to move from my seat, and Kevin grabbed my arm.

"You're an obstinate little shit. Shut the damn door I'll take you."

"There's a Marriott off the highway about a mile north of the airport," I said.

"This is not a wise decision. As a matter of fact it's a down right stupid ass uninformed decision," he said, and turned on the radio.

"I think any decision that doesn't include my staying with you would be considered bad in your opinion."

"What? You have got to be kidding me. Bitch if you think I'm like them government fools back there you're full of shit. If you think I'm trying to get you to stay with me so that I can drain you and the crew of all future information then you're not as smart as I thought you were." He turned the radio to an AM station and found the news. He looked disgusted with me, not hurt, just disgusted. I didn't care.

"Then why don't you want me to go with Tim? Why are you so hell bent on me staying with you?"

"I'm not hell bent on you staying with me. I want you to stay alive. It's my duty."

"Fuck your duty. I imagine you could interpret the crew's words to say what you want them to say as long as it tells you what you want to hear."

Kevin turned up the radio volume. "August the first, two thousand and twelve is not a day we will soon forget expressly if you're a resident of Foreman Oklahoma," the reporter said. "Two hundred and seventy-six children, ages ranging from twelve to the youngest victim, a seven-week old baby, have been murdered. Also among the dead are one hundred and eighteen parents and school faculty."

"You wrote about this," Kevin said. "It's been the lead topic in the sessions for the last week."

"Last night I heard The Preacher talking about Tim and Marla and some person named Albert."

"Finneaus Albert, he's the bomber. He's not going to stop until there's a thousand deaths."

"The Singer's song last night was, death begins and will not end until a thousand souls are released," I said.

"I need to go through those pages. The death count is at three hundred and ninety four, not even halfway to a thousand. He'll strike again and soon. The crew will tell us where to find him. I'll make a deal with you, we'll check into a hotel, sit down together and see what the crew has said in the last few sessions. How's that sound?"

I was thinking about his deal when I heard a siren and looked behind us. There was a police cruiser tailing us. Kevin put on the blinker and started to pull over. "Go," I said. "Outrun him."

"We're not going to outrun him," he chuckled. "Stay here and I'll take care of it." Kevin got out of the car and walked to the cruiser behind us. I adjusted the rearview mirror so I could see them. Kevin put his arm around the cop, which I thought was strange, and the cop patted him on the back. Their bodies were turned to the cruiser so I couldn't see them. After a few minutes, Kevin was back in the car, and laughing. "I went to school with that kid, good times," he laughed. "Let's get you checked into a hotel."

"Why'd he stop us?"

"We left the flashers on," he said and pushed the button to turn them off. "We must've forgotten when we got back on the highway. I told him that me and my lady were having a little tiff and things are chilled now."

When we'd arrived at the Marriot Kevin checked us in, and made sure I was safe inside the room. He went back to the car for the notebooks and to call home. I got some clothes out of the bag Jim had packed for me and headed to the shower. The water was cool and clean. I let it pour over me before I began to clean the soot off my skin and hair. I was devastated to the point of numbness. I held tightly to the sound of Jim's voice in my ear telling me to stay tough. I washed my hands and looked at the ring Jima had put on my finger. She didn't think I knew it was her mother's ring, but I knew. I'd given it to her on her sixteenth birthday. It was silver with little interlocking hearts that covered the front. It was a simple little ring. I affirmed my promise to Jima out loud. "I'll never take it off, not until I give it back to you."

I stretched out on the bed and turned on the TV to a local news station. They showed the grieving people in Forman, Oklahoma. Somebody's child, mother, sister, brother or father. It was more than I could endure. I flipped the channels, but it was the same on every network. The screen would light up with the depressed relatives and friends holding pictures of their loved ones who had been murdered. The bomb expert explained how the building had imploded. There was no way out for any of them. The local fire department was still searching non-stop for survivors. There was little to no hope of there being any. The bombs were filled with gasoline and other heat explosives. When the building fell it was like being trapped in a brick oven. Whoever might have escaped being crushed was cooked within minutes.

I turned the TV off and looked out the window. Kevin was sitting in the front seat of the car. He was using a laptop while talking on his cell. He seemed to be deep into the conversation and pounding on the keyboard at the same time. He picked up something from the passenger seat and looked down at it and then went back to pounding on the keyboard.

I went back to bed, closed my eyes and thought about Jim. "He loves you," that's what Fat Boy had said. "He loves you." *He loves the thought of me*; I told myself. He can't love the reality of me. I heard the electronic key in the door followed by a quiet beep, and then Kevin walked in carrying a small box.

"You need to rest," he said, flipped off the room light and pulled the bathroom door shut leaving a small sliver of light. "It's been a long ass day."

"You can say that again, but please don't."

"Go to sleep," he insisted. "I'll get you up early."

"What about you?" I asked. "You could use a little sleep yourself."

"Eh, I'm used to it. I don't require much shuteye." He set the box on the bed and took out my notebooks. "I swear girl you about wrote a novel in the last few days. Are they always so prolific?"

"My all time record for one session is twelve journals with each hand, twenty-four total over a thirty-one hour session," I said.

"Damn," Kevin said. "Your hands must have been about ready to fall off."

"I don't remember if my hands were hurting, but I do remember having to pee and being thirsty at the same time," I said. We both laughed for a second and that was the first time I had felt good, however brief, for many hours.

"Where do you go to?" he asked. "I mean when they're taking over."

"They take over?" I asked myself more than him. "I guess they do take over. It's hard to accept some obvious facts."

"It is," he said.

"I go where I want to go and that's all I'm going to tell you. That part's mine and only mine. How's your mother?"

"She's good. She misses me and wants me home. She's the same old Momma. Can I ask you a question?"

"You can ask, but I reserve the right to refuse an answer," I said.

"You should be a comedian you're so funny," he said. "Where do you think the voices come from?"

"Inside my head."

"Again funny," he said. "Seriously."

"I am being serious. I don't know. I don't think about those things," I said.

"You never question it? You must think about it at times, or at least at first you must have."

"No. I don't, didn't, never have. When it's not happening I don't want to think about it. I would rather do anything than think about them."

"You never read anything they say?"

"Not until recently," I said.

"Why?"

"I've never wanted to. I still don't want to. I sort of feel the need to at this point, but I don't want to."

"Why?"

"There's not an answer that's going to satisfy. Don't you see that you want me to act as if I care about them? I've spent years wanting nothing more than to get rid of them and live a normal life."

"Normalcy is overrated."

"Said the normal person. Where do you think they come from, God?"

"I think I do," he said. "What else could it be?"

"Evil?" I asked.

"They give you a road map to stop evil not perform it."

"You think it comes from God," I said.

"I don't know if I even believe in God. I believe in good. I believe there is good and there is bad. We all have the propensity for both. I believe that in the end good wins. I think the crew is what will help good to win."

My mind and body went cold. This was the very reason I never thought about the crew or questioned it. I couldn't live with this fear. I had to push it aside. I had to be on the outside of it, where my sanity lived. If I lived in them, studied them, or questioned their origin that's when I would lose my mind completely. I'd be nothing more than their puppet. "I can't talk about this."

"I promised I wouldn't do anything behind your back," he said. "Full disclosure." He sat on the bed, opened his laptop and signed onto a website. "This is my site."

The homepage was identical to the cover of the book with, Patient: Crew, written in black letters across the middle of the page. There were four tabs that ran along the bottom: about us—the books—the prophecy—the testimonials. He clicked inside each and let me view portions of them. The books were transcribed in their entirety, which I'm sure the publisher didn't like. The prophecy area was a meeting and study place that allowed everyone to give their interpretations of what the crew had written. Another section was filled with testimonials, and news reports of what the crew had foretold. There were twenty-seven thousand, one hundred, and seventy-five accounts.

"This is what I need you to see." Kevin clicked on the tab labeled, about us. There were five caricatures with bios attached to each. Fat Boy was at the top of the page, and looked a little like the old cartoon character Fat Albert.

His bio read; *Fat Boy is a founding father of the crew search team and a self-proclaimed crew maven.* The other four leaders had similar bios, and their caricatures looked like typical skinny white nerds. The only difference between them was their shirt color and shape of their glasses. They all went by their screen names. Alpheus6824, Megame, Durgin007 and Braindead1.

"You created all of this?" I asked.

"I didn't create it Megame did," he said. "He produced the website and we all contributed the content, but none of that really matters. What's important is that you know these are the people I sent the pages to. These are the people that can help us."

"I thought I told you to keep it to yourself. No sharing."

"That was before the school bomb. I told you then we needed help. I can't figure this one out by myself."

"Who are these people? All you are showing me is cartoon characters."

"We use the avatars for security so no one will know our true identities. Let me show you." He clicked on a little floating C at the bottom of the page, and a screen popped up that required a password. He typed it in, and that led to another page that required yet another password. It opened up a white web page that housed pages of the crew books rearranged and spliced together like pieces of a puzzle.

"Kevin, did you know who I was when we met?"

"No one knows who or where the crew comes from."

"Do these guys know?"

"No. Not that they aren't begging me every second but no I didn't tell them."

"Thank you."

"I got your back," Kevin said. He pecked on the keyboard and the screen ran quickly through different pages, and finally settled on another web page that asked for yet another password. "Can't be too careful. Here's where I download the new pages, the unpublished ones. The other Crewbies agree that these writings are much different from the published ones."

"Crewbies?" I asked.

"That's what we call ourselves."

"How are the writings different?"

"It's hard to say because we are just now able to compare them. The books are redacted. Words are taken out and at times whole phrases. They seem to be edited with great scrutiny."

"Do you think Tim and Marla edited them?"

"Yes, we do."

"What reason would they have for doing that?"

"Maybe they knew the sessions were prophetic, or maybe it's something as simple as an editor wanting it redacted because of space."

"Marla never discussed the publishing process. I didn't see what she did with the notebooks after I gave them to her."

"What did y'all do with the money from the book sales?" he asked.

I looked away. I wasn't disturbed by the question. I was bothered by the realization—my realization—of how little I actually knew of what had been going on around me for ten years.

"It's ok its personal I get it," he said.

"No I don't mind," I said. "The truth is I don't know. It was Marla's book. I guess she kept the money. I was always taken care of, and never wanted for anything. Tim set up an account for me in Sunny. I've got money. I guess I never had a reason to question anything, but now I feel a little stupid."

"Live and learn baby, live and learn," he said.

"But that's my point I've not done either."

"You need to get your head out of your ass when it comes to your writings, but other than that you've led a pretty amazing life. You've changed lives. The things you've allowed yourself to write have saved people, and kept other people from doing the wrong thing—really bad things—and even made a few people rich."

I wanted to throw up. "I don't care. I never wanted any of this, and didn't ask for it. I've always thought someday it would all go away. I thought if I wrote enough if I allowed them full access it would—someday—go away but the way you talk I know they'll never leave me. This is all I'll ever be."

"You can have a life. They don't take up all of your time," he said.

"Alone maybe, but what good is life without someone to share it with?"

"You don't have to be alone."

"I can't bring anyone else into this. I can't put this sort of burden on anyone. No one should ever have to live like this."

"Jim loves you. He wouldn't think that life with you was a burden."

"I can't, he deserves better. Jima deserves better. She needs a normal life."

"There you go again with all that normal talk. Normal is boring. Average is just that, average. There is nothing special about nothing special. You should give him the choice. You owe him that."

"I don't owe him, and I've made my choice. He's not involved. Understand? It's my business don't interfere."

"Yes'm I knows my place."

"Don't be that way. I wasn't being bossy."

"Everything is always so cut and dried with you."

"I think I get that from Tim. He wasn't a friendly type."

"That's the other thing I meant to tell you," he said. "I looked on every news site, every search engine and nothing not even a blog blurb on the car explosion at Tim's house."

"What does that mean?" I asked.

"It means that it's gone pretty high up the ladder, and someone is blocking the information."

"Government?"

"Ours and possibly others. It's not easy to completely block information from the Internet, but it can be done for a price and for the right people. This didn't come from the CIA alone this came from higher up. Maybe even the Whitehouse."

"I think that's a little dramatic. I've seen Tim make a lot happen from his laptop at home. What would the White House want with the crew?"

"What wouldn't they want? You don't realize it, but you have the keys to the kingdom in that pretty little head of yours. Anyone would love to have a little chat with you, and the crew."

"It's not like that," I said. "It's not like that at all. I don't ask them things they don't tell me things. I can hardly even understand what they're saying when they talk all at once. Something somewhere in my brain can decipher it. I can say it out-loud or I can write it down, but I can't simply tell you what they say."

"Have you ever tried?" he asked.

"No."

"Then it's not that you can't, it's that you won't," he said.

"I don't. I can't imagine ever talking to them as if they were human or alive." Kevin closed the laptop, and we sat in silence for a minute or two. My eyes were heavy. It was just a few short hours until I would meet Tim at the airport.

"What's wrong?" I asked.

"Nothing," he lied.

"What if the government watches your site?" I asked. "They could have read everything you've transcribed and already know who you are. If those were agents talking to people in Sunny do they know who I am?"

"They weren't asking about you."

"But you don't know do you? You said you didn't talk to them."

"I know because of how everyone reacted to their questions. They weren't talking about you. Get some rest." He reached into his back pocket, pulled a card out of his wallet and handed it to me. "I'll never change my email address, and I will always make myself visible one way or the other. I will do everything in my power to make it easy for you to find me. I will always be where you need me to be. You have my word on that."

"You're one of a kind Kevin, my number one and only friend. I'll never be able to thank you for everything you've done." Kevin was the first adult friend I had made outside of Tim and Marla. It wouldn't be easy, but I would have to force myself to disconnect from him as well.

"One of these days when you're safe and settled I want you to tell our story for the website, and the Crewbies. Tell everyone how we met, and how I'm the dark warrior the crew predicted. Tell them I was the one that saved you."

I laughed at Kevin as his chest puffed, and he wallowed in his own glory. "That's a deal Kevin. Some day I'll do that."

"Is that a promise?"

"It's a promise." He gave me a big smile, but the joy left his face as quickly as it came. He was hiding something from me. I could feel it. "What is it Kevin? What is it you're not telling me?" I asked.

"I don't know. What is it I'm not telling you? I think I've told you everything," he said trying to be funny, and then looked away.

I didn't push him. I thought it could have been about his mother, or something might have happened at the store where he worked. I didn't want to pry, and it didn't concern me greatly because I would be leaving in a few hours. Chances were I would never see or speak with him again. I fell asleep to the sounds of Kevin transcribing the journal pages for his Crewbies. I was sure Tim's plan wouldn't backfire, Kevin had my back and that I wouldn't be discovered. I knew the risk was big, but I also knew I had to have more control over my life. It was time for me to make my own choices and not just follow orders, but still I felt the need for someone on my side. Someone not involved with Tim or Marla.

15.

Kevin was sitting with his laptop on the bed next to me. I knew he had moved around during the night because the garbage was full of food wrappers and there were half-eaten snacks sitting on the floor next to him. He was holding a Styrofoam cup of coffee that was steaming.

"Do you have anymore of that?" I asked.

"Here take this one," he said. "I'm tanked up already."

"Have you been up all night?"

"I slept for about an hour. I'm good."

I wasn't sure how much of my stuff Kevin and Jim had packed. I was sure that only one bag of clothes was coming with me. I would leave the notebook sessions with Kevin to give him what he needed to catch Finneaus Albert. Tim would be furious. I would lie and tell him they burned in the fire.

"Are you ready?" I asked as I zipped the suitcase.

"I got us a late check out. There's no rush."

"There's no sense in prolonging the inevitable. I'm getting on that plane with Tim, and we might as well get to the airport so I can get my boarding pass."

Kevin looked down at his laptop. "It's just that…"

"It's just that what? What is it?" I asked, and again had a strong feeling in my gut that there was something he wasn't telling me, and now I couldn't ignore my curiosity.

"There's so much here that it's impossible to comprehend it any faster. The Poet goes on and on about the month of thousand deaths and warning that more candles are now burning low. I know it means more deaths are imminent. That's all I know from The Poet, more deaths. The Singer has been silent, and The Professor gives only lists of numbers that could be anything from GPS coordinates to lottery numbers. The Hippy is all about conspiracy theories, and how to always expect what would never be expected. He talks a little about Tim and Marla, but nothing specific. He refers to them as the guardians of the flower child—that's you—but doesn't say anything specific." He pointed the computer screen my direction. "Do you want to read it? See if it says something to you."

I pushed the screen back. "No I don't want to read it." My refusal to read the sessions did not make him happy, but I didn't have time to be concerned about Kevin or his happiness. I had to keep my mind sharp. If those agents were in Sunny looking for Tim that meant they were on his tail and could possibly be at the airport. I was certain he had a plan, and I had to be on my toes to follow through.

Kevin parked the car in the short-term lot. I opened the glove box and pulled out an envelope that contained the registration and car title. Tim had instructed me to take out the title and put it someplace safe inside the house, but in that moment I was happy I hadn't been obedient. I signed the title, and registration and handed them to Kevin.

"The car is yours."

"No, no, no," he said. "I can't take your car. No. This thing cost at least, well I don't know how much, but I know it cost a lot."

"What else am I going to do? Leave it here and let the city impound it or worse connect it to Tim, or me? It's better this way. You can get rid of it, trade it in or sell it. If anyone asks tell them you bought it on craigslist." He knew I was right and didn't put up a fight.

"I'll buy you another car when you come back."

"I'm not coming back Kevin," I said and opened the car door. "We both know that."

I left Kevin in the car and started walking to the front of the small airport. The outgoing upper floor was empty and the ticket area had one flight attendant monitoring it. I showed her my confirmation and she in turn asked for my passport and license, which I handed to her while making pleasant eye contact. Tim had told me that nervous behavior was as contagious as a yawn, and if I acted nervous the person I was interacting with would follow suit. The flight attendant stamped my passport and handed me a boarding pass. I took my suitcase and sat in the back of the secured waiting area against a wall.

Abilene Regional Airport is a two-room two-story building. Departures were up stairs, arrivals down. I could see both the entrance and the entire secured area from where I sat. There was the usual TSA guard and Abilene Police presence at the gates and exits, but nothing out of the ordinary. I had an increasing uneasiness while I waited for Tim. In the past I had always thought of myself as someone who could think in a quick efficient manner during whatever dilemma I might find myself in. I had planned my escape from this very type of situation thousands of times, and not one moment of the event happened as I'd thought it would.

The relief I'd felt when I saw Tim walk through the entrance was quickly overturned. He made it as far as the ticket counter before being surrounded by a dozen local police. The government men wearing dark suits and sunglasses were close behind waiting for Tim to be cuffed. I didn't see him enter the building, but there was no missing Fat Boy as he walked at a rapid pace straight to me. He took me by the hand then wrapped one of his huge arms around my neck and all but carried me to the door. We'd almost made it out when I heard Tim yell my name. I turned my head and our eyes locked for an instant. Tim began to scream in a high-pitched scratchy voice.

"There she is! Shanna! You idiots you're letting her get away!" Tim continued to yell and tried with all his might to point at me with his cuffed hands. Kevin pulled me out the door, down the ramp and into the parking lot. We were on the highway within a matter of minutes.

My entire body went limp with despair. I couldn't register a thought. I could only hear Tim's words, *there she is you're letting her get away*. He'd turned on me. It was never his intention to protect me. He'd lured me into a trap in hopes that Marla would be released; this was the only explanation I had. Words he said to me ran through my head. Tim said they had planned on running to Mexico and Marla would know where to meet us. What he didn't tell me was that the plan took affect after I was in custody. There were too many questions and not a single answer.

"Holy shit Kevin, they know who I am."

"Yes, I thought of that," Kevin said.

I remember very little after that exchange. When the crew came forward I could not abide it. I threw my head into the dash as hard as I could until I felt warm blood running down my face. Kevin pulled the seatbelt tight around my chest forcing me to stop. The air between my sanity and insanity became thin. I went away and allowed the crew to take over. I was done.

I felt Kevin lift me out of the car and lay me down. I opened my eyes and could see I was in a bedroom. I saw Kevin standing next to a woman almost as big as he was. They were talking, but I couldn't hear them above my own voice muttering the gibberish of the crew. I sang, recited poetry, gave lengthy lectures and repeated numbers for hours on end. When the crew was finished with me, I slept. Day turned to night and night to day. I had no awareness of time or space, and no need for normal bodily functions. I felt like a delicate vase floating in the air above a vast ocean, blue above and blue below. I could feel huge cracks forming inside my glass heart. When I dreamt it was always the same. Jim was in the water urging me to join him, but I couldn't allow myself to jump. I was afraid I would shatter and kill him with my shards.

When the sessions would begin Kevin tried to put notebooks and pens in my hands but I refused them, pushing—sometimes throwing—them aside. I spoke the crew's words for hours causing my throat to become sore and my voice weak. Exhaustion overcame me when they'd finish. At times when the crew was quiet, I heard Kevin talking with the woman. She asked him what the plan was if I didn't snap out of it. Kevin never answered her. Those hours and days were filled with an agony that is not easy to relive. It was the worst kind of pain I've known. I prayed for death, an end to it all. I envied Momma—she was the lucky one—the one blessed with death. I should have died with her.

I heard the crew using my voice to call my name. I didn't respond. My mind was no longer big enough for the eight of us. Something had to give, and I felt my choices diminishing. There was no sadness, anger, happiness or hope. Emotion did not exist. I felt nothing but pain tearing through my bones and twisting my heart. My only prayer was that death would come quickly.

Kevin and the woman took turns trying to feed me and make me drink. I refused. The woman said if I didn't eat or drink I'd die. Hearing her words fed my determination. The sessions became shorter as my body weakened. The final session lasted a mere five minutes, and then everything was silent. I didn't hear the slightest distant mumble only silence. I heard nothing but the slow beat of my own heart.

I slept deeply and dream free before I began to hear the woman talking to me. Her voice was faint at first, but soon I heard a rocking chair, and then her words in rhythm with the creak of the floor as the chair rocked back and forth. "You had better not be thinking you're going to die in my guest room. It is simply not going to happen. I see your eyes open and I see your face understanding me. Sit yourself up there, get that protein drink off the nightstand and drink every drop. Drink it slow and don't stop until you've finished it. Don't you worry about me I'll do the talking and you do the drinking. Otherwise we're packing you in that car of yours and dropping you at the hospital, but you're not dying in my guest room."

I tried to pull my body up to a sitting position. The little strength I had would only allow me to lean up on my elbow. I felt a sudden dizziness overcome me and the room was spinning. I steadied myself with the help of the nightstand. When I felt stable, I took the glass and balanced it on the bed with my hand and drank through the straw. It was cold, milky and strawberry flavored. My throat stung as the nourishment made it's way down. After a few sips I could feel my strength returning.

"Don't drink it too fast now you've not had a bite to eat or drop to drink going on five days," she said. I sipped the drink slowly and sat up a little more in bed to test my stability. "Easy does it, don't go too fast. You're a strong little thing and I have no doubt you'll be fine just take it slow. In the mean time I'll tell you about my boy Kevin. You may think you know that boy of mine. I'm here to tell you no one not even Kevin knows that boy like I know him. Kevin is as big as a house with the strength of a hundred men. He's also gentle as a kitten with a very fragile heart. He's a sucker for a pretty girl especially one in need."

"It's not like that with us. We're not like that," I said. I could hear my voice with lucid clarity. "We met at the computer store, and since then he's helped me more than you could imagine. I know how kind he is, but we're not doing anything other than being friends."

"I believe you, ' she said, and seemed more than a little relieved. "You don't have enough strength to conjure a lie and besides all that your stories match."

"Is he ok?"

"He's fine. "He's worried sick over you, but fine just the same. He's at the office. He doesn't want to be AWOL for too long or they'll send the cops for him," she laughed.

"The office?"

She looked puzzled. I could see the light bulb moment in her head as she tried to cover her comment. "I meant to say the store. A momma can dream a little. I like to tell myself he's a business man in a bank building downtown not just a store clerk." She let out a nervous laugh, and her rocking motion became erratic. She was lying.

"Will he be home soon?"

"I'm going to call him when we've finished our conversation. We'll let him know you've decided to dwell amongst the living once again," she said. "Keep on drinking every drop. Like I was saying, Kevin might look tough and most white people around here cross the street when they see him coming down the walk, but he's had a rough life not unlike you I suppose. He lost his father in a violent manner when he was just a child. Darrell, his father, was the only love I've ever known. We grew up together, lost our virginity in each other's arms and had fantastic dreams of dying together. Dreams don't always come true. I suppose you could argue that we did die together. Part of my soul has never been the same, and deep inside I can smell the decay of its death. Oh I've had my chances at other men, but I made a promise to Darrell and that's all I need. That promise keeps me on track. I have a purpose in this world—in this life—and I intend to fulfill it. Kevin has a purpose and from what I understand he made a promise to you, and intends to keep it." I closed my eyes and listened to the sweet soft southern flow in her voice. "My child has made precious few promises in his life, and just as he helps me keep mine I will help him in every way I can to keep his. Open your eyes and look at me." The rhythmic rocking stopped and she locked her eyes on mine. "Now I'm going to make you a promise. I will never forgive you. I'll make sure you're put away for life if you let my boy get himself killed while protecting you. Promises are the most important contracts you'll make. You should never make one without the resolve to follow it through. I know I don't."

"I promise you that if he is killed it will only be because I died first." I looked down at Jima's ring. My strength was returning, and with it bodily urges. I put a hand on my stomach and instantly knew it was time to run not walk.

"That's a good sign," she said aware of my distress. "It's the first door on the left."

Every sound I heard was clear and distinct. I had become accustomed to the muffled mumbles and didn't remember how wonderful sounds could be. I could hear my breath go in and out of my nose in rhythm with my heart, and the sound of pee splashing the toilet water. I even heard the sound of the rocking chair on the floor in the guest room next door. My stomach was a bit more settled and I didn't want Kevin's momma to come looking for me. I was still a little shaky on my feet and famished. My head was wonderfully quiet allowing me to hear Kevin's mother whispering on the phone as I re-entered the guest room.

"She'll be fine. We need to get some food in her." She saw me standing in the doorway, and abruptly ended the conversation.

"Was that Kevin?" I asked.

"He's on his way home and wants you to rest up until he gets here. It shouldn't take him more than five minutes or so." I sat on the bed. A sandwich with chips and a glass of milk was on the nightstand. "You eat that and you'll feel good. I can hear your tummy growling from over here."

"Thank you Mrs. Stewart."

"I would tell you to call me Momma Jade since that's what most of Kevin's friends call me. I don't see you as being a particularly warm woman so you can call me Jade."

"Thank you Jade. My name is Shanna Green. It's a pleasure to meet you. Your son is an honorable and honest man. He has been very respectful of me, and my...my...situation."

"I think your crew as you call it are a bit more than a situation. It appears to consume you. I believe they do this because you let them. Perhaps you could, and should have more control over them. Stop letting the tail wag the dog as it were. We all have a purpose, and we should live our lives accordingly. With that said—we can't let our purpose rule our lives or us—we are the masters. You need to lay down the law with them. Let them know who owns that body."

I laughed at her vernacular. "I don't talk to them."

"Well there you go. I can't help you if you want to pretend reality doesn't exist."

"I didn't say they don't exist. I know they exist."

"You think if you ignore them long enough they'll go away?" she asked.

"I think about them as little as possible."

"You could be right they might go away. The irony will be that as soon as they're gone you'll wish you had them back."

"I couldn't disagree with you more."

"I pray you're right. Life is not for the weak of spirit or body. Life's hard whether or not you have voices. Sometimes the gifts we return are the ones we end up needing the most." Her eyes wondered off, and she started to hum. I finished the sandwich and drank the milk. I heard a car pull into the driveway outside. I heard the door open and shut. Jade looked out the window and smiled. "There's my boy."

A few moments later Kevin walked through the bedroom door, took one look at me and lifted me up out of the bed. He hugged me as if we had not seen each other for years. His whole body jiggled as he laughed. "You're back," he said and set me down. I smiled for him, and then pushed him away. "You're back all right."

He talked like Kevin and had Kevin's smile, but he didn't look like the Kevin I'd met. This Kevin was wearing a suit and tie, clean-shaven and had a gun holstered around his shoulder. I sat up on the edge of the bed and began to search for two things, my shoes and an exit. Jade stood up from her rocker and carried it to the door, put it down and sat in it.

"You're a runner I can see it in your eyes," she said. She was right I was ready to run. He was one of them, and now he had me where he had wanted me the whole time. Kevin was not to be trusted.

"Just wait a second," Kevin said and lifted his hands in the air symbolically calling a timeout. He let his right arm down slowly, took the gun out of its holster and put it in the dresser drawer. He took off his jacket and handed it to Jade. "Calm down Momma you're fixing to rock yourself right off the chair." He smiled at her. She calmed in an instant and her rocking slowed.

"You're one of them," I said with disgust. "You must be having a good laugh over all this. You got me didn't you? Yes you got me."

"Don't let your imagination run amuck," he said. "If you mean one of them like Tim and Marla or, the CIA no I'm not one of them. I'm a detective with the Abilene Police Department that's what I am."

"You're government doesn't matter how you label it," I said.

"You found me I didn't find you, there's a difference."

"Huge difference," Jade said.

"So what now?" I asked. "What do you want me to do? But first in honor of our...what did you call it? Full disclosure? I got to tell ya, the crews gone on vacation and if I'm lucky it will be a permanent one. So what do you got now Fat Boy? Nothing."

"I was never out to get you," he said. "I didn't know who you were until I saw you write."

"What does that prove? You never told me the truth about anything."

"You've got it all wrong," he said.

"Explain it to her Kevin. You're not explaining so she can understand," Jade said.

"Momma stay out of this," Kevin spat back.

"I am merely trying to help. I don't understand what you're saying so I'm sure she doesn't either."

"Not now Momma," he said. "Shanna, there is nothing I can say to make you believe or trust me. I'm not even going to try."

"Am I free to go?"

"You have always been free to go."

"The windows are closed and door's blocked, but I'm free to go?"

"Momma move away from the door, and open it."

"You can't be serious," Jade said. "She's a runner."

"Momma, please move away from the door and open it," Kevin repeated. Jade got up, obediently moved her chair back into its place and opened the door. Kevin handed me the car keys.

"The titles still in it," he said.

"Where are my shoes?" I asked.

"In the closet," Jade said.

"I'll get them," Kevin said. "Momma, turn on the TV news. Shanna might be interested in the headlines." Jade turned on CNN, and the screen was lit up with reporters. It was a live shot from the helicopter flying over a building in Albuquerque New Mexico. Kevin sat on the bed beside me with my shoes in his hand. I couldn't take my eyes off the TV.

"This is day two of the search and rescue operation here at the Children's History Museum of Albuquerque, in New Mexico. Our fears and the fears of the nation are the same. We fear that no one will be found alive," said Pam Healy, on-location reporter. "The death toll has yet to be reported but officials have said it will likely be in the hundreds. The similarities between this bombing and the bombing just a week ago in Forman, Oklahoma has not escaped any of us here at CNN. There were four major explosions causing the building to implode or fall in on itself. The bombs were also fueled with gasoline that created fireballs and an oven-like affect on the building's interior."

"Did this happen yesterday?" I asked.

"Yes. There's going to be a lot of deaths, at least three-hundred," Kevin said.

"So now you're pushing guilt." I said, and put on my shoes. "It won't work."

"I'm not pushing guilt. If it were up to me you'd already be on the road far away from here, but it's not up to me. It's your choice. You need to choose where you go, and what you do next." He motioned for Jade to turn off the TV. "What I have decided to push is awareness. You can't fight an enemy you don't know." I stood up and looked around to see that nothing I owned was in the room. "Where's my stuff, my bag?" I asked.

"Your bag is in my room," Kevin said. "It's safe there, I know how possessive women are with that sort of thing."

Jade laughed, "Lord I raised a good boy. Thank you Jesus."

Kevin tried not to smile (this was the business Kevin) but he couldn't control the half-cocked grin that was on his face. "Everything else, the journals, your suitcase it's all in the car. I put my GPS on the dash, you can keep that and the tank is full." Kevin turned for the door. "Wait here one second let me get the files." He was out, and back in the room within seconds handing me four folders.

"What's all this?" I asked. I opened the folder on top labeled Timothy Todd. The first thing I saw was an 8X10 full glossy photo. It was a front view; no smiles mug shot. The second page was a side view of the same photo. The rest of the folder contained notes, and handwritten details of his employment with the CIA and dismissal. The next folder was labeled Marla Todd, and the one after that was Finneaus Albert. The last folder was labeled Shanna Green.

"That is everything I could find on Tim, Marla, Finneaus and you. It's a lot of detective work. It includes government records, and what the crew has said about each," Kevin said. "I transcribed as much as I could understand of your verbal sessions over the last few days, and uploaded it to the Crewbies. There's a copy in your folder." He looked down at the floor and moved his lips around as if he wanted to say more. "If you don't mind can I ask where you might go?"

"I don't fucking know," I said. "Is there a place where I'd be safe?"

"You don't have to leave," he said and locked on my eyes. "You can stay here free to come and go as you please."

"I'm better off on my own. If I'm lucky I'll find someone I can trust if there is such a person." *And if there's not I'll remain alone on my own.* I couldn't think of anything I wanted more right now than to just forget it all existed. I wanted to run as far as I could and then run a little further. I would go where no one would or could ever know the crew or me.

"I never gave you any reason to distrust me," Kevin said. "I never lied to you not once."

"You didn't tell me you were a detective," I said. "You said you were still in school. You said you worked at the store."

"All true. I am in school, and I do work for that store. All true," he said.

"That's right all true," Jade chimed in.

"I should have told you I was a detective, but honestly there was never a proper time," he said. "I knew the minute I told you I would be tossed out the door."

"You can bet your ass you would have," I said.

"See, that's why I didn't tell you. I knew I could help you. I'm the dark warrior. I am the one foretold by the crew, and if I wanted you in custody girl I'd have done it when I first saw you writing. Whether you believe me or not, that's up to you. I know who I am. I am the only person you can trust right now, and the only one who can help you."

"What are you going to do when I leave?" I asked. My resolve was weakening the longer I thought about all those children dying. A month of a thousand deaths would mean hundreds more would be murdered.

"I'm going after that fuck-wad Finneaus," Kevin said. "He's only half-way to a thousand and I'll be damned if I'm giving him the time to complete his sick fantasy. I'm going after his fucked-up ass and when I get him he faces the wrath of Fat Boy."

Jade walked out the door unnerved by her son's language. "That's enough for me. I'm starting supper and I'm setting three places at the table. It'll be ready in an hour." Kevin and I shared a laugh as she left the room a little lighter than it was before.

"Your mother is a good woman. I like her."

"I'm not going to let anyone hurt you. I'm trying to save your ass," he said.

"Why didn't you tell me?"

"I don't know," he said, put his head down and closed his eyes. He had the face of a man fighting a deep inner conflict. "I want you to gather your stuff and get the hell out of here. In your folder there's an envelope with a new name, passport, drivers license, birth certificate and everything you need to start a new life. Take it and go." He looked up at me, "that's what I want, but this has to be your choice because it's your life. I will accede to your decision."

"I want to stop him," I said.

"Not a chance, that's not an option. I can find this guy before he does it again. It would be easier with the crew's help, but I won't put you in danger."

"They're silent. They're not talking, not even a mumble. Can we do it without them?"

"I can do it without them," Kevin said. "There is no we just me. I got this. It's too dangerous for you to be involved."

"There's more danger in my being alone," I argued. "What if the crew comes back? How will I let you know what they've said? You need me to be wherever you are."

"I need you to be safe. The whole damned world needs you to be safe. Without you there is no crew."

"There is no crew now. What if they've gone to someone else?"

"They haven't," he said. "They're letting you rest."

"You don't know that. They could be gone forever."

"They'll be back. Patient: Crew book one, page forty-two The Hippy says: *When the flower child arrives at the point of no return man we have to   switch it off. We have to honor the sweet child in her time of weakness and need. It's groovy to go away and let the seedling heal so the flower can once again bloom; it's a heavy sacrifice for the whole.* They'll be back."

"When was that written?"

"Two thousand three. You could stay here. Momma can make sure you're safe."

"That's a year after I left Sunny. I need to be with you, to keep you safe." I wasn't sure if I was trying to convince him or me. I could smell Jade's cooking and hear her singing while pots and pans clanked in the kitchen. I could feel my mind waking up—transmitters humming. I was compelled to stop the killing and chaos that had been created. I was comforted by my enthusiasm to fight the enemy. "If I stay for supper will you tell me everything you know?" I asked.

"Full disclosure," he said.

A small dining room where Jade had set the table and lit the candles separated the living room from the kitchen. The living room walls were littered with family pictures. One wall documented every year of Kevin's life from birth to Police Detective. Every picture was that of a smiling family, none of the pain that Jade had described was evident. Above the sofa was a family portrait taken when Kevin was a toddler. His father was in his Police uniform, and Jade wore a light pink dress. She was holding Kevin who was wearing a little dark blue suit. I couldn't help notice how much Kevin looked like Jade. His father was a tall slender man with a long thin face. Kevin and Jade had the same chipmunk cheeks, and their eyes squinted to almost closing when they smiled. Their smiles were warm and genuine and overflowing with love.

"That's my favorite," Kevin said. "Are you ready to eat?"

"How old were you when this was taken?" I asked.

"Almost three. Six months later, he was dead."

She keeps it hung here in plain sight so that she can always live in that moment, I thought. I wondered what it felt like to have a little person come from your body and look like you. Was it like looking in the mirror of your own past?

"Supper time," Jade yelled from the kitchen.

"We better go sit, Momma don't tolerate tardiness when it comes to supper time," Kevin said and led me to the table. He pulled out my chair and made sure I was seated before walking around the table and doing the same for Jade. The meal with Kevin and Jade was the best I had eaten in years. Even food tasted better when the crew was silent. We had chicken-fried steak, mashed potatoes with white gravy, peas, carrots and dinner rolls. There was no conversation at first just a lot of chewing, drinking and mmm, mmm-ing. After every third bite or so Kevin would blurt out. "Momma you out done yourself tonight."

"Kevin tells me you are a social worker, and that you work with children," I said after I had eaten more than I usually do in a week's time.

"I am, I do and that's all I can say about that," she stated and then giggled.

"Momma can't talk about work and neither can I because most of what we encounter comes with a gag order," Kevin interjected.

"It must be quiet around here with only the weather to discuss," I said.

"Not as quiet as you'd think," Jade said and threw Kevin a knowing smile. They both laughed at their private joke.

"Rules are made to broken," Jade said. "Which reminds me, I was in that liquor store down on Fourteenth Street buying a bottle of cooking wine. Lord knows I don't drink the hard stuff, but you know I like to cook my pasta sauce with some burgundy. Well, they have a back room that takes up half the store and I was wondering why it was closed up with a locked door. I've heard rumors of kiddy porn being sold in that room, but you can't trust rumors. So I was talking to a man, one of the twelve I saw coming and going through the door to that back room, and I asked him what was back there. I said maybe there's an old bottle of burgundy in there I'd like to buy. I put my hand on the door knob before he had a chance to lock it, and six men jumped out of the woodwork to block my way. Maybe some rumors should be trusted."

"It would probably behoove the police department to get involved and make sure that place was shut down," Kevin said. "The owner of the store has a three-year old daughter. That can't be a wholesome atmosphere for a child." Kevin pulled a small note pad and pencil from his pants pocket and jotted down some notes. "You see Shanna we're on the same team, and if we can't share the knowledge we gain what good is being on a team. Sometimes the law get's in the way of us doing our jobs."

Kevin and Jade complimented each other—I envied their connection. I enjoyed being with them. It didn't mean I could trust them. It didn't mean they knew what was best for me. My thoughts continually drifted back to Tim and Marla. I trusted them. They were happy together too. I thought they wanted what was best for me. They had it all at least it seemed that way to me.

"Shanna, what's your wish right now?" Jade asked.

"My wish?" I had no idea what she was talking about. "I'm sorry I must've drifted."

"Momma has this game she likes to play around the supper table," Kevin said. "She especially likes to do this when one of my friends are around no doubt to embarrass the hell out of them."

"I do no such a thing, and I wouldn't call it a game," Jade said. "I simply like to see people's reaction to the question and then I like to hear the response. One can learn a lot about a person through their wishes."

"So what's the game?" I asked.

"If you had one wish this very second and you were assured it would come true what would it be?" I didn't have to think about that question. I knew my wish instantly. The room was silent. The heavy breathing and sounds of eating had ceased. I think even the crickets outside stopped their chirping while waiting for my answer.

"I don't want to be a victim—I wish I had this," I said. "I want this feeling of warmth, family and home. I want to be home, that is if I ever figure out where home is." The silence remained, and then Jade began to cry. Kevin looked at me with eyes that understood. "I'm sorry," I said. "I wasn't looking for your pity."

"No child," Jade said. "You don't need to be sorry." She cried out loud. It oddly reminded me of Marla's laugh. "As long as I am alive you have a home right here with me. That's a promise. I don't say that out of pity but out of love and only love."

"Thank you."

"She can't have my room," Kevin said, and let out a laugh that shook his body and the entire table with it. "It's time to get to work, are you ready?"

"I'm ready," I said. We left Jade at the table wiping her tears, and mumbling a prayer neither one of us wanted to hear.

16.

Momma's journal--May 11, 1985: You could do most anything with the light inside blessed to be with you. We can be everything along with one who'll be the guide. Listen with your eyes and know it by the smell. He'll be waiting just inside. When you least expect it, you've arrived. Run as though you know where you're going. Listen as if you've heard it before. Think louder and your voice will be heard. He's waiting. Needing his faith to become truth.

****

Kevin's bedroom was dark and masculine, unlike the rest of the house. Take away the bed and it looked more like a war room. The walls were covered with papers pinned around copied book pages. Every page was surrounded by newspaper clippings and official documents describing the event that was foretold by the crew. It was impressive. It felt right.

"That's just some long term stuff I've been working on," he said. "The left side is you." He had pictures of both Patient: Crew books and quotations from each of the crew. Beside the quotes were notes on who the crew might be, or where they came from. There were maps of Iran and Washington, DC with notes surrounding each. Nothing he had written was remotely close to the truth. "I was in shock when I first learned that you housed the crew," he said. "I've been looking for them since the first book debuted, and not once did I think it was some pretty little blonde from Sunny, Texas. I was sure whomever or whatever it was would be from Egypt, Iraq or Israel, you know—heavy beard, Monk type mystic. Every trail led in that direction. It was Tim, he wanted it to lead in those directions to cover his own tracks." He took the file folder marked Timothy Todd and opened it.

"Tim was never interested in the sessions. He never questioned me about them."

"Tim was an active government agent starting on or about the same time he was discharged honorably from the Army. He was with the twenty-third division security dispatch. He continued his security work by joining the FBI and was quickly recruited by the CIA when they learned of his contacts throughout Egypt and Syria. Because of the security work he did in the army he had a relationship with the Muslim Brotherhood and Hafez al-Assad; they considered him one of theirs. He fed them information prepared by the CIA and in turn they allowed him to be present during high-level briefings. I was forced to speculate most of the small shit because I don't have security clearance for the un-redacted files, but in the end it seems his cover was blown, and he was brought back to the United States. He reported to the Dallas bureau until the end of two thousand two. Should I go on?"

"Yes," I said. Everything they told me was a lie— make up a story and stick with it—it was all fiction.

"He continued his work for the CIA, mostly domestic until June of 0'two. He abruptly quit using his want to marry Marla and start a new life as an excuse. There's a lot more in here about his college years. We'll get to it in a minute."

"They got married in two thousand two?" I asked.

"Yes."

"How did they meet?"

"They met at the drug rehab clinic where Marla worked in Dallas. The clinic had a contract with the government for drug testing of the Agents. Tim needed a bit of help passing his tests so he buddied up with Marla— co-owner and Physician in charge. They met in 0'one and married in 0'two.

"Every word, everything was a lie. How could I be so stupid?"

"You were a kid. You saw what you wanted to see, what you needed to see. You needed a family and they gave it to you."

"I fell into their trap. How did they know?" I asked. "How did they know about the crew? How did I end up with them?"

"That's the creepy part," he said, reached into a bottom desk drawer, pulled out a bottle of whisky, took off the lid, wiped the top with his shirtsleeve and handed it to me. "Just a little to dull the nerve I'm fixing to hit." He didn't have to tell me twice. I drank once, swallowed hard and then drank again.

"Marla earned a bachelor's degree in psychology when her name was Betsy Holder. She owned a private practice in Abilene for eight years and during that time was a highly sought out psychotherapist. She had new and inventive ideas on how to treat chronic mental illnesses with non-traditional behavioral sciences." Kevin opened Marla's folder and found a picture of the book, Breaking Tradition. I recognized it as the book Marla would read to me on several occasions. It was her tool in convincing me that I was not mentally ill.

"I know the book," I said. My mind couldn't wrap itself around everything I was hearing. "She said Betsy was her roommate in college. They were best friends."

"She lived alone during her college years. The book made her semi-famous. She wrote about fictitious people and cases while claiming them to be real patients with real life success stories. Her practice grew after the book was published. People thought she was a miracle worker curing diseases like schizophrenia, bipolar and many others through behavior modification. She never used medications. The same way she had done for the fake patients in her book."

He flipped through the pages in Marla's folder, and pulled out three pictures. One was of a small bedroom furnished with two twin beds and a chest of drawers. Both beds were covered in blood. There were the shapes of two mutilated female bodies—one on each bed, tangled in the sheets and bathed in blood. The other two pictures were headshots of the girls when they were still alive. The attached police report said both girls had a glut of mental illnesses.

"What happened to these two girls? Did Marla, or Betsy do this?" I asked. I didn't want my mind to speculate I needed facts.

"Betsy and Marla are the same person," Kevin said.

"I get that asshole, but if Marla killed these girls why isn't she in jail?" I asked.

"We have what she told the police, and what was said in court. She claimed self-defense and took a plea deal. Most of testimony was sealed for the protection of the one witness," Kevin said. "She was contracted by two families to treat their daughters according to her methods written about in the book. Betsy locked herself, and those two girls in the apartment together—without medication. Betsy was the only one who came out, one week later, alive. She claimed the girls had joined their minds to become a single entity. They used the voices they heard to attack and try to kill her. Betsy's words were: "It was me or them". The Judge wanted proof of Betsy's treatment successes. She brought him the only case study in her book based on an actual patient. The witness was Anna Ruth Green." Kevin closed the folder and looked for my reaction.

"I don't know what you want me to say," I finally said, and took a long gulp from the whiskey bottle.

"What you're feeling. What are you thinking?"

"I feel nothing. I have no thoughts. I want to know what Momma said to the judge."

"The Judge met with Betsy and her lawyers in his chambers. Your mother was a witness. Nothing else is said about her. If it was recorded, we'll never know. Nothing is written, nothing is noted and all we know is that Betsy was acquitted. She changed her name to Marla, went back to school to get her PhD and eventually she became part owner of the rehab in Dallas. When she met Tim, he helped solidify her new identity and eliminated the old one."

"Make up a story and stick with it," I mumbled.

"What?" Kevin asked.

"Why did the truck driver take me to her?" I asked.

"She'd helped the drivers pass their drug tests in the same way she'd helped Tim. She was also giving them methadone and other drugs for extra cash. A few of the drivers started coming to her for help with their mental problems. The driver who picked you up in Anson was one of the drivers she had helped. He made a video of you and sent it to Marla. She recognized the face and instructed the driver to bring you to her. He's also the driver who brought Tim to Sunny. The photographer that Jim beat up was a private detective from Abilene hired by Tim to find you."

"She never left my side. She was with me day and night. Every second I was awake she was with me, documenting every word I said. I was never left alone," I said. I was trying to make sense of what Marla wanted from me in her reality. "If she went out of town, I went with her. I went shopping with her. I went with her to get a haircut. She would tell people I was her niece so they wouldn't ask questions. I never wondered what questions she was afraid of. She knew Momma? Why…why would she?"

"You'll never understand why. It's not worth the headache. It was a lie all of it. Marla, Betsy, whatever you want to call the bitch was a fake, and an opportunist. That's the only way to explain it and that's good enough for now."

"But she did help me," I said. "She's the one who knew writing would help me. She must have discovered it with Momma." That's the moment it began to make sense. She'd read Momma's case to me. That's what Marla had said, *here's a girl and she hears voices the same as you.*

"I believe she knew the crew writings are prophetic. When she told Tim, he quit the CIA and started relying upon the crew for information he could sell to his friends in the Middle East. Marla made a pretty penny off the books, and the crew gave Tim a perfect cover. He could never be accused of stealing information from the government because he didn't. If caught he would simply turn you over and secure his immunity. He used you until something went wrong, something unplanned."

"They didn't lock me up, and they were the ones that insisted upon my leaving and even secured a place for me to live, a place they controlled. What happened to Tim's partner? Who blew up the car?" I asked.

"Frank Argot was up for promotion and started poking around in Tim s old files. I think he caught on to what Tim was doing, and started to put the pieces in place. Argot met with Tim a month before the second book was printed. According to his notes, he questioned Tim about some large deposits of cash to his bank account. He asked Tim if he'd made any overseas trips recently—small shit like that—probably trying to spook him into saying something incriminating. After their meeting, Tim arranged the interview with Ceely Masters and fed her producers the information on Wayne Perkins. He sent you to Sunny and kept an eye on you, and used the private detective to be informed of what you were doing. The detective lost track of you during the move, and that spooked Tim. He must've thought Frank had found you and the gig was up. I don't know for sure but I think he took Frank out of the picture. Tim and Marla planned on running to Mexico. He blew up the car and Frank, and then Marla was kidnapped." Kevin took a breath and rubbed his forehead.

"Keep going," I said.

"Finneaus Albert," he said, and opened the folder. Inside were the crew sessions, and photocopies of a few pages from the books. "I know it looks as though I don't have much."

"How does he fit in with Tim and Marla?"

"As soon as I figured out who Finneaus Albert was the story was complete."

"Ok so who's Finneaus Albert?" I asked.

Kevin smiled and puffed out his chest. "Let me start at the beginning."

"You are joking right? We've been talking for the better part of an hour. Drop the drama."

"Do you have to piss on everything? I called the police in Oklahoma and got nowhere they're giving everything to the CIA. All I had to rely on was internal documents and the crew. I was looking through some of Agent Argot's files and found a name."

"How'd you get your hands on his files?"

"Momma. Social workers have more security clearance than the President. He was a single father of underage children. She requested his personal files, and the Central Ignorance Agency gave her a log in and password. Wham-bam-thank-you-mam and there it is on my computer screen, every case, every note and almost every thought Frank Argot ever had."

"You go Jade."

"Damn straight, Momma ain't no slack. I followed Frank's notes, mixed it with a little crew and out popped a connection." Kevin pulled my cell phone out of the desk drawer.

"That's mine," I said, and grabbed for it.

Kevin held the phone out of my reach. "Yes it's yours. It was ringing nonstop for an entire day and night. I never answered it, but I did listen to the voicemail. First, I'm going to tell you the connection and then you listen to the voicemail." He put the cell phone in his pants pocket.

"Frank started at the beginning—literally—with a birth notice. It didn't give us the names of Tim's parents, but it did give us the county and date of birth. The only school records he found were Tim's first year at Hardin Simmons University in Abilene." He opened Tim's file and handed me the school admissions document. At the bottom of the page, next to the question—responsible party—was the name Doctor George Albert circled in red ink. "Doctor George Albert leads us to Nurse Flora Albert, AKA Flora Todd, mother of Agent Timothy Todd, brother of Finneaus Albert."

"Stop talking like you're a fucking TV detective. It's fucking annoying. You got it fuck face?"

"Now that's some pretty talk," Kevin scolded.

"Shut the fuck up," I wanted the information straight like a first grade primer. See Tim run. Run Tim run. Tim turns on Shanna. Run Shanna run. "Tim and Finneaus are brothers?"

"Flora Todd gave birth to an illegitimate baby— Tim—at the age of fourteen. She finished school with the help of her Aunt, went on to study and become a Surgical Nurse. When she started working for Doctor George Albert, she was twenty-nine, and Tim was going on sixteen. Not wanting the Doctor to know she was a tainted woman saddled with another man's child she sent Tim off to boarding school. The Doctor and nurse fell in love, got married and had a son they named Finneaus. Are you still with me?"

"You could have just said half brothers. The Doctor must have known about Tim since he paid the college tuition."

"They met at some point, but it's not documented. We only know that Doctor George Albert paid for the first year of Tim's college. The crew has however talked nonstop about them. Finneaus is the bomber."

"You're positive, no doubts?"

"No doubts."

"Do we know where he is? Where he lives?"

"Yes."

"What are we waiting for?"

"Listen to the voicemail." There were sixteen calls from unknown. I looked to Kevin for an explanation. "There's only one voicemail. Listen to it."

"Shanna, where are you? You have to follow my instructions. Where are you?" a distraught Marla asked. Another voice could be heard in the background. I couldn't make out every word but got the impression Marla was being fed her lines. "He's got me. He says if you say his name he'll let me live. If you don't come soon and bring the crew he'll kill me. Where the hell are you? You owe me Shanna. You owe me." The line sounded muffled. She was talking with the other person, but it wasn't clear. "If you show up with cops he'll blow up everyone," she was crying. "Listen to the crew carefully Shanna and get here. Save me." The line went dead.

"When did she leave this?" I asked trying to push the right button with my shaking hands. Kevin took the phone while covering both of my hands with one of his. The warmth calmed me.

"Yesterday, an hour after the New Mexico bombing."

"He knows who I am?"

"She told you to bring the crew, to listen to the crew. She was covering."

"Where is she?"

"She's with him."

"Finneaus?"

"Yes."

"Where's he?"

"He lives in Sedona, Arizona. The crew gave us his address. They gave us everything. It's a trap. He's using Marla to get to the crew. He'll kill anyone who gets in his way."

"What the crew said, what I wrote is it in his file?"

"Yes, I think it's all there. When you were out you said a lot of things. I should have recorded it, but Momma wouldn't let me."

I took the Finneaus Albert folder and quickly scanned through what the crew had said. Joseph flat out gave his address. The Preacher talked about his motives. The Professor described the making of bombs, and The Hippy, Mother, Singer and Poet chimed in. Arizona wasn't close, and we needed to get on the road.

"I'm going to take care of this lunatic. You will not get involved. You're the pipe not the vessel."

"Oh good God in heaven. Please don't start with that crazy shit again. Pipe, vessel what's the difference? If I'm the pipe the one it flows through you have to take me. Without me, all you've got is an empty vessel." I headed to the guest room with Kevin close behind, looked around for anything I might have left, and then went back to Kevin's room.

"Get a suitcase packed."

"What?"

"We've got everything we need. Let's go, time's a wasting."

"No. You haven't read it all. It's a trap."

"I'm going that's that, enough said, let's roll."

"No. I can't risk it. No."

I started pulling socks and underwear from his dresser drawers. I opened another drawer and pulled out some t-shirts. "Where are your pants?" I asked. "In the closet?"

"No," he said and sat on the bed. "No Shanna you can't go with me."

"I promised Jade I wouldn't let you get killed, and I think you know that no one breaks a promise to your Momma. I'm not going to break that promise or any other promise I make from now on. I'll give you one right now. I promise if you don't get your ass up and get packed I'll go at it on my own." I sat on the bed next to him. "What are we going to do here? Argue it to death or go and get this son of bitch." He packed a bag, and we were out the door within ten minutes. Jade didn't try to stop us. She sat in her chair and bowed her head while the rocker made the floor creak in rhythm with her prayers.

17.

*T*he GPS was set for Sedona Arizona, eight hundred thirty-eight miles. Thirteen hours and four minutes later we would arrive, but until then I wanted more information. I held the folder marked Shanna Green in my lap. I wasn't afraid of what was in the folder—it was what it was. It felt invasive and a bit embarrassing to have a file about me. It created an inequality between us, and gave Kevin an unfair advantage.

"Sun's going down," Kevin said. "We'll arrive tomorrow morning."

"Tell me a secret," I said.

"About what? I haven't kept anything from you. You know everything there is to know."

"That's not what I'm talking about. I want you to tell me something that would be in your file if you had one. Something I would learn from reading your file."

"Oh I see where you going with this," he said and gave me a smirk. "You think that file gives me leverage. Read it. The worst thing in there is a consent form for a marriage license that you and Jim applied for in Abilene when you were sixteen. You probably faked the signatures so it could in theory get you in trouble someday, but it's unlikely." He laughed "Don't worry about it. You were young and no one would care because it was just a consent form. Otherwise, there are the birth and school records of an average girl living in Sunny, Texas. You disappeared for ten years, no doctors, no income and no other movement. You show up again after Tim was arrested."

"Is this all they know?" I asked.

"By now I'm sure they've sent agents to interview anyone who'd talk in Sunny. I'd say they know everything except for where you are right this second. They know about the house on the land and the hill people," he said and looked for my reaction. "They know who you are, and they have a warrant out for you as a person of interest. No one in Sunny knows anything about Tim, but some still felt the need to talk so they gave the agents the witch and evil seed bit. It's all in the folder. The CIA hung around a day or two and left without a credible lead. I talked to Jim a couple of days ago, and he said they grilled him good, but he'd never betray you. He didn't let them talk to Jima." Kevin took a sip of coffee, and again looked for a reaction. I gave him nothing. "He calls me from a payphone in Rotan, probably one of the last ones existing, in case they are tracking his calls."

"He calls you? He's called you more than once?"

"Yes, he has. Are you ok?"

"Yes Kevin. Yes!" I yelled. "I – am - fine. I am ok, and I'm going to kick you into next week if you ask me again. I'm fine. I want to know if Jim and Jima are fine as well. I want to know if they hurt Joshua Caleb."

"They're all good. I think Jim tries to keep things level for Jima's sake. He's called every day to ask about you."

"That's good, she should have a normal life," I said not giving in to my emotion. "Not so much chaos." Kevin didn't say anything else about Jim or Jima, and I was relieved. Talking about them ripped my heart apart. I put my folder in the back seat. There was nothing in it I didn't already know.

"You're not going to read it?" he asked. "One of the first things I did when I made detective was look myself up on the FBI database. I wanted to know me the way they knew me."

"It's just facts," I said. "It doesn't tell anyone who I am."

"Aren't you just a little curious?"

"No."

"Do you want me to fill you in on what the crew said about Finneaus?" he asked.

"I'd rather read it myself."

"Still don't trust me?"

"It's not about trust." We drove the next few hours in total silence. I started to doze off to the music of tire treads on the asphalt; it was a symphonic sound I had never noticed before. I felt the car sway and opened my eyes in time to see Kevin's body jolt awake from the drumroll of the breakdown lane's safety grooves. His arm went across my body and held me against the seat as he righted the car.

"We're going to stop ahead to get some food and coffee," he said.

"Good idea," I said. The sun was beginning to rise as we pulled into the Love's truck stop, a mile outside the Arizona state line. I stretched my legs and went inside ahead of Kevin in hot pursuit of the nearest restroom. After relieving myself I walked through the diner and joined Kevin at a booth. The room smelled like weary travelers and fried fish. The clinking of metal on porcelain as the diners ate mesmerized me. I found myself turning in the direction of whatever conversation hit my ears. Kevin started reading the Finneaus Albert folder to me before I could sit down.

"Slow down Kevin, I didn't hear most of what you said and couldn't understand the rest of it. I can hear people talking, real people talking all around me. Isn't it wonderful!"

"We don't have the luxury of slow right now. We're about two hours outside Sedona. We need to check into a hotel, get some rest and be ready for battle tonight." His demeanor and look had transformed into Detective Kevin Stewart.

"Just say it so I understand," I said. "I'm a fast study, just tell me what it is I need to read." He looked at me as if I were the most foolish person he had ever met. I felt an unfamiliar and sudden intimidation that made me want to crawl under the table. "What?" I asked.

"You need to read it all, both books and everything you've written since, not to mention the transcript of the verbal days. You need to know their style and rhythm," he said. His downward glare never left my eyes.

"We don't have time for me to read it all," I said staring him down.

"When I was fifteen and thinking I was all that, I started hanging out with some kids in a gang. South Houston was a breeding ground for those types back then. I decided they were what I should aspire to become. I saw these guys in high school with wads of cash, wearing the bling, and the latest pair of kicks. Most of my friends were going that direction anyway, and I didn't want to be left behind."

"What are you talking about?" I asked. "What does this have to do with anything?" I was frustrated and starving. "I need some food."

"Like I was saying," he continued. "One day around Christmas I decided I would go ahead and try to join one of those gangs. I had to accept, and pass a challenge for the privilege of getting the shit beat out of me, and only then would I be allowed to join." The waitress was at our table with three plates of food. The busboy was behind her holding three more plates.

"Hungry?" I asked.

"You know it," he said and arranged the food so that we could graze from plate to plate. Kevin continued with his story as we feasted on eggs-three ways, pancakes, waffles and a huge helping of hash browns.

The first story he told was about the gangs in Houston. His mother took him to the hospital after his beating and then moved them both to Abilene. His second story was about buying a fake ID so he could get a job as a bouncer at the Up Stairs Club. I couldn't, even if I tried, remember the rest of them, and I stopped counting at eight when I finished my last cup of coffee.

"You won't find one of those stories in my folder," he said as we entered the highway headed west towards Sedona. "Nobody knows those stories except me and my mother, and now you. It's a hell of a lot more than I've found out about you."

"So what's your point?"

"What the hell do you mean what's my point?"

"Isn't that why you told me all those stories? You wanted to make a point so make it already."

"My point is that you have no reason not to trust me. I have studied the crew, and I know we know they're right about this. I can show you how, and I will but it's ridiculous to think you could catch up to us in one night."

"Far be it from me to be ridiculous. By we and us, I assume you're talking about the Crewbies," I said.

"Don't be sensitive. It's a simple fact."

"Don't be so pissy," I retorted.

"I'm not pissy, I'm worried," he said.

"Me too." We drove for another hour before stopping at a motel off the highway. Most of them looked seedy, but we were lucky enough to find a small semi-clean place to stay. We got one room with two full size beds and took turns with the shower. After we had settled in Kevin again opened the Finneaus Albert folder.

"When I read the session about the month of a thousand deaths I knew it struck a cord in me."

"Ok," I said.

"It was in the first book," he held up the first page in the folder and then returned it. "I have to say something first. I have to say it so you understand, and then I don't want to be forced to explain myself again."

"Go ahead."

"I told you before, I don't know what I stand for outside the law. I don't know if I believe in God, Jesus, both or neither. I know I believe in something—something bigger than us. I believe the crew is a part of that something, or sent by that something to help us as a people. To help us change."

"Crazy Kevin," I mumbled.

"Shut it," he growled back at me. "I knew that the session sounded familiar and when I showed it to the others they reminded me of book one, page one ninety two, The Singer sings." He pointed at the page and followed the words with his finger as he read out loud. *"Some are not yet born and some just starting to live, but the man has made a plan and a thousand promises given. The time line now remains. From the four corners, the heat intensifies. The man has made a plan, and a thousand promises given. The time line now remains. Fueled from a gut of rage there's none that can stop Finn now, because the man has made a plan and a* thousand *promises* given. *The time line now remains.* It's obvious that The Singer is letting us know a plan has been hatched and Finn, aka Finneaus, is the man, and he's mad. He not only sings about the plan and who's creating the plan, he sings about the firebombs, the children who will die and the intense anger of Finneaus. Each session or day of writings has a certain leader, and the others give a basic commentary. This was The Singer's day, and this was his first writing of that day, or session. It's hard to tell which it is, day or session, because the books are different from the raw writings, but we're on the right track."

"The Singer was the leader that day. Did he say more?" I asked. "What about the others, did they talk about it?"

"No and no, not that time," he said. "It becomes more regular throughout the last pages of the first book."

He thumbed through the pages, and I moved to the other bed.

"What's wrong? Is it my breath?" he asked.

"No, it's me trusting you. Tell me what you know I don't need to see it," I said. Kevin had a goofy grin on his face, and wiped his eyes. "Are you crying? Big baby," I laughed.

"I'm not crying, but you did touch a little soft spot, thank you. Going forward, on page one ninety-eight it appears that Joseph the leader is in control for the session. Joseph says; *the master plan is set in stone and became reality when the butterfly flew away. He fashioned the sixteen tunnels of fire. Now, he lies in wait for an introduction.* In the same session he says."

"How do you know it's the same session?" I asked.

"It fits that way." He threw the crew book to me, and I looked inside. "In the books, each speaker is named but there's never a date or time. When you've read it enough times, you can figure out which sessions happened within the same time frame."

"Which is better the sessions or the book?" I asked.

"Your way is specific, and that equals truth not redaction," he said. "In the same session, The Hippy talked about sixteen tunnels of fire that *travel a straight line three times with one to grow on.* The Professor says, *if it were to travel by steam engine the news wouldn't reach the architect until the next day.* Both bombings consisted of four bombs fueled with gasoline and strategically placed in the four outer corners of each building. This is what caused the buildings to fall inward. The gasoline fireballs ignited everything in their paths creating four tunnels of fire traveling straight lines. It will happen four times total. Four bombings. There have been two so far. The Professor is letting us know the bombs were set off from a distance of at least a day's travel."

"How can you be so sure? How do a steam engine and architect equal this guy setting off the bombs from a distance? It doesn't say that to me, not at all. You're forcing it."

"I layer the crew sessions with the facts of the case and bombings. With Tim, Marla, and you wrapped around it and a little bit of me in the mix." Kevin stood up and started pacing. "I know it's hard for you to believe me at face value, but I have others that I confer with. We have all come to the same conclusion. You need to have faith," he said.

"Never, faith is the tool of the weak."

"Trust it, know that it is truth. On page two hundred, the last page, Mother says—Mother always speaks on the last page—nowhere but the last page. She says; *Bend a knee, say a prayer for the little ones we lose.*"

"I have to say something first. I have to say this so you will understand, and I won't be forced to explain myself again, ok?" I asked.

"Go ahead," Kevin said.

"I don't believe in anything good, bad or indifferent. I don't believe in any of it. I believe mankind has a need to be fooled into thinking there's more than this shit hole. There is nothing greater than us. We're at the top of the food chain and the only entity with more power than us is the earth, but we will win that battle some day. You want to create change? Take religion out of the equation, and then you can't blame your deeds on a god or a devil, you have to own it. The world will start to change in the instant we take all the blame we deserve." I started rummaging through the luggage.

"What are you looking for?" he asked with a smidgen of fear in his tone.

"A drink," I said. He handed me a bottle of water, and I knocked it across the room. "Libations!" I yelled. Kevin filled a hotel glass with whiskey he'd stored in his bag. I downed it. "Why Marla? Why did he take Marla?" I slowly drank another shot. Kevin sat silently across from me.

"The plan is made, the sixteen tunnels of fire and the three straight paths. I'm not sure what one to grow on means. In the second book, the plan becomes clear."

"Thanks," I said. Kevin took it all in stride, but I couldn't drink enough to disconnect from her words—the little ones we lose.

"No problem," he leaned over, and kissed my forehead. "Book two, page thirteen, The Poet makes a poem out of numbers." He fumbled around for the book and then the page.

"Stop it Kevin. Don't read it just tell me already," I said.

"The Poet makes up this poem, and it turns out the rhyming numbers at the end of each line are the exact geographical coordinates for Finn's house. Just a side note, those same numbers also won the Powerball a month before the first bombing. At that point, page thirteen to the end. Every session has at least one reference to the month of a thousand deaths. The sessions you wrote in Sunny are specific and in literal terms gave us his name, address and even his phone and social security numbers. We know who, what, where, and how, but not the why. Why did he take Marla, and why is he blowing up children?"

"I give. Why?"

"The crew," he sat on the bed. "He wants the crew. That's why he took Marla and it's why he's blowing up the children. He wants you—he doesn't know he wants you—because he doesn't know you possess the crew. We know that because Marla said to bring the crew with you."

"When you went verbal, do you remember anything during the sessions?"

"Very little."

"Do you remember sitting up and talking to me?"

"No."

"It was five AM, and you'd been out for two days and deep into the fourth session. You were going on five hours, and suddenly the talking stopped, you sat up in bed and turned to face me." He took his cell phone out of the cargo pocket in the leg of his pants, and handed it to me. "Push play and watch for yourself."

"You recorded me?" I asked before pushing the play button on the screen.

"I did. Momma was asleep. She knows nothing about this."

The video began. I was sitting up in bed with my head cocked to one side. It appeared to be me, but the look on this girl's face was far too cheerful. Both eyes were open as I talked with different voices making it sound as if there were seven people in one body, male, and female. I began to sing. "Everything set in motion won't back down won't let go. Set in motion set in stone." I struggled to breathe as I watched and heard the voice of The Singer coming out of my mouth. "We are the army we never fail, never fall. From within without and around all strive to destroy but we soldier on, we soldier on." The voice of The Singer seamlessly transformed into The Poet. "The loss not worthy of the cost. The history no need for mystery. The third brings forth the word. The voice humanities last choice. This is the last chance the final choice." The Preacher's voice took over. "God save us everyone as we enter the time of heavenly revolt. We have no power over the change that will occur as promised in the days of old." I watched as my body turned and held my hands together like a spout placing them in the palm of Kevin's hand. "Let the knowledge flow from the pipe to the vessel. Together let our voices be heard as one before all words are turned to dust. Let the church say amen."

241

"Amen," Kevin could be heard, but not seen on the recording.

"It's like a crazy acid flash," The Hippy said using my mouth. "Big brother dug his code name. Man called himself the butterfly. Finn fancied himself a stud, tripping all over the world man, and then suddenly it was peace from the butterfly, and Finn was left to fin for himself. Not cool. He freaked out. It's never cool to take away the people's power." I'd cleared my throat, and furrowed my brow before The Professor began. "We wait on the edge of the unknown for an explanation of life. We know that not a single element has eternal continuation. Everything that is will eventually meet its own demise. Not humanity, earth, or anything on it, not the planets, not the stars, not the universe that houses it all, nothing can escape the inevitable end of existence. And just as that fact remains another is created. For as sure as I am that death will occur, I am equally convinced in the certainty of birth." Joseph's voice took over. "Today, the endings take place in Albuquerque, New Mexico. From atop his perch, Finneaus will create chaos between the four walls of the past, present and future. Complete destruction. From a day's journey done in the split of a second. Today, he lives at twenty-three Jacob Lane in Sedona, Arizona. He's not alone, but he's the only threat. The numbers are 3696923849." I watched my head straighten and face the camera lens. Looking in my eyes on the recording as I heard the voice of Mother come out of my mouth was a guttural experience. "Do not doubt the force behind your actions." The recording stopped, and I returned the phone to Kevin.

"We, you and me, are the only ones who've seen this," he said. "And the only ones who ever will." He took a small video card out of the phone, went into the bathroom and flushed it down the toilet. "The numbers Joseph gave were to a cell phone that triggered the bombs in the children's museum to explode," he said, and sat on the bed.

It was almost noon we had driven all night, and I had consumed an inordinate amount of emotion. I was at the point of complete exhaustion. "Do you think Marla's alive?"

"I hope Marla's alive."

"That and a nickel won't buy you a hunk of cow shit," I said disgusted by that word—hope. "What's the plan?"

"Can we talk about the video?"

"No. What's the plan?"

"We'll sleep for a few hours. We'll find the house and stake it out for a few more hours," Kevin said.

"And after that?"

"I haven't gotten that far. Any suggestions you have would be appreciated," he said, and we slept.

18.

It was late afternoon when we'd arrived at the home of Finneaus Albert on twenty-three Jacob Lane. Kevin received an email from the Crewbies saying they were on their way, and would meet us at the hotel early the next morning. Our plan was to stake out the house and observe any movement. After that we'd head back to the hotel, meet up with the Crewbies and from there we'd figure out the rest. Our purpose was to stop him before he had the chance to hurt Marla or anyone else. We drove by the house once and saw the driveway was empty. We parked two houses down, across the street. It was a quiet neighborhood.

"I have a question," I said after the first hour.

"Ask," Kevin said.

"Why did you contact the Crewbies instead of the cops or the CIA?"

"I didn't contact the Crewbies; they contacted me. Those smart asses figured it out without me. I needed you to sit up in bed and slap my face. I can't call the law because the only hard evidence we have comes from the crew, and I can't take that chance."

"What about Marla?" I asked. "Do you think she's inside?

"I don't know," he said.

"This is a big risk for you. If this goes wrong, you could lose your job."

"If this goes wrong, I'll lose more than my job."

"I could leave. All you'd have to do is give me a head start. You can show the cops what the crew wrote, and they would arrest him."

He laughed at me. "First you beg me to tag along, and now you want to leave? I'm not calling anyone. I'm not turning you over to the feds. I need to prove Finneaus is the bomber without help from the crew." He turned off his phone. "Do you have an extra car key?"

I opened the glove box and took a key out of the owner's manual. "This is the spare."

"Put it in your sock down below the shoe level." He got out of the car, and hid his gun in the back pocket of his pants.

"What are we doing?" I whispered.

"Looking," he said. We walked at a normal pace across the street, down the sidewalk, and stopped under a tree that partially hid us. "Everything still silent in there?" Kevin asked and pointed at my head.

"Blissfully."

"I'm happy for you, little sister but I could use a bit of crew help right now so you let me know if they knock on the door. We've got to find something that implicates him. You can't build bombs of that caliber and not leave any evidence behind." We started walking again, this time with more stealth, staying away from the front, and stepping quietly beside a sliding glass door on the side of the house. I could see that the glass door led to a kitchen, small but typical. Kevin made a call from his cell phone, and a second later I heard a phone ringing inside the house. Four rings, and an electronic voice asked for the caller's name. Kevin hung up.

"He's not home, first down." Kevin tried to open the glass door, but it was locked. The fence gate, a few feet down, opened easily. "First and ten do it again." Kevin led the way slowly into the back yard and closed the gate quietly behind us. "No dog, that's another ten and now for the Hail Mary." We walked against the back of the house until we were standing in front of a large open window. "Touchdown," he said. The window was covered with a

245

sheer curtain, but the sun was at an angle that enabled us to see inside. A dining room sized table was covered with metal scraps, screws and broken glass. There were barrels of chemicals, fertilizer and six large gas cans. Kevin slid the screen open with ease and leaned inside. He took out his cell phone and started taking pictures.

"Will this be admissible in court?" I asked.

"These pictures are not—officially—being taken by me, but they'll end up in the right hands."

"How's that?"

"How doesn't matter. We've got to lock him up before he gets a chance to do it again." The wind blew the curtain onto Kevin's phone, and I leaned inside to hold it away from him. "There's enough shit in here to blow up Sedona."

I saw the man's movement a split second before I heard his voice. He was standing directly behind us.

"BOOM." The man's scream jolted Kevin, causing him to turn so quickly that his legs were tangled and he landed on his hands and knees leaving his butt straight up, in front of the man. The man bent over, put his hand and the Taser he was holding up to Kevin's ball sack and zapped him. Kevin froze for a moment then fell forward with a full-face plant to the ground. His body jerked. The only sound he made was a high-pitched whimper.

"Kevin!" I yelled, and dropped to my knees to help him. "Kevin, are you hurt?" He whimpered.

"He'll be fine," the man chuckled. "His love stick might never be the same, no great loss. But, now that he's otherwise occupied you come along with me little lady."

"I'm not going anywhere with you asshole." I stood up ready to fight.

"Oh, I think you'd better do as I say, little lady." He pulled the handgun from Kevin's pants and was pointing it at my chest. "I think this little piece of metal guarantees it." He was a short, slight man. Kevin could have crushed him with one blow (if Kevin could have gotten to his feet). The man wasn't much larger than me for that matter, but a bullet is faster than any fist. I obeyed when he led me inside through the sliding glass door. He poked the gun in my back forcing me to walk through the kitchen and into another room—probably a den at one time—and pushed me to the corner. "Sit down," he instructed.

"What do you want with us?" I asked. "Where's Marla?"

"We'll get to that in due time," he said while taking zip ties out of his pocket. He secured my hands in front of me, and then my feet. The room was small and clean. Nothing hung on the walls, and it was sparsely furnished with a desk and rolling chair. A twin-sized bed, covered high with blankets and thick sheets of plastic, was against the opposite wall. "Best you don't comment right now. We'll wait till your little buddy outside gets his bearings, and then us three will have a proper consultation." He took a roll of duct tape from the desk, and began to tape my legs from the toes to just above the knees. He taped from the elbows down, and around my wrists and thumbs. He ripped off a section with his teeth, put it over my mouth and went outside.

Sweat was running down my nose, making it itch and fueling my fear. I canvased the room with my eyes and realized I was sitting next to a hallway entry that probably led to the bomb making room. At the end of the same wall was another hallway. I couldn't see where it led, but felt sure it was a front door or entryway. I leaned over and stretched to look further down the hallway next to me and saw three closed doors. On the first door hung a plaque— the kind of thing you'd make in an elementary school art class—that read Finney's Lab. I listened carefully trying to hear anything other than the hum of the air conditioner motor. I made noises behind the tape on my mouth trying to call out Marla's name, and held my breath in case of a response. The house was silent. I tried again, and again with no response. I wiggled my hands and feet but the tape wouldn't loosen. I heard voices outside. I could hear Kevin yelling my name and then suddenly it was quiet again. A few seconds later, Kevin was being forced into the room with his wrists taped. His face was wet with sweat, and he was clearly in pain

"Sit down in that corner you big ape," Finneaus instructed Kevin. Kevin sat never taking his eyes off the gun being waved around at him. Finneaus pushed the gun against Kevin's head, and bent down to tape his legs. Kevin saw an opening and kicked Finneaus in the chest, which sent him sliding across the floor on his butt. Finneaus jumped to his feet and started waving the gun at me. "You hear me god blacky. Don't mess with me! I've been waiting on this introduction for a long time, and I ain't going to let your big ass ruin it before it even begins. Now put them feet out and together or I'll blow a hole in blondie's face. Any questions?" he yelled still waving the gun in my direction. "I thought not." Kevin obeyed and put his feet together while Finneaus taped him from just above the knees down to his toes, and then taped his mouth.

"Y'all thirsty?" Finneaus asked. He talked like a pleasant southern man. One wouldn't think anything of him if he hadn't had a gun in his hand. "Let's get you stabilized and we can have a swig of soda, and a little dialogue. How's that sound? Good? I think so just the same as you, boo. No talking," he pointed his finger at us both, first Kevin and then me as he left the room.

Kevin suspiciously stared at the bed that was covered with blankets and plastic. He sat up as tall as he could, and let his eyes follow the length of the thick plastic. I tried to follow his gaze, but slumped down quickly when Finneaus came back into the room carrying a tray holding three cans of Dr. Pepper and three straws. He put a can between the tape that secured my hands and pointed the straw to my mouth.

"People always saying he's not like us, something's missing in him." He sat on his knees. Our faces were no more than a few inches apart. He grabbed a corner of the tape across my mouth and ripped it off. My face stung as pieces of skin were ripped from my lips. He was smiling, and waiting with anticipation for my reaction to the pain. I smiled, and sipped the Dr. Pepper from the straw. "Hmm," he said, stood up, and giggled. He then carried a can of Dr. Pepper to Kevin, sat on his knees and slowly moved to face him. "You're a big one," he said and ripped the tape from Kevin's mouth. He put the can in Kevin's hand and the straw on his lips. Kevin stared him down with eyes as cold as steel. "Is it good? Do you like it? You're not as nice as the Y-chromosome, but the X's usually aren't. It's all about the hunt and gather with you. Am I right? I know I'm right. You just don't want to admit it, but I'm right. I bet I know as much about you as you do about me. You want to make a bet? Ok ten dollars, but we're going to have to make an appointment for a consult on that because first we have to get the test results."

Finneaus stood up, walked to the desk and opened a laptop computer. "If you will direct your attention to the screen over here." He pecked around on the keyboard, sat in the chair and rolled himself to one side of the desk. The screen lit up with a slide-show presentation accompanied by classical music. "The plan has always been to do this with limited exposure to collateral damages. Make a plan and stick to it, I always say."

The first slide was a picture of the Elementary school in Oklahoma taken before the bombing that slowly morphed into the rubble that remained after the explosion. "Page four—six hours dominating cable news," Finneaus said. The next slide was a picture of Marla holding the

Patient: Crew books. "She's the one who knows everything. They had me fooled. I'd have bet Tim was the intelligence, but it turned out to be his woman. She shouldn't have sold out. She should have refused. It's his fault all in all. We all know that's the real truth here. He didn't keep an eye on her. Only took me a second to snatch her. Boom—blow up the car. Boom—get the woman. It was easy once I got his attention, easy as pie in the sky. What good did it do me? That's what I want to know. What good did any of it do me? She couldn't produce the crew, couldn't do it. But she knew who could. You could, she knew you could."

The third slide was a picture of the bed on the opposite wall. There weren't any blankets or plastic over the bare mattress. "She shouldn't have been so stubborn. The Y's are always stubborn. I'd planned it for years. I thought everything over in my head a million and two times, and then a million and four times more. It was the only way to get their attention. They'd have no other choice than to warn people. It wasn't until I decided I'd kill a thousand people in thirty days that they finally said something. I figured it out, and I knew I was on the right track when the book came out with the warning—right there in that book—oh lord Jesus it was a thrill not to mention an honor. I mean…I mean…I didn't even write it down. I just started saying in my head. Did I say it out loud? No, I don't think so, but just the same they knew. They knew my every thought. I told her what I wanted. I told her what would happen. I told her everything I knew to tell her. She called you said you would bring them."

The fourth slide was of the children's museum in New Mexico, before the bombing. "I made her hold the phone. She pushed the final number. Page one, thirty-nine hours and counting on the national news networks, and a CNN special report. They're calling me the baby bomber. I'd rather they call me the bombardier. Wish in one hand, shit in the other," he giggled. "Am I right? You know I'm right. There's supposed to be a picture right here of the blowed up museum, but I couldn't fine one so's we'll just pretend it's there. All the same it's her fault, all her fault. She's to blame for that one. She tried to hurt me with that phone so I gave her a Dr. Pepper and then, then, then!" The final slide was of Marla lying on a bed with a pillow under her head, her arms across her chest. "Didn't take but a gulp and a swallow." He leaned his body to the side as if falling over and started to sing. "I'm a pepper, she's a pepper, wouldn't you like to be a pepper too?"

My heart raced. I didn't want to look at the bed. I didn't want to think about her body rotting under the pile of blankets and plastic. "Oh my God." I couldn't stop the words from coming out. "You killed her? Is she in that bed?"

"What's wrong with you?" Finneaus was confused by my outburst. "She ratted you out. She can't be trusted if she'd rat you out like that, and so easily. The crew they're happy. I know they are. I'm right about that."

"You didn't have to kill her," I said. "You didn't have to do that." I started to take another drink of Dr. Pepper through the straw.

"Shanna don't!" Kevin yelled. We shared a look of terror as we looked down at the cans of soda we'd been sipping.

"You poisoned her!" Kevin dropped his can to the floor.

"Now look what you've done," Finneaus said, jumped from his chair and ran into the kitchen. He brought back a roll of paper towels, and wiped the soda from the floor.

"Why did you break into my house?" he asked Kevin.

"I didn't break in. You forced me in."

Finneaus pointed at Kevin and his right hand began to shake. "You sliced the body open, stuck your hands inside the body and that's breaking, and that's entering in any medical journal. Agreed?"

"Sure man whatever you say," Kevin said. "What do we do now?"

"This is my conference." Finneaus pointed at Kevin with his shaking finger. "You stay out of it." He closed his eyes and mumbled to himself quietly. "One, two buckle my shoe. Three, four shut the door. Five, six pick up sticks." The next second his eyes popped wide open, and he grinned at me. "I always find a moment of reflection can put a mind straight wouldn't you agree?"

"Yes." I was afraid to say anything more. Marla was dead. I had no delusions about that fact. She was dead and probably under the blankets and plastic. Tim was in custody—telling the CIA who knows what—and we were the hostages of a lunatic.

"Ok then." Finneaus sat in the office chair, rolled to me, stopping only when the roller nudged my leg.

"Do you know my name?"

"I don't know." I knew his name. I also knew the question was trick.

"Well?" he pushed. "Times up." He rolled to the desk, picked up the gun, rolled back to me and held the gun against my head. His hand was still quivering. "Now, one more time. Do you know my name? It's a simple question."

"Finneaus Albert," Kevin yelled. "Finneaus mother fucking Albert."

"Did I ask you? Did I say a word to you? That's not fair, and now you've gone and ruined everything." He took the gun away from my head, and rested it in his lap. He started to cry softly then slowly he rolled his chair back to the desk and closed the laptop. "The presentation is over. You have successfully crapped on it all. I don't want to play this game anymore." He laid his head on the desk and became quiet; within ten minutes he was snoring.

"Look for something sharp," Kevin whispered lightly.

"She's under those blankets," I said.

"I don't know," Kevin said. "But if you ever wanted to see crazy there it is."

"She's there, under there." I couldn't look at the bed.

"Snap out of it. Yes she's probably there and if we don't want to join her we had better look for a way out of this." Kevin pulled his legs in an attempt to rip the tape. He tried to get up on his knees, but fell over every time. I looked around the floor for something sharp. It was one of the cleanest floors I'd ever seen. The room had a strong odor of pine cleaner, and bleach.

"There's nothing over here," I said.

"Nothing here either. We've got to get out of here. Don't talk, understand?" he looked at me in the same way Jade had when she forced a promise out of me—the promise that got me into this mess.

"Do you still have the key?"

"Yes," Finneaus stopped snoring and whispered. "I want to know the answer to that question myself. Do you still have the key?" He kept his head on the desk with his eyes closed. "You failed the sleep test. I'm not as crazy as you. You thought I was sleeping, and that's crazy, and you're even crazier for thinking you'll get away. Clean as a whistle this house is. Not a mouse in this house." He raised his head and looked at me. "Where's the key and what does it open?"

"I don't have the key. I forgot it," I said.

"I'll be nice one more time," he said and cocked his head to the side. He stared at me and then turned his chair quickly to look at Kevin. After a few long seconds, he turned his chair to face the desk again. He fumbled with the gun in his lap, slowly picked it up and rolled to me.

"I said I wouldn't I said I couldn't, and now you'll say I shouldn't." He got out of the chair and stood next to my head still fumbling with the gun. "Sun's a going down now it's time to speak or you'll be on your way to that great sunset in the sky." He rubbed the barrel of the gun down my cheek causing me to shake uncontrollably. My nerves were chaotic. I looked down at the ring and thought that not being able to return it to Jima would be my only regret. I knew that at some point if not now he would shoot me. "No time like the present," Finneaus said, cocked the gun and pushed it into my head.

"Come on man you don't want to do that," Kevin struggled with the tape.

"Of course I don't want to do it," his anger built with each word. He jabbed the gun barrel harder into my head.

"If you don't want to kill her then put the gun down!" Kevin pleaded.

"I don't want to. I have to. You're making me do it. Tell me where the key is and do it now or I'm going to dye her hair red in a second, man."

"Can I jump now?" I cried.

"Ok, ok, I'll tell you everything," Kevin said. "But put the gun down first."

"I'm not putting it down Jack rabbit dag nabbit. I'm shooting in five, four, three. I mean it I do I mean it." I closed my eyes and listened to my breath as it went in and out of my body. A sudden calmness ran through me. I thought about Jim and me when we were fifteen. We would sneak out of church during the invitation song, and make out. We had our own hiding place inside the garden shed not more than ten feet from the church's back door. That shed was a special place for us.

"Put the gun down Finn," Kevin demanded. "I'll answer all of your questions if you will put the damned gun down, and come over here."

"I get first question," Finneaus yelled while keeping the gun against my head. "I'm first in line, and there's no cuts."

"Ok, ok, you're first," Kevin said. "Ask me a question."

"Ask you a question and you'll tell me some lies."

"Only the truth, man. I'll tell you the truth." Finneaus tapped his foot as if in deep thought, but never took the gun away from my head. I could see the fear in Kevin's eyes. I gave him a little smile and a shrug. I had begged for death to come. I was ready.

"What's your name?" Finneaus asked. "And her name too."

"My name is Kevin, and her name is Shanna. Now put the gun down, please."

He pressed the gun harder into my head and giggled like a pathetic clown. I could hear Kevin scream "duck," but the sound was muffled by my pounding heart, and the gun letting out a soft—click.

"Wasn't loaded any-who," he said and rolled his chair back to the desk. He turned his back so we couldn't see what he was doing. "That was the stress test, and you both failed." He pointed the gun at Kevin's chest. "Want a take a chance or want a give some answers?"

"What is it that you want to know?"

"I said it once I said it twice, and I'm not going to chew that cabbage thrice," Finneaus said. "Let's get this chart in order. I need a history and physical in order to make the correct diagnosis." I knew right away what he was saying, but Kevin was confused. Marla had used the same terminology.

"That's such a broad subject. Instead of asking to know every minor detail, maybe you should be more specific," I said

He snarled at me. "Did anyone ask you to speak woman? Now do what your little dark friend here said and shut up." I put my head down, but not out of obedience or shame. I did it so that son of a bitch, crazy ass, scum bucket couldn't see the anger in my eyes. This was the first—and only—time in my life that I thought I could kill a person without regret.

"She doesn't mean anything by it," Kevin said. Finneaus kept his eyes focused on me. "Come on Finn look over here. I'll tell you everything. He slowly moved his head around to face Kevin, rolled the chair to him then quickly raised the gun to Kevin's head, cocked it and pulled the trigger, but again there was no bullet in the chamber. Kevin flinched. "Damn it Finneaus what the fuck are you doing?"

Finneaus giggled. "You're running out of chances Kevey. I'm not as stupid as I look. I saw you taking pictures of my lab, and my samples. I saw it all. I have it on tape so I can see it as often as I want. I heard you say touchdown like you'd found the gold you was searching for. What's the key for Kev? Huh? What's it for?" He stood up, smoothed his pants and started to twirl the gun with his fingers. "The way I see it is my way, and my way says you're a dirty rotten liar. I should kill you both, and use your bones for shrapnel. I'm hungry, and I like meat. I don't care if it's red, pink, black or blonde." He sat down rolled to the desk and put the gun in the top drawer. "I guess this is your lucky day Kevolater. How do you take your meat cooked?"

Finneaus clapped his hands, snapped his fingers and headed into the kitchen. He turned on the radio and started singing along with Kenny Rogers while cooking, singing especially loud on the chorus. "You got to know when to hold 'em, know when to fold 'em. Know when to walk away, know when to run." When the song ended, Kevin and I remained silent until the next song began and Finneaus sang along.

"Do you think he'll poison us?"

"No I don't," Kevin said. "I think that would be to fast for him. He likes to scare us. He wants to make us sweat. He had Marla a long time before he finally took her out."

"How are we going to get out of this? Did the crew give you any solutions?" I waited for a response. "Yeah, I didn't think so."

"Let's eat and get him talking to us like a friend. Maybe we can get him to loosen our hands."

"Do you think he's going to kill us?" I asked.

"He's killed over five hundred people most of them children in the last week. Yes I think there's a strong possibility that he could kill us, but I'm not going to let that happen. Are they still gone?"

"Yes Kevin they're still gone." I was pissed. I should have never gotten myself—let alone Kevin—into this situation. Every time I looked at Kevin, I saw Jade pointing her finger at me as a reminder of my promise. "If they come back, you'll be the first to know."

"I'm sorry I got you into this but I promise…"

"No more promises Kevin," I cut him off. "I can't handle any more promises."

"I love you," Kevin said softly. "I just want you to know that I love you like a family member, like a sister."

"No. You will not start that, not yet. We're going to get out of this. I don't know how, but we are and you are going home to Jade."

"If you say so."

"I feel the same way about you, like the brother sister thing," I said. The song stopped, and we listened to make sure Finneaus was still cooking. Kevin turned his legs and with great effort got to his knees and started shaking his upper body like a stripper shaking her tits. This was not an easy move for a man of Kevin's size, and would have been funny to watch had the situation been different. When he stopped shaking, I heard something hit the floor. Kevin froze and listened, Finneaus was still singing.

"What's that?" We heard footsteps from the kitchen coming closer. Kevin sat hard on his side. With his taped hands, he pushed whatever dropped out of his shirt under his legs. A second later Finneaus walked through the door.

19.

*H*e didn't take the tape off our arms. We waited until Finneaus had taken a bite or two before eating. The meat didn't have a familiar flavor, but it was tolerable.

"This is a very good supper," I said with a forced smile.

"I wasn't sure if you'd take to rodent, but it looks like you're a doing jest fine with it. You must be from good stock girly," Finneaus said.

I took another bite and happily chewed it despite my eyes tearing from holding back the gags. The tears ran down my face, but I continued to eat until my plate was clean never allowing myself to think about what I was consuming.

"Why are you crying Shanna?" Finneaus asked.

"I'm not crying. I think I might have gotten a bone stuck in my throat. Could I have something to drink?" *My acting was good* I thought, and with a little luck it would get Finneaus out of the room for a second.

"Swaller yer spit. I got a question to ask first, and then I'll leave you both to ponder the answer." Finneaus continued to enjoy his meal slowly without speaking. His facial expressions would change while chewing, and he would giggle and moan happily from time to time as if he were in another place where we didn't exist. Kevin finished his plate quickly, and began gnawing on a leg bone. I wasn't sure which made me sicker, being forced to eat a rat or watching Kevin enjoy eating a rat.

"Have you lived here long?" Kevin asked.

Finneaus showed no emotion as he finished chewing, and wiped his mouth on a sleeve. For no apparent reason, he began to giggle. "This is the question you want to ask of the man who is holding you hostage at gunpoint?"

"I was trying to make conversation. I meant nothing by it," Kevin said as he continued to chew on the leg bone.

"Let's make this clear. I didn't give you this disease. I didn't make you come to my house and snoop around my lab. You did it all of your own accord." He stood up, gathered the plates and set them on the desk. "What is my name?"

It was a stupid knee jerk reaction but I said it anyway. "Your name is Finneaus son of Flora." Finneaus walked quickly to me and slapped me opened handed across my face. I grunted from the pain but didn't scream. It stung and made my entire face flush with heat.

"Hey," Kevin yelled. "Don't hurt her for answering your question." He tried to get to his feet, but it was impossible. "Shanna, you ok?"

"Better shut up or I'll do worse to you," he said to Kevin then turned to me. "Don't use my mother's name in vain little shit girl. I bet you think you're cute, but I don't." He walked back to the desk and stood while typing on the laptop. When he had finished he moved aside, and the screen lit up with a news story about the Albuquerque bombing. He muted the sound. "I'm waiting for a visitor," Finneaus said. "Are you that visitor? If you are, you'll know my name and you'll know what comes next. If you don't then I have no use for you." He gathered the plates and left the room.

"We have to tell him," I insisted.

"Tell him what?" Kevin asked.

"That I'm the crew. What else can we do? He's going to kill us."

"I think he already knows."

"Marla didn't tell him everything or he'd have killed you and made me write by now."

"He knows enough be slow to speak. It can buy us time."

"Marla wouldn't have told him."

"You'd be surprised what people will do to survive."

"We have to do something. We can't just sit here and take the bullet," I said.

"Still silent?"

"Yes. I can't bring them back at will."

"Are you sure?" Kevin asked still gnawing on the bone. "Maybe they're giving you a choice."

"I've never had a choice."

"Maybe you can choose for them to come, and choose for them to leave."

"You're grasping at straws, and what in the hell are you doing with that rat bone?"

"I have to get on my feet. All I need is one good blow." He took the bone out of his mouth to let me see the sharp point he'd whittled with his teeth, and carefully put it in the tape below the palm of his other hand.

"Do you really think he did all of this, all the bombing and killing children just to get me?"

"To get to the crew."

Finneaus came back into the room. He typed on the laptop keyboard. When he stood to the side we saw a picture of a church on the screen. "This one was easy. Religious people are far too trusting. I told the secretary that a member of the congregation, who wanted to remain anonymous, had paid for a complete refurbish of the heating system. She didn't ask nary a question. She was more than willing to accept the fantasy as long as she'd get something for nothing," he giggled. "Who goes to a porn theater without wanting to pump it. What good is porn without pumping it, right Kevin? Am I right? The problem is that I don't like the lies. No more lies. I decided to not accept the lies when I read the first book.

The crew is all I listen to now, and they've been gone. I can't find them. I read both books a hundred and twenty eight times. After the first one, I started my own research and development. I have to find the crew. They know me. They've been waiting for this meeting. I'm sure it was in their chart."

"You're talking about the books?" Kevin asked softly. "Because I know the books. I know them very well."

"You know nothing," Finneaus snarled. "His wife, now she's the one who knew it. She had it all, and she was fool enough to let it go. But you know nothing."

"I know your name," Kevin said.

"Say it."

"If I say your name what will you do with us?" Kevin asked.

Finneaus crouched down beside Kevin. "I'd be more worried about what's going to happen if you don't say it. I can't let you walk out of here—not now—after all that's happened. You must know that."

"I'll tell you what I know, and you let us go," Kevin said.

"Well, well, well," he said, and went back to the desk and laptop. "It looks as if we got us a couple o' falderal fakers. You want to know what we do to fakers?" A video of a toe being cut off with garden shears appeared on the screen. It was an extreme close-up, and he turned up the volume. The owner of the toe was screaming in the background. I looked away as the shears began to cut the skin, and I noticed that Finneaus was not watching either. He had his back turned. His face was scrunched with disgust. It was a scare tactic. He could no more do that to someone than I could. The video ended. "You see that," he said. "No more games. I don't have time for games, and neither do you." He opened the desk drawer, this time he held up two guns. He pointed one at Kevin, and the other at me. "Tell me my name and do it now."

"Dark warrior," Kevin said. "You're the dark warrior prophesied by Patient Crew." Finneaus dropped his arms, and the guns pointed to the floor.

"It worked. Huh. I never thought it would actually work. I thought it could, but I never in my wildest dreams allowed myself to think it would. If you know my name it worked." He was giddy. "It was really a fluke. I've seen it work in the movies, but never thought it would really work. I studied on the theory for weeks, but then one day I said it's now or never so I just did it. I put the bomb in the car, snuck into their house and waited. I knew sooner or later those two suits would leave. I should have waited because Tim saw me, oh yes he saw me. I bet the feds think he did it, but that ain't so. Tim don't got the brains enough to build a bomb. Don't matter now, all's well that ends well. Honestly I didn't put that much thought into it."

"So what's next?" Kevin interrupted.

"I don't know," he said with a giggle. "Like I said, I hadn't put that much thought into it, but I guess next I want to meet them. I want to meet them immediately, right now all seven of them. I want to know where they are right now." He pointed the guns at us again. "Now!"

"You can't meet them," Kevin said.

"What?" Finneaus yelled. "Why? They know who I am or you wouldn't know, and you wouldn't be here. Tell them it's me. They'll want to meet me."

"It doesn't work that way," Kevin said.

"I don't care how it works," he pointed both guns at me. "I'm going to kill girly if you don't get the crew here in the next few minutes. Call them, and tell them to come or you're both dead. That's what we're going to do, call them."

"My phone's outside, remember?" Kevin said.

"You can use my phone," Finneaus said, and left the room.

"I sure hope you know where you're going with all this because I sure as hell don't," I fumed.

Kevin leaned over and I saw what he'd dropped from his shirt earlier. It was a cell phone. "Take it," he said. "Turn it on, and then mute the sound." I couldn't find either button as I fumbled and dropped the phone twice before Kevin wiggled closer to me, and picked it up. He pushed a couple of buttons. "They'll get my signal."

"Who, the crew nerds? We need the cops Kevin. Call the cops."

"He's not going to kill us," he argued. "You saw him. He couldn't even look at that stupid toe video."

"That church he showed us is the next target. We have to stop him," I said.

"No cops, not yet. Give the Crewbies enough time to get here and get you out."

"Get us out," I said. Kevin pushed the phone under his leg just as Finneaus entered the room with both guns pointed at us, and a cordless landline sticking out of his pants pocket.

"Call them," he said, and moved his body around so Kevin could reach up and grab the phone. "Call them, and tell them where you are. Tell them I'll blow us all up if they don't come alone. I see a police car, and I'll blow the whole block to smithereens. Tell them I just want a consult. I won't hurt anyone if they follow the treatment, and come in for the appointment. Go ahead now and call them."

"I can't," Kevin said. "There's not anyone to call."

"How do you contact them?" he asked.

"I don't. They contact me."

"I see," his shoulders slumped with disappointment. "What did they tell you about me? When did they know it was me? When did they know that I am the dark warrior? I need to know specifics here." He laid the guns on the chair and took a Patient: Crew book out of the desk drawer.

"Tell him," I whispered to Kevin.

"They know all about you. They've said your name over and over in the passages. I can take you to them in my car."

"No. They must come here," Finneaus said.

"They want you to come to them."

"No. They will come here. That's the plan," Finneaus insisted.

"The plan has changed because of what you did to Tim and Marla."

"No. Nothing's changed."

"It's the only way," Kevin said.

"They go to find the place of hell," Finneaus said quietly as he flipped the book pages. "They go to find the place of hell. Where is it? I saw it last time, and now I can't find it. They go to find the place of hell." He massaged his forehead and continued to mumble. "They go to find the place of hell. They will come here."

"*Onward they march never turning back. Their sights are made. Their minds meld as they go to find that place of hell that he created for us to dwell.* It's in book one, page thirty-three line six. The Poet," Kevin said.

"I know. I know that already," Finneaus said, frantically searching the book. "You didn't have to prompt me I knew it. You didn't give me enough time. It's not fair."

"Is this that place of hell?" Kevin asked. "Is that what you think? Because I think that's taking it out of context."

"This is not a debate, and I don't really care what you think." Finneaus said. "How do they do it? How do they know the future? Do they have a secret room where they go to meet God? They must get it from God. He's

265

the only one who knows that sort of stuff. How does he talk to them? See there it is," he pointed at a page in the book. "I had it all along I didn't need you then, and I don't need you now."

"Harvest time is around the corner. Everyone comes for a day of feasting, and prayer at the little brown church in the vale." Finneaus started to sing. "Oh come to the church in the wildwood oh come to the church in the dale. No spot is so dear to my childhood than the little brown church in vale. ' He hummed a little longer, and then pulled a cell phone from the desk drawer. With great care he pushed the power button, and placed the phone down gently beside the keyboard.

"The front of the church is very deceiving. It is much bigger than it looks. You see, the front part is the chapel, but the back is a gym that's where the party's at. Down the side—the part you can't see—that's the kiddie's classroom area. I had to cheat and use five for this one," he looked at Kevin and shrugged his shoulders. "I know what you're thinking but I had to." He pointed at the church's image. "You see if I set only four charges I could get the entire gym, classroom area and most of the chapel, but not the front. I had to be able to take the front down too. It makes better TV, and a more complete job. I also thought, I thought, Finn this'll get them talking about you for sure. You know since I changed the pattern and all. So you can see I had no other choice." He giggled and typed on the keyboard. "It'll all be going down in the morning. They start gathering at nine, and by ten they will be stuffing their pig faces just in time to have their happy bellies blown to bits. I'm hoping for at least four-fifty. It'd be great to hit nine hundred ninety before I blow up the ten of us, but I don't think that will be the case."

"They know who you are. There is no need for more bombs," Kevin said. "You've completed your mission."

"This is not a mission," Finneaus said. "This is a major discovery. We have the cure. The research isn't finished until you have the cure in the palm of your hand." He leaned back in the chair, and his giggle grew into a full-blown crazy laugh. His whole body shook while he picked up the guns. "You don't get the joke, but I do. They are waiting for me. It's my turn and I've got check, maybe even checkmate. It all depends on the attendance. It was low at the school and museum. Now, I need a big number. I'll play their game." Finneaus shook the guns wildly in his hands. Suddenly, I heard a loud POP as the gun pointed at Kevin discharged. Finneaus was in a panic, running from room to room, and then back with us throwing towels at me.

"Cover it up. Jeepers! Jeepers creepers the devils reapers! Look what you've done you little shit," he ran out of the room screaming. "You're a good for nothing waste of space. Look what you've done now, stupid shit boy. What good are you? What good are you?" He returned quickly with a bucket of water.

"Mother fucker," Kevin screamed. "You fucking shot my mother fucking foot mother fucker. What the fuck is wrong with you!"

"Can't do nothing right, can't never could do nothing. Just a waste of time and space," Finneaus rambled as he paced around the room careful not to look at the blood flowing from the hole in Kevin's shoe and foot. "Shush, shush don't yell."

"Don't tell me to shush you crazy mother fucker," Kevin yelled. "Damn you."

"The neighbors! Oh no! Oh no! Busy bodies every one of them." He looked out the one window in the room, which was covered with a heavy dark curtain. "Oh! Oh! There they come. Oh! Oh!" He ran to the front door area. I heard a series of beeps followed by a door opening. Kevin started to scream. I looked at him, confused for a fraction of a second, and then joined in. We both screamed so loudly we didn't hear it when Finneaus came back into the room, tape in hand. He covered our mouths tightly with the duct tape never looking down at the blood. "Cover it I said." Finneaus turned away quickly, doubled over and began to gag. "Cover it good so I can't see the red." Scream again, and I'll blow us all up."

I scooted closer to Kevin's foot. The shoe was blown apart in the center of the laces and blood was gushing from the hole I tried to gently pull the shoe off with my fingers, but Kevin cried out in pain with every tug. He pushed me aside, put his right toe under the left shoe heal and flipped the shoe off in one quick move. The shoe flew across the room and the bullet rolled out. He cried through the tape and began to turn pale.

I couldn't stand to see him in pain. It was easier for me to look at his mangled foot than it was his face. I pulled his sock off as gently as I could without being able to bend or maneuver my arms. Kevin laid down trying to breathe through his clogged nose. I held a towel up to his face and let him blow He put his taped arms up to my face, held my chin in his fingers, forced me to look into his smiling eyes, and then he laughed. He let out a burst of snot blowing laughter. I couldn't help but laugh with him.

After we had settled down and caught our breath, as best as we could through our noses, I strained to hear Finneaus talking with an older woman outside while tending to Kevin's foot. They were talking about the gun shot noise and screams but decided it must have been a backfire from the kid's car down the street. According to the woman, that same kid was arrested last week for drunk driving. The screaming, she was sure, must be some drunken teenagers up to no good.

"Better keep your doors locked," we heard Finneaus say. "You never know what kind of mischief could be living right next door." I'd finished wrapping

Kevin's foot with the towels and was wiping the floor when he walked inside.

"That was a close one. We have to be more careful when handling the equipment," he said, sat in his chair and rolled over to us. "Put the dirties in the water bucket, and put a clean rag over the top so's I can't see the red stuff. I'll bury it outside in the morning." He rolled over to the desk. I did as I was told.

"We can't let that happen again, but what do you expect for a know-nothing slob. This place is a pig's sty. Sun is a going down, but it's never too late to clean. These floors could use a good scrubbing. How can we possibly perform surgery here? Looks as though there's been a battle in this room. Crumbs everywhere." he giggled. "This will not do. No, this will not do. Everything needs some time in the autoclave." He got up from the chair, went into the kitchen, and returned with spray cleaner and rags, wearing a white doctors coat and surgical mask. He started with the desk, spraying and wiping the surface, the laptop screen, and then the desk legs. He dropped to his knees on the floor and started cleaning the baseboards.

"We'll have to get the dust mop going on these floors before we use the vacuum. I hope I've got enough bleach," he said and continued to scrub the baseboard. He carefully sprayed and wiped a small section before starting on another. "You can say goodbye to these short nights soon. Time changes in a few weeks, course I don't guess that matters a hill of beans." He giggled and started on the next section of baseboard. "We've got a little time here while I clean this room. Would you like to know the story of Finneaus Albert? You can have the exclusive."

Kevin made a grunting sound through the tape across his mouth. I was in awe, watching Finneaus turn from a mad scientist into a crazed gunman shooting Kevin in the foot then into a fit of lunacy at the sight of blood and immediately becoming the curious neighbor sharing an evening chat on the street, all within twenty minutes time. Now, he'd turned into the compulsive house cleaner and wanted to award us, his hostages an exclusive interview as if we were roasting marshmallows around a campfire. I wasn't interested in the story of Finneaus Albert, and Kevin's patience was making me sick.

Finneaus stopped cleaning. "Well, why didn't you say something?" He walked over to Kevin, and yanked the tape off his mouth. He turned to me. I closed my eyes, and braced myself as another layer of skin and lips was removed.

"I have to use the bathroom," I said.

"Hold it," Finneaus said.

"I have to go too," Kevin said. "We've been sitting here for a long time Finn; it's only natural to need relief."

Finneaus was disgusted at the thought of having to clean up after us if he didn't allow us to do our business. "I guess you've got a point." He picked up the bucket with the bloodied rags inside, and went into the kitchen. We heard him open the sliding door to the outside.

"Are you ok?" I asked.

"I'm good, just a little pain in my foot—and my stuff," he looked down at his groin. "I might not ever be the same, but other than that I'm good."

"Should I loosen the wraps?"

"No. You did a good job on those thanks."

"I'm tired of holding my tongue," I said. "I'm going to tell him. I can show him how I write, and tell him that the crew demanded he let us go." I checked Kevin's foot and it was hot. "I've got to get you out of here and to a doctor right away or your foot's going to get infected."

"I'm fine, I've lived through worse than this. Don't tell him. We can do this without him knowing." Finneaus came back into the house with an empty bucket. "Bedpan," he said and left the room, but not before informing us that we had five minutes and he would be listening. "Don't do any number two's, that's too messy. Don't piss on the floor," he yelled from the kitchen.

"How do you think I'm going to sit up enough to get on that thing? You've got to cut our legs loose or there's going to be a big mess," I said.

Finneaus came back into the room with a knife, and cut the tape on our legs from the top to the ankle. "I'll be around the corner with this knife in one hand and a gun in the other ready to turn you into stew meat if there's so much as one false move."

Kevin leaned away from me. "You go first. Take your time."

"This is insane," I said and fumbled to get my pants down. I was able, with great difficulty, to get the job done, but I don't know if Kevin was as successful. It wasn't sanitary or private, but it felt good to relieve myself and soon enough the ordeal was over.

"Throw a rag over the top," Finneaus demanded while waving the gun in my face. I took a rag from the stack he'd brought in for cleaning, and draped it over the top of the bucket. Finneaus kept the gun pointed at my head until I'd finished doing his bidding and had sat back against the wall. "Now then where was I?" he asked as he sat on the floor, put the gun beside him and started cleaning the next small section of baseboard—not paying attention to our loosened legs.

"You were going to tell us the story of Finneaus Albert," Kevin said.

"That's right. Finneaus Albert now there's a story. It all started when I was…hmm…I guess I was just turning five. I remember because I was about to start school. The Doctor was very proud of me. The patient crew knows this story I'd bet."

"Who's the Doctor?" Kevin asked.

"It's not time for the questions part of the evening," he yelled. "My father, George Albert, was the Doctor. He was a great man and an even greater Doctor. The whole town depended on him and his expertise. He was loved by all." He said with pride. "Mother was the Doctor's second wife, the first wife died with her baby during birth, or at least that's what I was told. Truth is, I think she was still amongst the living at that time because I had heard the Doctor and Mother talking about her. Why the interest if the woman's dead. They had me when Mother was well into her forties, of course Tim was born when she was younger and wanted children in her life." He looked down at the baseboard along the floor. "This needs to be painted. The sand blows so much around here. It takes the paint right off every surface. The Doctor had a sand experiment he did on Mr. Herman, my Sunday school teacher. The Doctor didn't like him or what he taught, or maybe it was the way he taught that he didn't approve of. Mr. Herman was all about love and grace whereas the Doctor was all about discipline and punishment." He sat back and relished in his memories for a moment, and then began to giggle. "I'm surprised the Doctor didn't force him to eat the sand. No, really, I'm just joking. The Doctor was an ethical man, and did it with hypodermics." He stood up and stretched before beginning the meticulous cleaning process again on the next wall's baseboard. "Now surely you can see how this wall needs a fresh painting." He smeared a red spot on the wall not ten feet away from where we were sitting, and where he had shot Kevin's foot. He stared at the red on his finger, and then turned his attention to the smear on the wall.

"Mr. Herman believed that no matter what a person did they could be forgiven. No one should feel guilt for the things that they had done because we are forgiven and washed in the blood of the lamb. Jesus already knows our deviant thoughts before we ever do the evil deed, and

he forgives without us even having to ask." Finneaus
turned his gaze to Kevin's wrapped up foot, and back to
the smear on the wall, and then to his finger. Kevin and I
held our breath. I could feel his anxiety. But, Finneaus
simply sprayed the wall and wiped it clean. He put the rag
in the bucket and walked into the kitchen, and outside
through the sliding glass door. Within a minute he was
back in the living room with a small jug of bleach, a can of
paint and a brush. He wet a rag with the bleach and ran it
over the blood splatter removing all evidence of its
existence.

"Mr. Herman had tired blood. The Doctor told
him about his experimental injections of the blood
cleansing solution. It took years of research. It was the
Doctor's passion. He would take me to the pound and let
me choose whichever dog I wanted, and we used it for his
research and development. If the dog didn't die from the
injections then he would try it on a patient, a human one."
He opened the can of paint, dipped the brush and began
painting the wall. "I remember the pup we named Frankie.
He was a cowardly little thing, but he proved to be an
excellent test subject for Mrs. Herman, Mr. Herman's wife.
The Doctor sometimes let me mix the chemicals and sand
for his research. Frankie helped the Doctor find a cure for
the diabetes in Mrs. Herman. A week after her first series
of injections she was eating anything she wanted, putting
three spoons of sugar in her coffee and munching donuts
by the dozens. She lived a good year before her heart took
her out. But, the Doctor had cured her of the sugar
diabetes—she didn't die from the diabetes. When Mr.
Herman came to him wanting help with his tired blood the
Doctor and I got another pup, and started our research.
Mr. Herman died two weeks after the Doctor started the
injection therapy. We were both sure the serum was good
since Buster had lived for at least six months on it. The
Doctor cured half of the people in this town, but still they

slander him. It wasn't his fault you know. I knew him
better than most, and I know it wasn't his fault. Ashes to
ashes dust to dust leave a shovel outside, and it'll surely
rust. After Mr. Herman died, his kids turned the Doctor
over to the fuck heads at the AMA. They started an
investigation the following week. Then they put him in the
jail. It was the beginning of the end for all of us. It was
their fault, everything was their fault and they used him as a
scapegoat, someone to lay the blame on just like you're
using me now." He carefully balanced the paintbrush
across the top of the can and went into the kitchen.
Kevin's nudge brought me out of the trance this hideous
story had put me under.

"Are you ok?" he asked.

"What do you mean am I ok? Are you ok? No,
neither one of us is ok. This guy is going to shoot us or kill
us with some sand chemical mixture of the Doctor's." I
pulled at the tape around my ankles. "We have a phone for
fuck's sake Kevin. Call the cops. Do you really want to die
just to protect the fucking voices in my head?"

"I'm protecting you it has nothing to do with the
crew, only you."

"It's not worth losing your own life."

"Yes it is. I know what will happen if the
government gets their hands on you, and it's worse than
being dead." Kevin shifted his legs and moaned in pain.
"He's not going to kill us. He knows we are his ticket to
the crew. Get the bone." I put my fingers between the
tape and his wrist and almost had it out when Finneaus
returned, and we had to quickly move back into place. He
put a jar of turpentine on the floor, and dunked the brush
in it.

"I love fresh paint. It makes everything smell new,
like nothing bad ever happened," he said.

"But something bad did happen, and something
bad is still happening." I was no longer capable of silence.

"Shanna!" Kevin admonished.

"Let her speak. I'd like to hear what the little girl has to say. It'll give the brush time to soak. Go ahead, you were saying that something bad is still happening?"

"Yes something bad is happening. You are the one doing the bad. You need to do what's right and let us go. If you don't let us go the crew will be angry."

His calm demeanor changed back into the giggly clown like man. "The right thing? I should do the right thing? You're a funny girly. What do you know about the crew? I know you know something I just don't know what that something is. Can't be much seeing as you're a girly."

"I know they'd be mad at you for what you've done. You need to let us go. The sooner the better."

"What happens if I don't let you go?" Finneaus asked. "There's no man more free than the one who has nothing to lose, and I got nothing."

"You've still got a lot to lose man, and if you let us go then we can help make things easier for you. If you show compassion," Kevin said.

"Compassion?" Finneaus giggled. "Compassion? Nobody ever showed me no compassion. They killed my mother when they threw him in jail. They had no right. She told me to make the bomb, and blow them up. She made me write her name on it. She wanted to make sure they knew it was payback for what they had done to the Doctor. I couldn't get it right. I just couldn't get it right. I tried everything, but nothing worked. They didn't show compassion," he started to cry.

"What happened Finn?" Kevin asked.

"Why do you keep calling me Finn? My name is dark warrior. Finneaus is a good for nothing waste of space, and never will be good for nothing neither. He can't even look at the blood and needles without puking or passing out. A stupid piece of cow shit," he wiped his eyes on his sleeve. "The Finneaus part of me may need help, but the dark warrior is fine as pie on his own and always will be. It's your fault. Every child that has died, and everyone who will die tomorrow, every person blown to smithereens is your fault, yours and the crew." He glared at Kevin. "There comes a time in every man's life when he has to stand up for what's right, and it's only right that I meet the crew. If they can take the liberty of writing about my life, what I think and plan, if they can get into my head that way then I deserve to meet them. I did the experiments, and I made the bombs work this time. This time I blew up the right people. It's you two that's the problem."

"You are so full of shit you can't see the light of day," I was fed up with the unceasing bravado. "You need to wake up and see what you've done, all on your own, alone. How can you sit there and blame something that exists—only in the imagination of its reader—for the destruction you've produced? The crew didn't create you, and frankly they could care less whether you live or die. We all have childhood demons. Get the fuck over it, and take the blame like a man. Dark warrior my ass."

Finneaus stood up and started to pace around the room. His rage was growing with every step. "I should take you down to that church, tie you to the top of the steeple and let you explode with the rest of them. But that's too good for you. You are nothing but a blasphemous wanton bitch who consorts with evil."

"Yeah that's right Finneaus, I'm the evil one."

Finneaus stopped pacing and dropped to the floor hard on his butt. He scooted across the room like a cowardly animal until he was against the wall next to me. He leaned his body against mine, put his head on my shoulder and whimpered. "He would say, 'I'm just trying to help people'," Finneaus whined. "And then he would slowly push the needle deep into their flesh. Most of the puppies were brave and tried to bite the Doctor, but Buster

276

was a sweet little puppy. He would let out a little yelp, lick his hands and beg the Doctor to stop. He never bit nor never nipped at him. The Doctor thought Buster was a coward, maybe he was. Mother told me to make them good Finny, and make sure my name's on every one. She said, they shall pay for their evil deeds. Whatever you sow so shall ye reap." He put his head in his hands, and began to bawl like a baby.

"She wanted you to make bombs?" I asked.

"She wanted me to blow up the courthouse. She wanted to kill the judge, and all the other people that put the Doctor in jail."

I opened my mouth to speak, and Kevin pushed his arms against my chest. I looked down, and saw the bone protruding from the tape. While Finneaus was busy wiping his nose on my sleeve, I quickly put my head down grabbed the bone with my teeth and carefully dropped it down to my fingers and out of sight.

"Shanna don't fight him he's right. The crew wrote about him he's the dark warrior," Kevin said, playing the good cop.

"What was in the injection, the one he put in Mr. Herman?" I asked.

"I'm not going to answer your questions," Finneaus straightened his body, and instantly became calm. "We have a lot to get done before the surgery tomorrow. Amputations are exhausting; we'll need our rest." He picked up his rag and began again to clean the baseboards where he'd left off, one small section at a time. He cleaned the remaining ones and touched the paint on the wall to see whether it had dried. "Still a little damp, but it'll be dry by morning." He picked up the paint can, brush, and jar of turpentine and carried them into kitchen.

"What in the hell are you thinking?" Kevin asked. "Don't get him upset don't do that again."

"Marla did the same thing to me when she wanted me to fall asleep. Self pity is hard work."

"Just don't go too far, got it?"

"And who's the jerk that didn't have a file on George fucking Albert? His name was on Tim's college application. How could you not think to check him out?"

"I did check him out and there was nothing but birth and death dates and medical school transcripts. There was nothing about him going to jail."

Finneaus passed by us without a word on his way to the front door. We heard a series of beeps, and then a computer generated female voice. "Security system activated." I waited until he had re-taped our legs and walked down the hallway to what must have been his bedroom before finally putting the rat bone between my teeth. I began cutting through the tape on my wrists. The plan was to pull my hands apart as much as possible, and then cut down the middle with the sharpened bone. It took half an hour to get a good tear in the tape, and then with one long rip my hands were freed. It was a glorious moment when I could use my hands to easily remove the tape from my legs and feet. I stood up and stretched, ignoring the urge to dance and sing a victory song.

"Hurry," Kevin whispered. "This could be another sleep test. Get my arms I'll do the legs." The tape came off his arms easily after I'd made a cut using the bone. Kevin, with his free hands, ripped the tape from his legs.

"Can you stand?" I asked.

"We're about to find out." The pain that ran through his body when he stood on the mangled foot was unbearable. "Lord Jesus Christ in heaven give me strength to go another mile," he cried quietly.

I put his huge arm around my shoulder but he had to lean down so far to use me as a support that he lost his balance. Sweat beads were streaming down his face as he leaned against the freshly cleaned wall. "We don't have the security code," he whispered.

"We'll have to be fast. I'll run ahead, start the car and pull up to the door. You walk as fast as you can and jump in, we're outa here. The neighbors will run outside to see what's happening when they hear the alarm. He won't shoot us in front of them." I was ready to put the plan into action. Kevin lightly laughed at our predicament. "What is it that you find so fucking funny?"

"I'll be lucky to take two steps without falling over, and when I do it's going to take more than you to get me back on my feet." Kevin slowly slid his back down the wall, bracing himself with his good leg while raising his mangled foot, and sat. His body blocked the hallway entrance into the room. "I'm willing to bet he has bombs in this house that are set and ready to go as soon as he hears the alarm. We can't take the chance that he'll blow up any more people," Kevin said. His breathing was labored, and his voice was getting weaker.

"What about the back door?"

"I saw an alarm keypad on the inside when I came in. You have to go. As soon as you get outside, call the police and tell them everything except your name. Here," he reached into his pocket and took out the cell phone. "Use this, wipe it clean and dump it when you're done." He looked down the hall. "Run and don't stop until you get to Abilene. Go straight home. Momma will know what to do." In my mind I was already out the door and halfway out of town, but my heart wouldn't listen. The consequences of leaving Kevin behind were unbearable to imagine.

"Do you think I'm going to Abilene and tell Jade I left her crippled son back at the baby bomber's house?" I sat on the floor next to Kevin. "We'll just have to think of another way." I could see my decision did not sit well with him. "Call the police Kevin. It's the only way out. We can't let him blow up that church."

"I know," Kevin said. He fumbled around with the phone trying to make a decision and looked at his texts. "Nothing from the Crewbies yet, but I'm sure they're doing their best to get here."

"Call them Kevin. Call the cops," I demanded. I got the key out of my shoe and put it in my pants pocket. "I'll wait by the door, and when we see them coming I'll leave. I'll get in the car and drive, or I'll just run down the street and hide. I won't let them catch me. The noise will confuse Finneaus. He won't have enough time to react."

"Too risky," Kevin insisted. "The police will block off the streets and the alarm will startle them so that any movement will be suspicious. They'd end up shooting you, and Finneaus will finish it by blowing up the whole block."

"Staying here another minute is the stupidest move we could make, call them!" I reached for the phone, but Kevin sat on it. "We don't have any other choice we have to call them now. You can't justify keeping me safe when so many lives are at stake."

"Stop it with your no other choice bullshit, and listen to me," he said. "You need to take this seriously. You write the future. Every word you write with those hands tells the future."

"Stop it Kevin, shut up."

"You stop it. Stop pushing it away, stop disconnecting from the truth. What you do is prophetic. When the world finds out who you are—well let's just say if you want to be hunted like an animal for the rest of your life then go ahead, call the cops." The cell phone vibrated in Kevin's hand as he held it out for me to take. We shared a look of fear, and looked down the hall for any signs of movement from Finneaus.

"It's from Megame they're three hours out. We just have to hang on a little longer. He's not going to kill us, we're his only link to the crew."

"No. We are not waiting another three hours besides how are they going to get inside? They can't break in because of the alarm. I was thinking I could stand outside his bedroom door, and you make a noise so he'll come out and I'll jump him. I can take him."

"There are three closed doors down the hall, which one is his bedroom? Is he in a bedroom? Is he armed? Is he listening to us right now? This isn't TV, it's real and in reality the good guys don't always win."

"Then call the cops."

"Three hours or less and they'll be here."

"You can't be serious Kevin." I couldn't believe the struggle I was having with a detective over calling the police on this crazy mass murderer. "He shot your foot!"

"That was an accident," Kevin scoffed. "Keep your voice down."

"Accident? Accident?" I whispered. Well let's just, what's that word you're so fond of—hope—he doesn't have another accident when he has the gun pointed at your head."

"Guns," Kevin said. "Are they in the drawer?" I walked softly to the desk and opened the drawer where Finneaus had put the guns, but it was empty.

"He has them," I said.

"Go in the kitchen and find something we can use as a weapon."

"I'm not going in there. He could be on the other side of that wall waiting for me to turn the corner before blowing my brains out. What if he's a light sleeper?"

"Go on," Kevin urged.

I made it to the doorway without making a sound. I could hear my heart racing inside my chest and then the beating turned to a hum, the hum turned into mumbles and the mumbles became voices. I walked back to Kevin who was motioning for me to go the other direction and saying something I couldn't hear. I sat on the floor and whispered in his ear. "They're back."

Kevin looked down the hall and signaled for me to be quiet. He pointed to the desk and wrote in the air above his palm to indicate tablets and pens in the desk. I walked quickly and opened the bottom drawer. There were some small note pads and I found pencils in the middle drawer. I sat next to Kevin and started to write.

20.

I wasn't jumping for joy when the crew returned, but I will admit to a more relaxed confidence that we would find our way out of the situation. My physical body went limp as I wrote. My mind fell into a deep dreamless sleep, allowing the crew to take over. I was unaware that I had been writing for at least an hour before Finneaus came into the room, nor was I aware he'd been recording me with a video camera. I woke up during the argument.

"You can't do that man," Kevin demanded. "Give me one good thing that will come out of it?"

"He who knows the future rules the world. I will be the good to come out of it," Finneaus giggled. "This is my discovery, and I will publicly claim it as such. I am Columbus and this is my America."

"You didn't discover anything."

I was still sitting against the wall. I opened my eyes partially, and could see through the slit that Kevin's hands and legs were again taped. I was holding the pencils, but the pads I had used were on the desk where Finneaus was sitting in his rolling chair.

"Would you like to ask Marla if she'd mind my taking credit?" Finneaus asked.

"It's not about credit. I don't care how much credit you take, take it all but you've got to know that if you publish it the situation gets worse. The dark warrior is called to protect her, not feed her to the public," Kevin said.

Finneaus stood by the twin bed that was covered in blankets and plastic. I couldn't see what he was doing, but I got the impression he was playing with the covering to taunt Kevin. "Are you sure, really sure, you're ready for this?" he teased.

"She's under there?" Kevin asked.

"Maybe so maybe not maybe you'll be there too, soon very soon." He rustled the plastic. "Tell me when."

"You're going to kill me? Then what? You can't kill Shanna because you have nothing without her. Do you think she'll do as you say? I bet you think she'll be your little puppet? She'd put the gun to her own head and pull the trigger before she'd do that." Finneaus went back to his laptop. He was typing and clicking the mouse while letting out a giggle here and there. Kevin was gnawing with his teeth at the tape on his arms, never taking his eyes off Finneaus.

"There it is," Finneaus proclaimed, "for all the whole world to see." He stood up with his arms raised high and his head thrown back glorifying his actions. "Ye shall know the truth and the dark warrior shall set ye free."

I closed my eyes and remained still. I wasn't ready to face this. I listened to the comforting hum that had returned to my head.

"I'm not going to kill her," Finneaus said. His back was turned to us as he sat in his chair and pecked on the keyboard. "I don't need you, but I don't know what I'll do with you yet. She however will bring a big price overseas."

"Price? What do you mean price?" Kevin was trying with all of his might to rip the tape around his arms. I looked up, caught his eyes and started to use one of the pencils to cut into the tape. We had a tear started, but within seconds of the ripping sound Finneaus was rolling his chair towards me.

"There she is," he said through a chaotic laugh. "Didn't anyone ever teach you that the code and the key should always be separated?"

"Yes, your brother did." I continued to pull on the tape around Kevin's arms. Finneaus pulled me away with intent, instead of brut force.

"He's not my brother. He's my half brother!" He yelled. "I don't want to hurt those pretty little hands of yours considering what they do and all, but I will if you don't cooperate." He laid my hands on my lap, one overlapping the other, and unrolled the tape. I lifted my left hand and slapped him. Full on, open palm, direct hit on his right cheek. While he was stunned and holding his face, I hit him in the gut and started to stand. He shoved the top of my head and pushed me to the floor, but I wasn't giving up. I again tried to get to my feet, and he kicked me in the knee and I fell face first into the wall near Kevin.

"You're a little spit fire aren't you?" He stood up, lifted his discount store fake leather boot in the air, and slammed it into Kevin's mangled foot. Kevin screamed. I held his arms in a sloppy attempt to soothe the pain I had caused. Finneaus giggled and put more tape over Kevin's mouth.

"You mother fucking son of a bitch," I yelled. The tape hit my mouth as soon as the word bitch came out. Kevin was sweating, and his breathing was shallow. I looked into his eyes and began to breathe long steady breaths. He soon followed my lead, and the blood came back to his face. I sat on the floor and held my arms out allowing Finneaus to tape them.

"You think I'm the enemy. I'm not the enemy, and everything will go much smoother if you don't think that way." He sat in his chair and rolled back to the desk, put the tape down and held up the notepads I had written on. "I knew they would send someone or at the least contact me. I just knew they would, but I never expected this. I never expected this." He read through the notepads. "This is far beyond what I'd expected." He stood up and

285

pecked on the keyboard. He moved aside and let me watch
the video he'd publicly uploaded onto the Internet. It was a
video showing both of my hands writing on the pads that
sat on my lap. My face was never shown, and only the side
of Kevin's leg was in the frame. I watched Jima's ring
dance with the movement of my hand. Finneaus excitedly
jumped around the room giggling and cackling with glee.
"How do you do it? Do they warn you, or knock on a door
deep inside you? I need to understand this." He replayed
the video while reading the pads. He mumbled to himself.
Kevin was moaning from the pain. I motioned for him to
close his eyes and rest, but I knew rest would not come to
either one of us until this nightmare had ended.

"Lookie, lookie we have over two-thousand hits."
It's going viral. That cake took only two hours to make,
and already it's being eaten alive." Finneaus looked down
at his watch. "I don't know. I just don't know what to do.
What do I do? What do I do? Hmm." He paced back and
forth across the room then turned to stare at me. "Yes, yes
I know," he said. He ripped the tape from my mouth. I
could feel blood from my lips running down my chin.
Finneaus quickly looked away, reached into his pocket and
pulled out a tissue. He held the tissue to my face without
looking and I leaned in to wipe my chin clean. He sat on
the floor next to me, putting his hand on top of my taped
hands.

"Would you do me a favor?" he asked. He was
calm, and his voice was low.

"That would depend on what it is you want from
me."

"That's an honest answer and I respect you for it,
but I still need you to do something for me."

"What is it you want?"

"I want your opinion on something. Do you think
I'll get good press for this, for discovering you, Patient
Crew I mean?" Every word he said had been well thought

over. He was as serious as shit. In less than a month this man had slaughtered hundreds of people most of them children, I was speechless. It is an element of life on earth for which there is no understanding.

"Both explosions, and all of the deaths have been reported continuously," I said while forcing calmness to be my mainstay. "People all over the world are devastated, and afraid. You've caused sadness, deep sadness. It's on every network, every news channel and all over the net. You've made the first page of every national newspaper. I would say the bombings are getting very good press, but no one knows who you are. They don't know your name."

"When I deliver the results of my discovery they'll all know my name. The whole world will know my name," he said.

"If they know your name they will hunt you down just to lock you up," I said. "You may think you've trapped the crew, but they've trapped you right back. Your name is all over their writings. Your name, address even your phone number is written. And every time your name's mentioned it's in conjunction with the bombings. If you tell the world about me they will want to see me write. When they read what I have written they'll know it's you who did the bombings. Looks like you're up against a brick wall."

"When you saw the news, did you cry for those babies?" Finneaus asked.

"No, I didn't."

"Neither did I," he whispered. "Couldn't take your eyes off the TV screen I'd bet. Everybody wants to see the blood."

"Can I ask a question?" I kept my tone calm. I wanted him to open up to me. I had read in some of Marla's books that it's better to remain friendly so that the crazy person in the room will trust you. Finneaus didn't have an instant response. He rubbed his temple as if it were hard to let me in that place where his thoughts lived.

"I think yes. You can ask me a question."

"Why did you do this?"

"We should let him sleep," he said. Kevin's eyes were closed and appeared to be asleep, but his body was stiff and ready to jump in a moments notice. Albee would say he was playing 'possum. This was my cue to keep Finneaus talking. "He's had a tough day." He looked down at his watch and tapped on the face. "Time is running out for a few more cradle lumps."

"You found me. You found the patient crew. You don't need to kill anymore," I said.

"It has been written, it must be done."

"Why? What more would you gain?" I asked.

"Gain?" Finneaus asked. "You think I do this for my own gain as if I get some sort of payment? I never gain from the experiments, and the dead are casualties of research and development. I do this because people aren't listening. We have the cure for humanity right in front of our faces, but nobody listens. The patient crew has been speaking for years, and they still don't listen. The army of our creator has started a draft and has begun to increase the ranks. My actions are noble. I have contributed to the army. We all have to make our sacrifices. We are all sacrificial lambs being led to the slaughter. We did it to ourselves, and now we all suffer alone in our misery. God does not cry for us." Anger flooded his face as his voice rose. "I was just a child and he took it all away! Every moment that should have been a good memory he tainted. She did nothing to stop it, acted as if life were filled with sunshine and roses. We had comforts before they took him away. We had a fine house, a big car and lots of food. After they took the Doctor, she went away somewhere deep inside and rotted there. She even smelt rotten. Day and night, and night and day she would say it. Build me a bomb, go down to that courthouse and blow them all sky-high Buddy." He stopped, took a deep breath and grinned at the distant memory. "That's what she called me because we were buddies."

He began to breathe in deeply, hold it, and then release slowly. "I taught myself how to control the anger while I was in Juvenile hall. The same courthouse that sent the Doctor away, and the same one that she wanted blew to smithereens was the one that convicted me of her murder. They locked me up until my eighteenth birthday."

"Did you blow up your mom? Is that how she died?"

"God doesn't ask us to do more than what we're capable of doing. I guess he made me able to do more than the average man. She was terribly mad when they took the Doctor. She wouldn't stop nagging me about it day and night and night and day continually, build the bomb Buddy and we'll show them. Never ending, from the time I woke up until the time I went to bed. She took me out of school because she thought they were a part of the broken system. When I answered a knock at the door and the man said we had to leave the only home we ever knew, well let's just say that was the last straw that broke the camel's ass," he started to giggle, but stopped himself with the deep breathing exercise.

"I hadn't finished it. I sure as shit didn't know it would kick that hard. I lit the fuse and ran for cover. The whole house went down. I was blown out the window, had to get over a hundred stitches in various places. It blew the windows out on the neighbor's houses. People heard it from all around. I got page ten in the B section. When I got out of lockup, no one even remembered what had happened. It was like time had gone on and forgot about me. I'd have been better off in jail for life. At least in there when they hate you, they just kill you. Out here they ignore you. Tim ignored me. He never visited me and never wanted anything to do with me until he needed something—then he came sniffing around."

"What did you do for Tim?" I asked.

"I was his mule," his face grimaced at the memory. "I went all over the world carrying nothing but a zippered notebook. It looked like one of those trapper keepers the kids would use in school, but it had a zipper instead of Velcro flap. I was curious so I'd read what Tim had written in the notebooks while I was on the plane. He knew everything before any of it happened. Sometimes he knew days before and sometimes years before. He knew it all and it was always before."

"How did you know it was the crew?"

"I asked, he told, I know," he said. "He didn't tell me the truth because it's sitting in front of me. He didn't tell me about you."

"What did he tell you?"

"That a group of prophets called crew gave him the word. Once, he even showed me a page. Looked just like what you wrote. He left me without so much as a boo." The morning sun began to break through the windows in the kitchen, and peek around the corner into the living room.

"How did he leave you?"

"Cut me off and left me high and dry only wanting more. He wouldn't return my phone calls and stopped paying my bills. I read the books as soon as they came out. I knew everything, but couldn't get no one to listen. Everyone just laughed at me. We'll see who laughs now."

"I want to make an agreement with you Finneaus," I said.

"What kind of agreement?"

"I want you to let those people in the church live, and let Kevin leave. No more death," I said.

"What's in it for me?"

"The crew is all yours." Kevin's eyes popped open and glared at me.

"Well now look who decided to join the party," Finneaus said. "I for one enjoyed your absence."

"That's the deal Finneaus don't listen to anyone but me. Listen to what I'm offering you," I continued my focus on him.

"A contract? You'll do what I say, willingly?"

"Yes, whatever you want as long as you follow through with your part of the contract, no more death. What do you say?" I asked.

"No," Kevin yelled through the tape on his mouth making it sound more like "O."

"This is my choice Kevin. I promised Jade, and we can't let him kill anyone else. We can't let this continue."

"O," Kevin was relentless. "O, o, o, o, o!"

"You don't have a vote," I said and turned back to Finneaus. "Well? Do we have a deal?"

"I don't know. Give me a second here, I don't know. I guess it could work. We would have to haul ass out of here and hide." He stood and began to pace. "I have a place in mind. It's a quiet place where we won't be found out. I can't say it out loud or Kevo here will follow us."

Kevin was making as much noise as he could. He tried to move to his knees, but his mangled foot wouldn't let him.

"It's been written. What will happen if I change the course of what must be?" Finneaus asked. "The crew might get angry especially The Professor—he's my favorite. I don't want to make him mad at me."

"It takes courage to create change," I said. "You can be the first to change the course." Kevin continued to struggle with the tape on his mouth and hands. "Can we take the tape off his mouth?"

"Es, es," Kevin yelled.

"Listen to me," I was stern as I spoke to Kevin and looked in his eyes. "You have to be quiet or we'll put double the amount across your mouth next time."

"You better listen to her," Finneaus marched over to Kevin, and ripped the tape from his mouth. Blood oozed from his bottom lip. I quickly put my shirtsleeve against it and pressed hard.

"I've got a feeling blondie here has changed sides Kevo."

Kevin started to talk, and I stuffed my shirt in his mouth.

"Let's do this deal Finneaus," I urged.

"What's the rush?" he asked. "Haste makes waste. Besides, I need a little more information. I need to kick the tires before I buy this car."

"We don't have much time; it's already morning. You need to take the bombs out of that church before it is too late."

"But you said it yourself that no one knows who I am so what's the rush? I don't feel good about breaking the prophecy. They've called upon me, and I must follow through. What has been written must be done. First, the church and then we'll leave."

"That's not true Finneaus. They've only talked about the plans you've made. This has nothing to do with prophesy. You created it. You can change your mind change your plans."

"How do they talk to you?" he stopped pacing. I leaned against Kevin in an effort to keep him calm.

"They don't talk to me they talk through me," I said.

"Tell them to do it now," Finneaus ordered.

"It doesn't work that way."

"Why?" he asked. "No deals until I know the history and physical.'

"It's not like having a conversation," I said. "I have no control over them. They come and go as they please."

Finneaus stood up, fidgeted around, sat back down, and then stood up again. His smile was broad; his eyes shifted out of control as he began to understand the crew. "What about the way you write? With both hands and all because I have got to tell you that shit freaked me out. Do they control it? Is it like a possession?"

"No, they don't possess me I'm ambidextrous."

"So Kevbot here…" he started.

"His name is Kevin," I interrupted.

"Ok, ok I get it. Kevin here is your assistant?"

"I'm nobody's assistant I can tell you that," Kevin said. Finneaus reacted by lifting his boot, and aiming it at Kevin. I caught the boot mid stomp with the side of my arm, and he froze.

"No more," I said. "No more hurting that's part of our agreement."

He didn't speak. He simply lowered his foot and nodded his head.

"Thank you," I said.

"How long have you had them in you?" Finneaus asked.

"Going on eleven years now," I said. "It hasn't been easy having something in my head that keeps me from doing what I want to do, and being who I want to be. You understand don't you Finneaus?"

His face relaxed as if the tension had been relieved in his muscles. "I do," he said.

"It's like always having company, and all you want to do is lay on your bed, watch TV, and eat a bag of chips, right?"

"Yes, that's exactly what it's like. I wake up every morning and hope it's empty in those rooms up there, but by breakfast the torture begins again. It's all I can do most days just to remember to eat and shit with all the activity going on up there." He hit his head with the palm of his hand.

"I've written for days on end without a break. Sometimes when I wake up, I don't even know what day it is." He nodded as I spoke and I knew we had found a common ground. "That's the part that makes me angry."

He sat on his knees in front of me rocking his body back and forth. After a few minutes he giggled lightly. I saw his face transform. The muscles tightened in his cheeks and his head twitched. He tapped his watch and giggled. "You almost had me there. I've seen more shrinks than I care to remember. I know all their tricks blondie. You are good though. You are good." He stood up in front of us. "Let's see what's happening at the house of God." After a few moves and clicks of the mouse the laptop screen lit up with a picture of the church.

"Shall we start the count down?"

"What about our contract?" I asked.

"Oh that was a nice thought sweet pea but I already got you, and having you is having the crew. No, I think we will blow up the church, and then I think we will kill the big black man. And then we'll complete the prophesy by blowing up the house, and a few others if my calculations are correct. I can almost guarantee they are."

"You better kill me you crazy prick," Kevin warned.

"Good golly gosh look at the big man trying to scare me. I'm so frightened," Finneaus forced his body to shiver with his giggles.

"If you do it I won't write," I said defiantly.

"When this house blows, we'll be twenty miles outside town and you will be writing."

"I won't write."

"I'll break your legs."

"I won't write."

"I'll kill you."

"I won't write."

Finneaus started pacing. "You will write for me," he screamed.

"I won't write, unless you make the deal and keep it."

"Let me talk to them now."

"It doesn't work that way."

"I don't care how it works. Fuck how it works. I want to talk to them face to face now. Right now."

"They don't have faces only voices."

"Then voice to voice. Shit woman I don't care just bring them out now. I want to talk to them." He started pounding his head with his hands, and mumbling incoherent words under his breath. He was frantic, and then in an instant he stopped, brushed his hair back with his fingers, tucked in his shirt and faced me with his hands clasped in front of his body. "Miss Shanna," he said meekly. "I'll execute that contract, but I'll need an amendment. I'll need to speak to the crew first. Man to prophet. It's my duty, and my right to test them."

"I can't. I don't know how to do that. I'm not lying to you."

Finneaus—defeated—walked down the hallway. He opened a door and I heard the sound of squeaking wheels rolling across the floor. He came back in the room pushing an old gurney.

"I know you don't care if I blow your head off you're like me that way but I also know—for whatever reason—you'll do anything to save your friend. Lets say we start with him." He rolled the gurney to the center of the room, and locked the wheels. There was a sheet of plastic covering it, and a pillow at the head. "All I ever wanted was to meet them, know them. Looks like they don't like me, same as everyone else. Same story different chapter."

"They wrote about you," I said. "They are why I am here. They are here with you. You're asking them to do something they don't do."

He went back down the hallway, and this time returned with a bag of salt so large he had to carry it over his shoulder. In his hand, he carried two buckets—one stuffed inside the other. He let the bag of salt fall to the floor and placed the buckets side by side under the head of the gurney. He pulled a rubber tube—it was probably three feet long—out of one bucket and laid it on the bed. "It's not much different from preserving a deer. You bleed em, gut em, and stuff em with salt. Cover em up for a few weeks to catch any left over muscle fluids, and you got yourself a hunk of Kevin jerky."

"You have their writings," I pleaded. "They wrote for you."

"All that's there is a poem about some seed that came from a flower. Didn't say a word about me didn't mention my name, not even in passing. I don't like The Poet. The Professor didn't say a word not a word. Ignored me just like the rest of them."

"He didn't ignore you. Give it time and they'll come back." He slowly walked to the bed covered with blankets and plastic against the wall. One at time, he lifted the coverings to reveal a sheet stained a brownish red.

"Just in case you think I'm not capable," he lifted the sheet that covered the upper part of Marla's body.

A white chalky cloud puffed out of her body, and wafted over his face causing him to gag and turn away. It was a briny smell that was similar to the smell of salty rot at low tide in Galveston. The first thing I saw was her hair. It was platinum blonde and thick as a horse's mane. Her face was wrinkled like a grape that'd been turned into a raisin. Her body was dusted with a white powdery substance. I kept my eyes on the hair. It was the only part that still looked like Marla. Finneaus covered the body, turned to

Kevin and pulled a gun from his belt. He cocked it and pointed the muzzle at Kevin's good foot. "After that let's go for a knee. I'll keep shooting until he's dead makes no never-mind to me. You get the picture?"

"I do I get the picture, but you're not hearing me Finneaus," I said. "They don't respond to me. I respond to them."

"They responded to my thoughts bitch. I think they can respond to his screams." He pushed the gun into Kevin's foot. Kevin screamed something I couldn't hear.

I didn't write. I spoke. I have no recollection of what they said or how long they talked. I blacked out the minute they began. I had a vision that I was sitting in a darkness filled with the most beautiful silence. I felt safe and protected. Utterly alone. No thoughts invaded the silence of that space. No proof of existence remained in me, yet I have never felt more certain of life.

21.

*T*he first sound I heard was Kevin calling my name. "Shanna, come back to me." I heard other voices in the room close by me, but I couldn't understand the words. I felt a hand on my cheek, and opened my eyes. The room was full of commotion. I focused on Kevin's face.

"There she is," he said. "She's awake. Don't clean that—it's mine. Don't forget the pee bucket." People were rustling around the room. I listened for him, but not one of the voices I heard belonged to Finneaus.

"I'll get her to the car," an unfamiliar voice said.

"Make sure you get the tape with her hair on it," another voice said.

"Let's hurry this up guys," Kevin said.

"Kevin?" I said. My throat was scratchy. "I'm thirsty."

"Get some water," Kevin told someone who quickly handed him a bottle of water. "Here you go. Drink it slow. Alpheus is going to get you out of here."

"Nice to meet you," Alpheus said.

"Pleasure," I whispered.

"Everything is good, I'll meet you in Abilene." He pressed his warm cheek against mine and whispered in my ear. "We did it." I sipped the water as reality came back into view. My head was throbbing. It felt like I was surrounded by a million-member drum core, and they were beating out an annoying rhythm. I focused on the room. I hadn't been moved, but the tape no longer bound me. I looked to my left and saw Kevin. He was happy, elated to be exact. I turned to my right, and saw a man at the desk typing on the laptop keyboard, next to him was another man. I didn't know either of them, but they both smiled at me briefly before turning their attentions back to the computer. Another man was sitting on the floor across the room. Alpheus was kneeling by my side, and on the floor next to him was the dead body of Finneaus Albert.

"The church?" I asked.

"The church is safe," Kevin said as he carefully turned my face away from the bloodied corpse. "No more deaths today."

"What's next?" I asked. I was ready to move, and more than ready to get out of that house. I stood and Alpheus helped me balance.

"Steady yourself for a second before you try to walk," Alpheus said.

"Megame and Durgin will take care of the digital trail," Kevin pointed to the desk, and the two men waved.

"Nice to meet you," I said, and waved. It felt normal, waving hello to someone new, but nothing about it was normal. They both glanced my way for a second and waived back.

"Braindead is in charge of the removal of all physical evidence," Kevin said, and pointed to Braindead who didn't look up as he continued picking up small pieces of tape and hair from the floor. "As soon as you get your balance, we need to get you out of here. Alpheus will drive you to the hotel. Pack, check out and head to Abilene." I sat on my knees in front of Kevin, and we held each other.

"We did it," I said. "It's over."

"You did," he said. "You were amazing, but it's not over yet."

"What are you going to do? What about your foot? You need a doctor."

"I'm fine don't worry. No more worries."

"We should get going," Alpheus sheepishly interrupted. He shook Kevin's hand, and we were out the door.

Alpheus drove. Not a word was spoken by either one of us during the short trip to the hotel. I went up to the room alone. Alpheus waited in the lobby. All I could think about was standing under a hot shower and letting the water wash the bad away. Within seconds of entering the room my thoughts were put into action. I locked the door, turned on the hot water and waited for the room to fog up before taking off my clothes. I stood under the hot water. I scrubbed my body. My mind was wracked with questions. What did the crew say to reverse the situation? When did the Crewbies arrive? How was Finneaus killed and who did it? Kevin said it was me. Did that mean I killed him?

Why did Finneaus believe it was necessary to murder hundreds of children? He never gave me an answer. Why? Was the crew a solution to a problem, or the creator of it? There were no easy answers to my questions, then or now. There would never be a perfect answer, but I hoped for a better one. I scrubbed the filth of Finneaus from my body, but I couldn't get him out of my soul. He would forever be a shameful mark on my spirit, one I can never forgive. After my body was clean I could no longer hold back the tears.

My heart ached. I cried for Finneaus out of pity for the things he couldn't control. I didn't want to carry the hatred I felt for him, but I didn't know where to put it. I cried for the families torn apart by the senseless acts of a lunatic. Most of all, I cried for the children; the innocence lost. A river of tears would never wash away what had happened. Tears didn't relieve the guilt I felt for not stopping him sooner.

I dressed and made sure nothing was left in the room before leaving the key on the nightstand, and going to the lobby to meet Alpheus. I found him with the three other Crewbies. All of them jumped to help with the bags. I drove my car with Alpheus and Megame as passengers. Durgin and Braindead followed behind in their car. I forced my curiosity to wait until we had entered the highway.

"What happened?" I asked. They both began to speak simultaneously making it impossible to understand either. "Slow down and start at the beginning. We have a thirteen-hour drive ahead of us, plenty of time to tell every side."

"We heard yelling," Megame was the first to speak. "We tried the front door with no luck and went to the back. That's when we heard the gun shot, and the next thing I know Kevin's yelling for us to break the door down and get our asses inside." Megame and Alpheus shared a laugh.

"What time did you get there?" I asked. "Could you hear anything that was going on inside?"

"We got there around six-fifteen. We could hear yelling, not like someone screaming but more like disciplining. You know like a mother does with her child," Alpheus said.

"Who was yelling, Finneaus or Kevin?"

"You were," Megame said.

"Could you understand what I was saying?"

"No, not really."

"Not really? I need to know what happened, and how it happened. Maybe I should just wait for Kevin to answer my questions," I said peevishly.

"What I mean is," Megame continued. "We could hear the tone of your voice but not the exact words you were saying. We heard the gunshot, and Fat Boy started yelling, you stopped. When we got inside you were out cold."

"We broke the glass door and went inside," Alpheus said. "Finneaus Albert was dead on the floor. Fat Boy was holding the gun. You were slumped over, at first we thought you had been shot but you were just sleeping. Then, we got started."

"Started on what?" I asked.

301

"Getting that video off the web," Alpheus was careful not to look at me as he spoke. "The one with the writing. We deleted it. That part was easy, but it had already been downloaded repeatedly. We couldn't get it off the net completely, and probably never will."

"What else?"

"The whole house was wired with nanny cams. We had to search out and destroy all of them," Megame said. I watched him through the rearview mirror as he talked. He was focused on Jima's ring.

"We got it all. I'm sure of it," Alpheus said.

"We'll see Al, we'll see," Megame argued. "We tried to leave nothing in the house with your hair or prints on it. We didn't wash it down, but we got the obvious. It's not like the guy's going to be able to tell his story. I think it's safe to say no one will ever question Fat Boy."

"Hey Meg, don't talk about that," Alpheus said.

"Why?" I asked.

"Fat Boy wants to keep things under wraps," Alpheus said. "We shouldn't discuss it."

"There's no rules about what we can or cannot discuss," I said.

"But Fat Boy said," Alpheus started.

"Fat Boy's not here man. What's his story?"

"I'll let him tell you, besides it's probably all over the news by now," Megame said. Alpheus turned on the radio and tried to tune in an AM news station.

"You won't be able to get a station while we're in the desert." I turned off the radio. "Speak."

"He's going to say he became suspicious of Finneaus after going through Frank Argot's files. He put two and two together, and came up with the solution." Megame was keeping it simple, careful not to give up the ship. He was being loyal to Kevin, and I respected him for that.

"He's trying to protect me. He could lose everything, but he insists on protecting me," I said.

"It's unlikely," Megame said. "He'll probably get a raise and promotion. Finneaus had the bombs set up to respond to a phone call. The final two phones were in his desk. One for the church, and the last one was for the house."

"Kevin saved a lot of people," I said.

"You both did," Alpheus said. "It'll save the government a boat load of money not having to prosecute the son of a bitch. They'll love Fat Boy. They'll for sure question his story six ways to Sunday, but in the end he'll be the hero."

"As it should be," I said.

A few hours later, we began to see the rock gardens of Albuquerque. A sign had been erected commemorating those that had died in the children's museum. Pink and blue ribbons were tied on the trees, telephone poles, fence posts and anything else that was stuck in the ground. *No more death today*, I told myself as we pulled into a rest stop inside the city limits. The guys filled the cars with gas and bought some snacks. I went inside to relieve myself.

The Crewbies were huddled in a tight circle and obviously speculating about the day's events and my role in them when I rejoined them outside. They quickly changed the conversation. "Would you like me, or one of us to drive?" Alpheus asked. "You must be exhausted."

They were being overly cautious around me, choosing their words carefully. I wasn't exhausted. I was however, more tired of wondering and not knowing. I felt as though I were the bride at a wedding but missed the kiss. I needed to have the ending to end it. Otherwise, the whole ordeal was ongoing and I was still running. "I'll drive, Alpheus you ride with the others and Megame will ride with me," I said. Alpheus looked a little pissed by his demotion, but took the orders in stride and got in the back seat of the chase car. Megame was cautiously thrilled and took his place next to me.

"What do you know about me? What has Fat Boy told you?"

"A lot less than that ring tells me. You want me to be honest?"

"That's all I want."

"I had most of it figured out by the time we got to the house. I've been reading your sessions as fast as Fat Boy could send them, and I knew that the seven crew members were part of one. I didn't know what or who that one was. I didn't know how they spoke either." Megame looked out the window in thought. "Just between me and you?"

"Of course," I assured him.

"Fat Boy's not a big talker, he keeps things close to the vest. He's going to make damn sure no one knows anything about you. He's going to explain the link between that CIA agent, and his wife to Finneaus. He's planted evidence, created some letters and other email documents using your phone because it was linked to Agent Todd's account. I know because I'm the one who showed him how. There's more, but I've said enough to get me killed already."

"So why stop now?" I asked.

"Because that's all I really know. Like I said, Fat Boy's not a big talker."

"What's his reasoning?"

"He wants to keeps them off your trail for a while, they'll have their hands full questioning Tim."

"Tim's got all my sessions. All he has to do is give one to someone at the CIA and they'll be looking for me."

"Kevin took care of that in the emails. Tim and Marla used you and the crew as code names for themselves and Finneaus. Kevin left the last pages you wrote on

Finneaus' desk. He'll tell the investigators that he saw Finneaus writing it, and they'll think the sessions Tim gave them were written by Finneaus."

"Do you think the CIA will believe it?" I asked.

"It's possible."

"I'm not leaving until I see Kevin," I said.

"He won't like that, he wants you gone before he gets home," Megame said.

"I don't care what he wants. I'm not leaving until I see him so you might want to get that message to him."

Megame took out his phone and started texting. "There's no guarantee he'll get this anytime soon."

"He'll get it."

I turned on the radio as we left Albuquerque. There was no need to search for the news. Every station was airing the latest reports surrounding the death of the baby bomber, and the hero that killed him. Detective Kevin Stewart was trending and well on his way to becoming a household name.

"We can confirm the name of the baby bomber is Finneaus Albert," Sonya Turner from KRBC radio said. "He lived and died on a quiet residential street in Sedona, Arizona. The police line starts six houses down from the crime scene on Jacob Lane. It's a typical blue-collar neighborhood. We have not been given an exact address nor have we been given access to the neighbors. The CIA and FBI are both involved here, as it appears to have some connection with the arrest of former CIA agent Timothy Todd, and his wife Marla Todd. They have demanded that no one even remotely involved in this case speak with the press, but our sources tell us that there are also connections between Finneaus Albert and former agent Todd's partner who was killed in a car bomb a few weeks ago."

"Question for you Sonya," Bill the news anchor said. "The Internet is buzzing about the Patient: Crew books that Doctor Marla Todd wrote. Some are claiming them to be prophetic. The bloggers are saying that Patient: Crew predicted the bombings, and even talks about a person named Finn. Have you heard about this or heard anyone else discussing this?" I turned off the radio.

"I guess it shouldn't surprise me," I said.

"Does it frighten you?" he asked.

"It does. What does your mother call you?"

"Huh?"

"What's your name? Your real name?" I asked again.

"We don't give real names."

"Why?"

"It's safer that way."

"Why? The first time I asked I was trying to pass time, but now I'm genuinely curious."

"We all talked about it and decided it was safer this way," he said.

"You're telling me you don't know any of their real names?"

"I know them and I'm sure they know mine, but we don't communicate that way—we're not friends we're colleagues—and it's better if we don't use real names with digital communications."

"So it's a nerd thing?" I asked while holding back a laugh.

"I don't know," he said with a pause as if he had done something wrong.

"Don't worry about it Megame, I'm just teasing you. Trying to lighten things up a little. I feel a need to be happy. I'm alive, and it's a good day to be alive. A good day for us, and the people in that church."

"We saved almost as many as we lost," he said. "I guess we broke even "

"That's right," I said, and suddenly felt a sadness wash over me. My body slumped with grief.

"I'm not good at the winning part. You should have ridden with Alpheus. He says you win some you lose some. I think about the losses, he's all about the wins."

"I didn't want to ride with Alpheus. I wanted to ride with you."

"Thanks."

"You're welcome."

"Ed."

"Ed?"

"My name is Ed, that's what my mom calls me," he said.

"Well then Ed, my name is Shanna. It's a pleasure to meet you," I said.

"It's a pleasure to meet you too."

"You're right we didn't save enough if we didn't save them all. Nonetheless I know that it could have been worse, and we could be dead now and then I would have broken two promises. I know now that I don't want to go out that way. I want to leave without debt, you know, without hanging promises. Does that make sense Ed?"

"It makes sense to me."

"Tell me about the Crewbies, about the website."

"We have dedicated our lives to Patient: Crew, the writings and to making sure we save them all."

"You've dedicated your life to them?"

"Yes. I study them, sometimes obsessively."

"I don't know who's the bigger nut. Me for hearing voices, or you for studying those voices." I laughed so hard he had no choice but to join me. We laughed a while, took some drinks of our soda and opened a bag of chips. The laughter healed both our souls a little more. It was much needed medicine.

"I met the guys on another prophecy site we were following."

"What prophecy site?"

"Garysays.com was the domain. Some person named Gary said he gazed into a bowl of extra virgin olive oil and could see future events. He was great, wildly entertaining but the only problem was that none of his visions came true. So he stuck with the distant future stuff that would happen in two thousand and eighty. Brilliant if you ask me since no one would be around to know whether he was right or wrong." Megame ate some more chips. He wasn't a kid, but he didn't look much older than one. The only feature that showed any amount of age was his receding hairline.

"We all started, the guys and me, talking about the Patient: Crew book we had read and agreed we should start our own website with the book being our study. From conception to execution was eight hours. It was meant to be a public area where people could discuss the book and how it had predicted things in their own lives. Within three months we had to increase our bandwidth and storage by two hundred percent just to accommodate all the hits. That's when we began to understand how important the books are. It's also when we decided to run our own study and research in the background, away from the crowd. We used their stories and proved or disproved them."

"What percentage is provable?" I asked

"Ninety-eight percent," he said. "Every phrase, and sometimes every word has a prophetic meaning to someone, and relates to many all at the same time. They are the most amazing books I have ever studied, and to think there are literally thousands of pages that we haven't been privy to. Tens of thousands of pages maybe even hundreds of thousands. Boggles the mind."

I glanced at Ed, and there he was with the same silly grin Kevin had when he realized who I was. "I'm no different from you. I hear the voices, and I've heard it said they tell a few future events. You guys are the ones who are amazing. I try to read the sessions, and they say nothing to me. We're no different, just two pieces of the whole."

"How does it happen?" he asked.

"I don't really know how it happens."

"Have they always been inside of you?" He asked. "I mean always with you or talking to you."

"I started hearing them when I turned seventeen."

"Do you ever wonder why they chose you?" He asked.

"Every second, of every day."

"I can understand that. I guess you might as well just accept it, and get on with your life. Kind of like dealing with a handicap or making lemonade out of lemons—not that your life is a lemon, or that you're handicapped," he fumbled with the words.

"I know what you're saying. Don't be nervous around me. I don't have many friends so let's try to make this work."

"I'd like that."

"Yeah, me too." I said.

We sang along to a Willie Nelson disc Jim had left in the player. Time flew by, and we were passing the Texas border as the sun set behind us. When we were about an hour outside the Abilene city limits, Ed became serious.

"What's next, another book?" He asked.

"I haven't given it much thought. The books were Marla's not mine."

"You're the pipe and we are the vessel it's up to us to make the changes you draft," Ed said.

"That's straight out of the book of Kevin."

"It's from the first book of Patient: Crew, page one, line one," Ed said.

"I did not know that."

"You don't read it?"

"No."

"Do you want me to tell you what it says?"

"You know it by heart?" I asked, amused. "How much of them do you have memorized?"

"All of it," he said proudly.

"Then by all means please recite for me." I turned off the radio, and gave Ed the floor.

"Patient Crew book one, page one. Joseph says and I quote, *the master craftsman through the purification of generations formed the pipe. Steel, that will not rust. An unbreakable force, it was put forth and tested in the flames. Always protected by truth. The pipe seeks its vessels to do the bidding of that which we draft. We call upon the foreordained dark warrior and his army. Follow as a limb near its root for the nourishment provided by the flow.* That's the only place in either book that you, the pipe, and us, the dark warrior and his army, are mentioned."

"We've had a pretty shitty couple of days," I said.

"I'd agree with that," Ed said.

"But what you just said made it a little nicer for me, less lonely."

"Don't thank me. I can't take credit."

"Neither can I."

"So no more books. Will you keep writing the sessions?"

"I don't see a river of choices. If I don't write, I lose control," I said. "I'm thinking we have to come up with a way to utilize the information in the safest manner, but no more books."

"We'll be in Abilene soon," Ed said. "You should park on the dark side of the street. Mrs. Stewart is expecting you. I'll wait until she turns the porch light off and meet the others down the street. We'll leave your car at the airport. Fat Boy figured since you already had a ticket to Mexico, your car being at the airport would throw them off track if they do look for you. They'll probably think you got on the flight after seeing Tim arrested."

"That's a good plan," I said.

"Fat Boy's always thinking six moves ahead. I probably won't get another chance to say this," he said and turned his body towards mine. "It's an honor to have met you. I've never really had a hero because I don't approve of that way of thinking. But, if I did have one it would be you."

"I just want to be your friend. There's not enough time for heroes and according to the crew the vessel is just as important as the pipe. Maybe even more considering the pipe was created, but the vessel was chosen."

22.

The porch light was on, and I could see Jade standing a few feet inside the door. "Come on in like you belong here," she whispered as I stepped on the porch. I walked inside. Jade turned the porch light off. She took me in her arms and openly wept. We stood like that for a good ten minutes before her eyes finally ran dry.

"Have you heard from Kevin?" I asked as we sat next to each other on the sofa. The TV news was on in the background.

"He called from the hospital. He's going to be fine and have a full recovery. The bullet hit a few bones, but went straight through." Jade began to sob again. "Oh lord I have got to stop this. I've been a blubbering idiot this live long day."

"It's ok. It's over," I said, and hugged her.

"You precious child, you kept your promise to me. He may be a little damaged, but you kept him alive."

"We're square, we kept each other alive."

"Yes you did," she laughed. "Yes you did. Are you hungry? Thirsty? What can I do for you?"

"Nothing. I just want to sit here and be still for a minute." I could see in her eyes the questions she wanted to ask. She could see the unwilling answers in mine so she pulled me into her arms, held me close to her chest and sang a lullaby while gently running her fingers through my hair. "Precious child you are to me, child of love, child of grace. Come close to me while I sing. How precious child you are to me."

I drifted to sleep. My dreams were filled with images of the past twenty-four hours. When one of those images would jolt me awake, Jade was there to soothe me back to sleep. She flipped from one news network to the next in an attempt to find any new information about the investigation, and Kevin. I woke up when the sun beaming through the window hit my eyes. I could hear, and smell food cooking in the kitchen. Jade peeked around the corner as I yawned.

"You up?" she asked, and then went back to work.

"I'm up." I stretched my legs and rubbed my eyes. "What can I do?"

"You can sit right there, drink a cup of this coffee and let me properly feed you," she said. It was of no use to argue, not that I wanted to. I sat up, and she put a steaming cup of coffee in front of me along with a plate of eggs. She brought in another plate of eggs for herself along with a full plate of pancakes for us to share.

We ate with the TV blaring in the background. She wouldn't turn it off until her son was home safe and sound. When he did come home, you'd have thought Jesus himself had made an appearance. Jade was jubilant as Kevin walked through the front door, after we had finished washing the breakfast dishes. I stayed in the kitchen to let Jade have a few moments alone with her son. He sounded strong and happy. Jade was singing and praying, kissing, and hugging all at the same time. I could feel an ocean of relief flow through my body.

"Where is she?" Kevin asked. He was bumping into the furniture trying to get around it with his crutches.

"Present and accounted for Detective Stewart," I said. He pulled me to his chest and squeezed me between his body and crutches.

"Come on over here now and sit down," Jade ordered. We sat on the sofa and stared at each other as if we'd never seen a more beautiful sight.

"You look good," I said. "No worse for the wear."

"I am good," he said. The smile left his face and was replaced with concern. "How about you? You ok?"

"I think so," I said. "I can't get him out of my head."

"Neither can I."

"I'm going to start lunch," Jade said. We had just finished a breakfast that would keep me full most of the day, but she couldn't sit and listen.

"In time it'll fade," I said.

"Just takes time," Kevin agreed.

"What happened after I blacked out?"

"He dug that gun into my foot and cocked it," Kevin said. His lip snarled as he remembered. "He never stopped giggling and just kept pushing it deeper. You pulled your hands free." He took my hands in his and examined them from the fingers to the elbow. "Nothing, not even a mark. You pulled your arms apart, and the tape ripped as though it was cut with an invisible knife. You ripped the tape off your legs the same way."

"What did he do?" I asked.

"Nothing. Nothing he could do. You were in his face. You never looked at your hands or feet. It was you in his face. Rip, your hands are free. Rip, your feet are free. You grab the gun with your left hand, throw it to your right hand and boom he's dead. You never missed a beat, in his face the whole time. Oh it was beautiful. You can talk to us asshole as long as it's on our turf. Mother fucker."

"Lord Jesus," Jade said from the kitchen.

"Are you ok Momma?" Kevin yelled.

"I'm fine," she yelled back.

"Did they really say that? Is that it, that's all?" I was desperate to know more. I needed to fill in the dark silence of that space where I was while they spoke. "Please, I need to know."

"It's not an exact quote, but it's close." Kevin kept his voice low so as not to disturb Jade. She stopped all movement in the kitchen in an effort to hear every word.

314

"He was pushing the gun into my foot, you remember that?"

"Yes." I closed my eyes and focused on Kevin's voice. I could see the room. The church was on the laptop screen. Kevin and I were on the floor with our arms, and legs taped. Kevin's left foot was wrapped in a white hand towel that was soaked in blood. Finneaus was hunched over us giggling.

"Your eyes were open. They were the eyes of a wild animal posturing to attack her enemy. You said, who is this one who scampers in the obscure. Seeking his prey like a depraved vulture? By the time you finished saying that—never leaving his eyes—your hands and feet were loose. I watched you pull your hands apart, ripping the tape like it was paper, and then do the same with your legs. You said, we would pray the lord to have mercy on your soul, but we refuse to throw our pearls before swine. His hands started to shake. He pushed the gun harder into my foot and tried to look away from you. You took his face in your right hand and pulled him close to your face. You said, man big brother is here right beside you. You're outa control. Your time has come."

Jade walked out of the kitchen and sat down on a dining room chair. "Oh lord Jesus help me in my time of trouble," she prayed. She was waving herself with an imaginary fan while rocking her body back and forth on the chair.

"Keep going," I said.

"Your left arm went under your right, and you took the gun out of his hand. I thought he would fight you, but he didn't. You said, a day without death would in some circles be seen as a miracle. You threw the gun in the air—over his arms—with your left hand, and caught it with your right. He didn't move, he couldn't. I put my hand over yours and then you asked, are you the one who means to hurt these three?"

"Three?" I asked.

"I know but that's what you asked. Then you asked, are you the one who seeks an audience, to commune with us? He said, yes. That's when you started to sing, turn out the lights the parties over." Kevin sat back. His breathing was heavy from the reenacted memory. "After we shot Finneaus you said, 92680. That's it. That's all"

"What do the numbers mean?"

"It's the security code for the alarm system."

"Was it me or the crew that was talking?"

"Your voice their words," Kevin said.

"I shot him?" I asked.

"We all shot him. You, me, and the crew."

"I need some iced tea." Jade stood up and went into the kitchen. "Anyone else need some iced tea?"

"I need some Momma," Kevin yelled. "Thank you." He looked at me and asked with his eyes if I wanted some. "Shanna too Momma, thanks."

"Why are you taking all of the credit for what you clearly didn't accomplish alone?" I asked.

"What?" Kevin asked. "I'm disappointed that you would see it that way."

"What other way is there to see it?"

"After all I've done for you bitch. Did you see my foot? Do you see it? It could have just as easily been my head."

"So that's why you're taking all the credit? You somehow deserve it? I can't believe you. You are a fame whore."

"Fame whore? Look who is talking, little miss subject of two books. Redacted books at that, I guess you needed to leave them wanting more."

Jade was standing in the living room with a tray of iced tea glasses in her hands, and a look of terror across her face. The terror turned to confusion when Kevin started laughing.

"Sometimes Kevin I hate you so much I want to see you in pain, you're such an asshole." I was laughing so hard I couldn't breathe. Kevin's laughs were tempered, however slight, by the pain in his foot.

"Don't worry Momma," Kevin tried to speak. "We're just letting off steam." We never again spoke another word about our experience or Finneaus Albert. We took our iced tea to Kevin's room. He had my folder with him.

"We need to update this," he said. He logged on to an official law enforcement website and printed some pages, then motioned for me to retrieve them from the printer.

The pages he printed were pictures of me. There was one of me at the grocery store, the Dry Goods and Feed & Seed stores. They had all been taken within the same time frame. There was a distant picture of the house on my land that must have been taken from the road, and a picture of Jim and Jima at the Parker house.

"They know everything about you," Kevin said. "The only thing they don't know is how you fit into the story. I was able to make Finneaus look like the subject of the books as well as the writer of the sessions. That was the easy part. Finneaus was the mule delivering his own message. The problem is that Tim is still talking about you, and telling anyone who will listen that you are the subject of the books and not Finneaus. The video Finneaus put on the Internet hasn't helped the situation. Tim was questioned about it. I'm just waiting for the report to come out." He printed another page. It wasn't a good feeling to see a picture of myself with the words "**WANTED FOR QUESTIONING**" printed in bold capital letters along the bottom and top.

"Why do I feel like I'm still on the run?"

"Because you are," Kevin said. "You can stay invisible, just not here. We left your car at the airport.

They know you were planning to meet up with Tim. I've made it so they think you got on another flight when you saw him get arrested. You'll take my car. I'll transfer the registration to your new name when you're settled. She's special so be easy with her. She belonged to my dad. He'd want it this way."

"Where should I go?" I asked.

"That's up to you," he said. He put the pages he had printed in my file and took out a sealed envelope. I have a good friend in witness protection. Inside this envelope are new names and socials. There are passports, and all the documentation you'll need to prove yourselves to anyone. There's some money in there too, not much but it'll get you where you want to go."

"The longer I stay the worse it is for you."

"For all of us," he said.

"There's a hair color kit in the car, do that first and buy some fake glasses. I put a throw away phone in the glove box. We shouldn't contact each other for a while. In time, the news will get old and someone will come along crazier than Finneaus. They'll have forgotten all about you, and the case will be marked solved and closed. I'll contact you first, ok? Unless there's an emergency—then you call Jade. Her cell number is in the envelope."

"What if?" I asked. There were a million endings to that question.

"Use your judgment. Trust it," he said and handed me the car keys. "I put the boxes of sessions in the car, yours and your Momma's. You can decide what to do with them. Your suitcase and bag are in there as well. I put some notebooks and pens in your bag—just in case."

"What will I do without you in my life Kevin?"

"You'll never have that problem. I keep my promises. I will always be here for you. I'm committed to you for life. I will always guide, guard, and direct you. I would give my life for yours."

"God forbid."

"God? Does that mean you're a believer?"

"Don't push it Fat Boy. But let's say, for shits and giggles," I couldn't believe what was about to come out of my mouth. "Let's say these voices I hear are from God, then why? What do they want? Why are they here? How can we make them stop so that nobody else has to hear them?"

"Maybe they want us to do exactly what we have been doing. Stopping shit before it happens. Giving us a heads up. If we know, we can't ignore. Maybe they'll stop when we've done a good enough job of listening."

"I don't think they'll ever stop, not even when I'm dead."

We hugged and held onto each other, and then we said goodbye. I left my dark warrior in the protection of his army, and knew he would be cared for. He is my brother. We would be forever connected.

23.

Kevin's car was predictably him, a nineteen seventies Jaguar XJ12. He wasn't joking when he'd said she was a beauty. The best part was that it housed the smell of Kevin. The tank was full. My mind was focused. I had another promise to keep. I entered the highway and headed west towards Sunny, and threw the hair color onto the back seat. I felt no sorrow. I had no regrets. I had killed a man and if faced with the same situation my actions would not differ. After every ending, whether good or bad, there is a beginning. This end was no different from any other. It was time to create a beginning for myself, by myself. The crew would forever be part of my whole. They would stay in the background of any life I chose. I would learn to accept what I'd been given and stop trying to be their master, but would never become their slave. I was their equal. We would walk the path together.

Life, or the prospect of it, had not been anticipated less than thirty hours earlier. In that moment I felt as if I'd jumped off Mount Everest, and landed on my feet. I was tough of body, and mind. I would live alone, but not lonely. I had a family with Kevin, Jade, and the Crewbies. When my thoughts took me to Sunny I would remember Joshua Caleb and my family that lived in the hills. I would think about Jima and find comfort in knowing she had the ring, and I'd kept my promise. Jim would be there in my thoughts. He's wrapped around every part of me. I would never love another man the way I loved him. I visualized myself living in a city, and waiting tables at the local diner.

Within a half hour I was driving past the burned out fields that led to my house. The trees had been burned to stumps, and offered little camouflage for the car, but I wasn't worried. I hadn't seen a government agency or police car for miles and while the trees didn't hide me, they couldn't hide anyone else either. The air still smelled of watered down ash.

The house had been cleaned and looked as if I'd never lived in it. Hung on the wall—next to the etched portrait of Momma—was an etching of me. The same artist had signed both. I looked in the bathroom and bedroom, and was not surprised to see all the toiletries and furniture removed. The kitchen was emptied as well. I pulled a pad of paper and pencil out of my bag and began to write a note. I wanted to thank Joshua and the Caleb clan for helping me, and taking care of the house. I was startled when I heard the back door open.

"It's just me, Joshua Caleb. I saw the car. I figured you'd be stopping by sooner or later." He stood in the living room with his hat in his hands and nodded. He wasn't much for affection, but then again neither was I. "I didn't believe the newspaper when they wrote you'd gone off to Mexico."

"Is that what they're saying?"

"It is. I don't want to keep you just wanted to make sure of things."

"I was writing you a note. I wanted to say thank you. I wanted to thank you and yours for what you did for Momma and me. I'll never forget you."

"I'll count on that," he said and smiled. I could see my own smile in his.

"I want you to own the land," I said. "It'll take some time to make it legal. In the meantime, I'll send you a letter that will say it's yours. It won't stand up in court, but at least it's something. When it's all said and done, I want to make sure this land stays in the family."

"Don't fret little one," he said. "It'll all settle someday. We'll take care of the land as we always have until it's needed again. No one can truly own God's property."

"That's a sweet thought but I don't think the government would agree with your philosophy." It would be nice to think Joshua and the family would be able to live in peace. Nice thought, but not practical. The media was as relentless as the law. If, and when they discovered the house, land or journals they would find the hill people.

"I'll leave Momma's journals where I found them. You'll keep them safe?"

"Safe and sound. I'm happy to have enjoyed time with you despite the hurriedness," he said, put on his hat and tipped it.

We shared a look of concern as we heard the sound of a truck pulling up to the house and listened as the visitor walked to the front door and knocked. "Shanna, you in there?" Joshua and I exhaled from relief after hearing Jim's voice.

"You should tend to your company, and I'll be going." After saying those words Joshua Caleb vanished out the back door. I grabbed the keys to the jag, and headed out the front door without saying hello to Jim. He followed close behind and helped me bring in the boxes of Momma's journals. We stacked them on the living room floor.

"Did you see Joshua?" he asked.

"I did," I said. "It's not safe for you to be here, around me."

"It's not safe for you either," he said. "Can I at least give you hug?"

"It'd be easier if you didn't."

"You're acting like this because you're sad. Anger always was an easier emotion for you to handle," he said. "You haven't changed a bit."

"I've changed more than you could imagine."

"Remember when we almost got married?"

"I remember losing the baby, and not being forced to get married."

"I remember begging you to marry me baby or not. You didn't talk to me for two months after that. It was because you were sad and being around me made it all the worse," he said. "I love you. Even if you can't hear me, even if you can't speak to me, I still love you. I won't lose you again."

"Well Jim life's unfair that way. Sometimes you don't get what you want or need."

"Do you love me?"

"Don't," I demanded. "Just don't."

"Why is it so damn hard for you to show emotion?"

"Don't," I repeated.

"I sold the land," he said out of the blue. "The equipment too." He looked at me and grinned.

"You swore you'd never sell that land. That's your daddy's land, family land."

"I sold it to Mr. Randall. He's not going to farm it. Only wants it for the mineral rights," he said. "That's all it's good for anymore."

"Why would you? What do you plan on doing?" He looked at me with that silly grin still on his face. I could easily read his mind. "No. You're not going with me. What about Jima?"

"She's ready to go," he said.

"What about your mother, Aunt Picky?" I argued. "Those two are not about to let her go. And what about Jason? Are you going to leave them to take care of themselves?"

"I think they'll manage," he laughed at my suggestion they couldn't live without him. "Besides, Picky and mom will probably enjoy the peace and quiet. Jason's going to take his share, and move to Sweetwater. He's going to school and will look in on the sisters."

"I can't say I'm unhappy for Jason. He hates it here," I said. "I know your mom can't be happy about you leaving, especially with Jima."

"It's not as bad as you think," he said. "They want a good life for Jima, and they know Sunny is a dying town. It's the best move for all of us."

"You can't go with me Jim," I said. As much as I wanted to remain angry it became impossible when I looked into his blue eyes, and saw the pain I was causing. "It's not possible. It's not safe."

"Why don't you let me decide what's safe for us," he said.

"Let you decide? You don't know what you're getting yourself into, not to mention Jima." I had to convince him that I was right.

"Listen Shanna."

"No Jim, you listen to me. I hear voices that tell the future. When I left and went to Dallas, I lived there with what I thought were good people. They weren't who they claimed to be, and only used me for their benefit. When the shit hit the fan they pushed me out the door and sent me here and almost succeeded in getting me killed. Of course if I'd been killed, I couldn't be buried here. Not with that slab of concrete over the family plot. Albee made sure she wouldn't have to spend eternity anywhere near me."

"She didn't do that, the town did," he said. I wasn't about to stop him from telling me this story. "Some of the same kids that started the fire were caught trying to dig up Anna Ruth's grave a few years ago." His face flushed with shame. "I'm not trying to make excuses for this town or anyone, but you've got to know."

"I've got to know what?" I asked the obvious rhetorical question. "If you're not going to make excuses then don't."

"Fair enough," he said. "But, it wasn't Albee."

"I can't stay, and you can't leave. At least not with me."

"You've been through some hard times. I know all about it," he said. He moved close to me and tried to comfort me with a hug. I rejected his touch. "I talked to Kevin after you left Abilene."

"He's always sticking his hand where it doesn't belong," I said. "First, he puts his hand on the gun, and becomes a national hero. Now, he wants to rejoin the long lost lovers. Did Kevin advise you to sell the land?"

"No, again you're jumping to conclusions. I called him. He didn't want to tell me anything, but I got it out of him," Jim said. "He explained everything. But none of that matters."

"You don't love me. You're just trying to save me." I had a response for whatever stupid excuse for following me he might come up with.

He stood, his hat in his hands, rocking back and forth on his boots. "My granddaddy wanted the land to better the life of his family, and heirs. I'm using it to better all of our lives. None of this matters a bit. Nothing you say or do will change my mind. You need me and I need you. The only thing I've ever needed is you, but you keep running away from me. This time I'm ready. If you run I'll follow. I'm not letting you out of my sight, not again."

"Where's the purpose in all of this?" I asked. "The crew will take care of me. They've proven themselves." I had to look away. I couldn't abide those eyes. I took off the ring, and held it in front of Jim. "I need you to give this back to Jima."

"Oh no you don't," he said and stepped back with his hands in the air. "You give it to her. You promised."

"I am sick and tired of everyone expecting me to…to…" I started.

"To keep your word?" he finished.

"I'm sure she will understand. Please, give it to her."

"Shanna don't do this to us again. Let me help you." He stepped closer to me and held my arms. "Don't do this to us again."

"There is no us. I'm doing what's best for you and Jima," I said. "I've already killed her mother. I'm not going to do the same to her, or you. That's it Jim. It's my decision and I've made it." I tried to pull away from his grip, but he held tighter. "Please Jim. Let me go." That's when Jima came through the door. Her eyes were red, and her cheeks were stained from crying. I could tell by the look on her face that she had heard our entire conversation.

"How could you let this happen?" I demanded from Jim. That was all I could utter. My spirit was crushed. My thoughts went back to Vickie when we were seventeen. She had the same look of bewilderment and panic on her face. "Come here Jima." I held out my arms and she ran to me with full force. I held her close and whispered in her ear. "Please don't cry." I sat on my knees so I could be face to face with her. She was taller than I'd realized, and I ended up having to look up at her so she joined me on the floor. "I promised you I wouldn't take this off," I said and gave her the ring. "Not until I could give it back to you."

"I saw it on the video. That's how I knew it was you," she said. "Big Jim saw it too. We all did. We showed it to Aunt Picky, and Grandma Pilly too. Don't worry, they're not going to spill the beans. They swore to me on the Holy Bible they wouldn't. Right daddy?" She put the ring back on the chain around her neck and stood up.

"I was going to tell you everything on our way out of town," Jim shrugged.

"We'd better get while the getting's good," Jima said. "No time like the present now is there?" Jima went

to the front door. "Well come on let's shake this town."
She was giddy with excitement and wonder of what might
lie ahead of her. I was about to be the sledgehammer to
her dreams.

I got my bag and headed to the door. "You need
to handle this Jim." I turned the doorknob and glanced at
Jima. "You can't go with me Jima. Your daddy will
explain."

Jima was on my heels as I went outside. She
reached out for my arm and I avoided her hold. "Daddy
do something," she screamed through her sobs. "Don't let
her go. Do something." Jima grabbed my arm with both
hands and pulled.

"Jima don't," Jim said and tried to pull her away.
She continued to pull on me, screaming.

"Stop this now," I said. "Someone could be
watching." Jim took my cue and led us back inside the
house. "It's too dangerous," I said. "That video you saw
was made by a very bad man. The world's full of bad
people, and some of them want to get me. If you were
there with me they'd want to get you too. Do you
understand what I'm saying?"

"The video was made by the baby bomber," she
said, her voice rough from screaming. "Everyone knows
that. The detective was the same man you went on the run
with. Besides all that, you're going to end up with us
anyway you shake a stick at it. You should just accept that
fact." She looked at Jim. "Can I show her?"

"Do it quick," he said. "She's right we don't need
to be here much longer." Jima ran outside to the truck.

"What is she talking about Jim?" I asked. "I've
tried to be patient, but the longer I stay, the worse it
becomes."

"I understand. Let her do this."

"Let her do what? Why are you making this so
difficult?"

"I could ask you the same question."

"She's looking for a happy ever after. It's cruel of you to let her think there'll be one." When Jima walked in carrying the Patient: Crew book I looked at Jim with great contempt. "Why does she have that book? She shouldn't have that book."

"See, it's right here," she said and pointed at the page. "It's book two, we bought it in Sweetwater the day after you left."

"Why would you let her?"

"It's better if she knows the truth."

"It's better for all involved if you two go, and live your lives," I said. "Forget about me."

"No! Wait, it's right here," Jima stood between the door and myself holding the book up to my face, but I didn't look. Prolonging the inevitable caused nothing but pain.

"Jima you've got to stop this. You're letting your brain trick you into thinking they are talking about you." I put my hands on her shoulders. "Don't read those books anymore. Don't let the crew or anyone else tell you how to live your life. I'm leaving—alone. You take care of your daddy, and he'll take care of you. I promise I will always love you, and hold you right here," I held her hand to my heart. "Now, we need to be tough. Don't follow me. Don't cry, and don't make a scene." I walked through the door and closed it behind me without looking back.

I set a course for unknown lands, and felt strong. I would be all right. On my own, and alone I would leap forward with confidence. I would create a life. I was a good five hundred miles down the road headed east, destination unknown, smack dab in the middle of nowhere and there wasn't much to choose from on the radio. When I did find a signal, it was talk radio, and the subject was, of course, the death of the baby bomber. The stories, reports, speculations and rumors of him would take a few years to fade into history along with all unimaginable stories of human violence.

On the five-year anniversary of the baby bomber's death a kid named Andrew Hunter would create a plan to blow up his middle school. His plan was to kill all two hundred and thirty people inside. He said he wanted to follow the path of his hero, Finneaus Albert. Twenty-four hours before Andrew was to carry out his plan a couple of strangers showed up at his parent's house. The next day Andrew hung himself in the holding cell. He left a note that read; it is written it must be done.

You, the Crewbies, are the vessels of all that is truth and justice. Multitudes go about living their lives uninterrupted because of you. It's not mere hundreds that you have saved—not by a long shot—it is billions. Two nuclear attacks have been thwarted along with numerous other terrorism plots. Bank robbers, rapists, murderers, thieves have all been stopped from doing their evil deeds. Great stories have been told about these legendary strangers who appear out of nowhere. Armed with the knowledge they mysteriously possess. As The Professor says, *the pipe spills out onto a reckless society if left without the vessels of certainty.*

I've lived a good life since last seeing the five of you. I've had my ups and downs as any person does. My journeys have been filled with adventure and I have been lucky enough to be surrounded by people who know and accept me, and my crew. There are not sufficient words in the human language to express my love and gratitude for you my dark warrior, and your army of truth.

I've never truly recovered from taking a man's life. It's the only darkness that remains. I don't know if it is an event that one can outlive. With this being complete I live a debt free life. All promises fulfilled.

The End.

ISBN-10: 069240886X
ISBN-13: 9780692408865
Available on Kindle and other Devices

Cover Art Copyright 2015 David Kaplan

Kapcom Publishing 2015

Ebook available on Amazon Kindle

PATIENT: CREW

A cryptic and fantastical adventure told from the point of view of Shanna, a farm girl from Sunny, TX. Her life has been consumed by seven voices. They control her mind and body and she can assuage them only by writing, using her ambidextrous skills. Born into scandal in the heart of a West Texas community, Shanna is forced to leave home at an early age.

Her therapist's tell-all book launches a manhunt and Shanna is forced to flee again, but a psychopath who wants the crew of voices for his own has other plans.

A compelling tale of loyalty, promises and truth.

Hannah Kaplan has authored screenplays, short stories and national magazine articles. This is her first novel.